# The Fur Trader's Lady

### Gabrielle Meyer

Belle May Press

Copyright © 2025 by Gabrielle Meyer

All rights reserved.

No portion of this book may be reproduced in any form without written permission from the publisher or author, except as permitted by U.S. copyright law.

Scripture used in this book, whether quoted or paraphrased by the characters, is taken from the King James Version of the Bible.

For my mom, Cathy VanRisseghem.

Because this is her favorite story.

# Prologue

ENGLAND,
MARCH 1803

Sweat dripped from her brow as Lady Charlotte Fairfax hurriedly filled a small bag with a change of clothes and the scant coins she'd hidden away. She stopped every few seconds to listen for noise outside her door, her gaze following the bar of moonlight slicing across the floor. She didn't have time to pack the dozens of expensive gowns hanging in her dressing room or take anything valuable from the only home she'd ever known. After leaving her guardian, Roger Rutherford, asleep in the study with a glass of bourbon in his hand, she would only have a few moments to make her escape.

A sound at the door made her pause, her pulse thrumming.

"Charlotte?" Roger's voice slurred as he shook her doorknob. "Let me in! I did not give you permission to leave me. I still have plans for you this evening."

Panic clawed at Charlotte's throat, choking off her breath. Blissfield Manor had been a sanctuary from birth, but in the two years since her parents' death, it had turned into her prison.

"Charlotte!"

Something fell against her door with a thud. Was that Roger?

"Open the door," he said a bit quieter, his voice low and thick. "Did I tell you that you looked particularly lovely in that gown I had made for you?" She could imagine his feline smile. "I thought I might show you my admiration."

Dread rippled up her spine, and she longed to scrub away the distasteful words. The offensive gown he gave her—and ordered her to wear—lay in a pile on the floor of her dressing room. The low décolletage had made her feel foul, while the looks he had given her throughout dinner made her want to crawl out of her skin. At the age of forty, he was more than twice her age.

She tiptoed across the thick carpet toward her desk where she'd placed Stephen Corning's letter. It had arrived for her that morning and only made its way to her hands because he'd sent it through his mother, the cook. Mr. and Mrs. Corning were the only people at Blissfield Manor who had not succumbed to Roger's false charm or deception. In a very short time, most of the servants who had been faithful to her parents and cared for her all her life had shifted their allegiance from Charlotte to her mother's dishonorable cousin. Those who had not cowed to his every whim had been replaced—and she feared the Cornings were next. Roger had turned everyone against her to keep her captive at Blissfield Manor.

"I promise to be kind." Roger's voice was weaker now, no doubt from the effects of the alcohol. "After all, we shall be married in less than a fortnight. You cannot deny me forever."

She would turn eighteen in two weeks and be free to marry whomever she wanted—but if she did not marry, Roger would be her legal guardian until she was twenty-one, as stipulated by her parents' will. For two years, Roger had kept her by his side, never allowing her to meet anyone who might become a prospective husband. He planned to keep that honor for himself the day she turned eighteen, and she had little power to stop him.

Charlotte paused at her desk, trying to steady her breathing, forcing Roger's words far from her thoughts. If she had any hope of escaping Blissfield Manor tonight, she must keep her wits about her.

Stephen's letter gleamed in the moonlight, allowing her to read his words once again.

*My Dearest Charlotte,*

*Your letter fills me with dismay. I'm sorry to hear that you have lost your parents and that Rutherford has become your guardian. I never trusted him, and it enrages me to know he has gained control over you. You must get away!*

*It is impossible for me to leave my post in Athabasca at this time. I am over two thousand miles from a ship, and it would take months for me to get approval to leave—if I was given approval—and many months after that to travel to you. You must steal away to Montreal and find a man named Reid McCoy. He returns to his home every three years to see his mother, and this will be the year. You must get to him before the beginning of May, or he will have already left for Grand Portage. He is an honorable, trustworthy man, and he owes me a debt for saving his life. If anyone can find a way to get you to me, it will be him. Tell him you are claiming the debt in my name.*

*When you get to the Rendezvous at Grand Portage, I will be there for the annual meeting and will make you my wife. Rutherford will have no control over you then. Make haste but be careful. He is capable of anything.*

*With all my love, Stephen*

Stephen's words were like an anchor of hope, the only solid thing she had to cling to in the past two years. When her parents had died, her father's earldom, along with most of his property, had transferred to his distant cousin, Harold Fairfax. But Blissfield Manor and a sizable fortune were left for Charlotte upon her marriage. Roger Rutherford was named her guardian until she married. He planned to make her his wife in less than two weeks, but until Stephen's letter had arrived, she had no way of preventing that inevitable nightmare. If she could get to Stephen and marry him, she would not be forced to marry Roger.

"I am losing patience," Roger said, his voice stronger than before.

Charlotte quickly shoved Stephen's letter in her pocket and returned to her dressing room to get a bonnet and a pair of gloves. Mrs. Corning had promised to have her husband prepare a carriage for her to ride into London, where she could book passage on the first available ship to take her to Montreal. If she was fortunate, Roger would not recover from his drunken stupor until late the next morning, and she would already be away.

Her doorknob shook again, and this time Roger pounded hard against the door. "Let me in, Charlotte. I'm in no mood to be denied."

With trembling hands, she set her bonnet over her auburn hair, praying Roger would tire of his quest. It wasn't the first night he'd come to her room this way, though he'd never forced an entry.

"I will get the housekeeper and have her open your door if you do not unlock it."

Would he? She grabbed her small bag and rushed across the room to the window. Her watercolors, charcoals, and paints sat in their place near her easel, along with dozens of canvases. She would have to leave them all behind. Nothing was more important to her than her freedom. If Roger caught her trying to escape, he would place a guard in her room at all hours of the day and night, she was certain. She only had this one chance.

Looking down into the moon-drenched yard, she saw the carriage waiting, just as Mrs. Corning had promised. A horse pawed restlessly at the ground.

"You've given me no other choice," Roger shouted. "I'm going for Mrs. Melton."

Silence filled Charlotte's room.

Mrs. Melton had become Roger's strongest ally against Charlotte. The new housekeeper wouldn't hesitate to open her door for the lecherous guardian. Terror filled Charlotte's heart, and she had no time to lose. She didn't think twice but crawled out of her second-story window and took hold of the trellis hugging the wall. Her dress caught on the weathered wood, forcing her to pause and untangle it. She had climbed this trellis as a child, often meeting Stephen at the bottom, where he had waited for her to run off and play. But it had been years, and she'd never done it in a long gown and with a bag in her hand.

She had no alternative. Carefully, but with urgency, she climbed down the trellis. When her feet touched the solid ground, she didn't waste a moment and untethered the horse before stepping into the light carriage. There would be no driver to see her safely to London, though she didn't care. The Cornings had been kind enough to offer this bit of assistance, and she would not ask for more.

With a flick of her wrist, she tapped the reins over the horse's back and pulled away from Blissfield Manor cautiously at first, not to make too much noise, and then faster when she was farther from the house. She reached into her pocket for Stephen's letter, needing to cling to something tangible, something linking her to a future hope.

But the letter was not in her pocket. Frantic, she reached into her other pocket, but it wasn't there either. She looked around the carriage, opened her bag, and even glanced behind her at the road she had covered, but the letter was nowhere to be found. Had it fallen from her pocket in her haste to leave Blissfield Manor?

There was no time to climb back up the trellis to retrieve the message—and if truth be told, Roger would find a way to draw out the information from the Cornings one way or another. He would learn her destination, and if the last two years were any indication, he would come after her. He wanted complete control over Blissfield Manor and her fortune. Her only hope was to marry Stephen before Roger found her.

Tears streamed down Charlotte's cheeks as she pushed the horse to a gallop and flew down the road, away from her beloved home toward an uncertain future in the dead of night. She would have to cross a frightening ocean, find a man she'd never met, and convince him to take her on a journey into the wilderness. If she made it that far, she would have to locate Stephen, a man she'd only known as a child, and do all that with the little money she had in her small bag.

The task felt impossible, but she would do whatever it would take to be free from Roger Rutherford.

# Chapter One



R ain blew against Charlotte's face and made her bonnet limp, but she hardly noticed as she stepped off the ship, soiled and painfully thin from weeks of seasickness. The ground dipped and swayed beneath her, making her stomach roll like the endless ocean she'd just crossed.

Somewhere in the middle of that ocean, she had turned eighteen.

Montreal spread out before her much like London had with its wharf full of peddlers and laborers and its streets muddy and narrow. Cargo filled the wooden docks, while men and women hawked their wares to those stepping off the boats.

"*Poisson à vendre.*" A stout French woman pushed a fish into Charlotte's face, touting its freshness, though the stench suggested otherwise.

The smell combined with Charlotte's dizziness, and she lost her meager lunch on the dock.

"*Je suis désolé.*" Charlotte apologized, turning her face away from the fish, trying to get a breath of fresh air. But no matter where she turned, the smells of the wharf assailed her.

The French woman scowled and stepped away from Charlotte, spouting profanity from her thin lips.

Charlotte wiped her mouth, desperation filling her gut. She didn't have time to be humiliated. She needed to locate Reid McCoy before it grew too late. With nowhere to stay and no money to rent a room, she would have to rely upon his kindness—if he was still in Montreal and not headed back to Grand Portage already. The only vessel leaving London the morning Charlotte had booked passage had stopped in New York before coming to Montreal and had taken longer than she had hoped.

But she was here now, and she would not waste another moment.

"*Excusez-moi*." Charlotte raced after the fish woman, speaking in French. "I beg your pardon. Do you know where Mr. Reid McCoy lives?"

The woman turned back to Charlotte, also speaking in French. "Do you plan to buy a fish?"

Charlotte lifted her filthy hands and shook her head. "I have no money."

"Then I have no information." The woman pushed through the crowd away from Charlotte.

"Please," Charlotte begged, following her. "I would pay if I had the money, but I am destitute. I must find Mr. McCoy this evening."

The French woman did not wait for Charlotte, disappearing into the crowd. Charlotte pulled her shawl closer, a shiver making her body tremble. She longed for a bath and a comfortable bed but feared she would be denied both. It had been weeks since she'd had a good night's sleep, constantly on guard, listening for the sound of a sailor who might stumble into her berth. Thank God for Mr. and Mrs. Ames who had traveled across the ocean with her. But once they had disembarked in

New York, Charlotte had been by herself. She'd sold her only other dress and the bag she had carried for a bit of food.

Leaving her with nothing but the worn clothes on her back.

A man stopped her. "Did you need information about Mr. McCoy?" he asked in French. His dark brown hair curled under his red cap, and he wore clothing similar to many of the other men on the wharf. An oversized white shirt tucked into short, dark trousers, with a red sash tied around his waist. The cares of the world had not yet wrinkled his face or hardened his gaze.

"Do you know where I might find him?"

"He lives up there." The man pointed toward a street that ran up a steep hill. "It is a stone house with a red door and a fence and a matching red gate." He frowned. "It is a long way. Would you like me to take you?"

She shook her head quickly, not wanting any help or any more attention than she absolutely needed. "No, thank you."

Charlotte started walking toward the street he indicated, bumping into a stack of wicker baskets near a bread stand. She grabbed them to keep them from falling, apologizing to a large man who yelled at her in French. As she backed away, her gaze landed on a man near the ship she had just left and she stopped short.

Roger.

He stood speaking to a sailor who nodded and pointed in her direction.

Charlotte spun on her heels and lifted her shawl over her bonnet and auburn hair. Her heart pounded so hard, she feared it might stop. Questions swirled through her mind, casting confusion on her surroundings. She tried to avoid a puddle but splashed into it instead.

The delay in New York had probably given Roger's ship just enough time to get to Montreal ahead of her, just as she'd feared. Had he been to Mr. McCoy's already?

She had no choice but to continue toward her destination and pray that Roger hadn't already turned Mr. McCoy against her.

Lowering her head, she moved around a stack of salt barrels, making her way from the dock to the thoroughfare, fear nipping at her heels. The steady rain soaked her tattered dress and heightened the smell of sewage emptying into the St. Lawrence River. Mud sucked her feet to the earth, slowing her escape.

She had prayed all the way into London and across the Atlantic that God would guide her steps and lead her to freedom. Now she added another prayer, that Roger hadn't seen her on the wharf. She couldn't imagine it was God's will for her to marry Roger. She couldn't bear a life as his wife. Surely, God understood.

Without stopping, she continued up the street, trying to blend into the commotion of the riverfront.

The streets grew quieter the farther she moved from the wharf. As the sun began to set, the rain continued to pour from the thick clouds above. Candlelight flickered in the windows as she passed buildings packed tight along the banks of the river. The smell of roasted meat mingled with the stench of the riverfront, threatening to upset her stomach again.

Turning, she made her way up the hill, casting glances over her shoulder. Her lungs ached and her feet throbbed. Her muscles, weak from lack of use these many weeks on the ship, burned with exertion. Growing lightheaded, she stopped and leaned against a home built close to the street. How much farther must she climb this hill before locating Mr. McCoy's home?

A party of men exited a pub, merriment spilling forth from the establishment. Shrinking back as far as she could into the shadows, she silently watched them pass, the smell of alcohol lingering in their wake. Living with Roger for two years had made her distrust a man when he drank. The voyage over had made her distrust a group of drunken men even more.

Once the merrymakers were out of sight, she hurried up the street again.

The rain turned to sleet. Charlotte coughed as she trudged along. And when the mud started to freeze and bite into the soft soles of her worn shoes, she was certain she would either die on this Montreal street or Roger would find her. She wasn't sure which outcome would be worse.

Just as she was about to give up hope, she saw it. A house that matched the description she was given.

"Dear Lord," she whispered as she crossed the street, her body shaking uncontrollably from the cold, "may this be the refuge I seek."

After opening the gate, she entered the yard, glancing once more behind her to see if she had been followed. Everything was silent as the sleet turned to shards of ice, pelting her exposed face and hands. She closed the gate and hurried up the path to the front door, where she knocked.

Light shone from within the home, spilling out one of the paned windows onto the frozen ground outside. Tantalizing smoke blew from a chimney, promising heat within, as the tree in the front bent from the wind.

The door opened, and an older man stood there, looking down his nose at her. "Yes?"

"Is Mr. McCoy at home?" Her voice quivered from cold and fear.

He pursed his lips and ran his disapproving gaze up and down the length of her body. She must look dreadful. Gone were the elegant gowns, elaborate coiffures, and soft slippers of her past. In their place, she wore the tattered and soiled gown she had not washed since escaping Blissfield Manor six weeks previous, the grimy strands of her auburn hair, and the thin-soled shoes she had not stepped out of since slipping them on her feet in her bedroom. She had wanted to be ready to escape any situation at a moment's notice.

Charlotte had left England as a lady and arrived in the New World as a common beggar. Yet—if she could find her way to Grand Portage and into the safety of Stephen's arms, it would be worth all her suffering.

"Who may I say is calling?" The man's long face drooped in wrinkled flesh.

She had not given her real name since leaving Blissfield Manor, and she was loath to give it now in case Roger inquired after her. Besides, Mr. McCoy would have no idea who she was. But he would know one name. "Please tell him I am a friend of Mr. Stephen Corning."

The butler studied Charlotte for another moment. "You may go to the servants' entrance and wait there."

Without further warning, he closed the door and left her alone in the bitter cold once again.

The lure of a warm kitchen took all indignity away from being sent to the servants' entrance. Charlotte had faced far greater pains in the past six weeks, and she was certain she would encounter many more in the coming months if Mr. McCoy agreed to her request.

Another light greeted her at the back of the house, where she found a window next to a simple door. After knocking lightly, it was opened by a woman who looked as unwelcoming as the man at the front.

"Well, come in then," she said briskly. "Don't stand there lettin' the heat out."

Charlotte obeyed and nearly fell into the kitchen from exhaustion. She rested her hand against the back of a chair while the older woman closed the door.

"The master is being summoned," the woman said with impatience. "Though why he should be bothered by the likes o' you is a wonder. Him seeing to his mother and already so late in the evening."

"Mr. McCoy is home?" The relief was almost more than Charlotte could bear. Without being asked, she sank into the chair, soaking up the heat from the large hearth.

"He is, indeed." The woman went about her work, placing a log on the fire and stirring a pot hanging on a hook over the flames. The smell of stew wafted out to tickle Charlotte's nose and made her stomach growl. A loaf of bread sat on a cutting board within reach, and it took all her self-control to keep her hands to herself. Without the dip and rolling of a ship, for the first time in six weeks, her appetite returned.

The woman did not offer food to Charlotte. Instead, she eyed her from time to time, no doubt to ensure Charlotte did not steal. Never in her life had people looked upon Charlotte with such mistrust. It was a shameful feeling—one she did not like—and made her wonder how many times she had looked down upon someone of a lower class simply because they were hungry or destitute.

*Lord, forgive me* was her constant prayer.

Charlotte removed her damp bonnet and set it on her lap.

Each minute that passed increased Charlotte's unease. Every creak, bump, or groan outside the kitchen made her heart leap. How long did she have until Roger found her?

When the interior door finally opened, Charlotte jumped at the sound and tried to stand, but lost her balance as the room began to spin.

"Whoa there, lass." A giant of a man crossed the room and took hold of her by the waist, settling her onto the chair again. Even in her state of distress, she was aware of his handsome features and kind brown eyes. "Mrs. Mallarme," he said evenly in a deep Scottish brogue, "why haven't you given the lass something to eat and drink?"

"And have every beggar at our back door?" the woman asked with a raised brow. "They're no better than stray cats, they are."

He tossed Mrs. Mallarme a disapproving look and then reached for a clay pitcher to fill a glass with milk. "I dinna have time for the lass to faint in my kitchen. Please get her something to eat."

Charlotte tried not to cower before the man. Had Roger already spoken to him? It didn't matter now. She had come this far and would not shy away from him. She was too weak and too tired to go on. He was dressed well, though he was not wearing a jacket, and the top button of his white shirt was undone. His tight trousers were tucked into the tops of his tall boots and displayed thick, muscular legs. His dark hair looked like it had recently been trimmed, though he wore it a little longer than most men. It waved in an unruly manner, forcing him to impatiently tuck it behind his ears. He was clean-shaven with long dark sideburns, the same dark brown as his hair. They gave his face a lean, powerful look.

She took the glass he offered and tried to drink like a lady, but her hands shook, and she spilled the milk on her bodice. Mortification heated her cheeks, but he didn't seem to notice.

He crossed his arms and stared down at her. "Why have you asked for me?"

"A-are you Mr. McCoy?"

"Aye."

"Mr. Reid McCoy?"

He nodded. "Aye."

Desperation poured from her with the last shred of energy she possessed. "And do you know Mr. Stephen Corning?"

Mr. McCoy studied her for a moment, curiosity and caution warring within his expressive brown eyes. "Aye," he said slowly.

The glass of milk continued to shake in her hand, so she set it on the table. She wanted to be as far from Roger as possible and did not wish to linger here any longer than necessary, but there were things Mr. McCoy needed to know. "And do you remember a debt you owe to Stephen?"

Mr. McCoy towered over her, his eyes dark pools of warning. "He saved my life. I couldna forget that."

Charlotte closed her eyes and bit her bottom lip in an effort not to cry. She had found Reid McCoy, and just as Stephen had promised in his letter, he owed him a debt—one that would hopefully allow her to travel with him to Grand Portage.

She opened her eyes and rose on shaking legs. "I have come from England to claim the debt, in Stephen's name."

"What gives you the right to claim such a thing?"

"I am his fiancée."

Mr. McCoy's gaze was first disbelieving, then wary, and finally annoyed. "You've come for money, then?"

"I-I do not want your money." She took a step toward him, her vision spinning. "I must get to Stephen—at Grand Portage."

Charlotte did not hear his reply.

Before Reid could answer, the lass's eyes rolled back, and she fell forward into his chest.

"Good heavens!" Mrs. Mallarme cried out.

Reid lifted the young lady into his arms, alarm tensing his muscles. He didn't have time to deal with this—he'd already had enough trouble with his mother, who was still weeping in her bedchamber. His plans to leave Montreal earlier that day had been canceled when he'd been forced to send for the doctor to ease his mother's hysterics. He'd spent his day dividing his time between the wharf, where his canoes were being readied for travel, and his mother's bedside, as she begged him not to go.

The lass weighed hardly a thing. Her dirty gown hung on her emaciated body—but her speech and the way she had carried herself left him certain she was high-born. The idea that a woman as young and educated as this could be the fiancée of Stephen Corning was too fanciful to believe. But how did she know about the debt, and why had she ended up begging on his doorstep if it were not true?

He turned to the housekeeper. "I suppose she'll have to stay the night."

Mrs. Mallarme's eyes grew wide. "You won't take her in, will you?"

He started toward the door to the front hall. "I owe her friend my life." Even if she wasn't Stephen's fiancée, she knew about the debt, and that was enough for him to honor his promise.

Hurrying ahead of Reid, Mrs. Mallarme opened the door, though she clucked her tongue.

The lass began to stir in Reid's arms as he walked up the stairs. When her eyes finally opened, panic filled the brown orbs, and she pushed against Reid's chest, though her strength was no match for his.

"There, now." Reid spoke in a low, calm voice. "I'll not harm you."

A fit of coughs overtook her, and when they finally subsided, she became limp. "Please," she begged, "where are you taking me?"

"I won't turn you out in this weather. Mrs. Mallarme is preparing a room."

Closing her eyes, she leaned into Reid's chest, breathing heavily. "And you're certain you know Stephen?"

"Aye." He tried not to smile. She sounded like a wee bairn looking for reassurance.

She clutched his shirt, her eyes still closed, as if she didn't have the strength to lift her lids. "And you'll take me to him?"

His humor disappeared. The thought of taking her into the wilderness was preposterous. Even if it was allowed, he doubted she'd survive a week. "That I canna do."

Panic returned to her large eyes. "But I must get to him. He's the only one who can protect me from Roger."

He had no wish to encourage her dramatics, but he didn't want to aggravate her either. "Things will look better in the morn."

She shook her head with more strength than he would have thought possible. "My guardian has followed me across the ocean. If he finds me, he'll force me to marry him—I have nowhere else to turn."

Mrs. Mallarme opened a door at the top of the stairs and carried a candle into the cool room.

"Light a fire, if you will," he said to the housekeeper, wanting to be done with this task. He had a dozen other things needing his attention on the eve of his departure. His men were just as anxious to leave and were already frustrated at the delay.

"I can't go back," the lady continued. "He'll force me to marry him so he has control of my inheritance. He's evil and will stop at nothing to get what he wants."

"She's delirious with fever, mark my words," Mrs. Mallarme said as she knelt near the hearthstones.

The stranger clutched Reid's shirt again. "I'm not delirious. He's kept me a prisoner in my own home since my parents died two years ago, anticipating the day I would come of age."

Reid set her on her feet and waited until she was steady, then he pulled the covers back from the bed. "Try to get some rest. I'll send for a doctor."

She reached for him as he turned to go. "Has Roger been here already?"

The desperation in her eyes and in her voice finally made him pause. "No."

"Please," she begged. "If he comes looking for me, do not tell him I'm here. He will lie to you and get you to believe what he wants."

Mrs. Mallarme glanced at Reid from her place near the fire, clearly annoyed and not convinced.

The girl clutched his arm. "I beg you, please give me sanctuary. Do not tell anyone I am in your home. If not for me, then do it for Stephen."

She was clearly distraught and afraid. He would give her his reassurance, if for no other reason than to calm her. "You are safe here. I will tell no one."

His promise seemed to drain her of her remaining strength, and she crumpled onto the bed. "Thank you. Stephen said I could trust you."

Reid had worked with Stephen Corning for two seasons, when Stephen had first joined the North West Company as an assistant clerk. The memory of the day Reid had almost died, when his fully loaded canoe had capsized and he had been knocked unconscious from hitting his head against a rock, returned in fuzzy details. When he had not surfaced, Stephen had dived beneath the icy waters and drawn Reid to safety. After regaining consciousness, Reid had sworn an oath to Stephen that he would repay the debt in whatever way Stephen required.

And now here the lass was, three years later, claiming the debt be paid in Stephen's name—at the most inconvenient time she could have chosen.

"I dinna get your name," he said.

Lifting her chin, the first glimpse of confidence shone from her brown eyes. "Lady Charlotte Fairfax, the daughter of the late Right Honorable Thomas Fairfax, the Earl of Warwick."

Mrs. Mallarme rose from her spot and rolled her eyes. "And I'm Lady Edith Mallarme." She snorted.

Reid had had enough of the servant. "Bring the lass some food and be quick."

With pursed lips, the housekeeper left the room—keeping the door wide open.

"My father *was* Lord Thomas Fairfax, the Earl of Warwick," Lady Charlotte said earnestly, her English impeccable. "His earldom was inherited by his distant cousin, but my mother's cousin, Roger Rutherford, was named my guardian until I'm eighteen." She could hardly speak through fits of coughing. "He wants the home and the money and cannot have them unless he marries me."

A knot of compassion twisted in Reid's gut, but it warred with his impatience. If her tale was true and she was in grave danger, Reid was honor bound to help her. The least he could do was show a little empathy. "There, now." He squatted before her. She was so young and so frail that he feared she would not live long enough to tell her tale. But for now, she needed to sleep. "Try to rest."

"I must get to Stephen," Charlotte said. "He told me that you could take me."

"'Tis impossible. European women are not allowed in the fur trade." And even if they were, she was in no condition to make the journey.

"I need to get to Stephen."

"It canna be done."

"Could you sneak me in?"

"'Tis over a thousand-mile journey, through lakes, rivers, and over miles of portages," he said with as much patience as he could muster. "'Tis no place for a lady."

Tears filled her eyes, and she looked away from him. Taking a deep breath, she wiped her face. "If you cannot help me, I will find a way to go on my own."

He hated tears—especially when they were shed by a bonnie lass who had more than her fair share of heartache. "There has not been a European woman in the fur trade for over a hundred and fifty years," he said gruffly, trying not to let her tears soften his resolve. "It proved too dangerous and taxing."

"But Stephen told me you could take me." She met his gaze again, desperation in her eyes. "It is the only hope that has sustained me through the difficult voyage to get here. He said if I ever needed help, you'd find a way to get me to him."

Her words were raw and troubling. "What can Stephen do for you?"

"Once Stephen and I marry, Roger will no longer have control over me."

"I will get word to Stephen, and he can return to you here in Montreal."

"No." Her eyes filled with alarm. "It would take months. Before his return, Roger would find me. I know it. And it would be too late. Besides, I have nowhere to live, nothing to eat, and no real skills to find work."

Reid would offer to let her live in his home, but his mother would never allow it. And his staff would have no way of protecting Lady Charlotte from her guardian.

"Take me with you," the lady begged once again, holding onto his sleeve. "I'll dress as a man and do anything required of me."

He stood and crossed his arms. It was out of the question. "The life of a fur trader is dangerous, unpredictable, and indecent for a lady. I could never allow it—I'd be putting your life in danger if I took you into the interior—not to mention my job."

Somehow, she found the strength to stand. "You are putting my life in danger if you don't. Please, let me go in dressed as a man."

Reid went to the fire and put another log on the small flames. No one would believe this young woman was a man—though they might believe she was a boy. It wasn't unusual for a boy of fifteen or sixteen to enter the fur trade as an assistant clerk—especially if he was well educated. Reid had entered as an assistant clerk when he was fifteen and worked his way up to a senior clerk. He was poised to become a partner and own his own share of the North West Company—ensuring an income that would provide for him and his mother for the rest of his life. He couldn't risk his entire career for Lady Charlotte Fairfax, no matter what he owed to Stephen.

Mrs. Mallarme returned to the room with a steaming bowl of stew on a wooden tray.

"There's a man to see you, sir." She set the tray on a table and nodded toward Lady Charlotte. "He said his name is Roger Rutherford."

Charlotte turned wild eyes to Reid and then scanned the room like a cornered animal with no way to escape.

Reid didn't know if the lass's story was true, but he couldn't hand her over to someone she feared either—at least not until he met Mr. Rutherford and knew the truth of the matter.

# Chapter Two

"You're safe in here, lass," Reid told the frightened woman, wanting to reassure her. "I won't let anyone hurt you."

Lady Charlotte tugged her dirty shawl tighter around her body and stared beyond Reid to the door. He'd seen that look before when he'd taken two young Chippewa children into his fur post after their parents had been killed by intoxicated voyageurs.

The children had huddled against the back wall of his living quarters, staying with him until they could be transferred to the district manager. Each movement or noise had made them jump no matter how many times Reid assured them they were safe. He had tried to communicate that he meant them no harm, but they escaped in the middle of the night and were found frozen to death a few days later. Had they trusted him, they would probably still be alive.

Trying to push aside the memory of the haunting fear he'd seen in the children's eyes, Reid placed his hands on the frail shoulders of the young woman. When she finally met his gaze, he saw intelligence and honesty behind the terror. "I will keep you safe. You have my word—for your sake and for Stephen's."

She looked deep into his eyes, and he knew she was gauging whether she could trust him.

"Stay here and dinna try to run. It will only make things worse." He had to bend to look her eye to eye. "Do you hear me, lass?"

Her nod was the only answer she offered.

Ushering Mrs. Mallarme out of the room, Reid followed and spoke low. "Did you say anything about her to the man?"

"Mr. Dorsey answered the door. He saw I was coming up the stairs and asked me to tell you."

"Did Dorsey mention Lady Charlotte?"

"I wouldn't know."

Reid hoped not. It would be easier to protect the lass if he could feign ignorance. "Quietly draw a bath for Lady Charlotte and find her something clean to wear as you launder her other things."

Mrs. Mallarme's mouth puckered with disapproval. "And where do you think I'll find something for her to wear? Surely, you don't expect me to give her my own clothes or go into your mother's room and ask for hers."

A headache began to build behind Reid's eyes, which didn't bode well for traveling on the morrow. When a headache came upon him, it could take days for it to subside, and only rest and darkness eased the pain.

"Just do as I say," he said a bit too sharply to the housekeeper, rubbing his temples.

Reid left Mrs. Mallarme and walked down the flight of stairs into the foyer. The butler, Mr. Dorsey, met him at the bottom.

"A Mr. Roger Rutherford is here to see you, sir." Dorsey gave a slight bow. "I showed him into your library."

Reid drew close to the butler and spoke just as quietly as before. "Did he ask about the girl?"

"He only asked for you, sir."

"I don't want you to mention the girl to anyone—not even my mother."

Mr. Dorsey nodded. "Of course."

Reid paused for a moment to try to ease the pounding in his head, then opened the door into the library. An impeccably dressed man stood near the fireplace, his back to the door. The contrast between this well-dressed gentleman and the poor wretch cowering upstairs was jarring.

Rutherford turned and smiled, stepping across the room, his hand outstretched. "Thank you for seeing me, Mr. McCoy. I'm Roger Rutherford."

Reid shook the man's hand. He was much older than Reid expected, with graying hair at the temples and age lining the creases at the side of his eyes. He exuded manners to a fault and walked with the practiced movements of a man trying to impress.

"What can I do for you, Mr. Rutherford?"

Rutherford clasped his hands behind his back and leaned forward. "I'm terribly sorry to drag you into my family troubles, but I have come looking for my dear cousin, Lady Charlotte Fairfax. She has gone missing, and I have reason to believe she might come here. Perhaps you've seen her? She's about this tall"—he held his hand up to his shoulder height—"with curly auburn hair and dark brown eyes."

Frowning, Reid indicated one of the chairs near the fireplace. Moving leisurely and deliberately, he took a seat in another. "What makes you think she would come here?"

Rutherford sat with an easy air, as if he had no cares in the world—yet his eyes were restless and shrewd. He took in the room, even as he gave his attention to Reid. "My cousin is . . . eccentric. She has been difficult, often running away, telling wild stories about her life, claiming I have mistreated her." His words were pained—and clearly rehearsed. "She was never the same once her parents died, though I have done my best to care for her. I fear for her safety."

Reid sat quietly, his hands on the armrests, showing no emotion at the man's statement.

"She believes herself in love with the cook's son, Stephen Corning," Rutherford continued. "When her parents died, she sent him a letter and convinced him that she was in danger. When she went missing several weeks ago, I knew exactly where to look."

Reid frowned. "And why do you think she'd come here looking for Mr. Corning?"

"A letter arrived from Mr. Corning just before she left London. After she was gone, I found it in her room. It indicated that you owed him a debt and might be willing to help her get to him."

His words proved Lady Charlotte's story about Stephen was true—but was Rutherford the evil guardian she claimed? Or was she simply a distraught woman mourning the loss of her parents and the sudden change in her situation?

Reid couldn't take the risk by handing her over to him. "I am sorry, Mr. Rutherford. I'm afraid I canna help."

Rutherford's eyes narrowed. "You can't? Or you won't?"

There was no reason to continue the conversation. No matter what Lady Charlotte's reasons were for getting to Stephen, she had been given permission to claim Stephen's debt—a debt Reid would honor with his very life. He stood to indicate the interview was over and waited for Rutherford to rise from his chair.

Rutherford took his time standing. "I will be staying at the Montreal House, near the wharf." His cheek muscle twitched as he stared at Reid.

"If you change your mind and you choose to help me, I can guarantee you will be compensated."

Reid had no time for men like Rutherford, especially on a day like today. He strode to the foyer and called for Mr. Dorsey.

The butler appeared almost immediately with Rutherford's hat and coat, which the other man took with practiced ease.

"How is your mother faring?" Rutherford asked as he put on his coat. "I would hate to hear she isn't well."

Reid froze as he walked across the foyer to the front door.

"It must cause you great distress to leave her in Montreal, all alone, and only return to her every three years." Rutherford slipped on his hat, but he glared at Reid. "It would be a shame if harm befell her while you were away"—a sneer curled his lips—"repaying your debt."

"What do you ken of my mother?"

"I told you. Stephen sent a letter to Charlotte telling her to come here. It was full of very useful information."

Mrs. Mallarme entered the foyer at that moment, two steaming buckets of water in her hands. She stopped short, her eyes growing wide at the sight of Mr. Rutherford. "Beg your pardon," she said as she hurried past them up the stairs, casting worried glances behind her.

Rutherford's shrewd gaze followed her.

"'Tis time for Mr. Rutherford to leave." Reid nodded to Mr. Dorsey. "Please see him out."

"I warn you, McCoy." Rutherford didn't move when Mr. Dorsey approached. "I will find Charlotte, and when I do, anyone who tries to get in my way will regret his actions."

The list of atrocities Reid had witnessed in the fur trade had hardened him against men like Rutherford, even if he was a threat. Murder, abduction, scalping, gunfire—and worse.

Reid's heart raced with the force of his anger at the evil he had witnessed and those who perpetrated it—men like Rutherford. "Mr. Dorsey, our guest is leaving. Now."

Rutherford didn't wait for Mr. Dorsey to haul him out. He left the house without another word.

Reid slammed the door behind him. He detested men who stooped to make threats—and hated the guilt he felt at leaving his mother behind while Rutherford's warning still lingered in the air.

Closing his eyes, he tried to rub away the pain. What choice did he have? He had to return to the interior, which meant he'd have to hire someone to guard his mother and servants until the threat passed.

"Reid?" His mother shrieked as she rushed from her room and gripped the railing, staring down at him. Her eyes were red and swollen from crying. She sagged in relief when she saw him. "I thought you left me."

He climbed the stairs two at a time and went to her. Putting his hand on the small of her back, he led her into her bedchamber. "I won't leave until morning, Mam. I told you that earlier."

She gripped his arm and allowed him to help her back into bed. Her white hair was in disarray, and she still wore her pink morning gown, though it was now evening. "But your faither . . ."

He nodded his understanding. "I ken."

"He left me, Reid, just like you leave me."

"But I come back, every three years."

She lay in bed, still clinging to his arms. "He came back every three years too—until—"

"I'm not Faither." The force of his statement made him pause. Would he ever forgive his father for abandoning them?

Kneeling by the bed, Reid took her hands into his, and tried to smile, though the mention of his father made the muscles of his jaw tighten. He moved the hair out of her face and spoke in a soothing voice. "I will return."

"Why didn't he want to come home?" Her eyes pleaded for an answer. "Why did he choose to stay—" Her voice broke. "With her?"

Reid didn't have answers for his mother. The only thing he knew was that instead of his father returning home fifteen years ago when he retired from the fur trade, Sean McCoy had chosen to stay in the interior with his Indian wife and children with no explanation to his legal wife and child. The betrayal had destroyed Reid's mother. But he wouldn't let it destroy him.

He had joined the North West Company to prove to himself, and to his father, that he could be a fur trader *and* a man of integrity—unlike his father. When Sean McCoy had heard that Reid joined the North West Company, he invited Reid to his home, but Reid wouldn't give him the satisfaction of seeing his son grown and prosperous. Instead, he chose to focus his energy on providing for his mother and pushing his father's memory as far away as possible.

"I promise to return, Mam."

She closed her eyes and finally nodded. "You havna taken a country wife, like your faither?"

"No."

"Promise me you willna."

"I willna take a country wife." Though he'd been pressured several times to marry the daughter of an influential chief to secure the trade, he had declined. He wanted nothing to bind him to the interior and nothing to prevent him from returning to Montreal when he retired. "When I become a shareholder, I will have a stake in the company, and it will allow me to retire comfortably just a few years after. We'll finally have peace."

Her breathing began to even out, and her grip on his hands loosened. After a day of crying, she finally fell asleep.

Reid bent forward and placed his forehead on their clasped hands, whispering a prayer of protection for his mother while he was away. He hated leaving. Hated the emotional toll it took on her, but he couldn't give up everything he'd worked these past fifteen years to secure. He wanted to become a shareholder if for no other reason than to give his mother the peace and joy she deserved.

Leaving her bedchamber, he closed her door softly and stood in the upper hall across from Lady Charlotte's room. The faint sound of trickling bathwater met his ears—yet it did nothing to dispel his headache. He had paperwork to put in order before he left in the morning—and now he would also need to find a guard for his mother.

When his gaze landed on the front door, the thought of Roger Rutherford filled his chest with fire. The man would be relentless in his pursuit, of that Reid was certain. The lass wouldn't be safe in Montreal or on the voyage to Grand Portage. She wouldn't be safe until she and Stephen were married.

Reid gripped the railing. Not only was he honor bound to protect the lass because of his promise to Stephen, his conscience wouldn't allow him to leave her unprotected. The only option he had was to take her with him, dressed as an assistant clerk. When they arrived at the Rendezvous in Grand Portage, he would hand her over to Stephen and be done with her.

If anyone discovered she was a woman between Montreal and Grand Portage on the shores of Lake Superior, Reid would lose all chance of becoming a shareholder—but it was a chance he would have to take.

Stephen Corning had saved his life. The least he could do was reunite him with his fiancée.

In the morning, Lady Charlotte would need to transform into a fifteen-year-old boy. It wouldn't be easy, but—if it be God's will—then they might have a chance.

Charlotte awoke with a start. The room was dark, and for a moment, she couldn't recall where she was. Her heart hammered as she gripped the covers and scanned the room. Bits and pieces of the previous night returned to her conscious mind. The warm bath, the sweet fragrance of lavender soap, the soft sheets on the feather-tick mattress. A full belly.

She'd found Mr. McCoy.

Easing back into the mattress, she looked toward the window. A slice of daylight rimmed the far horizon, and for the first time in weeks, it didn't dip and sway with the motion of a ship. She couldn't remember the last time she'd been so comfortable or felt this safe. She feared that the moment she stepped foot outside the bed, reality would crash back and she'd have to run again.

If only she could stay here forever.

But thoughts of Roger forced her from her bed. Pushing aside the covers, she left the warmth. When her feet touched the cold floor, a shiver ran up the length of her spine. Would it be light enough to look out the window and see if the house was being watched?

Charlotte tiptoed across the wide room and stood behind the drapery to peek at the snow-covered lawn. The world was blanketed in pure white crystals. They lay on the dark branches of the trees, the rooftops of the neighboring homes, and the ridge of the stone fence circling the property. Nothing stirred in the frozen scene, except the wisps of smoke curling from the chimneys along the road leading down to the riverfront. As far as she could see from up on the hill, Montreal spread out before her like a sleeping giant ready to stir.

If Roger hid in this idyllic scene, she could not see him.

Another chill ran up her spine at the thought of him. Would she ever know a day when she did not fear his appearance?

A knock at the door made her jump. "Lass?"

Mr. McCoy.

Charlotte still wore the oversized nightgown Mrs. Mallarme had loaned her the night before. A quick perusal of the room told her that her other clothes were nowhere to be found. She grabbed a blanket off the bed and pulled it onto her shoulders as she walked to the door. "Yes?"

"I must speak with you."

"Can it wait a moment?" Even though he'd seen her at her worst yesterday, the thought of the handsome fur trader witnessing her in the hideous nightgown made her blush.

"It canna wait." His voice held no patience for debate. "Will you open the door?"

"I'm not properly dressed."

There was a short pause, and then his voice was lower than before. "If you plan to come with me, being improperly dressed will be the least of your worries."

He would take her to Stephen? Hope flared in her chest as she flung the door open and found him standing in the dark hallway holding a pile of clothing.

Without waiting for an invitation, he pushed past her and tossed everything onto the bed. "Mrs. Mallarme went next door and bought some clothes from the gardener's son. They'll have to do until I can get your allotment from the company. You'll also find a pair of boots and some shears in the pile."

Charlotte held the blanket tight around her shoulders, her fisted hands resting on her chest. "Shears?"

Mr. McCoy finally turned to look at her. His gaze caught on her hair, which was unbound and falling around her shoulders in a curtain of lavender-scented, auburn curls. The muscles in his cheek worked a bit before he spoke. "It'll be a shame to see you lose those bonnie locks."

Her hand came up and she touched a curl, dread tightening her stomach. "Lose my hair?"

He stood at least a foot taller than her, his attractive face drawn into serious lines. "I am willing to take you into the interior, but only if you are willing to do exactly as I say. If anyone suspects you are a woman—for even a moment—we will both lose everything." His dark brown eyes held no room for discussion. "You will cut your hair, wear these clothes, and change your name. You will change how you walk, talk, and eat. Everything you've learned as a lady must be forgotten. The men in my employ willna think twice to spit, swear, or defecate in your presence—and you will not bat an eyelash. Do you understand?"

Swallowing hard, she tried to keep the revulsion from showing on her face. But if the alternative was marrying Roger, she would do what he said.

"I understand."

"It will take us at least six weeks to get to Grand Portage," he continued with the same stern voice. "You will be cold, tired, and sore. And then you will be hot, tired, and sore. You will be expected to do your job like everyone else. I willna go easy on you. We paddle for twelve hours a day, portage many miles, and sleep on the earth at night. No one will help you." He stared hard at her. If he was trying to dissuade her from going, he would be disappointed. He didn't know what it had been like to live with Roger the past two years.

"You'll be bit by mosquitoes, stung by wasps, burnt by the sun, pelted by hail, and soaked by the rain." His voice held little emotion. "You'll meet Indians along the way, and some of their customs will alarm you at best—horrify you at worst. You will see bloodshed, drunkenness, and disease." He stopped again, but she didn't move a muscle, afraid he might have second thoughts. "If you survive until Grand Portage and you marry Stephen, it will be in secret with a priest. You will be forced to return the same way you came. If Stephen canna persuade his superiors to let him forfeit his contract, you will return to Montreal without protection. If any of the men who take you back discover you are a woman, you'll be at their mercy."

A dozen thoughts assailed her, and common sense tried to prevail in her mind, but she could not risk a marriage to Roger. She would deal with whatever came, one step at a time. What other option did she have?

He waited for her response, but she didn't give one.

"Do you still plan to come?"

The blanket Charlotte wore did little to ward off the cold in the room. Her skin was covered in gooseflesh, and her teeth had started to chatter, but she straightened her shoulders with resolve. She would either arrive at Grand Portage to marry Stephen, or she would die trying. Either way, she could not remain in Montreal or go back to England.

"I do."

He studied her for a moment and shook his head. "I'm probably a fool, but I canna leave you here."

"Thank you," she whispered and bowed her head, so she didn't have to look into his dark eyes. She hated begging him to take her. If she wasn't desperate, she would never dream of asking him to risk everything for her.

"What do people call you—besides Charlotte?"

"My lady," she replied meekly.

He scoffed. "That'll never do. Do you have a pet name?"

"My parents called me Lottie." Just the thought of her parents, both gone so quickly, filled her with grief. If they hadn't died, none of this would have happened.

"That willna do either." He crossed his arms and looked her over from head to toe. "Charlie."

"Charlie?"

"From now on you'll be Charlie Crawford, assistant clerk in the North West Company."

"What will be my duties?"

"You'll learn as you go, but your main job will be to keep track of the inventory in my canoes. If you were a full-time clerk in the interior, you'd be responsible for transactions and record-keeping, as well as maintaining a daily diary for the shareholders. But you won't need to worry about those things, since you'll be in Stephen's care by then." He nodded, as if his perusal of her was satisfactory. "I'll take you to the main office before we leave for Grand Portage and write up your contract. There you'll be given your allotted clothing and other supplies to assist me on the journey to the Rendezvous."

"Why Crawford?"

"My mither's maiden name." He moved around her toward the door. "Be ready to go in ten minutes."

Ten minutes to turn herself into a boy? It used to take her lady's maid at least an hour to complete her toilette.

But she wasn't a lady anymore—at least, she wouldn't be again for a long time.

After Mr. McCoy left her room, Charlotte stepped over to the bed and looked down at the shears. They gleamed in the growing light, taunting her. Once she cut her hair, there would be no going back.

But what was there to go back to?

Picking up the shears, she went to the vanity and took a seat in front of the mirror. Her hair had always been her crowning beauty. Thick, curly, and auburn, it drew compliments wherever she went. But no matter what she had to do, getting to Stephen would be worth the sacrifice.

She took a lock of hair and drew the shears up to her head. She would wear it as long as Mr. McCoy and tie it back in a queue. Without thinking twice, she snipped the blades together and her ringlet fell to the ground.

A sob scratched at her throat, but she wouldn't let it escape. She had already shed far too many tears since leaving Blissfield Manor, and she was done with self-pity and pride. Her life and her inheritance depended on her playing the part of a boy, so she would do it with all her heart.

In no time, clumps of her thick hair lay in piles on the floor. After tying the remainder back with a black ribbon, she didn't even take the time to look at her reflection in the mirror. If she did, she might start to feel sorry for herself, and she had no room for that today. Instead, she went to the bed and studied the clothes.

Weeks of illness had made her painfully thin, but it hadn't diminished her female curves. If anything, it heightened them. She took a strip of linen that Mrs. Mallarme had had the forethought to provide and bound it around her chest. Then she pulled the white shirt over her head, securing the top buttons close to her chin. The sleeves were too long, so she rolled them up to her wrists and then put on the brown vest and coat. The trousers were also too big, but there was a belt in the pile, which she cinched tight around her waist. She placed the brown tweed hat, which matched the coat, onto her head. It was also too big, but it would do well to cover her hair. Finally, she pulled on the pair of woolen socks and laced up the boots that were oversized.

When she finally had the courage to look into the mirror, she stared at her reflection much longer than she'd planned. The transformation was complete. She looked like a boy and nothing like the proper young lady she had worked her whole life to perfect.

The tears came without warning.

Would she ever feel beautiful again? She hated herself for being vain when she was about to embark on the most dangerous journey of her life. But she hadn't seen Stephen in almost five years, and the last thing she wanted was to appear to him for the first time looking like an ugly, undernourished boy.

A fit of coughs took her by surprise, and she bent over with the force of them. Her throat felt raw, and her chest burned, but she couldn't reveal that she felt ill. Mr. McCoy might change his mind.

Wiping the tears that had come to her eyes with the force of her cough, she took several deep breaths and opened the door. Nothing in the room belonged to her, so she left everything where it was and went into the hallway. The house was quiet as her large boots flopped against the wooden stairs.

"Charlie?" Mr. McCoy entered the foyer through a door at the back of the room. He was dressed like a gentleman, with tan breeches, a white shirt, and a dark blue waistcoat with tails. His tall black boots looked like they had recently been shined, and his face had been shaved. In his hand he carried a top hat, while a black coat was draped over his arm. When he caught sight of her, he paused.

He was one of the finest-looking men she'd ever met. Refined, yet rugged. Powerful, yet compassionate.

His eyes traveled the length of her, and it took every bit of self-control not to fidget or shy away from his bold stare. If she stood before Mr. McCoy in gown, how different this moment would be. She would be poised and confident, not uncertain and embarrassed.

He nodded and motioned for her to follow him. "Mrs. Mallarme has prepared our breakfast, but we'll have to eat on the way to the main office. We are already late, and my men are waiting for me on the wharf."

She didn't say anything as she followed him into the kitchen. Mrs. Mallarme and the butler sat at the table, eating their breakfast. They both looked up when she entered.

"Mark my words," Mrs. Mallarme said, holding a steaming cup in her hands. "She'll make you regret your decision."

"I would like to leave before Rutherford returns," Mr. McCoy said to Charlotte, ignoring his housekeeper. "Take the sack of food there by the hearth and the pack by the door." He pointed to the things she needed to grab.

She wanted to ask how far they would travel today, but she didn't dare. The last thing she wanted was to annoy him.

"I said goodbye to my mither," Mr. McCoy told the servants, his voice deep with sorrow. "Mr. Jenkins will be here soon to start his guard duties."

"A waste o' time and money, if you ask me," Mrs. Mallarme said to the butler. "If the master just left *Lady* Charlotte in Montreal, his mother wouldn't need protection."

"That will be enough, Mrs. Mallarme." Mr. McCoy exhaled. "I've made my decision."

Guilt twisted Charlotte's insides when she thought about the danger she was placing these strangers in—especially Mr. McCoy and his mother.

She turned away from Mrs. Mallarme's cold stare and lifted the pack near the door. It was heavier than she expected, and she had a hard time putting it on her back.

"Here." Mr. McCoy easily lifted it with one hand and helped her put the straps over her shoulders. When he noticed her grimace, he said, "You better get used to it. You'll be toting a lot heavier packs in the coming days."

She bit her lip to refrain from protesting.

Mrs. Mallarme sipped her beverage as she nodded a knowing glance at the butler.

Charlotte straightened her shoulders and lifted her chin high. "I can manage, Mr. McCoy."

He grabbed his own pack, which was twice the size of hers, and slipped it over his shoulders. "Drop the mister and just call me McCoy—or Reid." He opened the back door and glanced out. "Pull the brim of your hat low and step fast. We have much to accomplish this morn."

The servants came to the door and waved goodbye to their employer. And though Charlotte hardly knew them and hadn't been well received, a part of her felt melancholy leaving the safety and comfort of their warm kitchen behind.

Wagon ruts scarred the alley behind the McCoy home. The mud had not yet melted, and a fine layer of snow still covered the world around them.

"Rutherford might be watching," Reid said quietly. "I want you to keep your head low and try not to walk like that."

"Like what?"

He nodded toward her. "Like . . . well, like that."

She frowned. "How am I walking?"

"Like you're trying to balance a pile of books on your head—all stiff and proper. You need to walk like a man. Bend your shoulders forward and widen your stride—and stop swinging your hips."

At the mention of her hips, her cheeks filled with heat. She had never watched herself walk before. Did her hips sway like he said?

Doing as Reid commanded, she adjusted her walk. It felt awkward and unnatural, but she would do whatever was necessary.

"I will watch for Rutherford and try to keep you covered. My men should have our canoes ready to go, since we were supposed to leave yesterday. Speak as little as possible and learn as much as you can. The less attention you draw, the better."

Charlotte nodded in understanding. As she struggled to keep up with Reid, the exertion made her chest tighten. She tried to suppress the need to cough until her eyes watered and her lungs burned. Finally, she had to give in to her body's demands.

Reid didn't slow his pace to accommodate her condition. Instead, he reached out and slapped the pack on her back. The force of the contact made her stumble forward.

Her eyes grew wide, and she stopped. "Why did you do that?"

He turned to look at her as he continued to walk. He cocked his eyebrow but did not smile—though she saw the laughter in his eyes. "I said I was going to treat you like all my other men—and when they cough, I slap their back."

She stared at him in disbelief—and then ran to catch up to him.

# Chapter Three

The Port of Montreal hummed with life as Reid walked alongside Charlotte—Charlie—down the thoroughfare to the waterfront. Thankfully, his headache from the day before had dissipated, but it threatened to return. He'd tried not to be impatient as he had taken her to the North West Company's main office. There she had signed a standard five-year contract under the name Charlie Crawford and been given two new sets of clothes and a pair of boots, which fit much better. Along with the clothes, she'd been given a blanket and a wooden cassette box, which held all the necessary writing supplies she would need as his assistant clerk. Paper, ink, a journal, several ledgers, and so on were tucked into the box she now toted awkwardly, along with the large pack on her back.

When she had laid eyes on the paper, she had fingered it tenderly, and he'd almost chastised her for the feminine behavior, but something had stopped him. He recognized the longing within her for something dear to her heart, though he didn't know what it might be.

He could have helped her with the burden she carried, but if his men saw him assisting the new clerk, they would raise their eyebrows for sure—and she would be teased incessantly.

Scanning the bustling wharf, he looked for signs of Rutherford but didn't see the older man. It would be easy to miss him in the crush of people and cargo lining the riverfront. Any of the dozens of warehouses, stores, and homes could hide someone who didn't want to be seen.

"Remember to walk like a man and keep your face down," Reid said quietly to Charlotte.

She jostled the cassette and almost lost her hold on it. "Do you see him?"

"No, but we canna be certain."

Thousands of wooden boxes, barrels, and drums had recently arrived from England and had already been inventoried. They would be carried in the large Montreal cargo canoes to Grand Portage. Tons of flour, salt pork, corn, rum, high wine, and the like would be hauled into the interior along with the trade items for the Indians. Kettles, needles, cloth, beads, hooks, rifles, and much more were used to trade for animal furs—and all of it was imported from England.

Hundreds of men worked along the shoreline sorting the goods that would fill hundreds of canoes leaving within the next week. Over four tons of cargo would be hauled in each one, along with ten to twelve men. Voyageurs were the heartiest men Reid had ever met. Most of them were French-Canadians. Their short stature and wide shoulders, coupled with their superior strength, made them ideal for paddling.

The noise and commotion filled Reid's ears like the incessant grinding of a gristmill. He much preferred the quiet of the woods over the bustle of the city. It would be good to return to the lakes and rivers he'd come to love.

"The voyageurs are made up of two different groups." Reid pointed to a group of men stacking packages into five large Montreal canoes in preparations for their departure. "The north men stay in the interior through the winter and only return to Montreal at the end of their contract, which might last from one to seven years."

She nodded as she observed the voyageurs at work.

"The pork eaters are over there." He pointed to another crew working independent of the north men. "They do not winter over in the interior. Instead, their job is to bring the cargo from Montreal to Grand Portage every spring and then to bring the furs from Grand Portage back to Montreal to be shipped off to England by fall. The two groups rarely work together because the north men have little respect for the pork eaters."

"Why do they call them pork eaters?"

"Because their main food item on the long journey from Montreal to Grand Portage and back is pork."

"They just paddle back and forth?"

"Aye. And stay in Montreal during the winter."

Charlotte watched the activity with keen curiosity. Color had returned to her cheeks and her brown eyes held a shine today that they had lacked yesterday. When he had gone to her room earlier, he had been stopped short by the transformation a bath and a good night of sleep had made on the lass—and her hair. He'd never seen anything like the thick curls that had fallen over her shoulders almost down to her waist. It had taken his breath away to see her standing there wrapped in a blanket, her face still soft from sleep. She was every bit a woman. For a second, he had thought twice about bringing the bonnie lass into the male-dominated fur trade, but then she had come downstairs dressed like a man, her hair cut short, and all the womanly curves hidden under her clothes, and he knew she was willing to do whatever it would take to get to Stephen.

"Hullo, *Bourgeois*!" Calum Roberson called to Reid from his place near one of the canoes, using the term designated for the chief trader. "Glad to see you could finally make it this fine morn."

Reid hadn't seen his good friend and long-time assistant clerk Calum since last fall when they had arrived in Montreal. Calum had left immediately for Scotland to see his mam and had recently arrived back in Canada. He was only five years younger than Reid but looked up to him as a mentor.

The old friends met with a hearty handshake.

"'Tis good to see you," Reid said with a wide smile. "How was your crossing?"

Calum didn't answer, because he had laid eyes on Charlotte. "And who's this wee lad? Planning to replace me, are you?"

It was time to begin the charade in earnest, and Reid said a quick prayer that it would work. In the light of day, Charlotte's feminine features were much more attractive than they had been the evening before. She was a bonnie lass, even with her short hair and trousers, but she could pass for a fair-skinned lad, too, if no one was the wiser.

"This is our new assistant clerk, Charlie Crawford," Reid told Calum. "He'll be traveling with us to Grand Portage."

"Ah!" Calum put his hand on Charlotte's head and rubbed her hat against her hair until it slid down over her forehead.

Indignation rose in her eyes, and her mouth twisted into a scowl. But to her credit, she didn't speak.

"An assistant of my very own to torture." Calum grinned, revealing a wide mouth with evenly spaced teeth. "But you're not a strong lad, are you?" He gripped her thin upper arm. "Did your mam coddle you and keep you away from the men's work?"

The indignation in her eyes turned to panic, and Reid knew he'd need to step in and make an excuse for the girl's lack of body weight or muscle. "The lad was sick crossing the ocean. It'll take a bit of time to put some meat on his bones."

Calum let go of her arm and lifted one brow. "It'll take more than a bit of time." He narrowed his eyes as he looked her over, his stern countenance an act for Charlotte's benefit, no doubt. Calum was the jolliest person Reid had ever known—sometimes to a fault. His humor could get wearisome after a time. "How old are you, lad?"

Charlotte swallowed hard. "Fifteen," she said, though it sounded more like a question than a statement.

Calum frowned. "You either are or you aren't."

"I just had my birthday," she said in a way that seemed to excuse her lack of confidence in her age.

With a laugh, Calum knocked Charlotte's hat off. "We'll make a man out of you yet."

Charlotte scrambled to grab her hat and pulled it down tight onto her head, scanning the riverbank, no doubt looking for Rutherford.

Reid crossed his arms and took his place between her and the thoroughfare, so one side of her was to the river and the other was protected by him. She was such a wee thing, she wouldn't be hard to hide. "He's just left his mither," Reid said, as a way of explaining Charlotte's awkwardness. "You remember how it was when you first joined. We'll have to go easy on him until he learns his way around."

"Easy?" Calum laughed. "I'll be anything but easy on him."

"We're already late." Reid tilted his head toward the brigade of canoes almost ready for departure. "Let's be off."

Reid led the way to the water's edge, where he greeted several men.

"I've already inspected the seams of the canoes," Calum told Reid. "And I've gone over the inventory list. All our cargo is accounted for." He presented the ledger he had been holding under his arm to show Reid that he'd done the work.

"How many men do we have?" Reid asked.

"Forty-eight, now that Charlie's here."

Reid gave the canoes a cursory glance, trusting Calum's inspection. "From now on, I want you to work with Charlie. Show him the inventory lists and explain what will be expected of him each day."

Calum nodded. "Will he be in my canoe?"

"No." Reid shook his head and realized he'd spoken too quickly. He took a little more time to explain. "I'll keep him in my canoe for now—until he's more comfortable."

"Comfortable?" Calum snorted. "You're getting soft, McCoy."

Reid located the guide who had been hired to take their brigade into the interior. Pierre. He was *Métis*, his father European, a fur trader, and his mother a Chippewa Indian. Pierre knew the best route to travel to Grand Portage and would lead the men, with Reid's approval, through the lakes, rivers, and portages. Beside Reid, who was a senior clerk and the highest-ranking officer of the brigade, the guide was the best-paid man in the group. After discussing a few trivial matters, Reid told him they were ready to leave.

"Time to move out!" Pierre shouted in French to the voyageurs in his vicinity.

The men took up their paddles and the one personal bag they were allowed and moved to the five canoes. Each person assumed their positions around the boats, all standing in varying depths of water. At the call of the guide, all the voyageurs, except the *avants*, who sat at the front of the canoes, jumped into their vessels at the same moment.

"Charlie," Reid said to the lass, "you'll travel with me in this canoe." He pointed to the one closest to them.

A movement caught Reid's eye. Rutherford stood near a warehouse, speaking with a bourgeois from the XY Company, one of Reid's rivals. If Rutherford had noticed Charlotte, he wasn't paying her attention, so engrossed was he in his conversation with the XY man.

"Quick, lass," Reid said under his breath, close behind her. "Into the canoe and keep your face toward the river."

"Roger?" she asked on a shaky breath.

"Aye. But dinna show any fear and dinna look for him. Just get into the canoe like everyone else."

She did as he bid, her footsteps unsteady as the canoe tilted slightly to the side.

Reid held it steady with the help of their avant, and she found a place to sit on a bench in the rear of the canoe.

At Pierre's next command, the avants pushed their canoes into the river and jumped into the stern, immediately directing their boats toward the rushing current.

"Strike!" At Pierre's call, the voyageurs dipped their brightly colored paddles into the muddy water, pulled back, and then lifted them out again, over and over, in a well-timed rhythm. Pierre called the synchronized movements for the first few seconds, but then the men fell into the natural pace of sixty-strokes a minute.

"We'll travel two miles downriver to Lachine," Reid said to Charlotte. "And leave the St. Lawrence River to enter the lake of the two mountains. There, at the head of Saint Anne's rapids, the last church on the island of Montreal will bid us farewell on our journey." Many of the voyageurs were Catholic, and they would stop at the church to pray for Divine guidance and safe travels. The church had been dedicated to the tutelary saint of voyages for this reason.

As Reid spoke to Charlotte, he watched Rutherford out of the corner of his eye. The Englishman took notice of Reid's brigade, as did many others on the wharf, but he quickly continued his conversation with the XY man.

Before long, Rutherford was out of view, and Reid turned his focus back to his canoe.

Charlotte sat beside him, her back straight, her shoulders stiff, and her chin high. She looked out at the river and did not glance behind her toward the life she had just left behind.

Reid offered a prayer for safety and protection, and asked God to help him do right by Charlie Crawford. Any number of things could go wrong.

It would take a miracle to get her to Stephen.

For almost an hour, the men paddled in perfect tempo, keeping to the rhythm of several songs sung in French and led by Pierre. Charlotte was familiar with many of the songs, but others were foreign to her, though she spoke the language fluently.

The wharf at Montreal had faded, and the empty countryside had opened before them. It didn't take long for the sun to melt the remaining snow and take the chill from the air. On both sides, the riverbanks were low, allowing Charlotte to see cultivated fields for miles.

"Where is my paddle?" she asked Reid, who sat beside her, his steady gaze watching the men, the canoes, the countryside all at once.

"Officers are not required to paddle."

"But you said—"

"I was trying to dissuade you." He spoke quietly, under the sound of the voyageurs' song.

The bench beneath her had grown uncomfortable, but she would not complain. "Nothing you could have said would be more frightening than my former life."

He finally took his gaze off the horizon and shook his head just enough to silence any further conversation about her past.

Behind them, the *gouvernail* of their canoe stood with a long pole. Reid had explained that the gouvernail, along with the avant, directed the course of the canoe. The avant sat in the front and watched for rocks, branches, or other snags that could damage the canoe, while the gouvernail watched the voyageurs paddle and kept their rhythm in synchronization. The *mileux* sat in the middle, and their only job was to paddle.

Two low-lying mountains with snow-covered tops came into view in the distance, capturing Charlotte's attention. She had never seen mountains before coming to Canada and was enraptured by them. Reid had told her they would veer off the St. Lawrence and take a tributary upriver toward a lake that sat between them.

"*Arretez,*" Pierre called to the brigade. Each gouvernail in each canoe echoed the command to stop, and all the voyageurs lifted their paddles out of the water.

The canoes continued to glide down the river at a slower pace, while the men pulled pipes and tobacco out of their bags, chatting comfortably with one another. There was a general sense of excitement among the men, which Charlotte marveled at. How could they be eager for the long trip ahead? She knew why she was anxious to get to Grand Portage, but what about these men? They had nothing to look forward to but turning around and coming back the way they had traveled.

"Every hour we stop for a break and smoke a pipe," Reid explained to her as he, too, pulled a pipe from his bag. "Each employee is given an allowance of tobacco as part of his supplies."

Charlotte nodded her understanding as the men filled their pipes with the leathery brown leaves and pushed them down with their fingers. Matches were produced and used to light the pipes.

"We break for as long as it takes to smoke the pipe." Reid lit his pipe and inhaled a draught of smoke.

Calum's canoe was beside Reid's, and he produced a second pipe, which he offered to Charlotte.

"No, thank you," she said kindly—and then remembered she was supposed to sound like a man. "I don't smoke," she said a bit deeper.

He pushed it at her and didn't give her a choice. "Everyone smokes."

Charlotte frowned and caught Reid watching her. A half smile tilted his mouth as he took another inhale of smoke.

Glancing around, she found every man smoking, without exception.

The voyageurs began to look her way, and for the first time since departing Montreal, she became the center of attention—the last thing she wanted.

"Is the boy too good to smoke?" asked one voyageur in French.

"Maybe his *maman* wouldn't let him," said another.

"His maman isn't here anymore," the first said, and the rest joined in laughing. "It's time he became a man."

"It'll put some hair on your chest," Calum said to Charlotte as he pushed tobacco into the pipe.

The others jeered her on, but Charlotte felt physically ill to think about smoking the pipe. Her father used to smoke when her mother wasn't looking, and she always liked the smell, but she had no desire to try it herself.

She pleaded to Reid with her eyes, but he looked away from her toward the riverbank, and she remembered what he had said just that morning. Everything she had learned as a lady must be forgotten. She should not so much as blush in their presence.

And she must do what they did if she wanted the charade to succeed.

With a slight nod, she allowed Calum to light the pipe.

"Just hold it to your lips and inhale through your mouth," Calum instructed.

All the men watched as she put the mouthpiece between her trembling lips. Reid turned his gaze back to her and observed her quietly.

Smoke spiraled out of the bowl of the pipe, scenting the air with the fragrance of sweet tobacco. It gave her a twinge of longing for her father, but she pushed all thoughts from her mind and took a deep breath.

The smoke filled her lungs and immediately began to burn. She coughed uncontrollably, forcing Calum to take the pipe from her before it fell into the river.

Reid pounded her back as the entire brigade roared with laughter.

The men went back to their conversations, but Reid handed a canteen to Charlotte. "Take a drink."

She looked at it warily. "Is it rum or whiskey or some other disgusting beverage I'll be forced to drink as well?"

He grinned. "'Tis only water."

Charlotte took the canteen and allowed the cool water to fill her mouth. It coated her throat and eased the burning in her lungs. But her eyes still watered.

Reid leaned back again and continued to smoke his pipe. The smoke left his mouth in a series of rings floating on the air as they dissipated into the clear sky above. "They won't leave you be until you're smoking a pipe like the rest of them."

She gagged at the thought of smoking that pipe again.

Reid grinned like before and continued to enjoy his break with the other men.

Water rippled by the edge of the canoe, and an eagle soared on the wind above the pine trees in the distance. Charlotte tried to steady her breathing as she listened to the boisterous laughter of the voyageurs.

"*Partir!*" Pierre called to the men. Some took another draw from their pipes, while others tapped the used tobacco into the river and put their pipes back into their packs.

Within seconds, the brigade sliced through the water again.

Just as Reid had told her, they left the wide river and followed a narrow tributary, twisting and turning their way into a vast lake. They paddled for another hour across the expanse and came to the other side. A quaint little church sat on a point of land jutting into the lake at the foot of one mountain, just as Reid had said. It was positioned so close to the water's edge that Charlotte wondered if they feared flooding. On either side of the church, hundreds of Indian lodges were scattered around the level ground, and just beyond the church, the lake narrowed again and turned into a series of rapids as far as she could see.

Charlotte held her breath at the sight of the Indian village. Never in all her life had she expected to see Indians. She'd read about them, even saw pictures, but she hadn't anticipated seeing them in person. While part of her shivered at the thought, another part of her was curious to see if the Indians looked and dressed like the books portrayed.

With expert ease, Pierre guided the brigade to the shore. Before the canoes touched the land, most of the voyageurs disembarked from the vessels right into the lake. One man from each brigade stayed in the cold water and held the canoes in place, while the others began to unload the cargo.

No one offered to help Charlotte leave the canoe, so she was forced to step into the lake like the rest of them. The frigid water filled her boots and wet her trousers, sending a shock throughout her body. The others didn't seem to be bothered by the inconvenience, so she had to pretend it didn't trouble her, either, though a chill caused her teeth to rattle.

Within fifteen minutes, twenty-thousand tons of cargo were unloaded and stacked on dry land.

"Why do the men get in and out of the canoes in the water?" Charlotte asked Reid, who stood watching the men work. "Why don't they run them ashore and spare their shoes?" Her own feet squeaked with each step she took and her body shivered.

"The bark used to line the canoes would be damaged by the rocks and gravel. The canoes only leave the water once they have been emptied. Then they are carried onto land."

As he spoke, four men surrounded each canoe and lifted them onto their shoulders as if they weighed nothing.

"The canoes are very light," Reid told her when he caught her look of surprise. "They are little more than bark and branches."

Yet they carried tons of cargo and almost a dozen men.

With practiced ease, the voyageurs flipped the canoes over and laid them on their topsides, and then, one by one, the men walked toward the church.

Reid and Calum stayed behind with the cargo. Calum found a rock to lean against, where he pulled out his pipe again and proceeded to fill it with tobacco.

Reid didn't sit, nor did he smoke. Instead, he faced the lake from where they had just come, his eyes on the horizon.

Thankful for the opportunity to stretch, Charlotte stood beside him, the sunshine warming her shoulders. She watched the Indian village in quiet awe. Men and women went about their work, barely taking notice of the new brigade, while children ran and played in the cold mud. Smoke spiraled from dozens of campfires, and the unfamiliar scents of cooking food floated on the breeze.

A priest opened the door of the church and waited silently for the voyageurs to pass inside. The solemn men removed their caps as they entered, many forming the sign of the cross before stepping over the threshold.

When all the men had disappeared inside, the priest followed, closing the door behind him. Soon, the sounds of prayers echoed across the still waters, enveloping Charlotte, warming her more than the sun. Should she have joined the men? As a member of the Church of England, she wasn't sure how these men would view her participation in their worship. Better to follow Reid and Calum's example and stay with the cargo.

But why had Reid and Calum stayed?

"Do you not believe?" she asked Reid after a few moments of silence.

He turned his gaze from the lake. "Believe?"

"Why didn't you join the others?"

"Just as the pork eaters do not work with the north men," Calum offered as he puffed out a plume of smoke, "the officers do not worship with the voyageurs."

But did Reid believe? It mattered little to her and her need to get to Grand Portage, but it made her wonder about the man who had risked everything to help her. Had he done it out of Christian duty? Or something else?

"Are you a believer?" Reid asked.

Was she? The question, shot back at her, made her pause. Until her parents had died, she'd had the faith of a child. She'd attended church regularly and had given her heart to Christ. But once Roger had come into her life, he forbade her to attend services. She had wondered where God was when Roger began to turn the servants against her and dictate her every step. She'd felt alone, as if God had disappeared along with her parents. She didn't doubt He was there—somewhere—she just doubted whether He cared about her anymore.

"I'm a member of the Church of England," she said as a way of explanation, not wanting to reveal her deepest doubts to this man.

His left cheek came up in a half smile that held more sadness than joy. "That isna what I asked."

She turned her attention back to the little church on the edge of civilization. "I don't know what I believe anymore."

"Aye." He nodded and didn't ask her to explain, yet somehow, she knew he understood. But was that possible? He was a free man, able to come and go as he pleased. He wasn't required to marry someone he didn't love—or marry at all, for that matter. His money was his own, his future belonged to him. He couldn't possibly understand.

"Many of these men are superstitious," Calum said to Charlotte, tearing her thoughts away from Reid. "Their religion has intertwined with Indian beliefs and folklore, and they will do everything in their power to appease each god they believe in, even the Lord God. Most of them would refuse to continue our journey if we did not stop here first."

"They consider this the true start of our journey," Reid told her. "They would not go any farther unless they received a blessing from the priest."

Much sooner than she expected, the men left the church, and without a word from Reid, they pulled straps out of their bags and secured them to the packages on shore. With amazing dexterity, they hoisted the goods onto their backs, pulling the carrying strap up and over their shoulders, allowing the widest part of the strap to rest on their foreheads. With the packages on their backs, they started down a path that followed the edge of the water, many of them running, and disappeared around a curve at the bottom of the mountain.

"I've never seen anyone carry a package that way," she said in awe.

"The straps they use are called tump lines." Reid nodded at a man just slipping his over his head. "It allows the men to use their whole bodies to carry the packs, freeing their hands for balance and to navigate some of the steep hills they climb."

Calum finished his pipe and took up his personal bag and cassette, much like Charlotte's, and followed the men.

"This carrying place is about two miles long," Reid said to Charlotte. "We canna take the canoes over the rapids, so we unload them and portage them to a spot below the rapids. The men will make two or three trips before all the cargo is moved from here to the next loading point downriver. They are required to make at least two trips, but they can make more, if they'd like. Calum records how much each man carries, and when we arrive in Grand Portage, they will be paid according to how much cargo they moved. He will stay with the cargo on the other end of the path." Reid stood with his feet planted wide and his arms crossed over his chest as he supervised the men. His muscles rippled under his tight trousers as he shifted positions to point to a large barrel that required two men to carry without the use of their slings. "See that the barrel of whiskey is taken first." He spoke in French. "I do not want it to remain here in the village any longer than necessary."

The voyageurs did as he instructed and hoisted the barrel between their shoulders. Off they went, running down the trail.

It took the men less than two hours to move all the cargo, and when the last twenty men returned to where Reid and Charlotte waited, they lifted the canoes onto their shoulders, four men to a canoe, and started down the path for the third time.

Reid put his pack onto his back and helped Charlotte with hers. Then he handed her the wooden cassette she'd received that morning, while he picked up his own large traveling desk, and they started down the trail after the last of the voyageurs.

As the men pulled farther and farther ahead, Reid took his time and did not rush Charlotte. Her muscles ached and her chest burned with the need to cough, but she would not give in to the cries of her body. If these men could do all the things she'd witnessed this day, then surely she could carry a wooden box and back pack. If she didn't do her share of the work, the others might start to suspect there was something different about her.

"You're doing fine, lass," Reid said quietly. Had he sensed she needed a little reassurance? "Just keep to yourself and dinna do anything that might draw their attention, and none will be the wiser."

They walked in silence for a long time, Charlotte breathing heavier with each step. The cassette became awkward in her arms, so she readjusted the burden and almost dropped it.

Reid stopped and nodded at her box. "Set it atop of mine. I'll carry it for a wee bit."

She shook her head, not wanting him to have to give her special treatment. She'd agreed to do her part.

His warm brown eyes invited her to take this respite. "You're still ill. You need to rest as much as possible, so you dinna become worse. You're doing my men and me a favor by getting better."

He wouldn't take no for an answer and was giving her a way out of her agreement—at least for now.

It took all her strength to lift the box high enough to set it on top of his, but the moment she released it into his care, she felt better.

He carried the extra weight with ease, and Charlotte couldn't help but admire his strength and agility. He was practically a stranger, and she was alone with him in the middle of the wilderness, yet she felt safe in his presence. It made her long for Stephen and the protection he would offer her once they were married—though the thought made her hesitate. She hadn't seen him in five years. When he left home, he'd been nothing more than a gangly seventeen-year-old boy. Had he filled out like Reid? Become a man in this wilderness? Would he make her feel as safe as Reid made her feel?

By the time they reached the next landing point on the Utawas River, the men had already filled the canoes with the cargo and were ready to continue.

The brigade followed the Utawas for the remainder of the day, passing smaller Indian villages from time to time. This river was much narrower than the St. Lawrence and had far more twists and turns. They stopped every hour or so for a pipe break until the sun kissed the horizon and Pierre called for the brigade to stop for the night. A clearing on the north bank revealed a common campsite with several fire rings of stones and charred wood.

Charlotte was exhausted and thankful for a chance to camp.

"Work fast," Reid called out to the voyageurs as they jumped from their canoes and immediately began to unload all the cargo once again. "There is a storm on the horizon."

Dark clouds rimmed the western skyline, hiding the sinking sun.

Charlotte left the canoe, her feet and trousers getting wet once again, and tried to stay out of the way as the voyageurs worked. Within fifteen minutes, the cargo was unloaded and stacked on dry land. Large oilcloths were tied over the piles in preparation for the storm.

After the cargo was secured for the night, they hauled the canoes on shore. Several men began to fix broken seams with a black, sticky concoction made from pine-pitch and grease, while a group of others erected two tents, using the poles that had lain on the bottom of the canoes that held the cargo off the hulls.

When the canoes were repaired, they were tipped over, and the men prepared their beds underneath. Some of the men went into the surrounding forest to gather firewood, while others produced food from boxes and barrels and prepared their evening meal over several communal campfires.

"Here, Charlie," Calum called to her from where one of the tents was being set up away from the cargo and canoes.

Charlotte joined Calum, who was helping the voyageurs with the tent. "We'll sleep in here tonight," he said.

She took a step back at the thought of sleeping with the strange man in such a small tent. "I-I thought I'd have my own sleeping quarters."

Calum laughed. "You *have* been coddled." He shrugged. "Only the bourgeois is guaranteed his own tent. If you dinna want to sleep with me, you can always sleep under a canoe with the pork eaters."

Reid stood by the river with Pierre, his gaze focused on the water they had just passed. Another brigade traveled downriver and would be upon them soon.

He turned and met Charlotte's gaze, and suddenly she wasn't as worried about the sleeping arrangement as she had been. She didn't know Reid well, but she could see in his eyes that something was wrong.

Leaving Pierre, he came to her side.

"The lad wants his own sleeping quarters," Calum said with a mocking bow. "We'll have to call him Your Royal Highness before long and start carrying him from the canoe to the shore so his shoes dinna get soiled either."

"Charlie will sleep in my tent." Reid took her by the arm and led her away from Calum. "I must speak to you."

Calum lifted his eyebrows but didn't say a word.

Reid's tent was set up several paces away from Calum's and a great distance away from the voyageurs. He opened the flap and allowed her to step inside. Following, he let the flap fall behind him.

"The XY brigade is about to arrive," he whispered.

"XY?" She frowned in confusion, speaking just as quietly as him.

"The XY Company, rival fur traders. They were formed by a group of disgruntled Nor'West men several years ago. They still follow our routes, and we cross paths with them almost every day." His mouth turned down in disgust. "They're despicable human beings."

"Is that why you're so concerned?"

"I wish it was as simple as that." He ran his hand over his face then rubbed his temples for a moment. "I saw Rutherford speaking to the bourgeois of their brigade on the wharf in Montreal."

Charlotte's pulse ticked in her wrists. "And?"

"There's a chance he either hired them to locate you, or—" He paused.

"Or what?"

"Or he came with them."

Her throat suddenly felt dry, and she couldn't breathe. "He could do that?"

"The XY men are always willing to take passengers—for a cost."

"But." She'd thought she would be free of Roger once she left Montreal. "How will we know?"

"They will most likely camp across the river from us. 'Tis not unusual to send some of my men to spy on them—and they'll send men to spy on us too." His brown eyes were filled with concern, and she knew she was placing him in a compromising situation. If Roger found her, he'd call her out, and Reid would lose his job.

"I want you to stay in the tent for the rest of the night," he said. "I'll have your cot brought in here with your other things and get you something to eat. You canna leave this tent for any reason. Do you understand?"

The few hours of freedom she felt on the river had vanished, and she became a prisoner to fear all over again. Panic clawed at her chest, threatening to overwhelm her.

Reid must have seen it in her eyes, because he put his hands on her arms and bent his head until she was forced to look at him.

"I willna let him harm you, lass." His voice was low, soothing. "But you must do as I say and try not to worry."

Warmth filled her chest at the look of strength and confidence in his eyes. When he straightened, he stood at least a foot taller than her, offering her a sense of protection she had not felt in years.

"I will try," she said softly.

He regarded her for another moment, then stepped out of the tent, letting the flap fall in place behind him.

The sounds of camp filled the evening air. Laughter, singing, and conversation mingled with pots clanging, wood crackling in the fire pits, and footsteps shuffling in the dirt. The merriment of the men grated on her exhaustion and fear.

In the empty canvas tent, with no way of seeing the world around her, she felt cold and vulnerable—and desperately alone.

She sat in the corner and pulled her legs up to her chest, wishing Reid had stayed with her. Setting her cheek against her upturned knee, she rocked back and forth ever so gently and tried, in vain, not to worry.

# Chapter Four

Darkness filled the camp and was only dispelled by the five rings of fire where the men sat telling stories, eating from communal pots filled with pork and beans, and smoking their pipes at leisure. The scene usually filled Reid with comfort and excitement, especially on the first night out from Montreal. But tonight, he sat near his fire with Calum, his back rigid, his attention on the banks of the opposite river, and his thoughts not far from the lass hiding in his tent.

"You're not yourself." Calum put another stick on the fire. "Something on your mind?"

Reid forced his attention back to his campfire. Where were his men? He'd sent them to spy on the XY camp over three hours ago. They should have returned by now with news. He hadn't been specific but had asked them to look for a passenger traveling with the brigade.

"Does this have something to do with the XY Company?" Calum asked. "You've been on edge since we camped." He frowned and nodded toward Reid's tent. "And what's wrong with the lad? Is he unwell? He hasna come out of that tent all evening."

"Homesickness is my guess." Reid took a draw from his pipe. "It hits some harder than others. He'll be fine in a few weeks."

Calum looked toward the fire and nodded. "I recall my first night out. I never knew such fear. It was one thing to leave Scotland and travel on a ship to Montreal, another entirely to leave civilization and know I was heading into the northwestern wilderness."

Reid could also recall his first night. He'd been scared senseless, but his fear had been overridden by his desire to prove himself to his father.

Charlotte, on the other hand, had far more to worry about this evening. The man she had traveled thousands of miles to escape could be on the other side of the river.

A commotion at the edge of the camp caught Reid's attention. He placed his hand on the pistol over his hip, always wary of animals and enemies.

His three spies moved into the firelight. At the front of the group emerged Alexandre Dupree, one of Reid's most trusted voyageurs. He'd been with Reid for years. If there was something to be done, the first man Reid considered for the job was Alexandre.

While the other two men found a place at one of the campfires, Alexandre came to stand before Reid. He was much shorter than Reid, with a square, muscular build. A red cap covered his dark hair, and around his waist he wore a matching red sash. An oversized white shirt and brown pants were similar to the ones the other voyageurs wore.

"Have a seat," Reid told Alexandre in the French-Canadian's native tongue. He took a clean plate and handed it to the voyageur, indicating the stew bubbling over their fire. "You must be hungry."

Alexandre helped himself to the food and settled back against a log.

It took all of Reid's self-control to allow the man to eat in silence. The fire crackled, an owl hooted in the distance, and the laughter of the men filled the night air. Even though the temperatures had dropped, the storm held off, blanketing the sky in low-lying clouds. A streak of lightning danced within the clouds, but the rain did not fall.

Calum didn't speak either, but silently waited. He stared into the flames, looking pensive after speaking to Reid about his early years as a young clerk.

"What news do you bring?" Reid finally asked in French.

Alexandre sat straighter and set his plate on his lap. "We had no trouble spying on their men. Most have already started to drink."

A common practice among the voyageurs—one Reid could not abide. He rationed the alcohol the men were allowed to drink on the trail, something not all bourgeois bothered to do.

"How many men?"

"It's a small brigade," Alexandre answered. "Maybe thirty men."

"And did they have a passenger?"

Alexandre nodded. "An Englishman."

Rutherford.

Reid leaned forward, his pipe in hand, studying the licking flames. Even now, there could be XY men spying on them as well. Charlotte wouldn't be safe if they stayed in proximity with the rival company. Reid would either need to pull farther ahead or stay behind. Neither one was a good option and would require him to make excuses to Pierre.

"Anything else?" Reid asked.

Alexandre shook his head.

Calum watched Reid from across the fire. "Do you ken the passenger?"

Reid had never lied to Calum—had made a point of never lying to anyone—but he couldn't risk letting even his friends know about Charlotte or Rutherford.

"There was an Englishman speaking to their bourgeois in Montreal. I wondered if they took him along." Reid shrugged, as if it mattered little to him.

The night was still young, and the men would be up late with the excitement of the new journey, but Reid hated to leave Charlotte alone any longer. Now that he knew Rutherford was with the other brigade, he would need to tell her—and make a plan.

"The day has been long." Reid stood and tapped his pipe into the palm of his hand. "I think I'll turn in."

Calum nodded. "Good night."

Reid started toward his tent, but the closer he drew, the more aware he became of the fact that he would be sleeping beside a woman—a bonnie one, at that. He'd chosen a life of celibacy, out of deference to his faith, while most other officers had brought Indian and mixed-blood women into their tents and fur posts. It hadn't been an easy path—and it didn't mean he wasn't tempted by the same desires as other men.

How much harder would it be to sleep in the same tent as a woman and continue to honor his vow to God?

A bolt of lightning flashed across the sky, followed close by a crack of thunder. The rain began to fall at the same moment the wind started to gust. It pushed and pulled the tall pine trees surrounding the encampment. The men rushed from their campfires to find protection under the large canoes just as Reid lifted the flap of his tent.

He stepped into the interior quietly, his back to Charlotte, and tied the canvas straps together, trying to rein in his thoughts.

It was dark within the tent, but the steady flashes of lightning allowed him to see the interior clearly.

When he finished securing the flaps, he turned and found Charlotte lying on her cot, the blanket pulled up to her chin, watching him closely—warily.

"I thought you'd be asleep by now," he said quietly.

"I couldn't sleep."

He doubted he'd be able to sleep tonight either.

She continued to clutch her blanket, as if it was a shield. Did she not trust him?

The tent was small—only meant for one man—but he tried to stay as far from her as possible in the tight space. He usually disrobed before bed, but he couldn't do that with her in the tent—at least not while she watched. Slowly, he slipped out of his coat and placed it on the trunk at the foot of his cot.

Charlotte silently turned her back to him, allowing him a bit of privacy.

He unbuttoned his shirt and took it off, laying it on his coat. Then he sat and removed his boots and socks. He'd sleep in his trousers—a small sacrifice for Charlotte.

The storm continued to rage, but within the tent, they were dry, if a bit chilly. Reid slipped under the covers and turned on his side, facing Charlotte.

She no longer wore the hat, and he had the opportunity to finally have a full look at her riotous curls. Without the extra length and weight, they were coiled tightly in thick locks. He'd never seen bonnier hair in all his days and wished she hadn't needed to cut it. Though it was shorter than before, he still wondered what it might feel like to run his fingers through all those glossy curls.

"Are you in bed?" she asked, cutting into his wayward thoughts.

"Aye." His voice was a bit thick.

She turned her head slowly, as if checking to see if he had told her the truth, and then she turned the rest of her body to face him.

Their cots were only about a foot apart. If he wanted, he could easily reach out and touch her curls.

Another flash of lightning lit up the sky, illuminating her beautiful face.

Ever since entering the fur trade, he'd been surrounded by Indians and half-blood women. Many were raised—and some educated—in the white man's ways, but all of them lacked the gentility bred and born to a woman of privilege. Even though he'd cautioned Charlotte to act like a man, he couldn't deny she was a woman through and through. He saw it in the curve of her hips, the tilt of her head, and the use of her words.

If any of the men looked close enough, they'd see it too.

He couldn't take his eyes off her, even if he had wanted. "I'm sorry you've had to stay in the tent all evening. It was a bonnie night, watching the storm roll in."

"Did your spies return?" She studied him as he looked at her, not dropping her gaze when their eyes met during a flash of lightning.

"Aye." He would have to tell her eventually. "Rutherford is with them."

She closed her eyes, her face pinching with despair.

"Dinna fash." He wanted to promise her safety, though he knew he could only do so much to protect her. "Their brigade is smaller than ours, so they will move faster than us. We canna go ahead of them, because they will overtake us again—but I can let them get ahead of us in the morn."

"Do you think he's going to Grand Portage?"

"'Tis the only place he can go, unless he plans to join one of the Indian villages along the way."

He hoped his words would make her smile, but they did not.

"He probably learned your brigade was leaving and thought to either apprehend me along the way or find Stephen at Grand Portage before we can marry."

Reid didn't bother to argue with her, since he'd come to the same conclusion.

"I'll need your help in the morning." Reid hated the idea of lying to his men, but he didn't see any other choice. "I'll tell the men you're too ill to travel. That will allow the other brigade to get a day ahead of us. They'll make better time and get to Grand Portage well in advance of us."

"What about Stephen? What if Roger gets to him before us?"

"Stephen must know Rutherford well enough not to trust him."

She nodded and worried her bottom lip, tucking it between her teeth.

"Will you help me, then?" he asked.

"I'll do anything I must."

They lay in silence for several minutes, the storm blowing against the canvas, rain pelting the oiled material enveloping them.

Charlotte looked small and vulnerable, and a sense of protection tightened Reid's chest.

"You should get some sleep, lass."

"I don't think I can, knowing Roger is on the other side of the river."

"I willna let him near you. You have my word." And he meant it.

She didn't say anything but simply nodded and then turned her back to him, wrapping herself into a small ball, shivering in the growing cold.

For the past two years, no one had protected her. He couldn't let her down now.

"Good night."

"Good night," she whispered.

Within moments, her breath evened out, and he hoped she had finally found rest.

Reid wouldn't be so lucky. The troubles that mounted around him would leave him worried long into the early morning hours.

A moan woke Reid just as the last of the storm rumbled in the distance. Darkness still cloaked the morning, and the sudden quiet beyond the tent was louder than the wind and rain.

Charlotte moaned again, her knees tucked up to her chest.

On instinct, Reid reached between the cots and laid his hand on her forehead. Her skin burned against his palm.

He wouldn't have to lie to his men, after all.

Reid left his cot and knelt beside Charlotte, the cold biting against his exposed chest. He'd been afraid of taking her into the wilderness, knowing she was ill after her ocean voyage, but there hadn't been any other options. He couldn't let her perish now.

"Charlotte." He said her name quietly, brushing wet hair off her brow. "Wake up, lass."

She moaned again and rolled away from his touch but did not wake.

Shaking her shoulders, he said her name again, needing to ascertain what ailed her.

Her eyes fluttered open, glazed over and confused. She pulled back from him as far as the cot would allow.

"'Tis only me," he said kindly. "You're ill."

Comprehension returned to her eyes, and she nodded, reaching toward her throat. "Water?" she rasped.

He brought the canteen to her and took off the lid. Gently, he cradled the back of her head, helping her sit up enough to drink the cold liquid.

As she sipped, her body trembled, and she pulled away from the canteen, squeezing her eyes tight. "My head," she whispered, her teeth chattering. "And my throat."

Reid took his blanket off his cot and placed it over her. "I'll find something to help you."

After tucking the blanket around her, like his mother had tucked blankets around him as a child, Reid looked for more symptoms. There were no rashes or spots, as far as he could see, and no other signs of illness. As the bourgeois of his brigade, all medical care fell on his shoulders or his assistant clerk's. The only doctor employed by the fur trade was stationed at Grand Portage. Each officer had no choice but to learn how to let blood, set bones, and cure all manner of diseases. Reid had no stomach for treating illnesses, and whenever someone else was available, he turned the task to a more skilled officer.

Today, it would be up to him to help Charlotte.

While he dressed, the men began to stir in the camp. Everyone would soon be awake, expecting to start their day immediately. Breakfast wasn't served until several hours of paddling were behind them, which meant they would pack their cargo as soon as they were awake.

Reid finished dressing and stepped out into the brisk morning. A hint of color rimmed the eastern horizon as several men climbed out from under their canoes. Mud caked Reid's boots, and water dripped from the pine needles encircling the camp.

"I need my medicine chest." Reid spoke in French when he saw Alexandre stretching near one of the overturned canoes.

Alexandre scratched his sides and nodded. "Is someone ill?"

"The new clerk, Mr. Crawford."

No one seemed alarmed at this news, since it was common for first-season men to become ill upon entering the trade. Everyone would expect Charlotte to rally, even if she was ill, and continue inland toward Grand Portage. She would have to be extremely ill, or near death, for them to stop for the day.

Alexandre moved toward one of the canvas-covered piles that had been emptied from Reid's canoe. Most of Reid's personal belongings and company-issued supplies were carried in his Montreal canoe.

Movement across the river gained Reid's attention. In the growing daylight, the XY men prepared to leave their camp. From his vantage point, it was impossible to make out the individual men so far away, but Reid didn't doubt Rutherford was among them.

The medicine chest was near the top of the pile, where it was always stored. Alexandre hefted it onto his shoulder and started toward Reid's tent.

"I'll take it." Reid intercepted the man, not wanting him to enter his tent. "The lad is very ill. I think it would be wise to wait a day or two before we continue."

Alexandre frowned but did not question his bourgeois.

"Find Pierre and tell him to come to my tent." Reid didn't wait for Alexandre to agree but left his side to return to Charlotte.

Calum exited his tent as Reid approached his own.

"We won't be leaving this morn," Reid told his assistant clerk. "The lad is very ill and will need to rest today. Spread the word among the men."

A frown creased Calum's brow as well. "What ails him?"

"Ague."

"Do you want me to bleed him?" Calum was far more skilled with medicinal practices and had a stomach for the task, knowing Reid didn't enjoy the job.

Reid clutched the medicine chest. Charlotte would probably have a better chance of healing if Calum cared for her—but it was a risk too great.

"The lad is comfortable with me. I'll see to his needs."

Questions shifted across Calum's gaze, but he didn't press Reid for answers.

"Set some water to boil," Reid said, "and bring me a cup when it's ready."

Calum nodded and set off to do Reid's bidding.

Reid entered his tent and found Charlotte tossing on her cot. Her blankets had slipped off, and she shivered uncontrollably. By now, sunlight had crested the horizon, filtering light through the canvas, revealing her flushed face and the sweat glistening on her brow.

"No, Roger!" she called out in her delirium over and over.

"Shh." Reid set the medicine chest on his cot and knelt beside her. He smoothed her hair back again and pulled the blankets over her thin frame.

She opened her eyes, but the fever dulled her gaze, and she didn't focus on Reid. "He's here," she whispered.

Reid shook his head and touched her brow. She burned hotter than before. Willow bark tea would take down her fever and offer her a bit of comfort from the pain, but it would not heal her. Only bleeding would balance her humours and restore her health.

He would need to wait until she'd had the tea to calm her before performing the bloodletting. If she continued to toss and turn, he could do more harm than good.

While he waited for Calum to bring the hot water, he opened the medicine chest and pulled out the glass jar of willow bark. Setting it aside, he found the four-bladed fleam, which he'd use to make the bloodletting incision. He also located the tincture of friar's balsam and the roll of lint.

Finally, Calum poked his head into the tent, a steaming cup of water in hand. His eyes traveled to Charlotte and then to Reid, as he scanned all the supplies Reid had prepared.

"Are you sure you dinna want me to do it?"

"Roger?" Charlotte tried to focus her eyes on Calum. She sat up, her face wild with fear. "You've found me!" She clutched the blanket to her chest and started to rise, but Reid held her down.

"'Tis only Calum. Not Roger."

"Roger?" Calum asked, his face twisted in confusion.

Reid shook his head. "Just set the cup on the chest and be gone."

Calum put the cup down and left the tent without another question.

With patience, Reid was able to calm Charlotte and get her to lie down again. When she was settled, he pulled out two strips of willow bark and set them in the hot water. While he waited for the tea to steep, he sat beside her and wiped her brow, whispering soothing words to settle her heart. His prayers wafted heavenward, much like the steam lifting from the cup. He'd seen sicker men recover and healthier men perish. He would hate to see this woman die when she had come so far.

When the tea was ready, he was able to help her drink some of it down, and as he waited for it to take effect, he prepared her for the bloodletting.

Stiff from sitting on the hard earth, he moved to a kneeling position and took her left arm in his hands, marveling at the softness of her skin. He placed a bowl under her elbow and gently rubbed her arm until she finally calmed down and stopped shaking.

"I'm going to bleed you now," he said very softly. "Have you been bled before?"

Her eyes were closed, but he knew she wasn't sleeping. "When I was a child," she said with a labored breath.

Reid opened the fleam and found the smallest blade. Taking a deep breath, he placed it against the soft inner part of her arm and pushed firmly.

She clenched her jaw but did not cry out.

Reid cringed, hating to cause her more pain, but it was necessary. He set aside the fleam and held her arm over the bowl with one hand, while he gently massaged her hand with his other.

After he bled her for a time, he applied the friar's balsam onto the lint bandage and wrapped it around her arm, putting pressure on the wound like the instructional book recommended.

When she was finally asleep, he stepped out of his tent. His stomach growled and his muscles were sore, but he was thankful to see the XY men were no longer in their camp.

"They left about two hours ago." Calum handed Reid a steaming cup of tea. "I saved you a plate of breakfast, if you're hungry."

Reid took the tea and swallowed it in one hot gulp. It burned down his throat and settled hard in his stomach. "Thank you."

"How is the lass?"

"She—" Reid looked sharply at his friend.

"I've got eyes," Calum said quietly, his gaze on the far banks of the river. "Only a woman would behave the way she did when she called me Roger."

Reid closed his eyes, thankful their tents were far removed from the other men. "You canna breathe a word—"

"Why'd you bring her?" His usual good humor was replaced by concern—and accusation. "Is she warming your bed? Is that it?"

Clenching his jaw, Reid stared down at his assistant clerk. "I'll have you hold your tongue. The lass is in danger and needs to join her fiancé at Grand Portage. She's running from the passenger traveling with the XY men."

"But why'd you agree to take her along with us?" He frowned. "She could get you in trouble."

"I owe a debt to her fiancé, nothing more." Reid stared hard at Calum. "I willna have you speak of this to anyone—not even Charlotte."

"Charlotte?" Calum's eyebrows rose high.

"I mean Charlie. And not a word. Do you understand?"

Calum rested his right hand over his heart. "You have my word."

Reid stepped over to their fire and took the plate of biscuits and boiled pork Calum had set aside. It had long since cooled, but he cared little.

"We willna break camp until Charlie is well enough to travel," Reid said, allowing no argument in his voice.

"The lass-lad is making you soft." Calum took a seat across from Reid, a smile on his good-natured face. "And now I ken why."

Reid wished he could be as lighthearted about Charlotte's presence as Calum was—but Calum had nothing to lose if someone learned about her identity.

# Chapter Five

An owl hooted in the distance, bringing Charlotte to her senses. She opened her eyes and blinked several times, staring at the stained white canvas hanging over her head. Her mouth felt like she'd been chewing wool, but her throat no longer hurt, and her head had stopped its incessant pounding.

Darkness shrouded the tent, and a chill pervaded the air. But she was neither too hot nor too cold. Had the worst passed?

She brought her left hand up to rub her eyes, which were heavy and gritty, but her elbow pinched where it was bandaged. Bits and pieces of the past few days came back to her, and she lowered her arm to her side.

Reid.

She turned her head and saw him lying on his back. Though it was dark, she could see him clearly. One arm was flung over his eyes, while his bare chest rose and fell in a steady rhythm.

In all her born days, she'd never looked upon a man without his shirt on. The sight did something strange within her stomach and created a quickening inside her chest. He was naught but muscles from waist to neck. Her gaze lingered on every rise and valley, marveling at the sheer beauty of the man before her.

If she'd had her canvas and charcoal, she'd draw a picture to capture the image forever. Instead, she'd have to commit his form to memory and draw it later, when she had the proper supplies.

But what would Stephen think if he found her drawing the image of a half-naked man she had slept beside in a tent—alone?

Her cheeks warmed and not from sickness this time.

Forcing herself to turn away from him, she lay there for several more minutes with no desire to sleep any longer. What time was it? How long had she been sick?

Her body was clammy with old sweat, and when she ran her hand through her curls, she found they were stiff from perspiring.

Oh, if only she could bathe.

But first, she needed to find the necessary.

Not wanting to wake Reid, she moved aside the blanket and sat up.

Her head spun for a few seconds as the cold air assailed her, and she began to shiver again. Her shoes were near the entry where she'd left them the last time Reid had helped her to the necessary in her delirium. She hadn't been cognizant enough to feel embarrassed at the time, but the thought of him assisting her with such a personal need was both humbling and distressing. Thankfully, he'd only aided her in finding a spot, and then he'd left her alone while she took care of her needs.

Still, her cheeks burned to think of it, and she realized that he was right in warning her that this journey would strip her of all decorum.

Slipping on her shoes, she untied the flaps and stepped out of the tent.

A multitude of stars arched across the wide expanse of sky with a full moon dimming them only slightly. The pine trees reached toward the heavens, black silhouettes against the magnificent backdrop of sparkling lights. The moon was so bright it sent shadows stretching across the quiet camp.

The voyageurs' campfires had dwindled with a small spiral of smoke drifting up from one closer to the water, but all else was silent.

Was Roger still across the river? She prayed he had moved on like Reid had hoped—yet a shiver of doubt overtook her. Was he watching her even now? Would he grab her if she wandered too far from camp?

Not wanting to find out, she took care of business as quickly as possible and then went to the water's edge to wash her hands and face.

The river was as cold as ice, but it was refreshing. Since her hair was so short, she cupped the water and poured it over her head, washing behind her neck and ears, trying to scrub away any trace of illness. She marveled at how easy it was to wash her shorter hair—maybe the only benefit from cutting it.

"Charlie?" Reid called quietly from near their tent, concern tightening his voice.

She ran her hands through her curls quickly, rubbing off the excess water, and then stood and made her way back to the tent. The moon was bright enough for her to see him move away from their tent and toward the woods behind.

"Charlie?" he called again, his voice desperate.

"Here," she said just as quietly, but urgently.

He turned and started moving toward her. He had not taken the time to put on his shirt, and the moon illuminated his bare torso, sending shadows over the dips and curves.

Her heart hammered at the sight.

Standing before her, in full motion, his muscles were even more glorious than when he was lying still. She had never imagined a man looked like that under his shirt. Did all men look this way? Or was it only Reid?

"Where have you been?" Fear and anger deepened his tone. "You should not leave the tent unattended, especially when you're sick."

"I had to—" He'd seen her at her worst, even helped her, so why could she not tell him what had pulled her from their tent? "I am feeling much better."

"You're wet." He reached out and touched her hair, sending a spiral of heat coursing through her stomach.

Memories of her illness returned. Him—always near, his touch soft and gentle, his words tender and encouraging. She'd been in and out of consciousness, but whenever she'd been awake, he'd been by her side, helping her drink the bitter tea, adding extra blankets when she had the chills, and bleeding her several times. She hadn't been so well cared for since she was a child.

"You'll get sick again standing out here in the cold." He put his hand on the small of her back and led her to their tent.

His touch was not only filled with concern, but it was also possessive—protective—and she liked it. Liked the way his hand felt against her back. Gooseflesh raced up her arms, but it wasn't from the cold. It felt good to have someone other than herself care about her welfare. It made her want to nestle beside him, sheltered under his muscular arm.

She chastised herself for such foolish thoughts. He was her protector—but only until they reached Grand Portage, and then she would never see Reid McCoy again.

Was it wrong to enjoy his attention while it lasted?

"How long have I been sick?" she asked.

"We've been in camp four days."

"Did Roger leave?"

"The XY men pulled out the first day you were sick."

She couldn't help but look over her shoulder.

"Dinna fash. Rutherford is several days ahead of us."

"What if he stayed behind somewhere?"

Reid shook his head. "It would be unwise. His guide would not allow it."

"He's been foolish before."

Reid's hand was still resting on the small of her back, but he slipped it around her waist and drew her toward the tent. "We'll trust God to protect you and guide your steps."

Heat radiated up her side, and she could no longer focus on anything but his hand and how wonderful it felt when he touched her.

Guilt assailed her, and she forced herself to think about Stephen. He was her intended. He'd proposed, and she had come all this way to accept. He would be waiting for her at Grand Portage.

The sooner she could get to him the better.

Now that Charlotte was well enough to travel again, the brigade made up for lost time. Wind pushed against Reid as the canoes sliced through the Utawas, heading downriver. After four days of lying idle in camp, the voyageurs were anxious to paddle once again—and paddle they did, at a remarkable speed.

Pierre selected songs that matched the mood of the men. Impatient and determined. "*Bon Jour, Jolie Bergere*," "*Brave Capitaine*," "*Vin Blanc*," and others.

Charlotte sat next to Reid in the canoe, dozing on and off, pale and weak. She'd insisted they leave camp, but he was still concerned that she'd relapse. Whenever they stopped to portage, he was adamant about carrying her things and even offered to carry her, when the others weren't near—but she refused, and rightly so. No matter how much he wanted to protect her, he couldn't coddle her or bring more attention to her than necessary.

Already the men were suspicious of the new clerk—and Calum couldn't keep his eyes off her.

Reid caught him watching her even now, and Calum simply grinned, tossing his voice into the voyageur song with abandon. Reid scowled at the younger man, a warning in his glare.

Up ahead, a series of rapids would require them to make three long portages, which would take them the rest of the day to accomplish. But at the end, they would be rewarded with the most majestic waterfall on their journey. It wasn't on the Utawas but a short distance to the left on an offshoot that flowed south. Called the Rideau River, it meant *curtain* in French.

Reid always enjoyed watching the reaction of a first-season officer when they encountered the falls—but he was even more eager to see what Charlotte thought.

For the remainder of the day, Reid oversaw the transportation of the goods in his care, thankful his men were well rested for the rigors of their duties.

When they had finished their daunting task, Reid and Charlotte took their time crossing the rugged terrain, stopping several times to rest.

Finally, they arrived at their campsite and found the men had already set up their tent.

A small Algonquin Indian village sat nestled across the narrow river, and the arrival of a brigade had brought out several men, women, and children to trade. They mingled with Reid's men, some sitting at the voyageurs' campfires, others standing near the banks of the river, showcasing their wares.

Charlotte stopped beside Reid. "Indians."

"Algonquin. They are closely related to the Chippewa, farther into the interior."

"Are they peaceful?"

"Aye."

Even though Reid rationed his men's alcohol, some of them pooled their rations together to trade with the Indians along the way. Sometimes, it led to fights and other trouble he'd rather not deal with so soon after Charlotte's illness. But he wouldn't worry her.

She yawned and placed her hand up to cover her mouth, her cheeks turning pink. "Excuse me."

"You'll be wanting to sleep, then," he said.

"I've been eager to find my cot all day."

Disappointment cut through him. "Do you think you could travel a short distance? I've something to show you."

"A short distance?" She frowned as they found their tent and he placed their things inside.

"'Tis not far. Just on the other side of those rocks." He pointed to the offshoot, less than a hundred yards away.

Curiosity lit her eyes, and she nodded. "I suppose I could."

He felt like a child again, wanting to grab her hand and run off to show her his surprise. Instead, they walked leisurely to the Rideau. As they drew closer, the sound of the falls filled the air with a distinct rumble.

"A waterfall?" Charlotte's eyebrows lifted in question, but he just smiled, certain she'd never seen another like it before.

Tiny blades of green grass sprouted up on the forest floor, and little blue flowers spread out like a carpet. Birds sang to one another, and squirrels jumped from branch to branch. Despite the late-season snowfall they'd had in Montreal, spring had finally arrived, and it was his favorite time of the year.

Before they reached the offshoot, he directed her down a path which would require them to do a bit of rock climbing. The men had remained at camp, and it was just the two of them, so he went ahead of her and reached out to wrap his hands around her waist to help her over a ledge.

She placed her hands on his shoulders and allowed him to assist her.

Her small waist felt supple beneath his hands, awakening a desire within him that came on so suddenly he paused after he lowered her to her feet. He allowed his hands to linger a bit longer than necessary, but she didn't pull away.

Instead, she looked up at him, uncertainty in the depths of her beautiful brown eyes.

Reid forced himself to step away from her—but took her hand into his. It was small and soft in his large one.

They descended the rocky ledges carefully, the sound of the waterfall drowning out all other noises in the awakening wilderness. Small buds gave way to tiny leaves just starting to turn the woods green and fragrant.

When they finally reached the falls, Reid stopped Charlotte.

He stood close to her, so she could hear. "Close your eyes."

She didn't question him but lowered her eyelids until her lashes rested on her smooth cheeks and allowed him to lead her the last few feet to the waterfall.

"May I open them?"

He turned her to face the falls, a spray of water misting over them. "Now."

She blinked several times, and then her mouth slipped open in wonder.

The majestic falls dropped over a straight ledge forty feet above the river, causing the water to fall in one sheet like a shimmering curtain. Sunshine sparkled off the top of the falls, making it appear as though the light dripped over the edge. Craggy rocks framed the falls on both sides, with trees growing out from the cracks.

Charlotte stared at the waterfall. "I've never seen something so . . . magnificent."

Reid had fully intended to admire the waterfall, since he only saw it every three years when he passed by, but he could not take his eyes off Charlotte. He thought of all the other things he treasured and wondered how much more he'd enjoy them if he could show them to her.

She walked to the water's edge and stooped down to dip her hand in the clear river.

Reid joined her and found her staring at her reflection.

There was little emotion on her face as she reached up and touched one of the curls that had slipped out of her queue. "I look like a stranger. So gaunt and homely."

He crouched beside her, looking at their reflections. His skin was darkened by the sun and exposure to the outdoors, while hers was light and delicate. His hair was almost black, while hers was almost copper in the sunshine. Their eyes were similar in color, but hers were wide and trusting, while his were hooded by years of hard living. Even crouched like they were, he towered over her slight frame, a reminder that she was at his mercy and under his care.

"You're one of the bonniest lasses I've ever seen." And he meant it—more than he intended. Throughout her illness, he'd felt strangely protective. In the past, he'd cared for sick voyageurs, but he'd never worried like he had the four days Charlotte was ill. When it was evident that she would recover, his relief had made him weak. He admired her more than any other woman before her, and it only added to her beauty.

"You must not come across many women, then." She tried to smile, but it didn't reach her eyes.

Their gazes caught in the water's reflection, and her face became serious. "But I thank you."

"Come." He took her hand and led her back to the path, not wanting to dwell long on his attraction to her. "You need to eat and get some rest."

He didn't let her hand go until just before they reached the path—and even then, it was harder than he expected when he did.

# Chapter Six

The revelry in camp was louder than usual as Calum and Reid sat near their campfire that evening after supper, while Charlotte rested in the tent. Eight Indian women had been brought to the camp by their spouses and given to the visiting voyageurs as a gift for the night. Several men had already gone off into the woods to take their pleasure and returned, just to hand the woman off to the next man waiting in line. It was a custom that did not sit well with Reid, but he could not stop his men from taking part. Indian men considered it a sign of welcome to the voyageurs to offer their women in this way, and the women willingly obliged, growing angry if their spouse did not make the offer.

An especially obliging woman laughed nearby, drawing Reid's and Calum's attention. She smiled at them, an invitation in her eyes. It was considered a high honor to be welcomed into the officers' tents.

Calum tapped his pipe into his palm and stood, impatiently pacing on the other side of Reid's fire. He stopped for a moment and glanced at the woman, then returned to his pacing. His gaze swung to Reid's tent, where Charlotte slept.

The fire crackled and then popped, sending an ember flying. It landed on the ground near Reid's feet.

"You said Charlie is promised to another?" Calum asked.

Reid's breathing slowed, and he narrowed his focus to his friend.

Calum stopped and faced Reid. "If you're not enjoying her *company*, why not allow her to sleep in my tent?"

Without taking his eyes off Calum, Reid stood. "I said you're not to talk about Charlie."

Calum came around the fire. "If I accept the offer of that Indian over there, I'll be complaining of some kind of disease in less than a week, just like the rest of these men."

"So don't accept the offer."

"But 'tis been a year since I was with Estelle." Calum ran his hand through his hair. "It could be months before I see her again. I don't think I can wait that long."

Calum had taken a mixed-blood wife in his second season, in *à la façon du pays*, or in the custom of the country. Marriage looked much different in the fur trade. Those who took part practiced an open arrangement, where a couple was considered married after the man presented gifts to the bride's family and the family approved. Once she moved in with him, they were "married," but both were free to leave the marriage at any moment, if they chose. In this way, many fur traders took brides, whether to strengthen an alliance, or to keep their beds warm. If they grew weary of the woman or decided to return to Montreal or Europe when they retired, many left their families in the interior. Some just passed them along to the next bourgeois who took over the fur post, and others sent them back to where they had come from. Very few remained, like Reid's father, to live out the remainder of their days with their country wives.

Estelle awaited Calum's return at the last fur post he managed in the *Folle Avoine*, or Wild Rice District. If Calum was not sent back there, he would hire a voyageur to collect her and their young son to join him wherever he was stationed. At least, that was his plan. If he chose to leave her in the Folle Avoine, she would have no recourse to demand he take care of her and the child. And if she did not wait for Calum, he had no power to enforce his marriage or parental rights.

"You will keep your distance from Charlie." Reid had not brought her this far to hand her over to someone who would misuse her. He crossed his arms, his muscles tensing. "I would not dishonor her with the suggestion—and she would not disgrace herself in accepting it."

Two new Algonquians—a man and a woman—entered the edge of light encircling Reid's campfire, drawing Reid's attention away from Calum.

"Are you the bourgeois?" the man asked Reid in broken French.

"*Oui*." Reid had seen this man in camp earlier. He wore several eagle feathers in his hair, marking his leadership among his people. "*Bienvenue*."

"I am son of Chief Tessouat." He stood tall and proud, his face betraying no emotions. "My sister, Wawetseka, is gift from my father to trader chief for this night."

Wawetseka kept her dark eyes lowered to the ground as her brother spoke. She was a beautiful woman, with long dark hair flowing to her waist. Clothed in a deerskin dress, the custom of her people, her ankles and forearms were bare.

Calum watched Reid closely, knowing where he stood on this issue.

Several voyageurs had taken notice of the new visitors, many of them stopping to watch. More than one cast appreciative glances at Wawetseka—and curious glances at Reid, probably wondering what he would do.

Reid had an important job as the bourgeois, and he took it seriously. Trade relations among the Indians were vital to the success of the fur trade. He could not dishonor Chief Tessouat by rejecting his daughter. Instead, he nodded thanks to the chief's son, who simply turned and left the camp.

Wawetseka stood quietly, awaiting direction from Reid.

Calum stepped to Reid's side. "I ken you dinna plan to enjoy the chief's gift. Do you mind if I do?"

Reid wanted to send the girl home where she belonged, but it would do no good. The chief would simply return her to the camp, angry that she had been rejected. With a quick nod, Calum was given his answer, and he took Wawetseka's hand and led her to his tent.

"Reid?" Charlotte opened the flap of his tent, her eyelids heavy from sleep.

"Aye?" He walked to her. "How are you feeling?"

"I'm fine." Her gaze landed on Calum, who paused and looked her way before slipping into his tent with the chief's daughter. "What's going on?"

This was one of the customs he'd warned her about when she'd begged him to take her to Grand Portage. He wanted to shelter her from the practice but knew it would not be the last time she was exposed to the custom. Each time they camped near a village, the native women would be presented to the men. It was simply their way and had been for over a hundred years since the Europeans had entered the northwestern wilderness.

"Young Mr. Crawford has not been given his turn," one of the voyageurs called out to the rest of the men. "If he's to be a man, tonight's the night!"

Several others rallied to the call, and one took an Indian woman around the waist, directing her to Reid's tent.

"This one should do," the voyageur said good-naturedly, while the rest laughed. He nudged the woman forward. "The young clerk's name is Charlie. He might not have any hair on his face or chest, but he's been cut from his maman's apron strings and ought to enjoy the freedom."

Charlotte frowned as she pulled the tent flaps close to her body.

Reid stepped in front of her, anger coursing like fire through his veins. "Leave the lad alone. He's been ill."

"What better way to make him well again?" The stocky voyageur laughed and slapped his thigh.

"Go back into the tent," Reid said quietly to Charlotte.

He couldn't see her but heard the tent flaps close.

Planting his feet, Reid stood before a dozen voyageurs and crossed his arms. "I allow you to do what you want, but I willna let you pressure the lad to join. Go back to your campfires and leave him alone."

The voyageur's smile fell, and he placed a possessive arm around the Indian woman's waist again, drawing her close to his side. "We were just having some fun."

"Have it in your own way, at your own fire."

As the bourgeois, Reid's authority was not to be questioned. The men turned without another word and left him. He'd gained a reputation in the fur trade as a devout man, but the voyageurs never tired in testing him.

Reid's tent beckoned with Charlotte—probably confused about what had just happened. If he was smart, he would let her fall back to sleep and enter the tent later, when he was tired and ready to sleep himself.

But at the moment, he was not tired. He was more awake than he'd been in weeks.

"Reid?" Her voice was quiet and uncertain.

He didn't debate another moment but opened the flap and stepped into his tent.

She sat on her cot, fully dressed, hugging her knees to her chest. The light from the campfire flickered outside the tent, sending shadows through the canvas, making her eyes dance.

Reid quietly turned and tied the flaps closed.

"Are those women in camp for the reasons I assume?" she asked.

He didn't bother to look at her but simply nodded.

"And Calum?" Her voice was low, disappointed. "Does he partake?"

She'd seen him taking Wawetseka into his tent. What more could he say?

He didn't undress but went to his cot and sat, facing her. "'Tis the way things are done."

She had taken off her boots but kept her socks on. She focused on her feet now and didn't meet his gaze. "And you?" She swallowed. "Do you need me to leave your tent for—?"

"No." His answer was quick and decisive. "I dinna abide the practice."

Charlotte nodded once and still did not look at him. "I'm happy to hear it."

"I'm sorry, lass. I hope the men dinna insult you."

"They think I'm a young man. You warned me about these things."

Reid gripped the edge of his cot, frustrated by all of them. "Even if you were a young man, 'tis still an insult, if you ask me."

She turned her smile to him, her eyes lighting with approval.

"Are you tired?" he asked.

Charlotte shook her head. "Are you?"

"No."

An awkward silence filled the small space.

"But we should try to sleep." Reid lay on his back, fully clothed. "Morning will come sooner than we'd like. The days are growing longer. We have several portages tomorrow."

The campfire grew dimmer, darkening the interior of the tent.

Charlotte also lay down and pulled her blanket up to her chin. She turned to her side and faced Reid. The distance between their costs felt like it was shrinking with each passing day, and he was afraid if he turned to look at her, it would feel like he was lying in the same bed as the lass—a thought that made every muscle in his body tense.

"How long will you remain in the fur trade?" she asked.

He continued to look at the sloped canvas ceiling. "I hope to become a shareholder at the end of this season. I'll know more when I meet with the other shareholders at Grand Portage. After that—" He paused. He had not given much thought to what would happen after he became a shareholder. In the past fifteen years, he had focused on only one thing—but what would he do after he achieved it? He would buy his mother that little cottage in the country that he'd promised her, but beyond that, he was uncertain. "I will probably serve another five to ten years in the interior, unless the shareholders find a position for me in Montreal or London."

"Do you enjoy it?" Doubt hovered in her voice, as if she couldn't imagine anyone enjoying this lifestyle.

It was dark enough that he felt it was safe to turn and look at her in the next cot. "There are things about it I enjoy." He thought about Calum sleeping with Wawetseka in the other tent while his wife and child awaited him in Folle Avoine, and Reid sighed. "And other things I canna abide."

Charlotte looked away from him and ran her finger across a seam in the canvas wall. "I miss home. I'll be happy to return to England when all of this is done."

He'd only known her for a week, but he already hated to think about the day he'd have to say goodbye.

Several weeks passed, and Charlotte grew accustomed to the rhythm of the voyageur life. They awoke with the sun, immediately loaded their canoes, and spent several hours paddling before they took a break to eat. Some days, they portaged many times, and other days, like today, they only had one or two portages. Always, they moved to the west toward Lake Huron and on to Lake Superior. Six days ago, they had left the familiarity of the Utawas River and had portaged through several independent lakes.

Tonight, their camp was much like all the others, though this one was situated on a peninsula of land jutting into a deep, tree-rimmed lake. Craggy rocks and bluffs pierced the sky, making odd-shaped silhouettes on the horizon. The moon was waning, offering less light and allowing the stars to shine even brighter. The days and nights had grown warmer, and the wilderness had become lush and green, creating a canopy in most camps. But here on the peninsula, there was nothing but a dark, starry sky above them.

A loon called in the distance, its sound echoing off the lake. The first time she'd heard the sound, she had thought it was a wolf howling in the distance and had cowered in fear. Reid had tried not to laugh as he told her the wobbling trill of the loon was no threat to them.

Calum had retired to his tent immediately after it had been pitched, complaining of a sick headache, and Reid had been called to another campfire to settle a dispute between two pork eaters. That left Charlotte alone, a rare thing, indeed. After she'd set the hominy to boiling, she'd rested against one of the boulders near their fire and pulled out her cassette. In stolen moments like this one, she used the company-issued paper and pencils and spent her time drawing.

Most of her pictures were pastoral scenes of the places they had visited, but she also had drawn a few of the voyageurs in camp, and one was of the brigade on the river.

Tonight, she would put the finishing touches on the picture she had drawn of Rideau Falls.

Reid appeared from the shadows, and her heart did a little flip at the unexpected sight of him. He wore his tan trousers and tall black boots. His white shirt was unbuttoned at the top, allowing his lapels to drape open, and he did not wear his coat.

"I spoke to Pierre. We'll enter Lake Huron tomorrow," he said, joining Charlotte. "We are more than halfway to Grand Portage."

Charlotte tucked her drawing inside her cassette, stood, and ladled some hominy into a bowl for him. "Another three weeks?"

Thanking her, he took the bowl and settled onto the ground, his back to a boulder across the fire from her. "If the weather is favorable." He took a bite of the steaming corn mush and nodded toward her cassette. "What are you working on?"

She looked at the inconspicuous wooden box. "It's nothing."

"Is it something Calum asked you to do?"

Calum had given Charlotte some menial tasks as she'd become more comfortable with the duties expected of her—though not as many as she would have suspected. For the most part, the other assistant clerk kept his distance from her, as did most of the voyageurs. Since the night with the Algonquians, no one pressured her or teased her about being coddled. They didn't even insist she smoke with them or participate in any other distasteful pastime.

Had Reid spoken to them on her behalf? If he had, she was grateful.

"It's nothing," she said again as she lifted the cassette to take it to their tent and away from his curious eyes.

Reid lowered his bowl. "What's in there?"

She hadn't shown her work to anyone other than her parents, because it was for her pleasure and nothing else. She had no desire to be criticized or laughed at.

"It's just a little hobby."

"May I see?" He set aside his bowl, his face expectant.

What would it hurt to show him? He'd seen her at her worst and treated her with more respect and admiration than before. Even if he found fault in her drawings, he would not belittle her.

Charlotte walked around the fire and placed the cassette on the ground, then took a seat beside him. She opened the box and lifted out the picture she'd drawn of Rideau Falls.

"It's nothing impressive." She handed the drawing to him with an apprehensive heart. "Just something I play at."

She watched his face as he looked at her drawing, holding her breath as she waited for his response. Why did it matter what he thought of her art? Would she be this nervous showing it to one of the other men in camp?

"'Tis incredible." He glanced up at her, amazement in his gaze. "You've captured Rideau Falls perfectly."

"I'm not finished with it," she explained quickly. "I'd like to add more shading here." She pointed to a section that had been shadowed the day they visited the falls. "And more foliage on the trees." She tried taking it back. "There's a great deal I should change, actually."

He held it out of her reach and shook his head, returning his gaze to the drawing. "'Tis perfect as it is, lass."

She stopped trying to take it from him and clasped her hands in her lap. "You're too kind."

"May I keep it?"

She blinked several times in surprise. He wanted to keep her drawing?

"I-I." She stuttered, unsure what to say. "It's not finished."

Reid held it, almost reverently, and met her gaze again. "I wouldna change a thing."

Charlotte squeezed her hands into fists, forcing herself not to take the drawing back. If he wanted it, she'd be honored to know it belonged to him. "Then it's yours."

"Thank you. When I return to Montreal, I will show it to my mither. I've always wanted her to see the falls." He looked past her at the cassette. "Do you have any others?"

"I do."

"May I see them?"

She'd already done the hard part in showing him one. What would it hurt to show him the rest?

Digging deep into the cassette, she pulled out a stack of pictures and handed them to Reid. "I've spent even less time finishing these," she said quickly. "They are rough sketches."

He looked through them, one at a time, astonishment lighting his eyes. "These are amazing. You should have them published when you return to London. People would be eager to see them."

The thought of publishing her work for the world to see was preposterous, but she appreciated his compliments.

She reached over to take the papers back.

But he came to the last page—the one she thought she had buried deep beneath her ledgers. Somehow, it had made its way back to this pile.

It was a drawing of him.

Without his shirt.

Charlotte's cheeks flamed with heat, and her hands began to shake. She wanted to take the paper from him and make some excuse about why she had drawn it, but she couldn't move. Couldn't speak.

Reid stared at the drawing.

What must he think of her? She had told herself not to draw him, but the temptation had been too strong. Every morning when she awoke and found him lying beside her, his bare chest had begged to be explored with her fingers. She had turned that desire into a picture, exploring the muscles with the tip of her pencil, instead.

"Reid." She said his name, her voice catching. But she didn't know what else to say.

He finally looked up at her, the firelight flickering in his brown eyes. There was no anger or embarrassment. Instead, questions shimmered in their depths, though he didn't voice them.

She reached for the picture, and he let it go without a fight.

"I—I'll burn it, if you like." She leaned toward the fire.

He reached for her arm and stopped her, pulling her back to his side. "You dinna need to burn it."

"I'm sorry I drew it." She choked on her words, his hand still heavy on her arm. "I-I was simply curious to see if I could draw a-a male body." Her cheeks continued to burn with shame and embarrassment. "Now that I know I can, I should destroy it."

"Dinna be sorry, lass." His voice was low, intimate as he slowly removed his hand. "I'm honored."

She wanted to throw herself in the lake and perish. He was only being kind, of that she was certain. What gentleman would allow a lady to be embarrassed if he had the ability to prevent it?

She took the stack of papers from him and stuffed them back into her cassette, leaving the one of Rideau Falls on his lap.

"If you slept with a shirt on, I-I wouldn't be tempted to draw such things." She stumbled through her words, trying to place the blame on him, when she knew it was her own weakness that had allowed her to draw the picture.

"You dinna like seeing me without a shirt?"

She swallowed. On the contrary, she liked it too much—but she couldn't tell him that. "I think I'll turn in early." She stood and lifted the cassette, needing to remove herself from the conversation before she dug herself in too deep. "It's your tent. You may do as you like."

He stood to face her, his back to the fire, his face in shadows. "If it bothers you, I'll not do it again."

"No." She shook her head. He had been kind enough to bring her along on this journey. She couldn't tell him how to sleep. "I-I'm fine. Good night."

She didn't meet his gaze—couldn't.

"Good night."

Charlotte entered the tent and let the flap fall behind her. Taking several deep breaths, she set the cassette on the ground and crawled into her cot.

Pulling the blanket over her head, she groaned. He must think she was the lowest sort of female, drawing a picture of him practically nude.

When Reid came into their tent later, she pretended to be asleep.

In the morning, when she woke up, Reid lay on his cot next to her, his chest just as bare—and just as superb—as usual.

And she was relieved—which made her more ashamed than before.

# Chapter Seven

Not a cloud marred the blue sky as the voyageurs pulled to shore, just a mile away from Grand Portage. For as far as Charlotte could see, Lake Superior spread out before her like a vast freshwater ocean. The shoreline was mountainous, with smooth pebbles and driftwood on the beach, and tall pine trees reached toward the heavens. Several voyageurs jumped from their canoes into the frigid water with excitement.

For two weeks, they had crossed this magnificent lake. Several storms had slowed their progress, but on the good days, when the wind was favorable, they had set sails in the Montreal canoes and had arrived at Grand Portage sooner than expected.

"Wash with haste," Reid called to the men. "I want to reach Grand Portage before nightfall."

The brigade had stopped to bathe and change into their cleanest clothes. Charlotte was thankful that she would have this opportunity, knowing she was just a couple hours away from being reunited with Stephen for the first time in years. She might have to greet him in men's clothing—but at least they would be clean.

Two men stood by the canoes, holding them in the water, so they wouldn't have to unload their cargo. Charlotte left her canoe, followed close by Reid. She stepped into the water, bracing herself for the cold.

After the night Reid had discovered her picture of him, she purposely erected a wall between them. It was the only way she could protect her heart. Soon they would be separated, and she didn't want to have any regrets. She was promised to another man, and she would honor that promise, no matter how difficult it might become.

It hadn't been easy to keep her distance from Reid—emotionally or physically—but she had done her best. She went to bed before him, awoke before him, and never went off with him alone to see the things he wanted to show her when they camped each night.

In turn, he had stepped back as well, and they had maintained a cool distance—though Charlotte missed their easy friendship.

Despite the cold water, the men began to strip down to their drawers to bathe.

Doing her best to avoid them, Charlotte walked to the shore, her back to the lake.

"There's a stream over there," Reid said behind her. "Beyond the outcropping. I'll watch to make sure no one disturbs you."

She clutched her personal bag and nodded but did not turn to acknowledge him. Yesterday, in preparation for their arrival, all the men—including Charlotte—had washed one set of clothes. Hers were in her bag, along with her company-issued soap, a brush, and a wide strip of clean linen she would use to bind her breasts. The one she wore was soiled from use, and she'd be glad to wash it with her other clothes.

The sun was bright and the air warm, but she knew better than to strip down to her drawers and risk someone finding her that way. Instead, when she found the stream Reid had mentioned, she walked right in, clothes and all.

The water was warmer than she expected, and she dipped underneath, allowing it to rinse every part of her body.

Over the past weeks, she had regained her health and the weight she had lost. Her muscles had become firmer with all the portages they had crossed, but she was still lean. She'd never felt healthier in her life. What would Stephen think when he saw her? Would he be shocked? Every time she looked at her tanned reflection in the water, it still surprised her.

Unbuttoning her shirt, she reached inside and unbound the strip of fabric around her chest. When it floated free, she washed it with the soap and threw it on shore, then she washed her skin. The soap was a luxury in this wilderness that she did not take for granted.

Keeping her shirt on, she buttoned it again and then took off her trousers, socks, and drawers. Staying under water, she washed those as well, and then threw them on shore next to her bag.

After her clothes were washed, she washed the rest of her body, including her hair. It was thick and unruly, but she didn't mind. It was growing quickly and might need to be trimmed again before her return trip to Montreal if she wanted to convince the men that she was one of them.

Just thinking about her return trip made her stomach tighten with dread. So many things were still uncertain. Would Stephen be allowed to return to Montreal with her? Would she go back as a clerk, with her own tent to sleep in? How would they convince their superiors to let a first-year clerk who had signed a five-year contract return to Montreal? If they did and she didn't have Stephen's or Reid's protection, would she have the same luxuries as she had coming? Who would shelter her from the pork eaters?

She took a deep breath and decided not to worry. God wouldn't forsake her now, would He? Hadn't God brought her to Reid? Maybe God still cared about her, after all. So far, He'd kept her safe from Roger and allowed her to come this far without serious incident. Maybe the rest of her plan would proceed as she hoped and she'd be married to Stephen before the day's end.

A deer came to the water's edge and dipped its head to drink from the stream. It didn't seem to notice Charlotte, and if it did, it wasn't alarmed.

She floated in the water longer than she should have, but thoughts of marrying Stephen brought on more worries. Would she find him as attractive as she found Reid? Stephen had been her childhood friend and nothing more. Though she loved him, she'd never had romantic feelings for him. If she didn't find him attractive, would it matter? He had offered to marry her and protect her from her guardian. Even if she didn't find him attractive, she suspected she would eventually love him. She already cared deeply for him, didn't she?

"Charlie?" Reid called to her from the other side of the outcropping. "Are you done?"

"Soon!" She scrambled out of the water, trying to pull her shirttail down to cover her bare bottom. The fabric stuck to her body, and she prayed no one had gotten past Reid. Without her binding, there was no way to hide her identity.

Working as quickly as she could without the aid of a towel, she stepped closer to the outcropping for privacy and slipped the shirt off. She bound her breasts with the linen and then put on her drawers. Her clothes were wrinkled and stiff, but at least they were clean and dry. She put on her shirt, buttoned it to her throat, and then put on her trousers and tucked her shirttails into the waist. Over her shirt, she put on her jacket, and then her boots, and pulled out her hat. After brushing her hair and trying to rub it dry with her hands, she finally put on her hat and stuffed all her wet clothes into her bag.

All the other men were in the canoes already, impatiently waiting for her—all of them except Reid, who waited on the beach.

More than one voyageur rolled his eyes at her, and several shook their heads. No doubt they thought she was an effeminate man who wouldn't survive long in the interior, but she didn't care. Not today. Not when she was so close to Stephen.

"Ready?" he asked her, and knew he meant more than her appearance. Was she ready to see Stephen? To get married? To leave Reid's side?

What other choice did she have?

"Yes."

His eyes were hooded and his jaw was set, but he nodded and indicated the canoes. "Let's be off."

The men sang their cheeriest song as they started toward Grand Portage.

Reid had explained to her that the XY men had a fort near the North West Company fort, but they did not coexist. If anything, there was usually fighting between the two groups, and the voyageurs were ordered to stay at their own forts. As a passenger with the XY Company, Roger would not be welcomed into the North West Company fort—but that might not stop him.

Charlotte had assured Reid that if she was caught, she would deny that he knew about her identity, protecting him from losing his job. She hoped it did not come to that.

Less than twenty minutes later, the brigade rounded a bend, and Grand Portage came into view. The North West Company fort sat in a large bay at the base of a mountain, with an island positioned in the middle of the bay. Jutting out from the land was a long pier where several boats were docked and being unloaded. Reid's brigade was not the only one that had arrived that day.

Cannon shot sounded from the fort, and Charlotte jumped. She reached out and clasped Reid's arm, but he only laughed.

All around her, the voyageurs lifted their colorful paddles and shouted in response. Grins split their faces as another cannon shot burst into the air and several men ran out of the fort to the pier to greet them. A NWC flag flew proudly above the fort, silhouetted by the brilliant blue sky.

With renewed strength, the pork eaters thrust their paddles into the water and went double time until they reached the pier.

"Bienvenue!" shouted several men in greeting when the canoes docked.

Reid was the first to climb out of the canoe and up the ladder to the pier. Charlotte followed, and then the others disembarked.

"Reid!" A man with brown muttonchops, dressed in the finest clothes Charlotte had seen since leaving London, clasped hands with Reid and grabbed his shoulder in greeting. "Welcome back."

"'Tis good to be back." Reid's smile lit his face and eyes. He turned to Charlotte. "This is my newest assistant, Charlie Crawford."

"'Tis a pleasure to meet you, Charlie." The other man extended his hand, and Charlotte took it. He had a strong, confident grip.

"Charlie, this is Joseph McDonnell, one of the wintering partners and a good friend."

"It's a pleasure to meet you, Mr. McDonnell."

"An English lad?" Joseph turned a surprised eye to Reid. "Where'd you find him?"

"He's my mither's kin." Reid was vague, but Joseph didn't seem to mind.

"Supper is just about ready," Joseph said. "Are you hungry?"

"Famished." Reid waited for Calum to disembark from his canoe and then the four of them walked up the wide pier to the fort's gate. A large meeting hall facing the lake dominated the stockade. Several other buildings fanned out around it, with a large open yard in front.

Outside the stockade, hundreds—maybe even a thousand—voyageurs milled about under the hot sun. Tents, canoes, and other temporary shelters spread out along the lake for as far as she could see on either side.

"The pork eaters are camped over there." Calum pointed to the right as they followed Reid and Joseph. "The north men are on that side." He indicated the left of the fort. "You won't see them mingling, if they have a choice."

"Where do the officers sleep?"

They stepped into the stockade, and the smell of campfire smoke wafted on the breeze.

"We sleep inside the stockade in dormitories. McTavish and Mackenzie have sleeping quarters in the Grand Lodge, since they are the founding shareholders. The rest of the shareholders have individual rooms in one building, while the clerks sleep four to six per room in another."

She'd be sleeping with other men on her wedding night? She hadn't even thought about it until now.

"Have you seen the men from the Upper Red River District?" Reid asked Joseph casually.

She held her breath, waiting for Joseph's answer. Stephen served in the Upper Red River District.

"Aye. I was just speaking to George McKay in the Great Hall before I came to meet your brigade. They've been here for over a week and plan to depart early tomorrow morning, since they have such a long trek back to their posts."

Tomorrow? Charlotte's stomach tightened, thinking how close they'd come to missing Stephen. What would she have done if he had left before she arrived? The very thought made her ill.

"Do you have business with one of the Red River men?" Joseph's blue eyes were clear and bright as he studied Reid.

"Aye." Reid did not offer more information, and Joseph did not ask.

A blacksmith, cooper, tinsmith, and others had set up their shops in the stockade and were doing brisk business as Charlotte and the others walked by. A group of men played a game inside the stockade yard that she had witnessed several Indians playing when they had passed through a village several weeks back. Reid had called it lacrosse. About two dozen men ran back and forth across the yard with sticks in their hands, trying to capture a cloth ball. Several were tackled in the pursuit, which made Charlotte flinch.

Joseph led them up a set of stairs onto a wide porch and through double doors into a large room. Dozens of tables lined the space, and they were filled with over a hundred well-dressed men laughing, drinking, and visiting. The din echoed off the walls and high ceiling. Two large fireplaces flanked the room, and at least a dozen glass windows looked out at the lake.

Was Stephen in this room?

Many of the men looked up when they entered and called out to Reid and Calum. Boisterous laughter grated on Charlotte's ears as she searched the room for her fiancé.

"The Upper Red River men are over here," Joseph said, leading them to the opposite corner of the room.

They were forced to step around tables and benches, and Charlotte jammed her shins against the unforgiving wood.

Several Indian women entered the room from the back door, carrying elegant platters, bowls, and steaming tureens. Fine china had been set before the men with silver utensils, glass cups, and linen napkins.

As they drew closer to the table against the far wall, Charlotte swallowed her disappointment.

Stephen was not among the Upper Red River men.

Maybe he had stepped away for a moment.

She scanned the room again, searching desperately for his familiar face. Had he changed so much that she didn't recognize him?

"Welcome, McCoy!" One of the men moved to the side and made room for Reid. Two others did the same, making space available for Charlotte and Calum.

"I'll see you later," Joseph said to Reid. "We have much to say to one another."

Reid shook Joseph's hand and took his seat across from Charlotte and Calum. His gaze skimmed Charlotte's, but he said nothing to her.

As the women served the meal, Reid spoke to the gentleman to his right. Charlotte could not stomach the food set before her, though it was delectable fare and a far cry from what they'd eaten on their voyage. Roasted chicken, boiled potatoes, gravy, cranberries, green beans, fresh bread, venison, blueberry sauce, and more.

"Did Stephen Corning come to the Rendezvous?" Reid finally asked his dinner mate.

"Corning's been ill," the other man said, shoving a chicken leg into his mouth. He pulled out the clean bone and set it on his plate.

"Ill?" Reid stopped eating and glanced at Charlotte. "Was he able to travel?"

"Forced to stay at his post on the Upper Red River. He wanted to come, but he was delirious with fever when we left him. Couldn't wait another day, since we have so far to travel." The man pulled apart a biscuit and slathered it with butter. "Might be dead, for all I know."

Charlotte fisted her hands and dropped them to her lap. She'd never fainted in her life, but she came perilously close now as her vision began to dim. She wanted to cry out that the man must be mistaken, but she held her tongue and swallowed several times, trying not to weep.

Stephen hadn't come to Grand Portage? Had possibly died?

Reid's eyes were hard as he looked at Charlotte.

She could only stare at him. What would she do now?

He nodded at her plate, indicating that she should try to eat.

But she couldn't. Her stomach rolled, and she was afraid she'd lose its contents on the table.

"Excuse me." She stood, needing to be free from the room before she made a spectacle of herself.

Reid wiped his mouth and watched Charlotte stumble through the Great Hall. He clenched his jaw and took a steadying breath.

"Excuse me." He stood and nodded toward her. "He looks ill. I better direct him to the lavvy."

Laughter followed Reid as he moved through the room to catch up to Charlotte.

He found her on the front porch clutching one of the posts, her face as white as her shirt.

"The lavatory is this way." He took her arm and led her across the length of the porch, down a set of steps on the side of the building, and around the back. When they reached the lavatory, he let her go. No one stood in the yard behind the Great Hall, and a quick check of the outbuildings told him they were alone.

"What will I do?" Charlotte placed her hands on either side of her face, tears in her eyes. "What if Stephen is dead?"

"You dinna ken if he's dead."

"What if he is?"

"We'll deal with it when the time comes."

"But what will I do until I know? I can't stay here—and I can't go back to Montreal or England without being married."

He rubbed the back of his neck. "I'll think of something. I won't leave you stranded."

"But what can I—"

"McCoy?" Someone called for Reid from the front porch. "Are you out here? McTavish wants to see you."

"I'm here," he called back. "I'm coming."

"I'll let him know you're on your way," the man answered.

As the founding partner, Simon McTavish was the most important man in the North West Company. Reid had only met him a handful of times, and none of those had been at McTavish's request. What could he want with Reid now?

"Wait a few minutes and then come back inside," Reid told Charlotte. "Stay close to Calum and hide your emotions. I'll find you when I'm finished with McTavish, and we'll decide what to do next."

"What about Roger? What if he sees me?"

"He willna be inside the stockade. You'll be safe enough for now." He paused and weighed the wisdom in his words. "Calum knows who you are. He'll protect you if something happens."

Her eyes grew wide. "Calum knows?"

"He's known since you were sick."

She nodded but didn't respond. He wished he could stay with her and reassure her—but he wasn't sure at all what to do with her now. And with McTavish summoning him, he had little time to worry.

He strode back to the Great Hall, his thoughts churning like the waves crashing into the shore near the pier. Had Rutherford been to see McTavish? Had he told Reid's superiors about Charlotte? What if he had? Reid would hate to lie and tell them he hadn't known about her identity, but she had asked him to do that if the truth was revealed.

And worse, what if Rutherford claimed Charlotte? He had a legal right to take her away. She was not yet twenty-one. The thought of Rutherford taking Charlotte as his bride made Reid's gut tighten with anger.

Heart thumping, Reid entered the Great Hall and went directly to McTavish's private quarters, uncertain what to expect.

No matter what happened, he would not leave Charlotte at the mercy of Rutherford—of that, he was certain.

# Chapter Eight

Reid knocked on McTavish's door and waited for an invitation to enter. It came immediately.

Three men sat at a round oak table in the middle of McTavish's private quarters. A map lay in the center of the table, with books holding the corners down. A canopied bed was tucked into the corner with a wash basin nearby. Bookshelves, a desk, and a fireplace took up another wall. Thankfully, the fire had not been laid, because Reid felt overly warm already. Would these men end his fifteen-year career immediately? Or let him suffer?

The room was situated on one end of the Great Hall and served as McTavish's sleeping room as well as his office during the Rendezvous. He came out with the first brigade of pork eaters from Montreal in the spring and returned with the last at the end of the summer.

"Ah, McCoy." Simon McTavish stood and extended his hand to Reid. "We've been waiting for you to arrive in Grand Portage."

Reid also shook hands with Alexander Mackenzie and Peter Pond. The three men owned more than half the shares in the company combined and oversaw the two thousand, five hundred men who made up the North West Company. Reid had no idea why they would seek a private meeting with him. He had made a request to purchase shares in the company, but that would require him to go before a separate board that brought the request to these men.

"What can I do for you?" Reid asked.

"Have a seat." McTavish pulled a chair out for Reid, then took his own. "Would you like some high wine?"

At the shake of Reid's head, McTavish continued. "We have a great deal to discuss with you."

Reid sat at the table and looked at each man, one at a time.

"We've called you here today because your sales numbers have caught our eye," McTavish said.

"You earned more than any other bourgeois for the last three seasons you served in the interior," Mackenzie continued. "That does not go unnoticed."

Reid began to relax. This was not about Charlotte.

"The XY men have moved into the Folle Avoine District." McTavish pointed to a spot on the map about forty miles west of Mille Lac on the Mississippi River. "Andrew Fraser held the post at Crow Wing on the Mississippi for the past five years and brought in some of the finest furs in the whole company."

"But this past year," Mackenzie interrupted, his aging face lined with frustration, "the XY men built a post two miles from Fraser and lured the Chippewa to trade with them, instead."

"We need you to take over Fraser's post." McTavish cut to the heart of their meeting. "And secure the trade, no matter the cost."

"Fraser retired this year and left a poor taste in the mouth of Chief Babisïgandïbe." Peter Pond finally spoke. He was the youngest of the men and an American. "Fraser left his country wife at the post, without children. She is the daughter of the chief."

"They call Babisĭgandĭbe 'Curly Head.' He is a well-respected chief of the Mississippi Band of Chippewa." McTavish ran his finger down the length of the upper Mississippi on the map. "He lives in a village at a place called Crow Wing. 'Tis some of the most fertile and rich fur country in North America. Crow Wing is also at the confluence of two rivers and well known by the Chippewa. If we lose the trade in that region, it will hurt our profits more than we'd like."

Reid took in all the information they had given him and nodded in understanding, though he had many questions.

"We need a man who will restore relations with Curly Head and create an alliance that will push the XY men out of the region." McTavish leveled his gaze on Reid, his bushy eyebrows covering the top of his eyes. "And we believe you are that man, McCoy."

Reid sat taller, amazed that these men had selected him from among all the other gentlemen in the fur trade.

"We've heard you would like to become a shareholder." Pond folded his hands on the table. "And we're prepared to make a deal with you. If you secure the trade with Curly Head and bring in the numbers we believe that post is capable of creating, we will grant your request at next year's Rendezvous."

Reid rubbed his palms on his pant legs under the table. This was what he'd been working for his entire career as a fur trader—to become a shareholder. All he had to do was secure the trade, something he'd done at several other posts. It seemed almost too good to be true.

"Will you take this post?" McTavish asked.

Reid didn't need to think twice. "Aye. I'll gladly go."

The three men seemed to release their breaths, and they all sat back, smiles on their faces. "Good!" McTavish said. "We hoped you'd say aye."

"We've gathered the best north men in the company and prepared your supplies already." Mackenzie explained. "We'd like you to set out in the next day or two. The sooner you can get to Crow Wing, the better."

Reid nodded. "I'll do whatever it takes."

"Good." Pond glanced at his fellow shareholders. "We hoped you'd have that attitude." He cleared his throat. "Since Curly Head is angry over the treatment of his daughter by Fraser, we believe the best way to seal an alliance with the chief is by marrying his daughter and restoring his faith in our company."

Reid stilled. "Take a country wife?"

"Aye." McTavish nodded. "We've heard Curly Head is angry because Fraser did not give his daughter children, which she felt was her right."

"We've been told you dinna have a wife." Mackenzie studied him. "Is that true?"

Reid fidgeted in his chair. "'Tis true." He hated to discuss personal matters with these men, but they needed to understand his choices. "I have no wish to get married."

The men stared at him, though none of them said a word. McTavish had taken a French-Canadian wife, and Mackenzie had married a mixed-blood woman—surely they wouldn't understand Reid's hesitation.

After a moment, Pond said, "We cannot force you to marry her—but we want you to do whatever it will take to make the alliance. Do you understand?"

"I do."

"Will you consider taking her as your wife?" Mackenzie asked.

Reid did not want to make a promise to these men he could not keep, but he would be foolish not to consider their request. "I will."

"There's one other thing we need to tell you." Pond leaned forward, his rotund belly making it difficult to place his forearms on the table. "We've learned you may have a connection to the bourgeois of the XY post, and that's another reason we've chosen you for this job."

Reid frowned. "Who would that be?"

Pond glanced at McTavish before continuing. "His name is Lachlan . . .McCoy."

"Lachlan McCoy?" Reid frowned. "I dinna ken the name."

"He's a mixed-blood man." McTavish leaned back in his chair. "His father is Sean McCoy. He's your half brother."

The air rushed out of Reid's lungs. His half brother?

"Your father was a Nor'West man before the company split," Mc-Tavish explained, though he needn't bother. "His son Lachlan joined the XY Company and has been tasked with stealing the rich Mississippi River trade in the Folle Avoine District from us."

Reid clasped his hands and rested his elbows on the table before bringing his fists to his lips.

"If you do this"—McTavish laid his hands on the map—"you will be greatly rewarded."

Silence filled McTavish's room as the four men waited for Reid's reply, given this new information.

He didn't need to think on it long. He would do this thing they asked—regardless of the cost. In one fell swoop, he could become a shareholder *and* send a message to his father. If Reid could secure the trade and close the XY post—because that's exactly what he intended to do—Sean McCoy would know his legitimate son was worth something.

"I will go immediately."

McTavish extended his hand and shook Reid's. "We wish you God-speed."

Charlotte's plight rushed back at him, and he paused. He couldn't leave her at Grand Portage, and he couldn't risk sending her off with the Upper Red River men to Stephen either. They might discover her identity and misuse her—and if Stephen was already dead, she'd be trapped there, with no one to aid her. If Rutherford didn't find her at Grand Portage, no doubt he'd travel to Stephen's post looking for her there.

No. Reid would need to take her with him to Crow Wing. He'd send a message to Stephen before they left the Rendezvous to come to her when he was well enough to travel. It was their only choice.

"I have one request," Reid said as the others stood, and he followed.

"Aye?" McTavish asked.

"I have a new assistant clerk who came out with me from Montreal. I'd like to take him with me to Crow Wing. He has potential, and I'd like to train him myself."

"Whatever you'd like," Pond said. "The lad may go with you. I'm sure he'll be thankful for the opportunity."

Reid shook the other men's hands and left McTavish's room, his head spinning with all the things he'd learned—and all the things he needed to accomplish to take down the XY post.

But first, he would have to tell Charlotte that she'd remain his clerk until Stephen could come for her—which might take several months.

He couldn't deny the pleasure he felt knowing he wouldn't have to say goodbye to her yet—but it was soon followed with apprehension. There was still a great risk that she would be discovered, and now that Reid was closer than ever to becoming a shareholder, he didn't want to compromise that opportunity.

Worse, he'd grown very fond of Lady Charlotte Fairfax—much too fond for his own good.

She was still promised to another man, and Reid would honor that promise. No matter how difficult it might become.

Supper had been cleared away, but the gentlemen had not left the Great Hall. Charlotte sat next to Calum, mindlessly listening to the conversations all around her. Some of the men were crude, their jokes making her ears burn. Others were deep in philosophical or religious conversations, starved from months of living at distant posts without other Europeans to discuss such weighty topics.

Calum told her that Reid had gone into the room at the corner of the Great Hall, and she had spent the past twenty minutes watching the door, waiting for him to exit. She felt like she was suspended over a deep abyss on a tight rope, worrying if she would make it across or fall into the unknown darkness. Reid had said he would not leave her stranded, but what did that mean? Would he send her back to Montreal with the pork eaters? Would he escort her to Stephen's post?

What would become of her?

"Drink." Calum pushed a goblet of wine toward her. "It'll calm your nerves."

The smell brought back memories of Roger in a drunken stupor, and she pushed it back to him. "No, thank you."

Calum turned and straddled the bench, his full attention on Charlotte. "You need to relax, Charlie."

She'd relax once she knew what she could do—and maybe not even then. What was taking Reid so long?

The door to Mr. McTavish's room opened, and Charlotte sat up straight, her back tight with anticipation.

Reid shook one of the men's hands and nodded. He did not smile, but the men who exited the room with him were smiling.

She wanted to leave the table and speak to him about what would happen next, but she didn't want to draw undue attention. He'd come to her when he was ready.

"You and Reid spent a lot of time alone in that tent," Calum said quietly. His eyes were glossy from the alcohol, and when she met his gaze, he offered her a lopsided grin. "I wouldna mind a bit of alone time with you myself."

Had he drunk too much? She glanced around to see if anyone had heard what he said, but no one seemed to pay attention.

She ignored Calum and focused, instead, on Reid, who was taking far too long to join them.

"Did you hear me, lass?" Calum asked.

Charlotte's heart picked up its rhythm at the word *lass*. She hadn't come this far to be discovered now.

"I think I'll join Reid." She rose from the table.

"Of course you will." Calum's grin did not falter. "Just save some for me."

She frowned as she moved away from him.

Reid turned from the other men and walked to the table where the candlesticks were kept. After he selected one, he lit it in the massive fireplace nearby and then met Charlotte at the front door. Together they left the Great Hall and stepped onto the covered porch.

The sun had sunk behind the mountain at the rear of Grand Portage, and the horizon above Lake Superior had begun to dim. Pink, orange, and yellow streaked the sky, creating a perfect reflection in the pristine lake.

"I'll show you to our sleeping quarters." Reid's voice was stiff and controlled. He held his hand in front of the candle to protect it from the wind.

He led her off the porch and around the Great Hall to a series of smaller buildings. They moved past the kitchen, which was still bustling with activity, past an apothecary, which had a line of patients waiting to be seen, and past a canoe shop, where several canoes had been stacked.

She didn't press him for information, and he didn't offer any, but her insides were bunched up in knots as she waited to know what he planned to do.

"Our dormitory is this way." They took a well-worn path to a two-story building with glass windows, two chimneys on both ends, and a covered porch, similar to the one on the Great Hall.

"The clerks sleep in this dormitory, but the shareholders sleep in there"—he nodded at the building next door—"in their own rooms."

Two men exited the clerks' building, as Reid and Charlotte entered a long hallway that ran the length of the building and housed a staircase. "Our room is this way." He led her down the hall to a room at the back. A single window faced the foot of the mountain, revealing a steep path in the dim light.

Two sets of bunks, a table, and four chairs were the only furniture in the room. Four hooks lined the wall next to the door. Reid set the candle on the table then hung his pack on one of the hooks. Charlotte was thankful to hang her bag on another. Her wet clothes had saturated the canvas fabric, and she'd be glad to hang them up to dry—but that was the least of her worries right now.

Thankfully, the room was empty. When Reid closed the door behind them, he leaned against it and sighed.

Charlotte stood in the middle of the room and clasped her hands together but didn't say a word. The room was growing dark, but the candle allowed her to see him clearly.

He met her gaze, and she thought she might cry from the look in his brown eyes. It was a mixture of empathy and frustration.

She hadn't thought about how this would affect him—had only thought about herself. Surely he had no desire to continue caring for her. He didn't owe her a thing. His debt to Stephen was paid. He'd brought her safely to Grand Portage and was not honor bound to take her any farther. She'd become an unwanted bit of baggage that he would now have to deal with, because he was a gentleman.

She'd never felt more alone or unwanted in her life.

The tears formed of their own accord before she could stop them. She swallowed, trying to prevent them from spilling over, but her chin quivered, and the first tear escaped, trickling down her cheek.

"Och, lass." Reid moved away from the door and gathered her into his arms in one fluid movement. "Dinna cry."

She buried her face against his chest, clinging to the lapels of his coat. She hated how she felt—hated that she had put him in this position. He was too good and too kind to be burdened with her problems.

His shirt was soft against her cheek, and he smelled of fresh soap, wind, and pipe tobacco. One of his hands cupped the back of her head, while the other ran up and down the length of her back. The muscles in his chest rippled with the movement.

"Dinna fash, I willna let anything harm you." He whispered the promise.

He'd said the same on the first night they'd met and then again when Roger was spotted traveling with the XY men. So far, he'd kept his word—but how could she ask him to continue? He had a life to live, one that did not include her.

His hands were warm and gentle, and she felt loved and sheltered in his embrace. It was everything she'd imagined his touch would be—and more.

Longing curled inside her belly, surprising her and stopping the flow of tears.

Reid's hand stilled on her low back, and his chest muscles tensed under her cheek.

She should pull away, but she didn't want to. She wanted to stay in his arms like this forever.

He was the first to pull back but only far enough to look into her eyes.

Something profound and powerful moved within the depths of his gaze—something that both frightened her and filled her with wonder.

She couldn't tear herself away from him, and he made no move to let her go.

"Charlotte . . ."

She marveled at the sound of her name in his Scottish brogue.

Footsteps echoed down the hall, moving toward them.

Reid let her go quickly. She had to reach for one of the bunks to support her, lest she fall.

The footsteps continued down the corridor, and Charlotte let out a shaky breath.

Reid moved to the window and stood there, looking outside for a long time.

Charlotte's legs began to shake, and she lowered herself to the bottom bunk. What had just passed between them? Had she imagined it?

"I'm being sent to the Mississippi River in the Folle Avoine District," he said quietly. "I'm to restore trade relations with Chief Babisĭgandĭbe."

"Is that a great distance from here?" she asked just as quietly.

"Another five- or six-week journey into the interior."

"Will you leave soon?"

"Tomorrow or the next day. I will meet with my men in the morning and look over all the provisions that have been prepared." He finally turned away from the window and put his hand on the back of a chair. "I have much to do before I can leave here."

She nodded but did not meet his eyes again, too afraid of what she might see. She wiped the tears from her face with the back of her sleeve, forcing her emotions to stay at bay. Her hands trembled, and she braced herself for whatever might come next.

"I willna leave you here, Charlie." He was back to calling her the name he'd given her in Montreal.

"What will I do?" She didn't want to cry again but wanted to face the future with as much courage as she could muster.

"The Upper Red River men are leaving in the morning. I will send a letter with their bourgeois telling Stephen where I will be stationed this winter. I willna mention you, in case someone else reads the letter, but I will make it clear that I have fulfilled my debt, and when he is well enough to travel, he can come and collect it."

"How long might it take him?"

Reid sighed and took a seat on the chair nearest the window—and farthest from her. "It will take the Red River men at least eight weeks to reach their post. If Stephen is alive and recovered, he will probably try to get away as soon as he's able—but it might not be until winter sets in, since there is much to be done when the north men return to their posts."

"How long will it take him to get from his post to yours?" She fisted her hands on her lap, afraid of his answer.

"If he comes in the winter and he has a seasoned guide, they will travel over the frozen lakes and rivers with a dogsled—but it would still take him at least six weeks. If he comes before the freeze, much longer."

Charlotte did the calculations in her head. It was mid-June now. "Four months?"

Reid nodded. "At least. It could be as many as six."

She stood and cradled her arms, trying not to panic. "And what would I do until then?"

"You will act as the assistant clerk at my post. Calum has taught you well, and what you dinna ken, I will teach you myself."

He'd do this for her? But why? He didn't owe her any favors. "I'll continue as Charlie Crawford?"

He stared at her for a long moment and then nodded. "Aye. Charlie Crawford, company clerk."

Charlotte paced across the room and tucked her bottom lip between her teeth while she considered his plan.

"There's no other option, lass."

The thought of continuing as a man for the next several months, with no guarantee that Stephen would come for her, was not what she had wanted or hoped for. She longed for Blissfield Manor and the comforts of home.

But she was thankful Reid was willing to help her, and she was determined he would not regret his offer. She would be the best assistant clerk he'd ever had, and she would do it without complaining.

"Thank you, Reid." She wouldn't let the emotion cloud her speech and make him sorry he'd allowed a European woman into the fur trade.

The candle flickered, sending shadows dancing over the planes of his handsome face.

Longing warmed her belly again, and she forced herself to look away.

It would be a long winter.

# Chapter Nine

The next morning, Reid sent a letter off with the Upper Red River men who took their leave from Grand Portage in great fanfare. As he watched them leave, he knew that if Stephen was alive, he'd receive the letter in about eight weeks' time. How would Stephen respond, knowing Lady Charlotte had come all this way to marry him? No doubt, he'd be honored and overwhelmed—and thoroughly besotted.

Just as Reid would be if Charlotte had come all this way for him.

Stephen wasn't a handsome or powerful man. He was a simple, kind, and steadfast sort. He was respectable and trustworthy and would put his own life in jeopardy to save another, like he'd saved Reid. Stephen had qualities any woman would seek in a mate. Charlotte had chosen wisely and would be fortunate to marry him.

But it still didn't set well with Reid. He struggled to imagine Charlotte married to gentle, unassuming Stephen. To share a life and a home—and a bed—with him.

Yet they had pledged their troth to marry. Stephen had written his proposal, and she had come across the ocean to accept. It was as strong a promise as any Reid had ever known.

And Reid would be loath to try and prevent it for any reason.

After the Upper Red River men were gone, Reid took Charlotte to the warehouse where their cargo was stored until their departure. Several of the north men assigned to their journey were already there, organizing the trade items into ninety-pound bales. The packages would be hauled with the north canoes, which were much smaller than the Montreal canoes and designed to navigate the narrower lakes and rivers of the interior.

Another beautiful day greeted them on the shores of Lake Superior, but the weather did not match Reid's mood. He'd not slept well the night before after his encounter with Charlotte, and he'd been irritated when she'd stood over his shoulder while he penned his letter to Stephen early that morning.

All around them, voyageurs and officers reveled in their summer break. Competitions of strength and agility were being held in the stockade yard, a feast was being prepared in the kitchen behind the Great Hall, and several men were laughing and singing on the front porch.

All of it grated on Reid's mood.

"Do you think someone will read your letter before they give it to Stephen?" Charlotte asked quietly, walking beside Reid as he inspected the supplies that had been prepared for them.

Reid stopped and pointed to several bales being tied by his north men. "I want the ropes tied tighter." He couldn't hide his frustration. "We canna afford for them to unravel along the way."

The men nodded and began to retie the packages.

"Could he come sooner than four months?" she asked, stepping around a barrel of rum.

"Here's the list of inventory." He handed her several pages that had been prepared by one of the company clerks before Reid's arrival. It was meticulous and there was no need to go over it again, but he couldn't abide Charlotte's questions. Not today. "I want you to ensure that everything on this list is here and accounted for."

She took the papers but didn't protest.

"I will see to our canoes." He walked away from her without further discussion, needing his space. He had sent for Calum, but the man had not come yet. He was probably still sleeping off the alcohol from the night before.

Several warehouses spread out before Reid, and hundreds of voyageurs moved back and forth between them, all packaging and preparing for the winter season. Over a hundred thousand tons of cargo were brought inland from Montreal each year. Every item was inventoried, divided, and painstakingly packaged into ninety-pound square bales. Fabric, blankets, knives, beads, fishhooks, alcohol, tobacco, axes, muskets, trade silver, tin goods, lead shot, traps, and gunpowder were sent to the posts to trade with the Indians for furs. Added to the trade items were the food stores, which included brown and white biscuits, beef, bacon, English and Irish pork, salt pork, Scotch barley, oatmeal, flour, sugar, split peas, corn, rice, and pemmican made from dried buffalo meat and cranberries.

Charlotte moved through the bales, the inventory list in hand, making notes with a pencil, glancing up at him from time to time in question.

Reid had not spoken to her about their embrace the night before, and he'd tried hard to forget it. He had lain in bed for hours, unable to sleep, thinking about how good she had felt in his arms. If they hadn't been interrupted, he was afraid of what might have happened. The desire to pull her closer had overwhelmed him.

But it wasn't just a physical desire he felt for her—and that was why he was angrier than a badger this morning. He enjoyed her company more than he ought to. If it was simply a matter of physical attraction, he could deny himself like he'd done these past fifteen years. But it wasn't that simple.

It would have been best for all of them if Stephen had been at the Rendezvous, ready to marry her and be done with it.

Calum appeared around the side of the Great Hall, walking sluggishly.

Finally. Reid impatiently strode toward the other man, anxious to accomplish one more task before it grew too late.

"You sent for me?" Calum squinted against the sun, as if it hurt. His clothes were mussed, and his red-rimmed eyes were lined with fatigue. He hadn't come back to their room until the early morning hours, and when he had, he'd smelled of stale rum.

"I have a favor to ask." Reid glanced around to make sure they were alone, and then he leaned in closer to Calum. "I need to leave the stockade for a few hours this afternoon, and I'd appreciate it if you kept an eye on Charlie. I dinna want to leave her alone."

"Leave the stockade?" Calum frowned. "Where might you be going?"

Reid had no desire to share all the details with Calum. The less he knew, the better. "I just need you to watch out for Charlie. Will you do it?"

Calum ran his hands through his dark hair and nodded. "I will."

"Thank you. I might not be back for several hours. I'll join you for supper this evening."

Reid clasped Calum on the shoulder and left him to do what he'd set out to accomplish.

He was going to the XY fort to find Rutherford.

Less than two miles away from the North West Company fort at Grand Portage, the XY Company had built their largest inland depot. It wasn't as large as the Nor' Westers' fort, but it served the same purposes. Reid had no wish to enter the stockade, knowing he'd be run out, but he had found an XY voyageur who had willingly agreed to find Rutherford for a price.

The sun beat down on Reid's back as he waited outside the gates for Rutherford to appear. It had been close to an hour since he'd sent the voyageur to look for him, and Reid was beginning to think the man had taken his money and had no plans on summoning Charlotte's guardian.

As the minutes passed, he felt for the butt of his pistol, which he wore at his side. He had no doubt that Rutherford was capable of anything. And with some of the stories Charlotte had told, Reid was determined to be prepared.

The gate finally opened again, and this time Rutherford appeared. He wore a suit similar to Reid's, with tight-fitting trousers, a white shirt, and a long-tailed coat. A top hat sat upon his head, distinguishing him as a gentleman in this place so far removed from civilization.

"I thought it might be you." Rutherford approached Reid cautiously, his eyes shadowed by the rim of his hat. Long side whiskers extended from his hair to his jaw line, and his mouth was firm. "What do you want with me?"

Reid did not have practice deceiving people, but he'd prepared himself on the two-mile walk with what he planned to say to Rutherford. "I couldna forget your visit in Montreal and thought I might be of service to you now."

Rutherford moved close enough for Reid to see his eyes. They were shrewd and calculating. "Do you have Charlotte?"

"No." It was the first of many lies he planned to tell Rutherford. "But I saw someone who fit her description."

Rutherford crossed his arms and stared at Reid. "Go on."

"Yesterday, when my brigade first arrived, I saw a young lad I'd not seen before. He was small and fair, with delicate features and auburn hair. It made me pause, so I drew closer to him and engaged him in conversation." Reid shook his head, as if he was stunned. "I'm convinced it was the cousin you are seeking."

Rutherford seemed to consider Reid's words for a minute. "How did you know I was here?"

"I saw you at the wharf the day we left, and then my spies told me there was an English gentleman traveling with the XY brigade that camped across the river from us the first night."

Rutherford's jaw was tight as he took a deep breath in and out. "What happened after you determined this person was Charlotte?"

"I spoke to the bourgeois in charge of his brigade and asked where the lad had come from and what he knew of him. He told me he'd just come from England and had signed on at the Montreal office under the name of Thomas Fairfax."

"That is the name of Charlotte's late father."

Charlotte had told Reid as much.

"Was she with Stephen?" Rutherford asked.

"After I suspected the lad was Lady Charlotte, I asked about Stephen Corning but discovered he'd been very ill and unable to travel to the Rendezvous. He was forced to stay at his post in the Upper Red River."

"So he isn't in Grand Portage." Rutherford's face filled with triumph. "Charlotte is probably devastated. I must go and find her."

"The lad asked to be transferred to the Upper Red River," Reid said quickly—and then forced himself to calm his nerves. "He left with their brigade this morning."

"She left this morning?" Rutherford frowned. "Are you certain?"

"I am." He didn't want to give Rutherford the truth about where Stephen was stationed, but he suspected Rutherford already knew, and if Reid's information wasn't close enough to the truth, Rutherford would not believe him.

Rutherford's gaze narrowed on Reid. "Why are you telling me these things?"

"You told me the lass was in danger, and I thought I'd help you find her. The wilderness is no place for a lady." He had to choke out the next words. "The sooner you find her, the better."

"I must find a brigade going to the Upper Red River immediately. Charlotte cannot marry a commoner and ruin her life." Rutherford's countenance changed, and he turned on the charm Charlotte had warned Reid about. "I said I'd compensate you for your help—I'm sure that's the real reason you've come."

Reid didn't want Rutherford's money, but he must continue this charade if he wanted Charlotte to be safe. Feigning embarrassment, Reid dropped his gaze and shrugged. "If you see fit to offer a little reward, I willna deny you."

Rutherford reached into his inner pocket and withdrew a wallet. He pulled out some currency and handed it to Reid. "I'm in your debt, Mr. McCoy."

Taking the money, Reid shoved it into his pocket. He'd give it away to the women who served their evening meals.

"If you'll excuse me?" Rutherford bowed. "I have much to accomplish if I'm to retrieve my cousin."

Reid matched his bow and then turned away from Rutherford, keeping his head high.

Everything about his encounter with the man made him angry, but he could think of no better way to keep Charlotte safe until Stephen could come for her.

He just hoped his letter would get to Stephen before Rutherford did.

The day had been warm, and Charlotte's head hurt from the glare of the sun. On top of the tedious inventory work, Reid had disappeared without telling her where he'd gone, and Calum had spent the afternoon hanging around the warehouse, teasing her like he used to. When she asked him if he knew where Reid had gone, he'd said no and offered no possible explanation.

She tucked the inventory list in her cassette and lifted it to bring it back to her room. All she wanted was a nap before the evening festivities. She'd been told by more than one person that there would be a feast, followed by a dance in the Great Hall, and everyone was expected to attend. It was the pinnacle of the Rendezvous, and the following day many brigades were expected to depart. Already, the Upper Red River men had left, as did another that had a longer journey to make.

"Where are you going?" Calum asked, stepping up beside her.

"To take a nap." She squinted as she surveyed the stockade, looking for Reid. "Have you seen Reid yet?"

"He said he willna be back until supper."

Where could anyone go in Grand Portage? Was he still in the stockade, seeing to business? Had he been called to a meeting? Or was he in the voyageurs' camps? But what would he do there? His disappearance baffled her.

Calum stayed close beside Charlotte as she followed the path to the clerks' dormitory. The closer she drew to the building, the more uncomfortable she became. Would he follow her to their room? It was one thing to share a room with several men when Reid was present—but an entirely different thing when she was alone with other men.

"Do you have plans for this afternoon?" she asked Calum as she stopped outside the building.

He opened the door and waited for her to walk in ahead of him. "No."

She didn't move. "Surely you have somewhere you need to be."

"Reid asked me to keep my eye on you."

He had?

"I'm planning to nap and won't leave the room until supper. You're free to leave."

He continued to hold the door open. "I have nowhere else I'd rather be."

Not knowing what else to do, she entered the building and walked down the hall to their room.

When they arrived at their door, Calum opened it and smiled.

She entered the room and set her cassette on the table. "You really don't need to stay. I'll be fine here on my own."

He closed the door and walked across the room to sit at the table. Their fourth bunkmate, a man Charlotte had not been formally introduced to since he'd stumbled in after she'd gone to bed and was snoring when she and Reid had left that morning, was not in the room.

"Have a seat." He pulled a chair out beside him with the toe of his boot.

What she really wanted was to sleep—but the thought of lying in her bed while he sat in the room was disquieting.

She sat down and folded her hands in her lap.

"Did Reid tell you why he is being sent to Crow Wing?"

"To restore trade with the chief in that region."

"And how might he do that?"

Charlotte shrugged. She had no idea how a person went about such business.

Calum's smile was callous. "He's planning to marry the chief's daughter."

Her breath caught. Reid planned to marry the chief's daughter when they arrived?

"I see he dinna tell you."

Swallowing, Charlotte tried to still the emotions flooding her chest. Why hadn't he told her?

"So you see"—Calum leaned forward and put his finger on Charlotte's hand, running it along the length of her small finger up to her wrist—"he's only using you, lass."

Charlotte pulled her hand back, repulsed by his accusation and touch. "Reid has been a gentleman."

"Gentleman or not, he's still using you."

"I think you misunderstand my relationship with Reid."

He put his hand on her shoulder and slid it down the contour of her chest. "Do I?"

She slapped his face, her heart pounding.

His eyes grew wide, and he grabbed her wrist, but he did not retaliate. Instead, he let her go and leaned back, smiling like it was all a big joke. "No one at this post kens you're a woman."

She stared at him, unsure how to respond.

"And you dinna want them to find out, do you?"

Charlotte stood. Why was he speaking about this?

He also stood and approached her. "So even if I had my way with you, you couldna tell anyone, could you? If you did, you'd have to admit you're a woman."

Panic seized her, and she stepped backward, bumping into the end of the bunk.

He came closer. "Now why not share some of that attention you've been giving to Reid?" He pressed against her. "I admit, it'll feel strange, making love to someone wearing men's clothing, but I imagine you're all woman underneath."

She pushed him away and ran toward the door, but he grabbed her wrist again.

"You dinna need to pretend with me any longer, lass. I ken who and what you are. Reid told me."

What had Reid said about her that would lead Calum to believe she was an immoral woman?

"Let me go, Calum." She tried to wrench her wrist free. "I'm not the kind of woman you think I am."

He pulled her tight against his chest, one hand holding her wrists together behind her back. When she tried to scream, he put his free hand over her mouth. "If you scream, someone will come, and you'll have to explain who you are. What'll happen to you then? They'll hand you over to your guardian."

Another jolt of panic raced up her limbs making her feel weak. He was right. Her only hope would be getting free on her own.

She tried, in vain, to pull away from him, but he was much stronger than she was. She began to pray, as she had during her years of imprisonment at Blissfield Manor, that God would find a way to free her from a man who meant her harm. She didn't know if God was listening then—or if He was listening now—but it was her only hope.

"All the good lasses are supposed to say no." He grinned and pinned her against the wall. She could not kick or punch or fight. He kissed her mouth, but she turned her head away.

"Dinna fight me, Charlie." He continued to smile, as if he truly believed she was putting up a fight as some sort of game. "If you'll let me, I'll show you what a real man is made of." He grabbed her chin and pressed his lips against hers.

She twisted her head out of his hands. "Don't." Tears gathered in her eyes. "Please don't do this."

"Do you think Reid was the only one who should enjoy your company? All the while he was turning his nose up at me for taking pleasure with the Indians, he had you to warm his bed."

She struggled to get free of him, but his grasp was relentless.

"I've been wondering what you're hiding under these clothes for weeks now." He yanked at her shirt. The buttons tore off and flew across the room. "Binding? I should have known."

The door opened and suddenly Reid was there. Charlotte glimpsed his horrified face a moment before he crossed the room and pulled Calum away from her.

Charlotte sagged with relief against the wall, trying to catch her breath.

"Are you mad?" Reid roared, shoving Calum against the opposite wall. His face was red as he grasped Calum's lapels and pushed him up the wall until Calum's feet were no longer touching the ground. "What are you doing?"

Calum put his hands on Reid's, but didn't try to get free. "Just having my turn."

Reid slammed Calum against the wall again, cracking his head against the hard plaster.

Calum winced.

Charlotte pulled her shirt together, tears streaming down her cheeks.

"Get your things and find another place to sleep." Reid shoved Calum away, causing the other man to stumble and fall. "If you so much as look at the lass again, I will make you regret that you have eyes."

Calum was a coward, Charlotte could see it immediately. He grabbed his bag and cassette and tripped out of the room.

Reid slammed the door behind him, breathing hard, fear making his eyes look wild. "Did he hurt you, lass?"

She could taste blood, and her bottom lip felt swollen, but that was the worst of it. Her muscles would probably be sore in the morning, and she might have a mark on her wrists where he'd held her, but she wiped away her tears. "I'm fine."

"You're not fine." Reid swallowed, his chest rising and falling as he took deep gulps of air. There was pain and anger in his gaze as he studied her. "Was I too late?"

"No." She shook her head quickly. "No. You were not too late."

Her shirt hung awkwardly from her clasped hand. She tried to gather it better, but part of her binding was visible. Calum's earlier comments returned to her. "What did you tell him about me?" Tears stung the back of her eyes, but she wouldn't let them fall again.

A crease wrinkled his brow. "Nothing."

"He thought—" She swallowed the shame, the tears falling despite her best effort. "He thought you and I—" She couldn't finish the sentence.

"Och, lass." He drew closer to her. "I dinna tell him anything except that you were hiding from your guardian. Anything else he believed was of his own making."

She tried to tighten the gap in her shirt.

Reid looked away and wiped aimlessly at his mouth. "I shouldna left you in his care."

"You didn't know." She sniffed and wiped at her tears, hating that she couldn't stop crying.

"I canna bear to see you cry, lass." He lifted his hand and wiped a tear with his thumb. "Or to think about what you just experienced."

She pulled away from his touch, suddenly wanting to make light of the ordeal. She hated to see pity in his eyes. "I'll need to find a needle and thread if I want to be presentable at the dance tonight." A sob caught in her throat. How preposterous her words sounded. Two years ago, she'd been allowed to attend the ball her mother hosted, and she'd been dressed in the most elegant gown she'd ever seen. Now, she was worried about a few missing buttons on her suit? "These are my nicest clothes, after all."

Walking away, she kept her back to him and surveyed the damage Calum had done. Three of the buttons were gone, and two hung by threads. "I suppose it doesn't matter what I look like." The tears refused to stop, so she wiped at them impatiently. "In England, I would care a great deal more."

"In England, you'd be clothed in the finest silks."

Her chin quivered as she thought about the gowns she'd left behind. Oh, how she longed to feel feminine again.

"You'd be the bonniest lass at the dance."

A button lay on the floor near one of the chairs. She bent to pick it up and saw another under the bunk. "My favorite color is purple." She was trying to make this moment less awkward, but she couldn't stop rambling. She got on her knees and reached under the bunk to retrieve the second button. "I never had a season in London, but if I did, I would have had at least one dress made of lavender."

Reid bent to pick up the third button, which was under the other bunk. "You would have turned every head in the room."

She was already on the floor, so she sat with her back against one bunk. She continued to clutch the front of her shirt and pulled her legs up to her chest. She rested her forehead against her knees, the tears falling as she thought about all she had lost—and what could have happened if Reid had not entered when he did.

Had God been watching—listening to her cries of help? Had He sent Reid to save her?

Reid sat on the floor across from her, his left leg drawn up. He draped his arm across his knee. "You dinna need all that finery for me to see you're bonnie, on the inside and outside."

She wiped at the tears again and licked her bleeding lip. Even though her hair was short, she wore men's clothes, and she was a blubbering mess, somehow he found it possible to tell her she was beautiful? The tears finally stopped. "I'm concerned you might be going blind, Mr. McCoy. You should see the fort doctor before we leave."

He reached out and handed her the button. Their hands grazed for only a moment, but it was enough to send a shiver up her arm.

"My eyesight is perfect."

"Then you are a liar—a far worse condition."

Reid smiled, but his brown eyes were serious. "I would never lie to you, lass. I have far too much respect for you."

If he would not lie to her, then maybe he would tell her where he had gone. "Why did you ask Calum to stay with me today?"

The smile left his face. "I went to see Rutherford."

Charlotte went still. "Did you find him?"

"Aye." His gaze didn't waver.

"Why?"

"I do not respect him."

She frowned. "What does that mean?"

"It means I lied to him. I told him I was there as a service to him and that I saw you here, dressed as a man." It was evident to Charlotte that it pained him to lie. "I also told him that I saw you leave Grand Portage this morning with the men going to the Upper Red River."

"Why did you do that?"

"So he will not follow you to the Mississippi River. When I left, he was already trying to find the next brigade going north."

Charlotte clutched the three buttons in her hand. "What happens when he learns I am not with Stephen? What if he hurts Stephen?"

"I hope Stephen gets my letter before Rutherford arrives. I warned him that someone might show up to claim his debt at the Upper Red River post. He will be prepared for Rutherford, and when Rutherford sees you are not with Stephen, Rutherford will leave there to find me again. It might take him months to learn my location." His voice grew quieter. "By then"—he paused, as if it was hard to say the words—"I hope Stephen has come for you."

She hoped so too.

# Chapter Ten

Light and laughter spilled out the windows of the Great Hall as Charlotte and Reid walked up the path. The moon lay low and bright on the horizon, reflecting off Lake Superior. Waves beat against the shore beyond the stockade, and revelers stood around two large campfires that burned bright in the yard. Both men and women moved in and out of the Great Hall. The Indian and mixed-blood women wore surprisingly modern gowns that would rival any Charlotte had seen in England. In the darkness, it was hard to distinguish them from their European counterparts.

"I wish I was escorting you to this dance with you dressed like one of those fine women," Reid said quietly. "Every man in this fort would be jealous."

Warmth filled her cheeks, and she was thankful it was too dark for him to see her response. A longing to be adorned like one of the women filled her so completely that she ached with it. How she wished Reid could see her in more than men's clothing. Even when she had gone to him in Montreal, she'd looked like a rag woman. The next morning, she'd been clean, but she'd been clothed in his cook's large, old-fashioned nightgown.

Every day since then, she'd been dressed as she was now.

But none of that mattered as long as she was reunited with Stephen at the end—at least, that's what she continued to tell herself. It was only vanity making her long to be beautiful again.

They walked up the stairs and across the porch. Lanterns hung from hooks, illuminating men laughing and talking with drinks in their hands. The women present were not the same women who had served their meals. These women were refined and well mannered. Some had such fair complexions she had a hard time believing they weren't European.

"Many of the shareholders' wives and daughters have joined us this evening," Reid commented as they walked past a group of four young women giggling and flirting with several clerks.

They passed over the threshold and into the Great Hall, where the tables had been pushed against the walls. The center of the room was full of men and women dancing. In one corner, three musicians played a waltz Charlotte had heard a hundred times. The familiarity of the song clashed with the knowledge that she was thousands of miles from civilized society.

"Some of the women here could pass as gentry from home," Charlotte said. "I had no idea they'd be so fine."

Reid handed her a glass of punch. "Many have fathers from Europe and mothers who are mixed-blood, so they are only a quarter Indian. Most are sent to Montreal—and even some to Europe—to be educated. The majority return to the interior, because they are not accepted anywhere else." He took a sip of his punch, watching the dancers twirl around the floor. "There is a whole race of people in the northwest that did not exist a hundred and fifty years ago before the fur trade began. They do not fit in anywhere else but here."

Charlotte watched the women in fascination. They dressed, danced, and flirted like the women she'd known all her life, though there were subtle differences. Their accents were unlike any she'd ever heard. Not quite the same as the Indians she'd encountered on their way to Grand Portage, but not quite French, English, or Scottish either. Most had dark hair and eyes, but some had blue eyes and lighter hair. There were even a few with red hair among them.

But all were beautiful and exotic to Charlotte, who felt woefully unattractive, though she wore a brand new suit of clothes, which Reid had purchased for her that afternoon after her other suit was ruined. He'd insisted, and she'd acquiesced, only to make him happy. It was chocolate-brown serge that matched the color of her eyes and made her hair look darker.

Calum entered the Great Hall, and she stiffened. She'd tried to beg off coming to the dance, not wanting to see him again, but Reid had encouraged her to come. He said it would be the last opportunity for civilized company until he returned this way again next year. When she told him she'd rather not, he said he'd stay with her then—but she didn't want to deny him the opportunity to visit with these people. They were his friends, his surrogate family—who was she to ask him to stay away?

Reid moved closer to her, though she didn't think he realized it.

Calum held a glass of sparkling red liquid while he laughed and joked loudly with several men and women. His movements were already affected by drink. He swayed but caught himself before falling.

Charlotte wanted to hate him, but she chose to feel sorry for him, instead. She'd been spared a horrible experience and was thankful that God had brought Reid at the right moment. It was yet one more atrocious experience on this journey, and she was determined not to let it define her.

"Do you dance?" Reid stepped in her line of sight so she didn't have to look at Calum.

"I love to dance." Already, her feet were tapping in time to the music.

"I do as well." He leaned close to her ear. "I wish I could ask you to dance."

Pleasure shivered up her neck, but she schooled her face to remain unaffected. Why was he suddenly acting this way? Was it the allure of the evening? The pleasure of fine company? Whatever it was, she'd like him to stop. It did funny things inside of her, made her feel things she'd never felt before—things she didn't think would please Stephen.

"Monsieur McCoy." An exquisitely dressed woman sidled up to Reid, her long eyelashes dipping to her high cheekbones in a beguiling way, as her ebony hair shined in the lantern light. "I have not seen you for a long time." She spoke in French, though her accent was not European. "I have missed you."

"Mademoiselle Tremblay, may I present my clerk, Monsieur Crawford?"

Miss Tremblay offered a regal curtsy, her full purple gown splaying out on either side of her. "It's a pleasure to meet you." She spoke to Charlotte, but her brown eyes stayed on Reid. "I have been waiting for you to ask me to dance," she said to him.

Charlotte tried to look away, but she couldn't take her eyes off Miss Tremblay's gown.

"I am not—" He paused. "I dinna think I'll danc—"

"You should dance," Charlotte said, not wanting him to refrain on her account—and needing a little space from the handsome fur trader.

"You see?" Miss Tremblay said. "Even your clerk wants you to dance."

Reid glanced in Calum's direction, uncertainty in his gaze making him hesitate.

"Go," Charlotte said, though in truth, she didn't feel like sending him away with this pretty woman. "I won't wander far."

He finally nodded and bowed to Miss Tremblay. Taking her arm, he led her into the group of dancers and began to spin her around the room.

An Indian woman appeared at Charlotte's elbow with a tray of roasted beef. "The meal is served."

Charlotte moved out of her way and noticed the table laden with food behind her. It was being served buffet style.

She hadn't eaten since breakfast, and her stomach growled. A crowd of people gathered around the food quickly. If she wanted to eat, she'd need to move fast.

"Mr. Crawford?" An older voyageur stopped before Charlotte with a woman at his side. There were only a few voyageurs in the room, and Charlotte had guessed they were the highly respected guides. The rest were the gentlemen bourgeois and their wives and daughters.

Charlotte nodded. "I'm Crawford."

"I'm Jean-Paul Michaud, and this is my wife Noemie." He bowed and his wife curtsied. "I will guide the brigade to Crow Wing."

"It's a pleasure to meet you." The three of them moved toward the buffet table, where they waited in line.

"Reid is an old friend." Jean-Paul's kind blue eyes softened. "He is like a son to Noemie and me."

Noemie nodded and smiled. She was a mixed-blood woman with silky black hair streaked with gray. Though she wore a beautiful red gown, her ears were adorned with beaded Indian earrings.

Charlotte warmed to this couple immediately and was thankful they would travel with her to Crow Wing. She also loved knowing they were Reid's friends. Somehow, that made her feel like she already knew them.

And even if Noemie couldn't know that Charlotte was a woman, it was a relief to have another woman nearby.

From where Charlotte stood, she had a good view of Reid as he danced with Miss Tremblay. The young woman was smitten with him—it was written all over her face. Did Reid know? He was attentive to his dance partner, holding her close, smiling while he listened to her speak.

Jean-Paul and Noemie followed Charlotte's gaze and then shared a secret smile of their own.

"Celeste will not let him go," Noemie said, "now that she has him back."

"Celeste?"

"Tremblay," Noemie provided. "She is dancing with Reid. He was her father's clerk for many seasons, and everyone thought they would marry."

Jean-Paul handed a plate to his wife. "You are spreading gossip, my love."

Noemie shook her head. "Everyone thought so—Celeste most of all."

"What happened?" Charlotte couldn't help but ask.

With a shrug, Noemie placed a scoop of roasted potatoes on her plate. "Who can tell in matters of love? A quarrel, perhaps."

Jean-Paul clicked his tongue. "Hush, Noemie," he chastised her gently. "Let them alone. If it's meant to be, it will grow."

"Sometimes a couple needs a little nudge." Noemie placed a biscuit on her plate and winked at her husband playfully.

"I would still be single if she hadn't nudged me all the way to the altar." Jean-Paul laughed. "My wife is a matchmaker," he explained to Charlotte. "Whether she's asked or not."

Noemie lifted her shoulder and shrugged. "I like to see people happy. Is there harm in that?"

Reid and Celeste were a handsome couple, and it was obvious Celeste still cared for him—so why had Reid not married her? Though Charlotte had spent six weeks with him, she realized she didn't know him well at all. He was a private man and did not give information away freely.

"What about you, Mr. Crawford?" Noemie asked. "Do you have a girl?"

Charlotte paused, her hand gripping the ladle of corn. "No."

"There are plenty here to choose from."

"Now, now, Noemie," Jean-Paul chided. "The boy is young. He has plenty of time before he needs to make that decision."

"No one is ever too young to start looking." She lowered her chin and studied Charlotte. "And he is a handsome boy—almost beautiful, if a man can be beautiful."

Charlotte turned away, pretending to survey the food options. She did not want Noemie looking at her too closely.

"Is there someone in this room that has caught your attention?" Noemie asked.

There was someone who had her attention tonight, but she would never admit it to Noemie—didn't want to admit it to herself either. Her gaze floated to Reid of its own accord. He was the handsomest man in the room. Taller than most, with broad shoulders, dark hair and eyes, and an air of confidence that made other men seem weak. But he was more than handsome—he was kind, courageous, and selfless. Any woman would notice—and many had.

"Ah, I see." Noemie nudged Jean-Paul. "Our Mr. Crawford has already noticed at least one person in this room."

Concern tightened the crease between Charlotte's eyebrows.

"Celeste is a beautiful woman," Noemie said with a knowing smile. "But you'll have to draw her away from Reid first."

Charlotte recoiled at the assumption the woman had made, but decided not to say anything, afraid she'd give herself away.

"Why don't we eat and forget about this matchmaking?" Jean-Paul pointed to a table. "Would you care to join us, Mr. Crawford?"

Charlotte did not want to join them and risk Noemie's prying.

"I think I will go onto the porch for some fresh air."

Jean-Paul nodded and led his wife away.

Charlotte left the buffet and skirted around the dancers to step outside.

"I was sad when you left." Celeste pouted and Reid tried not to sigh. It had been much the same with Celeste since she was old enough to bat her eyelashes at him.

"I had to return to Montreal. I told you that, lass."

She shrugged. "You could have taken me with you."

"It wouldna been proper."

"If you'd marry me, I could go anywhere with you." She moved closer to him than the dance required, her voice dripping with intimacy. "I'd go to the ends of the earth with you."

He'd tried making it clear to her that he wasn't interested, but it seemed Celeste needed another reminder. He stopped dancing. "I do not want to marry, Celeste. I've told you this."

She lifted a delicate shoulder and readjusted his cravat, her eyelashes lowering with suggestion. "And I told you I don't require marriage."

"Your father would not agree."

"I do not care about my father."

"I do." Her father was a wintering partner who had managed the Sault Saint Marie District. Reid had worked under him for several years before taking over his own post. He had nothing but respect for Monsieur Tremblay, though the older gentleman had spoiled his only daughter.

Celeste moved closer to Reid, brushing him with her body. "Are you certain?"

Reid had no desire for Charlotte to see him in this position with Celeste, so he stepped away from her and looked to see if Charlotte was watching.

But Charlotte was not with the Michauds, as he'd thought. And a glance around the room revealed she was no longer inside the Great Hall.

Alarm seized him, especially when he could not locate Calum either.

He didn't bother to excuse himself but left Celeste to find Charlotte. He wanted to run, call out for Charlotte, but he didn't want to bring attention to himself or her. Rushing onto the porch, he looked left and then right, his pulse throbbing in his ears—and then he saw her standing near the railing, a plate of food in her hands.

Relief made him weak, and he leaned against the doorframe. What was happening to him? He felt like a skittish colt.

Surely it was his debt to Stephen that had him acting this way. What would he say to Stephen if he handed Charlotte back misused or hurt? He couldn't live with himself.

Charlotte had not noticed him but stood in the soft light of a lantern, looking wistfully toward the lake. Wind ruffled the curls near her face, teasing them out of her queue. What occupied her thoughts tonight?

A new waltz started, playing softly on the breeze.

If they were anywhere else, he wouldn't hesitate. He'd asked her to dance. He'd use almost any excuse to hold her again—and dancing seemed like the best one he could think of.

The light did not reach beyond the porch, and an idea came to him.

His boots clicked across the wide planks as he approached her.

"You gave me a scare, Charlie."

Lowering her plate, she tore her gaze from the lake. Her eyes were large and beautiful, with long dark lashes. And when she looked at him in the soft light, she stole his breath away.

He stood beside her, collecting his thoughts for a moment. "I dinna ken where you went."

She put down a biscuit and rubbed her fingers together, scattering crumbs on her plate. "I'm sorry I pulled you away from your dancing partner. You looked like you were having a good time."

A group of gentlemen stood nearby, and their laughter overpowered Charlotte's words. He almost missed what she said.

"'Tis true." He took her plate and set it on a table near the window. "I like to dance."

Reid started toward the steps on the end of the porch and tilted his head, indicating she should follow.

Charlotte pushed away from the railing and crossed the porch, following him down the steps and into the inky darkness. Her new suit fit her well and showed him how much she had filled out since starting their journey. No longer was she the sickly thin woman who had knocked on his door. Now she was healthy and fit, her cheeks glowing with a rosy shine. He wondered about her womanly curves and how she kept those hidden but would never ask.

"Reid?" She stopped at the base of the stairs and reached into the darkness.

Her body was silhouetted by the light from the porch, but where he stood, it would be impossible for her to see him.

"I'm here." He reached out and took her hand. She gave it to him willingly, clasping it with both of hers.

"What are you doing?" she asked breathlessly.

No one had ventured to this side of the building, but the music and laughter had followed them.

He guided her to stand before him, though he still could not see her face. He held both of her hands in his own and rubbed the tops with his thumbs. "I'm going to dance with you in the dark."

She was quiet for a moment, and he wished he could see her eyes.

"We'll imagine 'tis a grand ballroom in your bonnie England," he said as he sensed her hesitation. "Filled with a thousand dripping candles and we will not be afraid of the light. Everyone will see us together—and no one will think twice."

Though he could not see her face, he hoped she smiled.

"Can you imagine it, lass?" he asked on a whisper, wishing it were true.

"Aye," she said, emulating his Scottish brogue.

His chest expanded at the sound. "And what are you wearing in this fancy English ballroom?"

She paused and then said, "I'm wearing a green silk gown."

"Not purple?"

Again, she hesitated. "There are too many purple gowns here tonight."

Did she mean Celeste? "And what about your hair?" he asked, drawing her into this make-believe moment.

"I'm wearing it up—with diamonds tucked into the curls."

"No." He shook his head and reached up to touch her silky hair. "'Tis long again and you're wearing it flowing freely to your waist, just like the morning in Montreal."

She inhaled. "What will people think?" she whispered with a smile in her voice.

"Tonight"—he took another step toward her—"we dinna care what people think. This dance is ours and ours alone."

Without another word, she lifted her left hand and placed it on his shoulder, then raised her right hand, still tucked inside his, into the air in preparation for the dance. "I'd be honored to dance with you."

He filled his lungs with the scent of her and slid his right hand around her small waist. The sound of crickets melded with the strains of music as they began to dance.

Though it was dark, he waltzed with her over the grassy floor with a canopy of stars overhead. The music was muted but still magical, as he spun her in his arms.

"You're a lovely dancer," he said after a moment. "If any of those men inside were dancing with you now, without seeing you in trousers, they'd never think you were a man."

His hand rested on the small of her back now, and he longed to draw her closer, but he refrained.

She didn't belong to him.

It was time to bring up a subject that would remind them of who they were and what they were about.

"Stephen Corning is a lucky man."

Her back tensed, but she said nothing.

"Will you ask him to leave the fur trade after you're married?"

She was silent for a moment before she answered. "Once I'm married, I will inherit Blissfield Manor and a tidy fortune. He will have enough to keep him busy managing our affairs." She then added quickly, "Unless he wants to remain here."

Reid couldn't imagine why Stephen would want to be an ocean away from Charlotte.

They danced for several moments, each in their own thoughts, before the music came to an end.

Neither one made a move to pull apart. Reid's eyesight had adjusted, so he was able to see the outline of her face in the darkness.

She looked up at him, her soft breath warming his chin.

"Thank you for the dance, Charlotte."

"Thank you for everything you've done for me." She finally took a step back and gave an elegant curtsy, and he could almost imagine her in that green ball gown she spoke of. "The honor of this dance was all mine."

She was a bonnie lass, even in trousers and a suit coat. But her engagement to Stephen was not an obstacle he could overcome, nor did he want to. Just as he'd told Celeste, his course was set, and he would remain steadfast. He would not give up the quest to become a shareholder, even if he had the opportunity. He'd worked too hard and had too much to prove to himself and his father.

Stephen Corning had saved Reid's life, and as far as Reid was concerned, his debt was not paid until he could hand Charlotte over to Stephen's care. Yet, what kind of a person was he, having these feelings for another man's fiancée?

Not any sort of man he respected.

Reid decided in that moment that he would be the man Stephen expected him to be. He would not allow himself to get into another situation with Charlotte that was so intimate.

He would be honorable, no matter the cost.

# Chapter Eleven

A wet day greeted Charlotte as they left the clerk's building the next morning. Sometime in the middle of the night, clouds had moved in, and the rain had started to fall. It wasn't a hard or steady rain, but a misty one that hung in the air and clung to her clothing like little beads of glass.

"Our brigade should be ready to depart soon," Reid said to her as they carried their personal things to the warehouse where the cargo was stored. "I'd like to be off before the fort is awake, or it will take us longer to leave."

Charlotte dipped her chin so the brim of her hat would protect her face from the rain. She had no desire to experience the extravagant departure she'd witnessed for the other brigades either.

The voyageurs assigned to Reid were gradually gathering in the warehouse. Charlotte recognized a few from her work with the inventory, but for the most part, this was a new group of men and women she'd not met. Besides Noemie, there were three other Indian and half-blood wives who would be traveling with them to Crow Wing. One had a baby in a papoose slung over her back, and another had two small boys clinging to her buckskin skirt.

"It's a dreary day to begin," Jean-Paul said to Charlotte and Reid when he spotted them. "But better to start out poorly and finish well than the other way around."

Charlotte smiled warmly at his words.

"It's good to see you again." Noemie put her arm around Charlotte's shoulders in a side embrace. "You disappeared last night before I could introduce you to a few of the young ladies."

Reid's head turned sharply at Noemie's words. "Charlie is young."

Noemie put her hand on Reid's arm and smiled up at him. "You were even younger when you entered the trade, and I remember you had a bit of fun with the girls."

Charlotte lifted her eyebrows at Reid's embarrassment.

"Keep your matchmaking ways to yourself," Reid cautioned the woman with a wink. "We don't need any trouble on this trip."

Noemie only chuckled at Reid's warning.

"Noemie means well," Reid said quietly as he led Charlotte away. "But she can be a little heavy handed when it comes to romance. Just try to ignore her."

Charlotte had already determined to do just that.

"Since you're the only clerk I have now, you'll be doing the things Calum—"

She flinched at the name.

Reid put his hand on her upper arm. "We've seen the last of him. He admitted what he did was thoughtless, but I still threatened to share a few of his secrets if he foolishly chooses to share ours. He's still sleeping off last night's celebration and will be going to Rainy Lake, which is in the opposite direction we're traveling."

Nodding, Charlotte straightened her spine and forced herself to put Calum behind her. "Go on."

He lowered his hand. "As I was saying, you'll be doing his job now. I dinna have any other clerk but you."

The reality that this job now fell on her shoulders was an enormous responsibility. Would she do it correctly? Would Reid be sorry he had to take her along?

"We will travel across Lake Superior for another two weeks, then we will cut inland and head west to the Mississippi. On this journey, your job will be to oversee the cargo and keep track of how much the men carry. When we get to our post, your duties will change, but I willna burden you with the details now. Are you ready?"

Her cassette sat next to her on the ground. The three outfits she owned were either on her person or in her bag. She was as ready as she'd ever be—even though she was moving farther away from home than before. Knowing Reid would be with her made the leaving more bearable. "I'm ready."

He gave her a brief nod and a smile of encouragement, then he leapt onto a wooden box and lifted his hands to quiet the group. He was so tall, he hardly needed the box, but it gave him a commanding presence that silenced his men.

Reid wore brown breeches, a white shirt, and a dark blue coat. A white cravat was tied around his neck, and black boots came up to his calves, hugging his muscles. He was strong and handsome and completely in command of his brigade. Charlotte felt proud to stand with him as he took off his black top hat and put it under his arm to address the others. "There is no chapel for us to visit, so before we load our canoes to leave, I'd like to offer a word of prayer and commit this journey to our Lord."

The voyageurs took off their red cloth caps, and Charlotte followed. Everyone bowed their heads, and some made the sign of the cross.

"Dear Heavenly Father." Reid took a deep breath and then let out an exhale, his words filled with reverence and awe. "Your Word says that in his heart, man plans his course, but it is the Lord who determines his steps. May You guide our feet and protect us as we go. May we not stray from the path You have set before us—and into dangers unknown—but follow Your will, wherever it may lead. May our actions please You, and may we bring Your name and Your Word to people who do not know You. We dedicate this trip to You. In the name of Your son, our Lord and Savior, Jesus Christ, amen."

"Amen," the rest echoed.

Reid opened his eyes and nodded at the group. "Let's be off." He jumped from the box, and the group went into motion. The voyageurs pulled out their tumplines, secured them to the ropes on the bales, and then pulled the straps up to rest on their foreheads. They took off at a steady clip toward the lake.

This was a heartier group of men than the pork eaters. These north men were tough and seasoned, many of them having never left the interior once they had arrived. Some even born there. They were not softened by the luxuries of civilization but hardened by life in the wilderness.

A more joyful group of people Charlotte had never encountered. They sang and teased, many of them filling the warehouse with cheerful laughter.

The day took on a rhythm similar to the ones Charlotte had come to know on the journey to Grand Portage, though this time, she had far more responsibilities. The cargo was moved from the warehouse down to the pier, where ten smaller north canoes were waiting for them. These canoes were about half the size of the Montreal canoes and did not have seats built into the vessels. Instead, the passengers sat on the packages, with Charlotte in a different canoe than Reid.

The rain did not let up, and the clouds hung low and gray over the lake. It didn't rain hard enough to stop their progress, so they paddled along the shoreline for almost twelve hours before Reid called an end to their long day.

By the time Charlotte stepped out of the smaller north canoe and into the water of Lake Superior, she was soaked to the skin.

As the men emptied the cargo onto shore, Reid approached her, his eyes filled with apprehension. "I'd like to continue sharing a tent with you."

Charlotte hadn't considered their sleeping arrangements until that moment. "Isn't the assistant clerk assigned his own tent?"

"Aye." He didn't meet her gaze as he watched the men work. "But I dinna like the idea of you being on your own. I'd like to be able to keep an eye on you—especially at night." And especially after what Calum had done—though he didn't voice that memory.

It seemed strange to be given a choice to continue sleeping in Reid's tent. Was it wrong to want to? She told herself it was his protection she craved and nothing more. But she couldn't deny a desire to be with him, both day and night, and it frightened her. What would happen when all of this was over? Would she be content with Stephen?

Or would she still desire to be with Reid?

"Will anyone think it strange?"

"If they do, they willna say." He planted his feet on the rocky beach. "I'm the bourgeois, and they willna question my authority."

"Am I allowed to say no to you?" she asked quietly.

His gaze finally fell on her, his eyes hooded, rain dripping off the brim of his hat. "You're always allowed to say no to me."

A gust of wind blew off the lake, pushing against Charlotte's back as his words settled into her heart. She couldn't think of a thing that he would ask her that she would need to deny. Reid was honorable and trustworthy, and sleeping in his tent would pose no threat to anything but her heart.

The rain began to fall harder. They'd need to make their shelter soon.

She'd feel safer sleeping in Reid's tent. It was that simple.

"All right." She nodded. "I'll share your tent."

He didn't respond, but he shifted his stance, and she knew he was pleased with her choice.

The wind continued to blow, whipping the canvas as the men tried to secure their tent. Jean-Paul and Noemie would also sleep in a tent, but the others, including the women and children, would sleep beneath the canoes.

"Shouldn't the children be in a tent?" Charlotte asked as Reid tried to get their campfire to light. It smoldered, and the smoke burnt her eyes as it thrashed about in the wind.

"They are born into this wilderness," he said, as if that was explanation enough. He squatted by the pitiful fire, trying to stoke it to life, but finally sighed. "This is useless."

"What did you say?" Over the howling wind, she was uncertain she had heard him correctly.

"Nothing." He tossed the flint and steel back into the box where he'd found them. "We'll have to eat cold biscuits and pemmican for supper."

Picking up the tinder box, he went to a voyageur in charge of rationing food supplies and took several biscuits and a handful of pemmican, then he nodded for Charlotte to follow him to their tent.

She had not eaten the food they called pemmican yet, but she'd inventoried the ninety-pound bags they had brought along for their sustenance. There were twenty bags of it in all.

When they were inside the tent, Charlotte tied the flaps closed.

Water dripped from her hat and made her boots slosh. Her clothing clung to her skin and weighed several pounds heavier than usual.

"We'll need to get out of our wet things." Reid set the food on his cot. "We don't want to become ill."

Charlotte had been wet on this journey before, but never this wet. Her clothes wouldn't dry for hours if she sat in them. But what about her other clothes? Weren't they also wet? They'd been exposed to the same elements as she had. Only their blankets were dry, having been stored in the center of the oiled canvas.

The wind blew, slashing rain against the slanted walls of the tent.

Reid took off his wet coat and hung it from one of the poles. It dripped against the grass beneath them. His back was toward her as he unbuttoned his shirt and slipped that off as well. His muscles bunched and lengthened as he hung his shirt next to his coat.

He looked over his shoulder at her. "Are you getting out of those wet things?"

"I've nothing else to wear."

"Wrap up in your blanket." His answer seemed like common sense, though under any other circumstances, she'd never think of it.

Sighing, she turned her back to him also and started to undress. Before she took off her shirt, she pulled the blanket off the cot and draped it over her shoulders. Then she removed her shirt, thankful the binding was still snug, and then her trousers.

The space was tight, and their elbows bumped.

"Pardon me." Heat filled her cheeks, despite the cold, knowing they were both undressing.

"I'm finished." He went to his cot.

She kept her long drawers on, though they were wet, and wrapped the blanket tightly around her. Even though everything was covered, there was still a level of intimacy she couldn't deny as she turned and found Reid sitting on his cot bare chested, with his blanket wrapped around his waist.

He didn't look at her, and she was grateful for the small level of privacy he offered.

Without speaking, she hung her clothes from another pole, sat on her own cot cross-legged like she'd seen the Indians do, and faced him.

After saying a prayer, he handed her a hard sea biscuit. They had been baked twice, to help preserve them for the long journey, and were difficult to eat. She usually soaked them in her tea, but she didn't have any tea either.

"I'm sorry about the cold meal," he said.

"I had worse on the ship coming over."

He chewed on his biscuit for a minute, then lifted a piece of the leathery pemmican. "It is made of buffalo meat dried in the sun, pounded, and then mixed with grease and sometimes dried berries." He looked closely at the pemmican. "This one looks like it has cranberries."

She took it and inspected it herself. Trying not to wince, she held it up for him. "It looks like it has hair as well."

Reid made a face, and she couldn't help but giggle.

He took it back. "The biscuit will have to do for tonight. Usually, we boil the pemmican in water for an hour or two and then add vegetables and flour to make a stew. It's called rubbaboo."

Wrinkling her nose, she teased him. "I can't wait to try it."

He smiled and set aside the pemmican, studying her for a moment. "I admire you, Charlotte."

She tugged the edges of the blanket closer together, uncomfortable with his praise and attention.

"Are you curious why?"

She shook her head—though she was very curious.

"I dinna ken another lady who would accept everything you've accepted and do it so gracefully."

"I haven't had much choice." She looked down at the biscuit in her hands, thinking back to the reasons she'd come to North America. "This life is hard, but the one I left was much worse."

"You've had a choice. Even though your circumstances brought you here, you've done everything without complaining."

"I haven't handled everything well." Her tongue felt for the scab that had formed inside her lip from Calum's attack.

"You've done better than most first-season clerks." He held the biscuit but didn't take another bite. "Better than I did my first season."

She set her biscuit down. "That's hard to believe."

"I'm proud of you." He nodded. "Very proud."

His praise made her cheeks warm—his praise and his bare chest.

How would she ever look at Stephen and not compare him to Reid?

"When we arrive in Crow Wing, it will be a hard life." He set the biscuit down on his cot and leaned forward, putting his elbows on his knees. The closeness of the tent meant he wasn't far from her. "I wouldna have asked you to come, if I dinna think you could manage."

The mention of Crow Wing brought back the memory of what Calum had told her about Reid's plans. She'd all but forgotten after everything that had happened, but now the words came back in full force.

Reid was planning to marry the chief's daughter—in just a few weeks.

Would it be wrong of her to ask him about it? Did she even have a right? He didn't owe her any explanation or reason.

Yet she wanted one.

A gust of wind rattled the tent, making Reid pause for a moment as he waited to see if the stakes would hold.

Charlotte sat across from him, holding her sea biscuit, but not eating. Her hair was curliest when it was wet. It had grown since she cut it, and now, out of its queue, it coiled around her face in the most becoming way. She ran her hand through it in a habit she'd adopted since joining him, causing the thick strands to soften.

Without her clerk's clothing or the hat that often hid her hair, she sat across from him wrapped only in a blanket, and he questioned the wisdom in suggesting they share a tent.

He found her more attractive with each passing day.

"You said you will try to restore trade relations with the chief." She probed him with her eyes, and he sensed she wanted an answer to a question she was not asking.

"Aye."

"How?"

He leaned back off his knees and took his time answering, wondering what she really wanted to know.

Darkness seeped into the tent and with it, the cold. His skin rose in gooseflesh, and he wished he had another blanket to wrap around his shoulders.

"There are many ways to restore trade relations," he said hesitantly. "The Indians are very receptive to gifts, so we give them liberally."

"The XY men don't give gifts?"

"They do."

"Then what other ways can you strengthen your ties?"

"We treat them well—" He stopped. "What do you really want to know, lass?"

She didn't meet his gaze, and her cheeks turned pink in the fading light. "I heard you will marry the chief's daughter."

Calum. He was the only person Reid had told.

Reid stood, needing to move his restless legs. If only he had more space.

Why had Calum shared the information with Charlotte? It didn't concern her.

"Is it true?" she asked.

"I dinna ken what I will do." He walked to the tent opening, but didn't move it aside. "I once made a promise to my mither that I would never take a country wife."

"And now?"

"Now." He sighed, turning back to look at her. "Now, I think I made that promise in haste. If I canna restore the relationship with Curly Head, I will fail at what I set out to do, and I wonder if breaking a promise to my mither is as bad as falling short of my goal." At Grand Portage, he'd told the partners that he'd consider their request. It had been a way of appeasing them. But now, Reid wasn't so sure. Perhaps he should think about marrying the chief's daughter with the intent that she would be his one and only bride. Others had married for lesser reasons and found love.

Could he?

Charlotte toyed with a loose thread of her blanket. Something stirred in his heart as he studied her profile, partially hidden by her magnificent hair. It was a feeling he'd never experienced. Equal parts attraction and affection, and the desire to share everything with her. If he felt a fraction of this for Curly Head's daughter, perhaps he could make a life with her.

Yet—he didn't want to feel this for any other woman but Charlotte.

"The only thing I know is that life doesn't always go according to our well-laid plans," she finally said, lifting her beautiful brown eyes to him. "Sometimes, we are forced to do the very thing we never thought we would do."

He was afraid of that very thing. If he gave in, what would prevent him from ending up like his father? A man who had sacrificed one family for another. But what was more important to him? Honoring a promise or reaching his goal—a goal that would also benefit his mother?

"'Tis getting late," he said. "We should try to sleep."

Charlotte was already wrapped in her blanket, so she simply lay down and turned her back to him.

Reid sat on his cot for a long time, thinking about his choices. There wasn't much time to decide his course of action. When he arrived at Crow Wing, he would have to make up his mind about whether he would pursue Curly Head's daughter. But he didn't have all the information he needed either. Was a marriage necessary? Or was there another way to create an alliance with the Mississippi Band of Chippewa?

"I dinna want to make the wrong choice," he said softly.

She was quiet for a moment. Then she whispered, "None of us do." She shivered and tried to pull the blanket tighter. He couldn't help but think they would stay warmer if they shared a cot—but he stopped his thoughts from wandering in that direction. Hadn't he promised himself he wouldn't put them in a position of temptation?

But hadn't he done that very thing by suggesting they share a tent? Yet how could he protect her from dozens of men if she wasn't near him?

"We simply do the next thing." Charlotte turned to look at him. "Hoping it's the right choice, and then deal with the consequences if it's not."

"But what if the choice I make does not please God?"

"God is bigger than our mistakes." Her voice was gentle, but a look of conviction and certainty filled her eyes as she continued. "He knows we don't have all the answers, and I think that's why He gives us faith." She paused, as if to consider her words. "Even if we take the wrong step, it's an opportunity to learn something about ourselves and about God. My journey has shown me that grace and mercy go hand in hand with faith. When we make a mistake, if it's done in faith, grace and mercy are there to lead us back to the right path. I'm not always certain that God hears my prayers, but I must move forward. And He has been there, each step of the way, showing me what to do when I need to make a choice, or if I've made the wrong one."

Her words calmed him. He didn't have all the answers, but he served a God who did. Even if he wasn't certain which way to go, he prayed God would lead him back if he made the wrong choice.

"I'll pray He makes my decision clear," Reid said.

"I'll pray for you too."

Reid lay down on his side and studied Charlotte in the dying light. She looked at him openly and did not shy away from his gaze.

"Thank you, my lady."

She smiled, yet there was sadness in the lines of her mouth. "I've almost forgot I'm a lady."

"I could never forget."

They lay like that for several minutes, until Charlotte's eyes grew sleepy, and she finally closed them.

Reid did not fall asleep for a long time but lay in his cot, thinking on her words and wondering why God had allowed his path to cross with Lady Charlotte Fairfax.

# Chapter Twelve

A five-week trip had taken them seven, and they were still not at their final destination. Heat and humidity bore down on the brigade as it wound its way around another bend in the narrow Mississippi River. On both sides of the river, the woods were thick and lush. Mosquitoes plagued the men as they paddled, forcing them to travel in the middle of the river, as far away from the riverbanks as possible, where the worst of the insects resided. Reid's patience had been tried to the point of breaking with the number of accidents and illnesses they had encountered on the journey.

On top of the difficulties, the blinding sun had produced a headache that throbbed behind his eyes, and the heat warmed the water, bringing with it the smell of rotting fish. His stomach turned with the pain from his head, and he wanted nothing more than to lie in a cool, dark room—but there was no opportunity. Already, it was mid-August and there was much work to be done before the Indians came to trade. He could not afford another stop, even if it was a short one.

In the canoe next to him, Charlotte watched him closely, concern and empathy in her gaze. During their last pipe break, when he'd done nothing more than lean over the side of his canoe and dip his hands into the tepid water to wash his face, she'd suggested they stop and make camp, but he'd firmly said no. Their final stop on this nightmare of a journey would be their wintering post, come what may.

Now, slicing through the water, he was thankful he'd insisted they continue, as he saw smoke rise from a distance not too far downriver. Several of the north men had left wives and children behind at the post. They would have planted gardens, tied fishing nets, and laced snowshoes in preparation for the winter. There would be a great celebration when the men finally returned after being gone several months.

"We're drawing close," Jean-Paul called from his spot in the lead canoe. "Not much farther."

Once they arrived, they would be busy settling in before nightfall, but it would be good to finally sleep in a feather-tick bed again, to have a roof, four walls, and a floor beneath his feet, and to have a fireplace that did not require cooking outside. The post that Andrew Fraser built was five years old, so it might need some improvements, but it would be easily inhabited.

Jean-Paul led the men in a lively song of "Alouette, Gentille Alouette," as they paddled with precision. Reid closed his eyes, thankful the guide was capable, but wishing he could ask them not to sing. It made his head hurt worse, though the song was necessary for the voyageurs to keep up their pace.

"XY Company post ahead," Jean-Paul called out, stopping the song of the voyageurs.

Reid opened his eyes, and the first thing he saw was the red-and-yellow XY Company flag high above the stockade along the banks of the river. It hung limp on its post, with very little wind to make it snap in this humidity.

Just outside the post stockade, three Indian tepees, covered in birch bark, were in residence. A family went about their work, stopping to watch Reid's brigade paddle by but showing no sign of recognition.

A shout within the stockade soon brought out a dozen or so men. They ran out of the post gate and shot pistols in the air, calling out threats and obscenities.

Several of Reid's men answered the call and returned their own threats in response.

"Do not engage," Reid ordered his men. "Stick to the course and save your energy. Our fight is much bigger than a few cowardly remarks they can throw at us."

It only took a few minutes to paddle past the XY post, and Reid refused to give them more attention than they were due. He wanted to search the crowd for his half brother, but from this distance, and because he didn't know what his brother looked like, he kept his face forward. There would be time to meet his brother later, but that time was not now.

"*Alouette, gentille alouette, Alouette, je te plumerai.*" Jean-Paul picked up the lyrics where he'd left off, his jolly voice reminding the men that they had a job to do.

Not more than a mile downriver, they came to Curly Head's village. About three dozen wigwams were scattered around the clearing, with women and children working close to their homes and the men working down by the riverbanks, fishing and building canoes.

Several children ran to the river to wave at the brigade as it paddled past, and the voyageurs called out their greetings in Chippewa. "*Aniin!*"

Reid didn't look closely at Curly Head's village either. There would be time enough for all those connections. He wanted to arrive at his post and get settled before he turned his attention to trade relations.

The North West post wouldn't be far now. McTavish had said it was about two miles from the XY post and a mile from the village.

Reid squinted against the glare of the sun. Just downriver, smoke spiraled into the thick, hot air. A handful of clouds marked the large blue sky, and thick forests of oak, elm, and maple lined the riverbanks. The Mississippi at this place was narrow enough he could shout across and be heard. To the right, the Crow Wing River joined the Mississippi with a channel divided by a small island that looked like the wing of a crow and gave the location its name. Reid had learned that this area had been inhabited for centuries by the Chippewa and was home to the chief of the region. It had long been a key location for the North West Company to trade—and why the XY Company had sent their men.

Sweat and moisture from the humidity covered Reid's body, making him want to jump into the river. When they arrived at the post, they would unload the canoes, sort the inventory, and then store it. Reid and Charlotte would move their things into the bourgeois's private quarters and see that all the voyageurs and their families were also properly housed.

Then, maybe, he'd take a dip in the river before turning in for the night.

It didn't take long to finally arrive at Reid's new post—and when they did, he stared in disbelief.

A quiet hush came over the brigade as the paddles stilled in the water.

The site chosen for the post was at the top of a valley, with visibility for passing Indians, yet protection from enemies. It was an ideal location, for which Reid was grateful—but what stood before him was not what he had expected.

Charred wood remained where the post had once stood. What was left of the long row house and stockade reached to the heavens like jagged black scars. A campfire burned where the fire ring remained in the corner of the previous stockade, and a woman stood near it, stirring a large caldron. Behind her, a string of clothing hung from one of the burned posts to another. She stood alone in the fort. When she caught sight of the brigade, she began to wail, as if in mourning.

Anger burned deep in Reid's gut. "The XY men," he said under his breath.

Furious shouts rose from the voyageurs, and Reid did not stop them this time.

"Let's turn around and burn their post!" one of the men yelled, lifting his multi-colored paddle high in the air.

Others shouted their agreement, but Reid put his hands up to silence them. He must set the tone of their post now, or he'd never gain control.

"We'll go ashore and inspect the post," he called out to his men, the need to seek revenge burning deep in his gut. He forced himself to say what must be said, though he fought the truth of it. "Vengeance is mine, saith the Lord. We will not retaliate." At least, not yet.

Several men shouted their disapproval, but they obeyed his command. The gouvernails directed the brigade to shore, and the milieux paddled. Before the canoes hit land, several men jumped out, and they began to unload the cargo, like usual.

Reid stepped out of his canoe, his back sore from sitting for so long, and his head pounding—now for other reasons. His shoes filled with water as he waded through the river to get to the bank.

He would not have a bed to sleep in tonight, after all. He and Charlotte would have to continue sleeping in the tent until the post could be rebuilt.

Frustration tightened his muscles, and he started up the bank to the site of the post. Charlotte was not far behind. It was a bit of a climb to get on land, and when they did, they were met with an even greater loss than he'd first suspected from the river.

What remained of the post would need to be torn down and rebuilt from scratch. There was nothing worth saving. If anything had withstood the fire, it had been stolen, for nothing remained inside the soot-covered row house.

The woman at the fire continued to wail, and none of the men could silence her. She knelt on the grass and put her face to the ground.

Her husband was one of the milieux from Reid's boat. When he came to her, he spoke to her gently, and she finally sat up to speak to him.

Reid was thankful she had quieted, as the sound had grated on his headache.

Noemie also joined the lady. She took her hand and spoke softly in Chippewa, her face growing more and more alarmed with each passing moment.

"What happened?" Charlotte asked, her hands on her hips. "Where are all the women and children the men have been waiting to see?"

Reid kicked at a felled pike from the stockade. "If I had to guess, I'd say the XY men did this, but I dinna ken where the women and children are."

"Why?" She turned to him, confusion on her brow. "Why would they do this?"

"Because they are despicable, as I've told you." He rubbed his temples and took a steadying breath, trying not to let his anger transfer to her. "They did this in defiance of us. Now, instead of going right to work with the Indians, it will take us weeks to rebuild—not to mention what it will cost. I planned to take over an operational fur post, with bedding, cooking utensils, furniture—the rest. Now, I will have to take from my cargo, which was intended for trade, and that will eat into my profits."

Noemie left the woman and came to Reid and Charlotte. "Abequa is in deep mourning," She said to Reid. "XY men burned the post down three weeks ago. Her only child was killed in the fire." Her eyes were filled with sadness. "The voyageurs from the XY post lured the other women away, promising them food, shelter, and gifts."

"Surely they will return now that their husbands are here," Charlotte said.

"Some might, but that is not the way of the People," Noemie said patiently. "They are not bound to these men and can leave them at any time, if a better opportunity arises. If the women like living with the XY men better, they will stay there."

"What about the children?" Charlotte frowned. "Don't these men have rights to their offspring?"

"Children are the property of the mither," Reid explained. "Faithers have no rights to their children in this culture."

As the news of what happened spread among the voyageurs, great unrest grew. Violence sprang to the eyes of the men, and several pulled weapons from their personal bags with the intent to bring harm on the XY post.

"Do something," Charlotte said urgently to Reid, "before they kill someone."

He clenched his jaw, his head aching worse than ever. "I will handle the situation."

Three men started for their canoe, but Reid called out for them to halt. The din of angry voices had grown so loud he lifted his pistol and shot it into the air.

All forty-three men quieted.

Reid returned the smoking gun into its holster and met the eyes of his men. "I ken you are angry—I am too. But they want us to fight.

They want us to focus our energy on retaliation and not on our work here." His head hurt to the point he thought he might vomit, but he breathed through his nose and kept his voice steady. "I ken you've lost your families, and I'm sorry. I canna imagine your anger or pain. But I must remind you that you are first and foremost *engages* to the North West Company, and your job must come before all else. You knew that taking an Indian wife in à la façon du pays meant that she could leave for any reason, at any time. Remember that you can win her back, if you so desire—but on your own time."

He walked across the uneven ground to look at another group of voyageurs to his right. "Your time is required here for now. We must rebuild this post in all haste. We will build it better and stronger than before, and we will defend it at all costs."

A shout of agreement arose from the men.

"If you are angry, turn your anger into hard work and show the XY men that you are not easily defeated. We will grow from this, and we will be better because of it. We will capture the trade and send them home penniless."

Another shout lifted to the sky.

"After the cargo is secure, we will immediately tear down what remains of this post. Tomorrow, half of you will begin to cut and prepare the trees necessary to rebuild, and the other half will prepare the footing for the new post. To save time, we will rebuild on the original foundation." If they had good weather and the men did their work efficiently, they might have a place to inhabit in a month.

Nods of approval moved around the group as the men spoke amongst themselves.

"Let's go to work." Reid was the first to lift a charred picket from where the stockade had stood, and he walked it away from the fort and hurled it down the side of the slope and into the valley below.

The others soon followed.

"I'm going to get some willow bark tea heated for your headache," Charlotte said when he rejoined her.

"How do you ken I have a headache?" He squinted as he addressed her.

She lifted an eyebrow but didn't respond. Instead, she went to the cargo and found the medicine chest and set to work.

It would be a long day.

Sitting on her cot at the end of the day, Charlotte stretched her aching muscles and cringed when a spot in her neck pinched. Earlier, she had watched Reid join his men in removing charred timber, even though he was in considerable pain. She couldn't stand around and just watch, so she had also joined the work. The sooner they had the spot cleared, the sooner they could build their winter quarters.

Soot covered her hands, face, and clothes. The humidity and heat had made her sweat like she'd never sweat before. She didn't have a mirror readily available, but if she did, she'd probably laugh or weep at what she must look like.

Just beyond the tent, she had lit a fire and prepared a simple meal for her and Reid. After they'd eaten, he'd been called away to settle a dispute between two voyageurs. One claimed the other had drunk his evening dram of rum. Charlotte had silently watched Reid walk away, his shoulders stooping under the weight of his responsibilities and the headache that hadn't let up all day.

Now she waited in the tent, wishing she could take a dip in the river. She could hardly stand how filthy she felt, but she didn't dare leave the tent until Reid returned. He'd be worried about her disappearance.

"Charlie?" Reid's footsteps returned to their tent site.

"In here." She stood and opened the flap of their tent.

Beyond the circle of light from their campfire, the world was dark. There was no moon to light their path, and the haze of humidity in the air made the stars dim and faded.

Reid's eyelids drooped, and his face tensed with pain. He was also covered in soot, and he no longer wore his coat but had long ago abandoned it to roll up his shirtsleeves. "Would you like to join me at the river?"

"I thought you'd never ask." She smiled and picked up the pile of clean clothes and soap she'd set out for just that reason and then exited the tent.

"I'll just be a moment." He entered their tent, and she could hear him combing through his things to find his clothes and soap as well.

When he finally left the tent, he had a bag slung over his shoulder. "I saw a place that will make a nice bathing spot a little way downriver."

Many of the voyageurs had already gone to bed under the canoes, which had been set up behind the post and away from the river. A symphony of crickets serenaded from the lowland near the valley, and an owl hooted in the distance.

They walked down into the valley and across the level ground until they came to the banks of the Mississippi. Water moved by at a steady pace, though the current wouldn't be too strong to swim. Darkness surrounded them, but their eyes adjusted enough to pick their way through the tall grass. Reid directed her to a spot where the riverbank dipped and they'd have easy access to the water.

It wasn't the first time they'd taken a nighttime swim. Reid turned his back to her and unbuttoned his shirt while she removed her coat, trousers, and boots. Like usual, she would leave her underclothes and long shirt on for modesty. It wasn't an ideal way to bathe, but far better than not bathing at all.

After she took off her socks, she grabbed her bar of soap and tiptoed into the river, then dove beneath the surface. The cool water sent a shock through her body, but it was an instant relief from the heat and grime.

She came up, wiping her hair back, and let out a contented sigh.

"Are you in?" Reid asked.

"Yes." She still had her back to him and kept it that way.

He entered the water and immediately dove under as well. The splash touched the back of her head.

When he came up, he was beside her, and he moaned with contentment. "I've been looking forward to this all day."

She turned to him then, seeing only his head above the water. "I'm sorry about the post. I know it's not what you expected or hoped for."

Reid sighed. "No, but 'tis what we have. Thank you for all your help. You did as much work as any man today."

"I couldn't sit back and watch everyone else work."

"You could have, but you didn't." He tilted his head back and dipped his hair into the water again, rubbing his temples. "This is making my headache ease."

She wanted to rub his temples for him, but she didn't dare get close. Instead, she began to use the soap, first washing her hair and then the other parts of her body that were exposed, all the while trying not to watch Reid do the same.

They worked in silence for many minutes, splashing, dipping, and scrubbing.

When they were finally done, neither one made a move to leave the refreshing water. They tossed their bars of soap onto the riverbank and allowed the water to rush by them.

Charlotte's feet touched the rocky bottom, and she tried not to think about the fish swimming around her feet. Early on during her trip into the wilderness, she'd eased into the idea of bathing in the clean lakes and rivers that abounded in this place. Reid had assured her that there was nothing in the water that would bother her, and she took him at his word.

"I'm planning to visit Curly Head tomorrow."

Reid's statement brought Charlotte's head up.

"Lachlan has probably been to see him several times," he said.

"Lachlan?" Charlotte frowned, not sure who Lachlan might be.

"My half brother."

Her eyes grew wide. "Your *what*?"

The current had pushed her closer to him.

"My father was a fur trader with the North West Company, but when he retired, he chose to stay in the interior with his country wife and children." His voice was low and filled with raw emotion. "The bourgeois of the XY Company is his son from that relationship, Lachlan McCoy."

"Reid." She moved closer to put her hand on his arm. "I'm sorry. I had no idea."

It was the first time she'd touched his bare skin other than his hands. His muscles responded to her touch, bunching beneath her fingers. The feeling sent a shiver up her arm, and she pulled back.

Neither one said anything for a moment, so she finally asked. "Have you met him before?"

"No. And I never wanted to, but I won't have that choice anymore."

They bobbed with the ebb and flow of the current. "So it was your brother who burned down your post?"

"More than likely, though I doubt he realizes I'm the bourgeois."

"What will you do?"

He shrugged. "I'll do what I was sent to do. Take back the trade."

"Which is why you'll be meeting with Curly Head tomorrow."

"Aye."

"And his daughter?" she asked quietly.

He simply nodded.

She needed to know what he planned to do, even though it wasn't any of her business. Boldness made her ask. "Have you made a decision about her?"

Reid lifted his hands out of the water and smoothed back his wet hair. She followed the course of the water dripping off his large biceps and back into the river. Warmth pooled in her stomach, and she had to take a deep breath and look away.

It was getting harder and harder to ignore her attraction to him.

He lowered his arms under the water again. "I dinna have enough information to make a decision yet." His voice was heavy. "I'm still praying about what to do."

A fish jumped farther out in the water, splashing down with a little plunk.

The story of Abraham and Sarah came to Charlotte from the book of Genesis. God had made a vow to Abraham that his descendants would outnumber the stars in the sky. But when God was slow to give him and his wife a baby, they took matters into their own hands, and it brought nothing but trouble to them.

"Do you believe God has made a promise to you concerning your work in the fur trade?"

He was quiet for a moment but then nodded. "When I was a child, I asked God to place the desires in my heart that He wanted me to reach for. Becoming a shareholder was one of those desires, so I've always believed it is God's will for me."

Her heart pounded and her body trembled. She sensed she was speaking a truth that he needed to hear—and not just because she didn't want him to marry the chief's daughter. "Then, don't you believe that He can accomplish that without you taking a country wife?"

Reid frowned, clearly deep in thought. "I suppose He could, though 'tis hard to see how."

She went on, a little quicker. "Consider what happened to Abraham when he doubted God's promise and took his wife's handmaiden into his tent." Her cheeks warmed at the implication, but she wouldn't let it stop her. "He suffered the consequences. If God made a promise to you, don't make a decision based on your doubt." She was quiet for a heartbeat, and then she whispered, "Maybe that's the answer to your prayer."

Charlotte didn't move as she waited for him to respond.

Peace settled over his face, which was no longer strained with pain or worry. "Mayhap it is."

She was still close to him—too close—but she didn't want to move away, didn't want to put distance between them.

He reached up and touched one of her curls near her temple in a way that she'd come to love. But this time, his finger grazed her skin, and he paused, looking deep into her eyes.

She didn't move—didn't breathe. Everything within her wanted his touch—craved it. She wanted to feel feminine and desirable. Loved.

Reid trailed his finger down her cheek, following its descent with his dark eyes. And when his finger stopped near her mouth, his gaze stopped there too.

Charlotte held her breath as she waited for what might come next. She wanted him to kiss her, and the shock of that truth made her swallow.

His gaze lifted to rest on her eyes, and the desire she saw there made her want to be closer to him.

Picking her feet up off the river floor, she allowed the current to carry her closer to him, until her body was gently pressed against his.

The fabric of her binding and her shirt kept her from touching the bareness of his chest, but it didn't take much to imagine what it might feel like if they were skin to skin. Her stomach fluttered with anticipation, and warmth enveloped her from head to foot.

Reid's hand slipped from near her mouth and wrapped around to cup the back of her head. His other hand slid around her waist, holding her close, making her feel small and vulnerable—yet, somehow powerful in his arms.

The current pushed against them, but he was strong and unmovable.

Her hands wrapped around his back and rested on the bare skin.

"Charlotte." He whispered her name in a raspy voice, his lips close to hers. "I canna kiss you, lass, as much as I long to." His accent was thicker than it had ever been, but he did not let her go. "It wouldna be right."

She wanted just one kiss, one chance to see what it would feel like to be cherished by this man she'd come to care for. Throwing every sensible thought from her head, Charlotte pushed up on her tiptoes. "Then I will kiss you," she whispered, and placed her lips against his.

It was all the invitation he needed.

Pulling her closer and lifting her off her feet, he took her mouth fully against his, deepening the kiss with a passion she felt all the way to her toes.

She allowed her hands to explore the muscles in his back, as she'd always longed to do. His moan surprised her, but it seemed to strengthen his own desire, and he deepened the kiss yet again.

Her lips tingled and she was out of breath, but she didn't care. She'd never felt anything as exquisite or beautiful as this kiss. Instead of quenching her desire, it fueled the longing deep within her and frightened her with its intensity. This one act of passion communicated more between them than words could ever do.

Her body melded against his and she felt both lost and found, all at the same time.

"Charlotte." He finally pulled back, his chest rising and falling with breathlessness.

She closed her eyes, immediately ashamed that she'd given in to the temptation to kiss him. What must he think of her?

Releasing him, she fought the current and swam backward to put space between them. "I'm sorry." She lowered even farther into the water to let the coolness relieve the tingling in her lips. It did not wash away the feeling but intensified it.

"*You're* sorry?" He looked toward the riverbank, running his hand through his hair. "I'm the one that should be sorry. I was tasked to look after you and give you to Stephen unsullied—yet I'm the one who kissed you."

She lifted her chin out of the river, wiping the water from her lips. "I kissed you—you have nothing to be sorry for."

"I think we both kissed each other, lass." Reid put his hands on the back of his head, sadness and dismay filling his eyes. "It canna happen again."

Mortification overcame her, and she wanted to sink beneath the water and never rise again. She felt chastised, and rightly so. Nothing had changed between them. She was engaged to another man, and Reid was her superior, a fur trader living a world apart from her life in England.

She had to redeem herself in some way, but she didn't know how. "I won't let it happen again." And she wouldn't.

He turned and faced the opposite riverbank. "I'll wait until you're dressed."

She swam to the embankment and stepped out of the water, her heart heavy and her limbs shaking. She'd had a taste of something she could never have again. The knowledge of what she could not have was worse than not knowing.

Quickly, she took off her wet shirt, pulled on her clean clothes, and moved to a rock where she sat with her back toward the water to brush her hair, thankful for the solid bit of earth beneath her. "I'm finished," she said over her shoulder.

He moved through the water and came to shore.

She continued to brush her hair until he was dressed and came to stand before her.

His face was filled with several emotions, the least of which was regret. When he offered his hand, she took it, and he pulled her to her feet and surprised her by wrapping her in a tight embrace.

"I care deeply for you, Lady Charlotte," he whispered against her hair. "Too much to let this come between us. I will continue to protect you and keep you safe for Stephen—and when he comes, I will let you go into his care, thanking God that I had the privilege to know you."

But that was all this could be. He didn't need to say it for her to know what was on his heart.

She closed her eyes and leaned against him, grateful that Reid McCoy had come into her life.

Together, they returned to their tent. He went to his cot, and she went to hers.

But sleep did not visit her.

Thoughts about Reid's trip to Curly Head's village—or rather, Reid meeting the chief's daughter—kept her awake long into the night.

Would Reid one day kiss the chief's daughter as he had kissed her?

She wept silently at the thought.

# Chapter Thirteen

Construction on the row house began early the next day. Charlotte felt helpless, yet in awe, as she watched the men prepare the logs for building. As a clerk, she wasn't required to participate in the manual labor demanded of the voyageurs. Even if she was, she would have no idea how to help. She'd never witnessed the construction of a log building and found the work fascinating. Reid had drawn up a plan that morning, and the men had gone to work immediately.

The row house would be a hundred feet long and twenty feet wide. It would consist of seven connected rooms, with the centermost being the bourgeois's main living quarters. On the north end there would be three large bunk rooms for the voyageurs, and on the south side, next to the main living space, there was a sleeping room for the bourgeois, a storage room, and then on the very end, a trading room. Those who had families would be responsible for erecting their own cabins behind the row house.

Because they had not brought nails, as nails were too heavy to carry long distances, the row house was built in the *pièce sur pièce* method. The men would notch out a groove in a long post, bury it in a corner of the building, and then stack the logs on their sides, securing them in place by sliding carved ends into the groove of the buried post.

The first section the men worked on was the bourgeois's living quarters, storage room, and trading room. Next would come the voyageurs' rooms.

"If this heat would let up, the men would work faster," Noemie said as she brought Charlotte a bucket of water and a ladle. Charlotte sat beneath an elm tree, recording the activities in her journal. Reid had cautioned her to write as if she were Charlie Crawford and not Lady Charlotte, because the journal belonged to the North West Company and would be read by the shareholders.

What she wanted to record was the kiss from last night, because she feared one day she would believe it had just been a dream. But she could never write down such a thing, for fear someone would read it and discover she was a woman—and because it would be best if she tried to forget it altogether.

Things had been awkward with her and Reid that morning, though she'd tried to pretend otherwise. Every time she looked at him, she remembered the feel of his skin beneath her hands, the press of his lips to her mouth, and the weightlessness she'd felt in his arms.

Charlotte took a sip of the cool water, trying to wash away the thoughts, and thanked Noemie. "I fear a storm is the only thing that will break the heat." She tried to sound normal, though her world had been upended the night before. "I've already witnessed several of those storms in this country." Wind, thunder, lightning, hail, and even a funnel cloud had been produced during the last. Until she was out of the tent and in a solid building, she would prefer not to endure another.

Reid had gone into their tent ten minutes before and now stepped out in his finest suit of clothes. His boots were polished, his hair combed and pulled back into a queue, and his tailcoat looked recently brushed.

He was going to see Curly Head, just as he'd planned, and she would go with him to record the event. She had already changed into her best clothing as well and had gone through the motions of making herself presentable—though her toilette was nothing like it had been when she was a lady.

She set her journal in her cassette and picked up the wooden box.

Reid was preoccupied with his cravat when she approached, but he stopped fussing with it and met her gaze.

"Are you nervous?" she asked.

"Does it show?"

"Only to those who are looking closely." She forced herself to smile, for his benefit, and was rewarded with his smile in return.

But something shifted in his eyes. "Charlotte—about last night—"

Jean-Paul's whistle preceded him as he approached from the rear of their tent. "It's a beautiful day to visit a chief." The voyageur guide was also dressed in his finest clothes.

Along with Jean-Paul, the interpreter also joined them. He was a mixed-blood man who looked more Indian than French and made Charlotte nervous with the way he watched her. He had been hired to help negotiate with the Chippewa. Though Jean-Paul and Reid spoke the Indian's native tongue, the North West Company had supplied the interpreter so there would be no misunderstanding.

Smiling in his jovial way, Jean-Paul clasped his hands. "Are you ready, Reid?"

Reid fidgeted with his cravat again and nodded.

Charlotte shifted her cassette in her hands, wishing they hadn't been interrupted and Reid could have finished what he wanted to say. But it wasn't to be, and perhaps that was for the best.

Two voyageurs approached, laden with packages on their backs.

"Gifts for the chief," Jean-Paul said to Charlotte when he noticed her curious gaze. "And his pretty daughter."

Reid didn't wait for Jean-Paul to explain more. Instead, he began to walk toward the north and allowed everyone to move in beside and behind him.

Reid walked between Jean-Paul and Charlotte. His mind should have been focused on his upcoming meeting with Chief Curly Head and everything he must accomplish, but he couldn't stop thinking about the woman beside him. He'd lain awake for hours the night before, the memory of their embrace lingering long into the wee, still hours of the morn. With Charlotte's soft breathing in the next cot, he'd come to accept something he had denied for a long time. He was in love with Lady Charlotte Fairfax. And, if the way she had responded to him was any indication, her feelings ran deep for him, as well.

Instead of denying his need for her, he had encouraged it, even allowed her to respond. But it wasn't fair to her, or to Stephen, and he was a fool for letting it go that far. Worse, now that he knew he loved her and knew how it felt to hold her close, he was more miserable than before.

He was almost certain she had been crying last night after their kiss, but he had known, deep in his being, that if he had tried to comfort her, they would have much more to regret this morning.

The headache that had disappeared while he had bathed returned in full force now. It made his mood sour, and he let out a frustrated sigh.

"Are you not well?" Charlotte asked, concern deepening her frown.

"I'm fine." But he wasn't, in body or soul.

And by the look in her eyes, he could see she didn't believe him, and she wasn't doing any better.

"The chief lives in his village year-round," Jean-Paul told the men who followed him. "He is the leader of a courageous group of warriors who defend this area from their mortal enemies, the Dakota."

Charlotte swallowed hard as her gaze came up and she surveyed the thick woods all around them. Was she afraid the Dakota would suddenly appear? At the moment, their only enemies were the mosquitoes. He swatted at one that pierced the skin on his neck. The others also brushed them aside, a slap resounding in the still woods every few seconds.

Beside them, the Mississippi ran high with all the rain they'd had in the weeks leading up to their arrival. It rushed south, around a bend, and out of sight.

The noise from the village met their ears before they saw it. A dog barked in the distance, and the smell of campfire smoke drifted to them on the humid air. Children's laughter mingled with the hum of conversation.

Reid took a deep breath, preparing himself for the meeting.

"Curly Head lives in a wigwam near the riverbanks," Jean-Paul said. "He is much respected by his people and the traders who have worked with him in the past. There has always been good blood between Curly Head and the North West Company until Andrew Fraser abandoned the chief's daughter."

"What do you know of her?" Reid asked as he moved a branch aside to allow Charlotte to follow with her cassette.

Jean-Paul took a few steps before he answered. "I served with Fraser for the past three years, so I had occasion to see Daanis many times. She and Noemie became good friends."

"Daanis." Reid tried her name on his lips.

"It means *daughter*," the interpreter supplied.

"She is Curly Head's only daughter." Jean-Paul pushed aside another low-hanging branch. "She was given to Fraser when he first took over the post. She was no more than a girl of maybe fourteen."

Reid was familiar with young brides, having heard of them being given as early as age eleven—but Fraser was a man of at least fifty. What did a girl of fourteen think of that match? Had she been agreeable to it, or had she been forced by her father?

"How old is she now?" Reid asked.

"Nineteen, I believe." Jean-Paul looked ahead, down the trail. "Despite the age difference, I believe she may have loved Fraser—at least, she was devoted to him. But when she was at her father's village this spring—" Jean-Paul's voice was low and serious, so unlike his usual self. "Fraser left without saying goodbye. She knew he would not return. Curly Head was angry, and she was heartbroken."

"Is that not the way of à la façon du pays?" Charlotte asked, her eyes searching Jean-Paul's face. "Either party may leave at any time?"

"Oui," Jean-Paul said. "Though it is not always a mutual decision. Curly Head waited a long time for his daughter to be old enough to marry a North West Company bourgeois. His tribe gains a great deal from the alliance." He glanced at Reid. "He's been eager to meet Reid."

The trees cleared, and Curly Head's village came into sight. Reid counted thirty-one wigwams scattered about the clearing. The long, low shelters had rounded tops and a narrow opening to let out smoke. Birch bark covered the sapling structures, and animal hides were used as doors.

Women and children sat in various places, weaving baskets, grinding grain, drying meat, and tanning hides. The few men in camp were along the riverbanks, working as before.

Two children stood near the path playing a ring and pin game. They each held a stick with a leather cord tied around the end. At the other end of the cord, a wooden disc was attached. The children tossed the ring up and tried to catch it on the tip of the stick.

One little girl saw the traders enter the village, and she called out their arrival to everyone within hearing distance.

Soon, the villagers stopped their work, and many of the children ran up to Reid, all speaking at once. They knew exactly who the bourgeois was, and they knew he would be the one to offer gifts.

"Give the wee bairns some candy," Reid told one of the voyageurs who carried a pack.

The man dutifully removed his burden and took out striped candy.

Charlotte set her cassette down and took the candy from the voyageur. She bent to the children's height and handed a piece to each one, a smile lighting her face. One of the children grinned up at her, and she briefly placed her hand on the girl's cheek. The act was so feminine, so innate, Reid had a brief moment of panic that the other men in his company would notice, though none seemed aware of the subtle gesture.

One of the smallest children toddled with uneven steps, making her way to the group. She was naked and dirty, but she had the biggest eyes Reid had ever seen. Her hair was long and dark and hung around her shoulders in snarls. When she reached her hands toward Reid, he lifted her off the ground and held her in his arms. She put her dusty hands on his face and grinned.

He couldn't help but grin back.

Charlotte straightened, and she also smiled at the young child. "Do you think she wants a piece of candy?"

"I'm fairly certain."

The little girl took the stick of candy with her dirty hands, and it went right to her mouth.

"The chief's lodge is this way," Jean-Paul told Reid.

He tried to set the little girl down, but she started to cry. On instinct, he turned to Charlotte, a question in his eyes.

She just shrugged and laughed. "She seems to like you."

With little choice, he continued to hold the girl and followed Jean-Paul through the village, toward the chief's wigwam, with the children in tow. They surrounded the men, laughing and speaking all at once in their native tongue.

When they were just a few feet away from the dwelling, the animal hide door opened, and a woman stepped out. She paused when she saw the approaching group. Just behind her, a man also exited the abode. He was dressed like Reid with tan breeches, tall black boots, a white shirt and cravat, and a dark red tailcoat. When he straightened to his full height, Reid stopped in his tracks, a younger version of his father standing before him.

Everything in the village faded from Reid's sight as he looked upon the man he assumed was his half brother Lachlan McCoy. Though he could see the traces of his half-blood mother in the dark eyes and chiseled cheekbones, everything else about him bespoke his Scottish heritage.

He stood eye level with Reid, but he wasn't as surprised at seeing Reid as Reid was at seeing him.

"It's good to see you again, Daanis," Jean-Paul said to the young lady.

She gave a brief nod then glanced from Reid to Lachlan.

Instead of cowering or shying away, Lachlan bowed before Reid. "You must be the North West Company bourgeois." He stood straight again. "I am Lachlan McCoy, factor at the XY Company post. I hope you enjoyed your welcome to Crow Wing."

Visions of Reid's post, burned to the ground, made fury rise within his gut—but he wouldn't reveal that to Lachlan. It would only make him happy to see Reid weakened by anger.

Daanis was beautiful as she stood beside Lachlan in a long maroon dress, similar to the clothing the women wore at Grand Portage. Her black hair was not styled like the other women, though. Instead, it was split down the middle and worn in long braids, which snaked over her shoulders and rested on her chest. Several necklaces adorned her neck, and long, beaded earrings hung from her earlobes, jingling when she moved. Now she stood completely still, watching these two men closely.

Reid guessed his brother assumed he was the bourgeois but did not know his identity, nor was he expecting to come face-to-face with his father's only legitimate son today. Reid would take deep satisfaction in knowing it would come as a shock.

So Reid also bowed, being deliberate and slow, and perhaps haughty, in his greeting. "'Tis a pleasure to finally meet you." He straightened and lifted his chin. "I'm Reid McCoy, son of Sean McCoy, formerly of the North West Company."

Disbelief and shock registered across Lachlan's face, and Reid took pleasure in seeing it. Behind the shock, a new emotion rose in Lachlan's countenance, one that surprised Reid.

Lachlan was ashamed.

Reid knew what it was, because he'd felt the same when he thought of his father's illegitimate family.

But Lachlan quickly masked his feelings. "I dinna ken you'd be the bourgeois sent to this region. My faither has spoken of you often."

"I dinna ken you existed until just a few weeks ago."

Lachlan narrowed his gaze, but Reid refused to show his brother how this meeting affected him. He still held the child, and when she squirmed to leave his arms, Reid realized he'd been holding her a little tighter than necessary. He set her on her feet and nodded at his entourage, catching Charlotte's concerned gaze.

She offered him the slightest nod of encouragement.

Reid looked back at Lachlan. "We've come to meet with Chief Babisĭgandĭbe."

Daanis lifted the flap and indicated the wigwam. "He is here."

"Thank you." Reid motioned for Charlotte and his men to follow him.

Lachlan shared a glance with Daanis, his eyes communicating something Reid could not decipher, though it was evident they knew each other.

Reid stepped toward the wigwam, but Lachlan did not move.

"You are a proud man," Lachlan said, his jaw tight and his eyes hard. "But you willna win this battle." He shared another brief glance with Daanis, then looked back at Reid. "You should pack your canoes and find another place to trade, for you will be put to shame here."

Reid clenched his fists and did not back down, nor did he answer. Instead, he moved around Lachlan and bent low to enter the wigwam.

The interior was dark, and it took a moment for his eyes to adjust.

Along both sides of the wigwam were reed mats and animal furs, which the Indians used for beds at night and seating during the day. A ring of rocks sat in the center of the room and held the smoldering fire.

At the far end, a shelf boasted various cooking utensils and family items. Furs, trading blankets, and dried plants hung from the walls and ceiling.

The wigwam smelled of smoke and herbs, and humidity made the air thick and stale.

What would Charlotte think of this home? It was so far removed from the grand manors of her childhood that it might come as a surprise.

He watched her expression as she entered. If she found it unpleasant, she did not show her thoughts or emotions.

She continued to amaze him with her resiliency and poise.

Sitting on the floor of his wigwam, Chief Babisïgandïbe smoked a pipe. His hair, for which he'd been given the name, was long with tight curls. He wasn't an old man, but neither was he young. Reid guessed his age to be about forty.

"Aniin," Reid said in greeting to Curly Head. "I am Reid McCoy, the new bourgeois of the North West Company fur post." He bowed, his back still tight from encountering Lachlan.

Curly Head motioned for him to have a seat at his left hand. The others followed behind and sat on both sides of the wigwam. Charlotte next to Reid and Jean-Paul on the other side of Charlotte. The interpreter sat to Curly Head's right.

The flap closed, but Daanis did not join them. Her voice was heard through the thin walls of the dwelling, beseeching Lachlan, though Reid could not make out what she said.

"Welcome," Curly Head said to Reid in English. He continued in Chippewa. "I have been anxious to meet the new bourgeois."

Reid understood most of what he said, but the interpreter still spoke. Since Charlotte was not familiar with the native tongue, he was thankful for the translator.

"I have been eager to meet the chief as well," Reid said earnestly.

"As you see, new traders have come," Curly Head said in Chippewa, referencing the XY men. "They give gifts and make friends with the People."

"I bring gifts too." Reid opened a pack and pulled out a red coat. "This is for the chief."

Curly Head took the coat and admired it, nodding several times.

"And this is for your daughter." Reid hesitated as he took out a coral and blue gown. It had been shipped to Grand Portage from Montreal that spring and from England before that.

Charlotte's eyes lit up at the sight of the gown and then quickly dimmed before she lowered her gaze. He could only imagine how much she longed for feminine things. He wished he could give them to her, but it would be many months before she could wear a dress again.

Reid handed the gift to Curly Head. "I have more." He pulled other items out of the packs. Guns, ammunition, beads, high wine, cooking utensils, and cloth.

After Curly Head accepted all the gifts, they shared a pipe. Charlotte did her best to follow the custom, but Reid noticed she did not inhale the smoke. When the ceremony was complete, Curly Head spoke again. "I have worked with the North West men for many years." His face lacked emotion as his words were interpreted.

"And we are thankful for your trade and friendship."

"Fraser was a good man," Curly Head continued. "But he left my daughter without a child of her own."

Reid glanced at Jean-Paul. How could he apologize for Fraser's lack of an offspring?

"But new traders have arrived." Curly Head didn't allow Reid to respond. Instead, he lifted his hand and pointed to several items, which Reid assumed were gifts from the XY men. "They promise good things to my people. And their bourgeois has asked to make Daanis his wife. It would be a good alliance for the new XY Company."

He watched Reid's face closely as the words were interpreted.

Reid tried not to let his anger or concern show. Who knew what lies Lachlan had told them or what promises he had made? He'd already shown Reid that he was ruthless with the burning of the North West Company post. What else was he capable of?

"I want my daughter to be happy," the chief said. "But I do not know the other bourgeois or his people. I do not know their company or how long it will last. I know your people, and I trust your people."

"We thank you for that trust and would like to keep it."

The chief nodded. "My daughter will be given to you in marriage, and we will make a new alliance with your people. Does this please you?"

The interpreter shared the chief's words, and Reid held his breath.

Charlotte sat as still as stone beside him.

No one spoke as the fire popped and sizzled.

Anger burned in Reid's gut from seeing his brother and being reminded of his father's abandonment. For some reason, his father had chosen Lachlan over Reid. The pain from that rejection squeezed Reid's chest and made his head pound even more. When would his father's choices no longer hurt? When would he finally have a chance to show his father that he was worth loving? Worth coming home for? If Lachlan won, it would prove to his father that Reid was unworthy of being called his son. He couldn't let that happen.

If Reid didn't marry Daanis and she was given to Lachlan, there was no way Reid could gain the trade. The People were loyal to their chief.

Yet he couldn't take Daanis as his country wife. Not only had he promised his mother, but he had no wish to perpetuate his father's sins.

More importantly, he had no wish to disappoint Charlotte.

Reid's heart tore from being pulled in so many different directions.

Curly Head waited patiently, and Jean-Paul watched Reid closely. If Reid rejected her outright, the chief would be deeply insulted—something he wanted to avoid as well.

"My post was burned before I arrived," Reid finally said.

"I have heard this."

"I am rebuilding, but it is not yet ready."

Curly Head didn't respond.

Reid looked to Jean-Paul for wisdom. The man clasped his hands, his face grave. He also knew the need for this union—they all did. It wasn't just Reid's future on the line. The entire North West Company would suffer if they lost the trade with the Mississippi Band of Chippewa in the Folle Avoine District.

And Reid could almost guarantee that he'd lose his chance of being a shareholder.

Yet how could he dishonor his promise to his mother and himself?

The moment had come, and Reid was still uncertain—but he had to say something. "I canna consider your offer until my post is finished." It was not what he wanted to say, but the fear of losing to Lachlan stopped him from refusing the chief completely.

Curly Head was known as a man of few words. He watched Reid closely, his face hard as he spoke. "You must rebuild. My daughter will help."

Reid began to sweat, knowing his entire mission rested on this relationship. He couldn't end it now.

"I canna bring a wife to an unfinished fort." Reid hoped the chief would not grow angry and make a rash decision to give Daanis to Lachlan. "All of your people are welcome to visit, but I must work hard to have everything in place before winter."

The chief revealed nothing, but then he finally nodded once. "I will keep my daughter in my tent until your post is ready. We will speak again."

Reid let out a shallow breath. He should have said no and not given the chief hope, but he couldn't bring himself to cut this tie. It was too important—vital for the company's success. It wasn't personal. It was a business alliance.

Yet, marriage wasn't just business. It was a lifelong decision with repercussions that could affect generations.

Thankfully, he'd been given more time, but the reprieve would not last forever.

# Chapter Fourteen

Hours after they returned from Curly Head's village, Charlotte sat near the cold fire pit, her cassette before her. Pulling a fresh sheet of paper from the box, she set it on top and lifted her pencil. She wanted to capture the image of the women and children working in the large garden that had thankfully not been disturbed by the XY men. The men building the Crow Wing post, which was now known as Fort McCoy, were also in her sight. Log poles had been buried at all four corners and every ten feet along the exterior walls of the row house. There were several more weeks of work to be done on the building and stockade, but the bourgeois's rooms should be ready within the week.

Reid had said very little on their walk back to the fort. When they had arrived, he changed into his work clothes and left her without a word. She had wanted to ask if he was pleased with how things had gone, but it was evident that he was not. The tension in the wigwam had been so thick that Charlotte had fairly suffocated from the displeasure of both parties. Not only was Curly Head disappointed, but Jean-Paul had also been angry.

From where she sat near the tent, she saw Jean-Paul approach Reid and lead him away from the other men. She could not hear what they said, but it was clear that Jean-Paul was questioning his bourgeois—something that was not often done, and for good reason. Reid's back was stiff, and he shook his head once, indicating their conversation had ended. He walked away from Jean-Paul and disappeared around the building.

Charlotte wanted to keep her mind off the chief and his daughter, so she ran her pencil on the surface of the paper, laying the foundation for the fort. After the walls and roof were on, they would build rock fireplaces in four of the rooms, which would offer much-needed heat for the winter months and a way to cook their meals. Charlotte had never cooked a meal for herself until she'd joined Reid's brigade, but now she was adept and found she enjoyed food preparation.

Birds chirped high in the trees, and squirrels scampered on the ground. There was still no wind and the air was sticky, but she wouldn't complain. She'd weathered worse on the trip here and liked the heat better than the cold.

"Are you drawing again?"

Charlotte jumped at the sudden appearance of Reid, and her pencil slid across the paper, ruining the picture she'd been creating. For some reason, embarrassment warmed her cheeks at being caught in an idle activity. She started to put away the drawing, but Reid stopped her with a hand to her shoulder.

"Dinna stop on my account." He squatted next to her and looked at her drawing. "'Tis a bonnie likeness you've given to the bairn and his mither." He pointed at one of the babies in her drawing.

Even though he'd given her permission to continue, she still slipped the paper away and stood to begin supper.

"I ken you're unhappy with the way I handled the meeting today." Reid also stood, his shoulders drooping under his unseen burdens.

Did he think she'd criticize him as Jean-Paul had?

"It is not my place to question you." She bent to start the fire, but he again squatted next to her and took the flint and steel from her hands.

She had been disappointed that he hadn't been firm with the chief concerning Daanis, but Reid was in charge of his own affairs. As soon as Stephen came for her, Charlotte would never see Reid again.

A prospect that tightened her throat every time she considered it.

"Jean-Paul is unhappy because I dinna accept the chief's offer, but I dinna ken what else to do." He struck the steel against the flint several times until a spark landed in the kindling. "I'm here to get the trade. If I had said no, then I should pack up and leave, as Lachlan said."

"Don't give up now." Charlotte wished she could put her hand on his shoulder to offer comfort. "But you don't need to give in either."

"I have bought some time, but I'm afraid I gave the chief false hope." He put more kindling on the fire and blew until it was ablaze. "I've only prolonged the issue until the fort is built."

"Do you think Daanis wants to marry you?"

Reid shrugged as he looked into the flame. "She probably has no choice. 'Tis clear the chief desires an alliance with the North West Company. 'Tis the only reason he hasn't given her to Lachlan. I'm glad of that."

Daanis's and Charlotte's situations were not entirely different. Charlotte had been given no choice when it came to marrying Roger. If she hadn't escaped, she'd face a similar fate as Daanis—marrying a man she did not choose. Did Daanis want to be the wife of another fur trader? Had anyone asked her?

A low rumble in the distance brought both their heads up, and Charlotte spied a wall cloud on the western horizon. Panic formed in her chest, and she had to swallow the fear back down.

They were in for another storm, and there was very little to protect them.

Supper was hardly over before the first clap of thunder shook the ground. Its noise filled the valley and rushed up to the campfire where Reid and Charlotte put away their dishes.

"Go inside, lass," Reid said, knowing how the summer storms frightened her. "I'll finish here."

She winced at the lightning. "Are you certain?"

"Aye."

She didn't argue but went into the tent as the first few drops hit his head.

Reid finished putting away the last of the dishes and turned back to the fire, glancing briefly at the sky.

Lightning flashed again, and another clap of thunder filled the thick air. Hopefully this storm would clear the humidity and allow them some comfort—without doing damage.

A figure suddenly appeared at the edge of the campfire. Reid frowned, irritated that he'd have to deal with another issue. As the bourgeois, though, he had little choice, even on a stormy night such as this. On any given day, it could be as serious as a physical fight between a voyageur and his country wife or as simple as a dispute over a game of cards.

But it wasn't a voyageur who approached. A woman walked up to Reid's fire. He stared in disbelief and confusion as Daanis stood before him, her beautiful face illuminated by the flickering flames. She was a breathtaking sight to behold, especially with the wind whipping her unbound hair around her shoulders. It pulled at her dress and tossed the tassels of her shawl.

She was the last person he'd expected to see.

"What can I do for you?" he asked with a thick voice. Was she in trouble? Did she or her father need assistance?

Daanis glanced toward the unfinished fort. They had made some progress on the row house, but it still looked like a scar on the earth. "My father spoke to me when you left." Her English was practically flawless. "He says I will marry you when the fort is complete."

Reid tensed at the announcement. A mosquito stung his hand, and he slapped it, then flicked the frustrating insect aside. "I told your father I would speak to him when the fort is finished, but I dinna make any promises."

Daanis met his gaze through the flames. "I lived here once before," she said calmly, as if the storm wasn't pushing and pulling at her from every angle.

"Aye." He moved closer to hear her over the wind. "With Fraser."

"We had a good life, until he left."

Why was she telling him these things? "Why have you come, lass?" he finally asked. "Do you need something?"

Lightning flashed, followed by a burst of thunder. Reid flinched. The wind picked up strength, and the rain started to fall harder. They should be inside a shelter, but she didn't seem to notice or care.

"Are you not pleased with me?" Her eyes finally showed a hint of insecurity. "We waited all spring and summer for your arrival—and now you do not like what you find?"

It was just as he'd feared. He'd insulted her by not accepting her father's offer. Had she come all the way from her village to hear it from his own mouth? What would drive a woman into a stormy night to seek approval from a stranger? Was she that desperate to marry Reid—or was she simply desperate to please her father and find some security?

Empathy for this young woman wedged its way inside Reid's heart, and for the first time since hearing about her, he finally saw her as more than a means to an end. She was a woman with few choices, desperate to survive in a world that cared little for her. Her plight was so much like Charlotte's, how could he not care?

"'Tis not a matter of liking you," he said. "I am not ready for a wife."

She stood before him, her gown speckled from the rain. "I will stay and be your wife." She nodded. "My father desires this for me. He trusts your people."

"You're getting wet, lass." He approached her. "I will take you to Jean-Paul and Noemie's tent, and you can stay the night with them. I'll return you to your village in the morn."

She put her hands on his arms and stopped him, desperation in her eyes. "Will you have me? It would please my father."

It might please her father, but would it please her? Had she come because she wanted to be his wife or because it was her father's wish?

He squinted, confused by her appearance and her plight, though part of him was pleased that she was choosing him over Lachlan. But he didn't want to hurt her nor give her a reason to hope. And now was not the time to discuss such a serious subject. "Not now, lass."

Disappointment filled her gaze as rain spattered against the fire, making it sizzle. It smoked and smoldered as the light faded.

"We will speak of this another time," he assured her. "I must get you to safety."

The rain began to fall in torrential waves, pummeling against them with abandon.

Charlotte opened the flap of the tent and called to him. Surprise splayed across her face when she saw Daanis.

"I will take Daanis to Noemie and be back soon," he yelled, hoping his words would be heard over the storm.

He didn't have time to wait for Charlotte's response. Instead, he led Daanis toward the tent on the opposite end of the valley. The storm intensified, whipping the trees and thrashing against the canvas tents. Streams of water rushed down the hill toward the river. Under the over-turned canoes, the voyageurs would weather the storm as best as they could, though they would be as wet as if they were uncovered.

Hail began to pound the earth as Reid and Daanis arrived at Jean-Paul and Noemie's tent. The couple was shocked to see them standing in the storm and immediately invited them in.

Charlotte would be alone and frightened—and very confused. Reid wanted to race back across the valley to reassure her but could not take the risk of leaving the fragile shelter of Jean-Paul's tent.

The wind thrashed and the hail pummeled against the fabric, threatening to tear holes in the musty canvas above her head. Charlotte lay awake on her cot, her heart pounding and her body trembling from the force of the storm. Lightning lit the interior of the space, and she was reminded that Reid was not on his cot, his reassuring presence making her feel safe. Instead, he was somewhere in the storm with Daanis.

Why had the chief's daughter come, and where had Reid taken her? He'd yelled something, but she hadn't heard him, and he'd turned away before she could ask. It seemed unlikely that he'd take her back to her village in the rain, but where else could they have gone? Would he come back tonight? What if he was hurt?

She hated being alone, especially during the storm. Just like she'd been alone during those frightening days on the ship and before that in her room at Blissfield Manor when she lay awake, afraid of Roger. She'd been desperate to escape. Yes, she'd found protection with Reid, but after five and a half months of running, was she truly safe? If Stephen was dead and did not come, or if Roger found her before she could marry Stephen, she would be forced to return to England with her guardian—and all of this would be for naught.

Was Daanis just as desperate as Charlotte? Was that why she had come out in this storm? The thought of seeing her and Reid standing together, of Daanis clinging to Reid's arms near the smoldering fire, made her heart hammer uncontrollably.

Charlotte sat up, her throat tight with fear. What if Daanis had come to change Reid's mind? He'd been so uncertain today—could the beautiful woman convince him he needed her, after all? What if he took Daanis as his country wife? Was that where they had gone, to speak to her father?

Jealousy and panic waged an ugly battle in her heart. She told herself that none of it mattered—that Reid was free to do as he pleased. But the truth was that it did matter—a great deal—because Charlotte had fallen in love with Reid McCoy. And had probably been in love with him for a long time.

The realization brought on unexpected tears—especially knowing that he was somewhere out there with Daanis. She lay down on her side and pulled her knees up to her chest, hugging them tight. The tears ran down the side of her face and dripped into her hair, but she didn't wipe them away.

There was no sense in loving Reid. It would only make things more difficult when she had to leave him.

A bolt of lightning filled the sky as another crash of thunder reverberated across the earth.

As she lay on her cot, she had to believe that God had brought her this far for a reason—and it couldn't be to fall in love with Reid. She had come to marry Stephen, risking everything to get to him. She forced herself to believe that in time she would grow to love him the way she loved Reid. It was the only way to bear the pain that tightened her chest. She was doing God's will, wasn't she? But if she *was* in the middle of His will, then why did it hurt so much? Did that mean she wasn't doing His will? Had He abandoned her in this wilderness?

Confusion and fear mingled with the thrashing wind. She buried her head under her blanket, trying to drown out the sound of the storm and her doubts.

Memories of the Bible stories she'd read as a child returned to her, and she realized that most of the people in the middle of God's will had suffered. Joseph in prison, Moses trying to convince Pharaoh to let the Israelites go. Ruth and Naomi when they were widowed. Esther in the king's palace, unsure if her entire race of people would be destroyed. Each of those people had been serving God and crying out for His divine will—even while they suffered. Could Charlotte be like those people? Could her suffering be part of God's divine plan for her life? Could it somehow prepare her for what God had in store, just as it had prepared all those other people?

A small measure of reassurance filled her heart. Maybe disappointment and heartache didn't mean that God had abandoned her. Maybe it meant that He was closer than ever, working out a plan she didn't see or understand. One for her good and His glory.

Though the thought offered a bit of comfort, it didn't take away the pain.

The hail ceased, but the rain and wind continued to shake the tent. She didn't want to think about Reid, so she turned her thoughts to Stephen, just as she'd done on the long voyage across the ocean, before her heart had been captured by the handsome Scottish fur trader. What might Stephen look like now? How might he have changed? Now that she'd been in the fur trade for several months, she had a better understanding of how he lived and what occupied his time, making it easier to picture him.

As she tried to conjure up an image of her intended, praying he was still alive, she started to imagine him tall and broad-shouldered, with dark brown hair and matching brown eyes. And for some reason, he no longer had an English accent—but a Scottish brogue.

Of course, none of those things reminded her of the young blond-haired, blue-eyed Stephen Corning of her childhood. It wasn't fair to compare him to Reid. Stephen was a good, faithful friend, and he was the one she had chosen. He was the reason she had come and met Reid to begin with.

If she wanted to love Stephen one day, then she would need to start saying goodbye to Reid now, and the only way she could think to do that was to put distance between them. They had become good friends and shared far too much with one another. That would have to end.

It was the only hope she had of preserving her heart.

# Chapter Fifteen

A week later, with the humidity gone, Charlotte could breathe again. Sunshine warmed her shoulders and brought a fresh wave of green to the valley. The clear blue sky was crisp, and the river flowed fast and true from the rain.

The night of the storm, Reid had finally come into their tent after the worst of it had eased and told Charlotte why Daanis had come. Charlotte had been relieved that Reid had not married Daanis, but she had said little to him about it then—or in the days that followed. After her own realization that evening, she had purposely put space between her and Reid, which wasn't difficult. He was driven to complete his fort, working from sunup to sundown alongside his men, with little time for anything else.

Charlotte wondered why he worked so hard on the fort. Because the sooner he completed it, the sooner he would need to address the chief about Daanis again.

It wasn't long before the bourgeois's quarters were ready to be oc-cupied and Reid was overseeing the addition of furniture, which his men had built for the trading room, the main living quarters, and the bedroom.

Charlotte had earlier overseen the placement of the cargo in the storage room and had spent all morning setting up the trading room—but she had not entered Reid's quarters. She assumed she would have a place in the row house, but Reid had not shared his plans with her or invited her to see the progress.

Instead, she walked to the edge of the valley near her tent, her cassette in her hands, to write in her journal. There had been little time for such matters, but the shareholders would want a recording of their activities at the end of the year.

"Mr. Crawford." Noemie called to Charlotte as she crossed the distance from the row house to where Charlotte sat. "The bourgeois has asked for you."

Charlotte put her journal in her cassette and returned the box to her tent before joining Noemie.

"Isn't it exciting?" the older woman asked. "Soon, the post will be finished, and we'll have a celebration."

Charlotte had heard rumors about a celebration, but Reid had not shared those details with her either.

"Reid has promised a party, unlike anything this country has ever seen," Noemie rambled, "to celebrate the completion of the post." She bent to speak in a conspiratorial voice. "I also wonder if he'll announce a marriage between him and Daanis as well. He has been working very hard to finish the fort, and I know she is anxious to come."

Dread thudded in Charlotte's chest. Daanis had returned to the fort twice since the night of the storm, and she had spoken to Reid on both occasions, though Charlotte had purposely not asked him about the visits.

Had they reached an agreement? One Reid had not told her about?

"I might make a match for Reid yet," Noemie said with a twinkle in her eyes.

How could Reid withstand Daanis's, Curly Head's, Jean-Paul's, *and* Noemie's prodding?

"Don't look so forlorn, Charlie Crawford," Noemie said as she misunderstood Charlotte's morose. "Maybe we will finally find a young maiden for you at the celebration. There will be many to choose from."

Charlotte steered the conversation away from Noemie's matchmaking and toward the row house. Half the men worked on the building, while another half buried the posts that made the picket stockade. There would be bulwarks in the front corners for defense and a wide gate to be closed when they were not open for trading.

There were a few cabins being built behind the row house and one was for Jean-Paul and Noemie. It was only a one-room home, but Noemie was proud as could be and continued to chatter about having a cabin all her own. It wasn't hard to turn her attention away from matchmaking to other matters.

Finally, they arrived at the row house, and Noemie motioned toward the center. "He's in his living quarters."

Half the row house stood complete, with walls, a roof, and oiled paper for windows. Two heavy doors faced Charlotte, one to enter the bourgeois's living space and the other to enter the trading room. Charlotte opened the one leading into the living space, and it took her eyes a moment to adjust to the darkness.

Straight ahead, a fireplace dominated the far wall, with an iron crane for cooking over the flames. A rough-hewn cupboard was close by with metal pots and pans, clay bowls, and silver utensils. In the middle of the room, a table sat with four generous chairs tucked in around it. The floors and walls were made of wide planks, and the rafters overhead were ready to store more goods.

Two windows flanked the door, and under each, there was a desk. One for Reid—and one for his clerk. His desk already held his cassette. She walked to the other desk and stared down at a stack of paper and a box of charcoals.

Where in the world had they come from?

"Do you like your gift?" Reid's voice came from behind her.

He stood in the doorway leading into his sleeping quarters, his coat gone, and his shirtsleeves rolled up to his elbows.

"Where did you get the charcoal pencils?" she asked.

"At Grand Portage. I planned to give them to you when we arrived—but other things garnered my attention."

Charlotte ran her fingertips down the length of the box, debating if she should accept his gift—but she could not refuse. "Thank you."

"You're welcome." He stepped aside and indicated that she should join him in his sleeping quarters. "I have another surprise for you."

Curious, she walked across the room and discovered that the door led into a hallway—and not his bedroom. It was about ten feet long and had a door at the opposite end. There were also two other doors, about halfway down the hall, that faced one another.

"The door at the end leads to the storage room and trading room," Reid told her, "so you dinna need to go outside when it gets cold."

"That's very thoughtful."

"The door on the right is my room. And the other one is your private sleeping quarters." He smiled, watching her closely. "You willna have to brave another storm under a tent, lass. If I could have built it faster for you, I would have."

He'd worked night and day for her? Not Daanis? Charlotte bit her bottom lip to stop it from trembling. Affection for this man filled her to overflowing, and she had to turn away from him, lest he see how his words had impacted her.

He opened the door to her left and she found a small room, about eight feet by ten feet, with an oiled paper window, a narrow bed with a grass tick, several hooks on the wall, and a cane chair.

"'Tis nothing like you deserve. But I hope you'll be comfortable."

She was so touched by his gift she struggled to find the words. "It's perfect."

"So you like it?"

"I do. Thank you, Reid."

A smile lit his face, and he seemed very pleased with himself. "Feel free to move your things in here and make it your own. I have work to do with the men on the other side of the row house." He moved away but stopped, his hand on the doorframe. "I am looking forward to having the fort finished soon. I've missed spending time with you, lass."

Was that the other reason he had been pushing himself to finish so soon? He missed her?

She missed him, too, more than she could ever admit, and she had to work hard to hide her emotions as she asked, "How much longer until the fort is complete?"

"At least three weeks."

She wanted to ask him what would happen with Daanis once the fort was ready, but it wasn't her concern—and she was afraid of what he might say.

"You can start cooking in the fireplace tonight, if you'd like," he said.

"I might not know how. I've only cooked over an open campfire." She tried to smile and match his good mood.

He grinned, and her heart expanded at the sight of it. She loved to make him happy, loved how he looked when his countenance was light.

"I'll make something special. As a way to thank you."

"You dinna need to thank me." His smile did not dim. "But I'll finish my work early tonight to enjoy your meal."

With that, he left, and Charlotte stood in her room for several minutes, soaking in the newness of the row house. Her window looked at the back of the stockade, and if she could see through the oiled paper, she would have a view of Jean-Paul and Noemie's cabin site, with the tall trees and blue sky beyond the stockade.

She should be pleased to be inside, where she would be safe from storms, but she couldn't deny how much she'd miss the tent and the time they'd spent there together.

Despite her resolve to keep distance between her and Reid, he had found a crack in her weak façade. With his care and thoughtfulness, he'd opened her heart wide again.

In the future, especially with the privacy the row house provided, she would have to be more diligent to keep him out.

It felt good to eat a meal sitting at a table again with Charlotte. She had used the store of flour Reid was allotted and had made fresh biscuits to go with the roasted venison one of the hunters had recently brought in. She'd also found squash from the garden and had baked it and then mashed it with a bit of maple sugar.

Reid had worked long and hard that day, but all his troubles washed away as he sat across from Charlotte. A single candle on the table flickered, highlighting her high cheekbones, wide mouth, and expressive brown eyes. But the candle also revealed something he didn't like to see. There was hesitation in her gaze, as if she was uncertain or even wary.

Since the night of the storm, or even perhaps their kiss, something had changed between them. He wasn't sure what it was, or why it had begun. He was anxious to speak to her about it, afraid he had done something to disappoint her, and longed to ease the tension so they could return to the camaraderie they'd had from the start.

"Have you moved all your things?"

"There wasn't much to move." She took a small bite of squash, not looking up from her plate.

"Do you need anything?"

She shook her head.

He couldn't bear this awkwardness. One of the things he loved about Charlotte was their ease of conversation and the comfort he took in her friendship.

"What's bothering you?" he finally asked.

She pushed her food around her plate with her fork and didn't meet his gaze. "The fort is almost complete."

"Aye." Was she unhappy with the row house? He'd worked hard to get it ready for her, and she'd seemed very pleased with it earlier that day. Her joy was the thing that had kept him going until supper.

"I've heard there is to be a party."

Was it the party that bothered her—or was she trying to change the subject? "'Tis customary to have a party to celebrate the completion of a fort. Do you not want one?"

She nibbled on her bottom lip for a moment. "Will Curly Head come?"

"I hope so."

"And his daughter?" She finally met his gaze, the uncertainty palpable. "Will she be there as well?"

"Aye," he said slowly. "Daanis will be there."

"I suppose she'll be wearing the pretty gown you gave her."

Realization dawned, and he couldn't help but smile. "Are you jealous, lass?"

Was that what had come between them? Was Charlotte jealous of Daanis? Memories of the night they'd kissed in the river resurfaced, and his heart pounded hard. He knew Charlotte cared for him, but he didn't allow himself to think about how much she might care.

Indignation rose in her face, and she sat up straighter. "Of course I'm not jealous."

He didn't believe her, and her reaction pleased him.

A sudden pounding came at the door.

Before Reid could rise to answer, the door crashed open. Jacques Doucette stood on the threshold, breathing deeply. Reid stood, his pulse thumping hard at the panic he saw in Jacques's eyes. The voyageur was new to Reid, but he was young and strong and had proved to be sober and levelheaded.

"What's wrong?" Reid asked.

"It's the men." Jacques spoke in French. "They have gone to the XY post and stolen back their wives."

Reid was not a man who cursed, but he was tempted to give way now. For over a week, there had been almost no contact with the XY men, and he preferred to keep it that way. The only task the North West men had was to win the trade. It would not serve them well to make war with their rivals, yet that was exactly what would happen if they behaved so boorishly.

Reid didn't wait for any other information but stormed into the night.

Charlotte rushed out of the row house to follow. He wanted to tell her to stay inside, but it was the right of the assistant clerk to attend to such matters. He'd kept her from many tasks a clerk was usually responsible for, and he didn't want the others to start to notice.

A commotion near the voyageurs' campfires mingled with the cry of a baby. Six additional women and at least a dozen children of varying ages were among the overturned canoes and campfires.

Two women were in physical altercations with their former husbands, fighting to get away, while the others sat or stood around the fires cautiously watching. Children huddled against their mother's skirts, and only one child was clearly happy in his father's arms.

"Who is responsible for this?" Reid demanded when he entered the light of the first campfire.

One of the women used Reid's interruption to break free, and she ran away from the gathering, toward the darkness. The man she'd been fighting with ran after her, but Reid called him to halt.

"Let her go," he thundered.

The voyageur stopped, turning murderous eyes on Reid. "I have my rights!"

Reid ignored him. "I will ask again. Who is responsible for this?"

"I am." Andre was the tallest of the voyageurs and the most competitive. When he wasn't working, he was organizing contests of strength, agility, or skill. He squared off now, facing Reid with his hands on his hips. "The XY men stole our women, so we went and stole them back."

These men knew the custom of the country just as Reid did. They knew these women had the choice to come or go at will, and if they went, it was their decision. "As your bourgeois, I demand that you let these women go." His anger boiled from a place deep within. Wasn't Charlotte running from a man who would force her to marry him if he could reach her? "If I hear you are keeping them here against their will, you will be taken into custody and brought to the district manager at Fond du Lac for punishment."

He spoke in French, knowing that all the men would understand—and some of the women.

Charlotte stood on the outer fringe of the campfire light, quietly watching—but Reid kept her within his peripheral vision. If something went wrong, she'd be the first he'd protect.

"I will not have you bring more wrath against our post." How could he stress the importance of focusing their energy on their work and not on fighting? He'd tried—daily—but it seemed to fall on deaf ears.

"Maybe it's the XY men who have brought wrath upon their post," Andre said. "They destroyed our home and stole our women." His voice burned with indignation and fury. "We are weak if we do not take back what is ours."

"We are not weak." Reid took a step toward Andre. "We are wise."

Andre took the wrist of his Indian wife and hauled her to her feet. "*I am strong.*"

The woman winced at being handled in such a way. It was clear she was with child, though whose baby she would bear might be a mystery—maybe even to her—but she was in no condition to be treated that way.

Reid took another step closer to Andre while addressing the woman in her native Chippewa tongue. "Do you want to be with Andre?"

Fear lined the edges of her eyes and mouth, and she shook her head in a barely discernible movement.

"Do you wish to return to your other man?"

This time she nodded.

"Then you may go, and if Andre bothers you again, he will face punishment."

She tried to pull away from Andre's hold, but he would not give her up so easily.

"I fought for her, and she is mine," Andre said. "She and my children were mine many years before the XY men showed up."

Reid could think of a great many things that were his before the XY men appeared—namely his father. Hadn't Reid's father been his before he learned of Lachlan McCoy presence in the world?

"No." Reid placed his hand over Andre's and began to pry his fingers loose. "She has the right to come and go. She is not your property." He gritted his teeth as Andre refused to budge. Reid had been forced to take other men into custody, but he hated how it divided the loyalty of the men. "Unhand her, or I have no choice but to arrest you."

The woman cowered, holding her swollen stomach with her free hand.

Finally, Andre let her loose. Thankfully, Reid was close enough to catch her, or she would have fallen into the dirt.

"This is not the end," Andre said to Reid. "I will have what is mine, one way or another."

"If you try to take her again, against her will, you will have to answer to me." Reid stood his ground. "Who else would like to leave?" he asked the women and children. "I'll escort you back myself."

Three of the remaining women stepped forward, their children in tow.

Reid didn't speak for a moment as he looked at each man in turn. "None of you are allowed to visit the XY post without my consent, do I make myself clear?"

Several of the men nodded, though Andre jutted his jaw and refused to agree with Reid.

"If anyone goes there without my consent, you will immediately be suspended from your work and will be transported to Fond du Lac." His gaze landed on Charlotte, who watched him with little expression.

"I want everyone to return to their campfires," Reid said. "Jacques and I will take these women to their home."

As the women gathered their children and the men begrudgingly returned to their campfires, Reid stepped over to Charlotte. "Return to the row house. I dinna want you out here with these men and you canna come with me."

She nodded and was about to turn away, when she faced him again, concern etching the lines around her mouth. "Be careful."

He would be careful—if not for himself, then for her. He didn't like to think about what might happen to Charlotte if something happened to him.

# Chapter Sixteen

T he woods were dark as Reid and Jacques led the small band of women and children along the overgrown trail toward the XY post. They had already passed Curly Head's quiet village where several Chippewa had watched them go by in silence. The night air had cooled, and the earthy smell of wet soil filled Reid's nose. No one spoke as they walked, which allowed Reid to hear angry men approaching before they were spotted.

Reid lifted his hand, and the group of women and children came to a stop. A moonless sky caused a dome of sparkling stars to shine vibrantly above. His eyes were adjusted enough to see the trail and the dense vegetation to their right, but the bright torches coming around the bend illuminated a far more dangerous landscape.

"Halt!" Reid called to the advancing men. "I have some of the women and children."

The first of the XY men stopped when he saw Reid.

It was Lachlan. Behind him, at least a dozen men bore rifles, axes, and other weapons.

"Go ahead," Reid said to the women and children behind him. "Join your men."

They did as Reid directed, moving around him and Jacques.

"These are not all the women," Lachlan said to Reid, his face illuminated by his torch. "Where are the others?"

"They chose to remain behind."

Lachlan said something to his men then advanced again, this time with only two others. The rest began their retreat to the XY post.

When Lachlan was just a few feet from Reid, he spoke again. "My men will not be happy until all their women return."

"You ken as well as I that they are free to come and go."

Jacques stood silently beside Reid, while Lachlan's men stared at him.

"You had better watch your back . . . brother." Lachlan's eyes narrowed. "Our battles have only just begun."

"I have no wish to fight you." Reid was not a man of violence, though if driven to such action, he'd defend anyone under his care.

"You're a coward then?" Lachlan sneered in Reid's face. "You must not be a McCoy after all. Mayhap someone else sired you while my mam warmed Faither's bed at his fur post."

Rage burned hot and fierce within Reid's gut, and spots dotted his eyesight as he balled his fists and took a step closer to Lachlan, anger forming the words he'd longed to say since he was a lad. "You're the illegitimate son, not me."

The blow came before Reid was prepared, and he staggered back, pain radiating from his eye to the back of his head.

It only took a half second for Reid to find his foothold, and he barreled into Lachlan's gut with his shoulder, knocking his brother and the torch into the mud. Reid fell on top of him, throwing punches blindly.

Lachlan punched Reid's jaw while trying to get out from under him. He bucked and pushed, but Reid would not let him move. The fury and resentment he'd felt for his father's second family pulsed through every muscle and sinew of his body.

Someone pulled at Reid from behind, tearing him away from Lachlan.

"Do not waste your strength," Jacques said. "He is not worth the trouble."

Reid's chest rose and fell rapidly as he watched Lachlan—wiping blood from his lip with the back of his hand—slowly rise.

His men stood with their torches, watching and waiting, hatred in their eyes.

"You will regret today," Lachlan said as he straightened to his full height and adjusted his coat, wiping his lip again.

Reid yanked himself free of Jacques. "I only regret that I dinna get a chance to finish what I started."

"It will be finished one day," Lachlan promised. "And you will be sorry." He turned and followed his men without looking back at Reid.

"I'm sorry," Jacques said to Reid as they started back to their post. "But I did not see that ending well for either of you."

Reid didn't reply, his anger running too deep to form any response he'd be proud of.

They followed the path to Reid's post without a word.

Many of the voyageurs still sat around their campfires, though most of them were silent when they saw Reid and Jacques approach.

Leaving Jacques with the men, Reid entered the half-formed stockade. The faint light of a candle flickered through the oiled paper windows in his living quarters. He'd never been so thankful that Charlotte was waiting for him—but would she still be quiet and withdrawn?

Tonight, more than any other, he wanted to speak to her, to share his frustrations, his pain, and his anger with someone who knew him, and, he hoped, cared for him at least a little.

He worked his jaw back and forth and winced at the pain. His eye was swollen shut, and he cringed at how she might receive him.

Opening the door slowly, he found Charlotte sitting at the table, a piece of paper laid out before her.

His heart turned at the sight of her. Even though she was dressed like a man and her hair was short and pulled into a queue, he still found her the most beautiful woman he'd ever met. It wasn't hard to picture her hair long and unbound, a pretty dress accentuating her form.

"Reid!" She pushed away from the table and was across the room before he could close the door. She touched his face with gentle fingers. "You're hurt."

He put his hand over hers, not wanting her to pull back but to stay this close for as long as possible. Just for tonight, he needed her tenderness and care.

"Aye."

"Who did this to you?"

"My brother."

She stared helplessly at him. "What happened?"

He closed the door and walked to the table and sat, his anger still brimming as he told her all the horrid details from the trail.

She stood, a frown wedged deep between her brows as she listened. When his tale was done, she sat again in the chair she'd been occupying and toyed with the paper in front of her.

"What do you have there?"

"A *courier du bois* arrived while you were gone." She swallowed and turned the paper to face Reid. "He traveled day and night to come here, and he's exhausted. I gave him a few biscuits, and he is now asleep under his express canoe near the river."

Reid's lips parted in concern. The courier du bois were the fastest men in the fur trade, independent voyageurs who were paid well to carry news throughout the territory. Their expert paddling, combined with their knowledge of the interior, made them indispensable to the traders. They were rarely sent unless the news was dire. Had something happened to his mother? With Rutherford somewhere in the interior, he had not worried about her safety since they'd left Montreal.

Reid pulled the flickering candle closer to the paper, struggling to read the scrawled penmanship with his good eye.

"The letter was addressed to you," Charlotte said, "but when I realized it was from Stephen, I opened it. I hope you don't mind."

Stephen? Reid looked up quickly, his pulse thrumming in his ears. He was both relieved and deeply disappointed that Stephen had sent word. "He's alive?"

She nodded.

He squinted and could finally make out the words. He read them aloud. "McCoy, I received your missive and am thankful that you were able to transport my cargo from Montreal. I will leave as soon as I am allowed and will meet you at Crow Wing. Stephen Corning."

Reid leaned back in his chair, a soul-deep sigh on his lips. Stephen was alive, and he was probably on his way to retrieve Charlotte. Within just a few weeks, she might be gone. Forever. He wanted to be happy for her—but he didn't have the strength of character to pretend.

He loved Charlotte Fairfax with his whole heart and soul, and to act as if he didn't was a waste of his energy. Yet—he couldn't tell her how he felt, because it wouldn't be fair to her or Stephen. And it wouldn't change anything. Instead, it would make everything worse.

Even if Charlotte was not betrothed to marry another, she could not stay in the interior as his wife. It was against the rules. And he could not ask her to live as his mother had lived—with uncertainty and a visit every three years.

The silence stretched until Charlotte couldn't stand it another moment. She stood and walked to her desk and placed the letter into her cassette. Even though it was addressed to Reid, the letter was hers. She stood near her desk, facing the window, but saw nothing.

She wanted Reid to say something—anything. She wanted to be happy that Stephen was finally coming, but she only felt a keen disappointment. How had she allowed herself to hope that he would never come? She didn't wish him ill—but part of her had somehow started to believe she could continue this ruse with Reid indefinitely. Though, what would be the eventual outcome? How could it end well for either of them?

"Have you nothing to say?" she finally whispered.

"What would you have me say, lass?"

She didn't know, and that was what troubled her. Did she want him to be just as disappointed as she was? But why? To what purpose? Did she want him to be happy? Relieved? Ready to be done with her?

Would that make it easier to say goodbye?

Shaking her head, she moved toward the medicine chest.

Reid pushed back his chair and stood. He reached out and stopped her.

"I'm a fool for saying it, but Charlotte, you must know how much I've come to care for you." He rubbed his thumb on her arm. "The thought of never seeing you aga—" He paused. "I canna stand the thought."

Tears gathered in her eyes, and she could do nothing but nod as she turned to face him.

"I think back to how frustrated I was when you showed up in my kitchen." He lifted his hand and touched one of her curls as his voice lowered. "Now I'm frustrated for a far different reason."

"And I think about how frightened I was to go on this journey." She put her hand on his and met his sad gaze. "Now I'm frightened for it to end."

He drew her into his arms and held her. She fit so perfectly against him—but even as she took delight in his touch, guilt washed through her, as she belonged to another. There was nothing inappropriate about Reid's embrace—but after what happened in the river, she knew how quickly things could change. No matter how much she cared for him, she could never let it go that far again.

Charlotte pulled herself out of his embrace and let out a long, low breath. She wasn't excited about Stephen's eventual arrival, but she would have to find a way to accept it—to anticipate it with joy.

"What will happen once Stephen arrives?" she asked.

He put one hand on the back of his chair. "There is a missionary priest at Fond du Lac. Stephen will probably take you there and marry you in secret."

"And then?"

Reid furrowed his brows. "Then your husband will decide what is best from there."

Was Stephen capable of protecting her like Reid? She'd always thought so—had staked her life upon that assumption—but now, knowing the rigors of the fur trade, would Stephen know what was best?

"If you were to counsel him?" she asked.

"I'd tell him to never leave your side again." His voice was so low, so intimate, so full of longing her heart raced. "If Stephen desires to leave the fur trade and return to England with you, then you should go with all haste." He didn't move as he watched her. "If he doesna want to leave"—Reid shook his head, as if that would be the most foolish decision of his life—"then he'll be forced to leave you at Fond du Lac and return to his post in the Upper Red River district. And you'll have to continue as a clerk until you can return to the Rendezvous at Grand Portage in the spring—and then back to Montreal with the pork eaters at the end of the summer." He put his other hand on the back of the chair to face her. "But I dinna think he'd make you do that. I think he'll break his contract and take you home as soon as he marries you. I canna imagine a man wanting anything less."

His words stirred the longing in her heart, but it was a longing for Reid and not for Stephen that warmed her. She hoped Reid's guess was correct, however, and that Stephen would break his contract and return to England. Because the thought of doing all of that on her own was daunting.

Silence filled the space again.

Reid's eye continued to swell, and the skin had turned from a light purple to a deeper purple.

Without asking him, she went to the medicine chest on the shelf and took out some lint and witch hazel. "If you'll sit, I'll treat your wounds."

He pulled his chair out and sat, his hands on the table.

Charlotte brought the items to the table and wet the lint. A waft of the sweet-smelling astringent drifted to her nose. She set down the bottle and drew closer to Reid as he watched her.

As lightly as possible, she dabbed the skin near his eye with the witch hazel, wincing when he grimaced. "Sorry."

She blew on the raw wound where his skin had split, and his face began to relax.

"I've missed you, Charlotte."

"I've missed you too."

"I ken I disappointed you somehow. Things have not been the same between us."

She folded the piece of lint and put more witch hazel on the clean cloth, then she dabbed at the scratch on his chin, not knowing how to respond. She couldn't tell him the distance was because of love—not disappointment.

"If this is about Daanis and the night of the storm—"

"You owe me no explanation."

"But I want you to understand." He stilled her hand on his chin and met her troubled gaze. "I've made up my mind. I dinna plan to take her as my wife. I willna let her be a pawn in our trade war. I'll find some other way to do my job."

She admired him for it more than she could say, especially because it might cost him a great deal—*if* he could follow through with his plan.

Charlotte recorked the bottle and set it in the medicine chest. "What if she is not a pawn? What if she wants to marry you?"

"It changes nothing. I made a promise to myself and my mither. I willna take a country wife."

"But she's—she's beautiful."

A disarming smile turned up his lips. "You're the bonniest lass I've ever set eyes on."

It was a preposterous lie, of course. Especially dressed as she was. "Don't jest, Reid."

"I'm not." He looked down at his hands. "Do you ken how difficult it was to share a tent with you all these months?"

Suddenly her mouth felt dry, and she longed for a sip to cool her. "Reid." She forced herself to look at the cassette where Stephen's letter was resting. It was dangerous, these waters they were treading. "Stephen is coming."

"I ken it well, lass." His face and voice were somber, and he sighed. "But do we need to keep a wall between us? I miss you."

She knew he didn't mean the literal wall that was now separating their sleeping quarters, but the invisible one she had placed around her heart. It was hard enough to know Stephen would take her away from Reid—but even harder to think of leaving Reid on bad terms.

She didn't want to waste these last few weeks with him. "No, there doesn't need to be one."

"Good. Because I couldna stand to live with you and not have the pleasure of your friendship."

"Friendship is all it must be."

"Aye." He nodded once. "And so it shall."

Even if it could not last, she would force herself to focus on the present. It was far better than dwelling on a future uncertain and shadowed with grief.

# Chapter Seventeen

Toward the end of September, the post was finished, and Reid was pleased. The stockade was sturdy, the row house was well built to withstand the harsh winter, and the North West Company flag flew with pride in the warm wind. It waved against the brilliant blue sky as a testament that Reid and his men were here to stay.

"Throw open the gate!" Reid called to Jacques. "'Tis time to celebrate!"

Over fifty men and women stood inside the stockade and cheered as Jacques and Jean-Paul pulled the heavy gates open. Curious Indian men and women stood outside the thick walls, waiting to enter. Over a hundred people had gathered, knowing Reid would treat them to high wine and small gifts. There would also be dancing, games, competitions, and food.

Curly Head appeared with Daanis at his side. The chief walked stoically into the stockade, watching the festivities unfold. He and his people were proud and quiet, but Reid longed to make them feel welcome. He wanted Curly Head to continue placing his trust in the North West Company.

Charlotte stood apart, almost as stoically as the chief. A wistful smile lifted her lips as she watched four little boys playing their own version of lacrosse in the dusty yard. He marveled that she could find any joy at all in this world so far removed from the luxuries of her homeland.

With each passing day, Reid's respect and admiration grew for Charlotte. How many English ladies could survive what she had endured—and continue to smile?

She glanced up and caught him watching her. A shy look softened her face and warmed his chest. Though things had become more comfortable with her again, there was still a gap between them that he feared would never be crossed again.

Reid turned his attention to Curly Head and Daanis. The young lady had visited the fort several times over the past few weeks, often to spend time with Noemie, though she had made her presence known to Reid each time. Her behavior was similar to the night she'd visited him during the storm. She hinted that she wished to join him at the fort, yet he was more and more convinced Curly Head had sent her and that she had not come on her own accord.

"Welcome," Reid said to Curly Head in his native tongue. "I hope you enjoy the celebration."

"Your fort is finished." It was not a question but a statement from Curly Head.

"Aye."

"You are ready for a wife." He spoke in English, and his meaning was clear.

Reid was more prepared for this meeting, knowing Curly Head's allegiance was with the North West Company, though it could change quickly. "I have much work to do before winter comes. I am not ready for a wife."

A flicker of anger passed over Curly Head's face, while something akin to fear danced in Daanis's eyes.

"You do not like my daughter?" Curly Head's jaw tightened. "XY man like my daughter."

"I like your daughter." Reid had to step lightly. "But I canna marry her now." He had no intention to marry her ever, but he couldn't be that firm with the chief. He needed more time.

"I do not wish to give my daughter to the XY man. His company is not good. Your company is bigger and better." Curly Head studied Reid, as if contemplating his words carefully. An uncharacteristic twitch jumped in his eyelid. "I will wait until winter."

Daanis dropped her gaze and looked at her hands, disappointment weighing down her shoulders.

"I work with North West Company since I was born." Curly Head continued. "I work with you now. I will send my people to your trading room."

The unexpected pronouncement surprised Reid. He'd expected more pressure from Curly Head. Was the chief trying to please him so he would take Daanis as his country wife? The alliance would benefit Curly Head as much as it would Reid.

At the moment, it mattered little. Reid was just thankful for the trust the chief had placed in him. He would work hard to keep that trust and continue to build it, hoping it would be enough when Curly Head discovered Reid had no plans to marry Daanis. "Your people will be welcome. I will be fair and honest."

Curly Head nodded once then stepped back. Their conversation was over—at least, for now—and Reid was given more time.

Reid turned his attention to Daanis. "Would you care for some high wine, lass?"

Daanis glanced at her father. He narrowed his gaze at her, as if in warning. She turned to Reid with a smile, though sadness lingered in the depths of her eyes.

"I heard you were celebrating." Lachlan appeared at the open gate with a half dozen of his men, his chest puffed out in self-importance. He wore buff breeches, a white shirt, and a blue tailcoat. If Reid passed him on a Montreal street, he'd have no idea that Lachlan had been raised in the interior. Lachlan exuded refinement, and Reid wondered for the first time if his father had sent him to Montreal or Europe for an education. The very thought infuriated Reid for reasons he couldn't begin to understand.

If Lachlan had been bruised from the night they'd confronted each other on the trail three weeks ago, the marks had faded. Reid's own eye was almost restored to normal, though the deeper wounds of resentment and hatred still festered.

"Aye." Reid stood with his feet wide apart and his shoulders stiff. He had not invited his brother or the other XY men, but if they wanted to celebrate Reid's accomplishment, he would not try to stop them. "We're celebrating the establishment of the grandest fort in the Folle Avoine District."

"You had better hope it doesna catch fire again." Lachlan laughed, and his friends joined him.

Reid balled his fist, ready to punch the grin off his brother's face.

All around Reid, the North West men stiffened at the comment, and several took angry steps toward Lachlan and his men. Vengeance burned in their eyes, and Reid knew if he didn't stop them, a fight would break out, threatening the goodwill of Curly Head.

"Avail yourself of my hospitality," Reid said loudly and evenly to Lachlan for everyone to hear, "but not my patience." He turned to address his men. "This is a celebration. Any man who lifts a hand to our guests will be punished to the full extent of my power."

Anger simmered among the men, but they understood his meaning. There wasn't a voyageur among them who didn't understand the delicate intricacies of trade relations.

"Daanis." Lachlan moved to Daanis's side, acting as if he hadn't heard Reid. He bowed before her. "It does my eyes good to see you again, lass."

A smile warmed her lips, and all traces of sadness disappeared from her face.

The others soon returned to their celebration, though Curly Head watched his daughter closely.

Lachlan did not hide his attraction to Daanis, and it was clear the young lady had feelings for him as well. If Curly Head allowed her, Reid suspected Daanis would join Lachlan that very moment. But she would not leave her father's home unless he approved.

Reid would have to appease the chief every chance he could get and be generous in his gift giving. He would have to be confident and trustworthy, reassuring the chief that his company was superior to Lachlan's if he wanted to stay in the chief's good graces.

Reid did not imbibe often, but it was time to toast his achievements in the presence of his brother and Curly Head.

"Let us raise our glasses to the North West Company." Reid glanced at the side of the row house where Charlotte stood. She watched him carefully and met his gaze with an encouraging smile.

The voyageurs lifted their cups, as did a few of the Indian guests, some of them accustomed to European traditions. Lachlan and his men refrained.

"To the North West Company!" the men cheered.

After everyone took a drink of their high wine, Reid lifted his glass again. "And to our honored guests, the Mississippi Band of Chippewa Indians. May you always feel welcomed."

Again, the men lifted their cups. "To our honored guests!" they said in unison.

There were toasts made to Reid, to the stockade, to the women who had prepared the food, and to the other guests who continued to trickle into the celebration. As the sun began to set, sending a cascade of pink, yellow, and orange streaks across the vast sky, the men pulled out their instruments to make music. A fife, a fiddle, and a *guimbarde*, which Charlotte called a mouth harp, were all that was needed, and the group was soon dancing.

Despite Lachlan's presence, Daanis stayed by Reid's side, watching the others dance. The glow in her cheeks was a bonnie sight to behold. She spoke of Fraser and the many celebrations he'd held at the fort as well as the time he'd taken her to Grand Portage the year before he left. Even though he'd abandoned her, she spoke highly of her first husband, and Reid sensed her desire to continue being the bourgeois's wife—whether that was with the North West Company bourgeois or the XY Company bourgeois, he could only guess. Either way, it was a coveted position for most Indian women. It afforded them luxuries that their people did not enjoy, and it allowed them to offer those luxuries to their loved ones. It was also a status symbol for many women, even though it did not guarantee stability.

For Curly Head, it meant many other things, namely protection from the fur company and their men, should he need it—as well as much needed trade goods.

Charlotte stayed on the outskirts of the group on a bench against the row house. She did not have a glass or cup in hand, and she did not dance, but she looked as if she was enjoying the spectacle around her.

"If Reid willna ask you to dance"—Lachlan stepped up to Daanis—"I will."

Daanis turned to Lachlan, her eyes glowing, but Reid took her hand on impulse. "If you'll have me," he said, "I would love to dance with you."

She looked between Lachlan and Reid and then glanced at her father.

His stoic expression did not change, but it must have communicated something to Daanis, because she nodded at Reid and walked beside him to the center of the yard. It didn't take long to realize Daanis was an accomplished dancer, nor did it take long for the others to see their bourgeois had joined in the fun.

The music became livelier and the dancers louder. Daanis smiled—truly smiled—for the first time since he'd met her, and he found himself smiling back.

The dance ended, and everyone clapped for the musicians. They responded by starting up another song, this one a variation of a quadrille. It wouldn't be fair to monopolize Daanis, especially with so many men present, so Reid handed her off to Jacques and made his way to the bench where Charlotte watched.

"Have you had something to eat?" he asked as he stood beside her, a bit breathless.

"I have." She continued to watch the dancers, her foot tapping to the tune.

"Why haven't you joined in the dancing?"

Charlotte nodded toward Noemie, who stood with a group of young Indian and mixed-blood women. "I'm trying to avoid our matchmaker."

He grinned. "May I sit with you?"

In answer, she moved over to make room.

The bench was small, and their shoulders brushed. Though the touch was light, it filled his whole body with awareness of her.

She glanced at him and held his gaze for a moment, communicating all that was needed. Charlotte was just as aware of him as he was of her.

Daanis laughed as she danced with Jacques, who was spry and animated.

Lachlan stood on the opposite side of the gathering, also watching Daanis, his gaze hooded. His men were spread out among the stockade, though none had joined in the dancing. Reid didn't expect trouble from them—unless they drank too much—but he would watch for any sign of disorder.

It would be a long night.

Reid and Charlotte sat silently on the bench. The quadrille ended, and the musicians began a waltz. Only those men who had a female partner stayed to dance, while the others dropped back to watch. Lachlan moved quickly to capture Daanis in his arms.

He held her close, dipping his head to speak to her, and gazed at her with a familiarity that suggested intimacy. Reid watched them, noticing Curly Head's disapproving stare.

"Daanis is a beautiful dancer," Charlotte said quietly as she studied the chief's daughter.

"Aye." He smiled and leaned closer to Charlotte. "But she's not as good as another lass I know."

A smile graced her lips, and Reid allowed himself to relax even more.

But as the evening progressed and Curly Head took his leave, Reid watched Lachlan and Daanis together. Without her father's presence, Daanis stayed in Lachlan's company for the remainder of the celebration, her actions and behaviors suggesting that the chief's daughter and Reid's half brother were closer than he'd first suspected.

September was usually Reid's favorite month because of the brilliant blue skies, pleasant warm days, and cool, starry evenings. This year was no exception, and he found himself looking forward to the end of the day when he and Charlotte would sit outside to enjoy the beauty of the northwest wilderness. It had been a week since the celebration and business had been good.

Inside the trading room this afternoon, Reid met with Red Bird, one of the men he'd come to know from Curly Head's village. The door was propped open, and the lure of the beautiful weather drew Reid's attention. Beyond the open gate of the stockade, the Mississippi River meandered south, while the trees along the riverbanks had just started to turn different shades of yellow and red. The mosquitoes had disappeared, and the lush wildflowers grew in the nearby valley. This was why he loved this country so well.

"Are you pleased?" Reid asked Red Bird, handing him the wool blanket they had agreed upon for the final fox fur Red Bird had presented.

Red Bird nodded and said his farewell. "*Giga-waabamin menawaa.*"

"Giga-waabamin menawaa," Reid replied.

Reid leaned against the counter as he watched Red Bird take his leave. In the adjoining storage room, Charlotte was taking inventory. After a week of trading, they'd already made several transactions, and she wanted an accurate accounting of the furs they had taken in.

A shadow passed over the window in the trading room a moment before a man appeared at the door. He was dressed in black breeches, a white shirt and cravat, and a royal blue tailcoat. The tall hat he wore just barely grazed the top of the doorframe as he passed through.

Reid frowned, disbelief making him straighten. "Joseph?"

Joseph McDonnell, the man who had greeted Reid when he'd arrived at the pier in Grand Portage, entered the trading room, a grin on his face. "McCoy!"

Reid moved around the counter and met Joseph in the center of the room, taking his hand in a hearty shake. "What brings you to my post?"

Visits between bourgeois were rare but welcomed. Sometimes they were simply out of boredom, but that usually didn't start to occur until the long days of winter set in. During the late summer and early fall, most bourgeois were too busy setting up their posts to make calls. The only other reason for a visit was to pass along news—and not always good news. Reid hoped Joseph wasn't here on bad tidings.

"I was placed in charge of the Folle Avoine District after you left Grand Portage." Joseph took off his hat.

"I hadna heard the good news." It was an honor and privilege to be placed in charge of the richest district in the North West Company. That honor was not given lightly. Joseph was a good, honest, and fair man. He was also smart and hardworking. But he would not come all this way just to share the news of his promotion. "I hope you'll stay for a while," Reid said.

"My business should not take too long. I'll only stay the one night." Joseph glanced around the trading room, approval on his face. "I'd heard you had to rebuild. You've done well in a short time."

"My clerk deserves the praise for the trading room," Reid said with a bit of pride in Charlotte. "He is organized and intelligent."

"Your clerk is the reason I've come." Joseph grew serious. "A courier arrived at Fond du Lac from the Upper Red River District. He had a missive from an Englishman named Roger Rutherford."

The air rushed out of Reid's lungs as he stood perfectly still, forcing his face not to reveal his shock.

"Mr. Rutherford believes an English lady has infiltrated the North West Company to find a man named Stephen Corning. She wasn't with Corning in Red River, so he said you might ken where she's at."

Reid shook his head, his heart pounding hard against his ribs. "I dinna think I can help you."

"Why would Rutherford think you ken where the lady might be?" Joseph crossed his arms and watched Reid closely.

At any moment, Charlotte could leave the storage room and Joseph would start to question her. If he'd been given any description of Charlotte, it wouldn't take him long to suspect she was the lady he sought. Reid had to keep Charlotte hidden for as long as Joseph stayed at the post.

"I'd be happy to answer your questions. I'll close the trading room, and we can speak in my private quarters."

"Where is your clerk?"

Reid hated to lie—but he couldn't tell Joseph the truth or he would put Charlotte in danger. No doubt Joseph would be compelled to apprehend Charlotte until Rutherford could get to her, and Reid could not let that happen.

"I sent him to a nearby village to bring gifts to the chief." It was a common enough practice for clerks and one Joseph wouldn't question.

It seemed to mollify the district manager, and he left the trading room ahead of Reid.

The bright sunshine made Reid squint. He didn't know how he'd warn Charlotte. If he didn't tell her that Joseph was here, she might join them, and then Joseph would be doubly suspicious.

He led Joseph into his quarters from the outside. "Just make yourself at home. I need to get some tea from the storeroom."

Joseph set his hat on the table and surveyed Reid's home, just as he had his trading room.

Reid opened the door into the hallway, closed it behind him, and then proceeded down the hall to the door leading into the storage room. He found Charlotte there, sitting on the floor, her cassette beside her, counting a pile of fur. A flickering lantern sat nearby, since there was no window in the dim room. Without looking at him, she held up her hand, indicating that he not speak until she was done counting. But Reid had no time for her to finish her task.

"Joseph McDonnell is here," Reid whispered as he went to the store of tea and pulled out a bag. "He's the new district manager of the Folle Avoine, and he received a letter from Rutherford."

Charlotte's head whipped around, her face turning white almost instantly. "Roger knows I'm here?"

"I dinna ken." Reid crouched down to face Charlotte. "But he told Joseph that I might ken where you are, and that's why he's here. I told him you went to a neighboring village to trade with the chief. I need you to stay here until I come for you. Do you understand? Do not show yourself to Joseph or anyone else." Reid stood, needing to return to Joseph. "I'll be back as soon as I'm able—but he's staying all night."

Charlotte nodded. "I'll not make a sound."

Reid left her in the storage room, closing the door quietly, and then walked back down the hall. He took a steady breath before he reentered his living quarters.

Joseph stood near Charlotte's desk. Her journal sat on top, and he had it open, thumbing through the pages. It was the property of the North West Company, and he'd warned her not to write anything personal in the journal, but Reid's pulse ticked higher as Joseph read her entries. Thankfully she had her cassette with her in the storage room, because if he had looked in it and found the letter that Stephen had sent them, Reid would have a very difficult time trying to explain it away.

Reid stirred the coals in the fireplace and put a few pieces of kindling on the glowing embers. He blew on the sparks until they caught the wood on fire, then he put a few more pieces on top of the flames. The cool teakettle hung on the iron crane, and Reid lifted it off, filled it with some water from the reservoir in the corner of the room, and set it over the fire to heat.

"Are you hungry?" Reid asked. "I have some biscuits."

"No, thank you." Joseph left Charlotte's desk and took a seat at the table.

Reid joined him while he waited for the water to heat.

"Tell me why Mr. Rutherford thinks you ken where the lady might be," Joseph said.

Sighing, Reid knew he must tell Joseph some of the truth. "Rutherford visited me in Montreal the day before I left. He believed his cousin might seek me out, based on a letter he had in his possession." Reid explained how Stephen Corning had saved his life and how Reid had promised to repay the debt. "I told Rutherford I couldna help him find his cousin, and then I left the next day." Reid hated lying to his friend. "When we arrived in Grand Portage, I met a lad who went by the name of—" Reid paused, as if to recall what the lad had said. "Thomas Fairfax, I believe. I was suspicious that he could be the cousin Rutherford was seeking, so I thought I owed Rutherford the courtesy of telling him what I saw. I visited him at the XY Fort at Grand Portage and told him."

"In his letter, Mr. Rutherford said you thought the lady—or lad, as it were—headed to the Upper Red River District, but when Rutherford arrived there, he could not locate his cousin." Joseph continued to watch Reid with a critical eye. Could he see through Reid's lies? "He found Stephen Corning, but Corning denied all of this. He said he never wrote Lady Charlotte a letter, never told her to go to you, and had not heard from her."

Reid lifted his hands and shrugged. "I wish I could help Rutherford, but I dinna ken any more than you." He leaned back in his chair. "What do you make of this?"

Joseph sighed. "I'm not sure. I just wish I hadna been drawn into the mess."

"Where does Rutherford think she went?"

Without blinking, Joseph said, "He thinks she's with you."

"That's preposterous." Sweat gathered under Reid's collar. "I dinna have his cousin—I dinna even ken if the lad I spoke to in Grand Portage was really her."

Joseph glanced at Charlotte's desk and nodded at the journal. "I remember meeting your clerk in Grand Portage. He was a quiet young lad with reddish-colored hair, if I recall."

"Aye." Reid nodded.

"Mr. Rutherford told me in his letter that his cousin has the same color hair."

"I remember him telling me the same."

There was a pause as Joseph brought his attention back to Reid. "I wish your clerk was here to answer some questions."

"What does my clerk have to do with this?"

Joseph absently scratched his sideburns and shrugged. "I dinna ken if he does or not."

"Mr. Crawford is from a Welsh family. His faither is my mither's distant kin. He's a good lad. I'm sure he'd be happy to speak to you if he returns while you're still here."

Nodding, Joseph stretched out on his chair. "I believe you, Reid. I've known you for years. You're one of the most honest men I've ever met. We may never know what happened to Rutherford's cousin."

Shame burned deep in Reid's gut, but he'd lie as much as necessary to keep Charlotte safe. "I wish I could help Rutherford. He's probably afraid for her."

"I think he's more angry than afraid." Joseph tapped the tabletop. "He sent the courier ahead of him but said in his letter that he's on his way to the Folle Avoine District to look for her himself. He'll probably come looking for her here."

Reid tried to appear neutral at hearing the news, when really, he was afraid for Charlotte. If Roger showed up before Stephen, then she'd still be at risk.

"But I'd rather speak about other things," Joseph said. "Have you finally taken a country wife?"

He didn't want to speak about Daanis either, but he'd rather they discuss her than Charlotte. "I've been a wee busy."

Joseph chuckled. "McTavish told me to pressure you to marry Curly Head's daughter, if I had the chance. So consider yourself pressured."

Reid smiled, but he didn't find humor in the situation. Joseph had taken a country wife and had several children with her. He wouldn't understand Reid's hesitation.

"I've heard Curly Head's daughter is a bonnie lass," Joseph said.

"Aye." Reid nodded. "Right bonnie, indeed."

Joseph laughed and reached across the table to slap Reid's shoulder in fun. "Dinna forget you're sent here to work, even if you have a bonnie lass to keep you distracted."

If Joseph knew the bonnie lass distracting him was not the chief's daughter—but the very lady he'd come looking for—his friend would not be smiling.

It had been hours since Reid had told Charlotte that Mr. McDonnell was at the post. Night had already fallen, though it hardly mattered in the windowless room. She'd extinguished her lantern long ago and had lain on a pile of blankets, trying to sleep while she waited. But sleep had not visited her. Thankfully, her eyes had adjusted to the darkness, though all she could see were the packages, barrels, and furs stacked in the room. If she had a book, at least she'd have a distraction from the worry that had entered with Reid so many hours ago.

Occasionally, she heard the men's muted laughter. The longer Reid kept Mr. McDonnell pacified, the safer Charlotte would be, so she waited as patiently as possible, thankful the men were occupied with happier things.

"You can sleep in my clerk's room." Reid's voice sounded closer. He must be in the hall. "He willna mind."

Charlotte sat up on the blankets, her pulse thumping a little harder.

"Are you sure?" Mr. McDonnell asked.

"Aye. He's an agreeable lad. He'd insist." A door creaked open, and Charlotte imagined Reid showing Mr. McDonnell into her room with a candle.

Thankfully, she had nothing in the room that would give away her identity. Since everything she owned had been given to her after entering the fur trade, her room looked like it was occupied by a male clerk of the North West Company. The only thing she had in her possession that might suggest she was not a man was her drawing of Reid—but that was in the bottom of her cassette, which was with her in the storage room.

"If you need anything, my room is just across the hall," Reid said. "Good night."

"Good night, McCoy. Thank you for your hospitality."

"My pleasure."

The door creaked closed, and Reid's footsteps faded back down the hall.

Where was he going?

Charlotte sat in the dark again, the sound of her breathing the only thing to keep her company. Surely Reid had not forgotten about her. Was he waiting for Mr. McDonnell to fall asleep before he came to her? The wall of the storage room was shared with the wall of her sleeping quarters. They were thick, sturdy walls made of logs, but still, they didn't mute the sound of voices altogether.

Time passed slowly, and Charlotte lay down again. She closed her eyes and tried to sleep—but a sound in the trading room made her sit up again.

The door connecting the storage room to the trading room quietly opened, and Reid stood there with a candle. He motioned for her to follow him.

She stood and tiptoed out of the room, careful not to trip.

When she was in the trading room, Reid quietly closed the door and took her hand, leading her to the opposite corner of the room. He set the candle on a shelf next to a few biscuits he'd brought for her.

"Does Mr. McDonnell suspect me?" she whispered.

"I think he did at the beginning, but our friendship is old." Reid shook his head, his mouth turned down. "He trusts me when I say you're not here."

Charlotte placed her hand on his arm. "I'm sorry you had to lie for me."

He put his hand over hers. "I'd do it a hundred times over if it kept you from Rutherford." Reid's dark brown eyes were filled with concern. "He's on his way here, lass. He could get here before Stephen. There's no way of knowing."

Charlotte dropped her hand, a knot forming in the pit of her stomach. "Did Mr. McDonnell tell you?"

"Aye."

"When will he get here?"

Reid shrugged. "He probably arrived at the Upper Red River just after Stephen received my letter and sent one to you. Rutherford would have spent some time looking for you, pressuring Stephen, and convincing himself you were not in hiding there. Then he sent the letter with the courier du bois, which probably took two weeks to get to Fond du Lac." Reid rubbed the palm of his hand against his temple. "He might be here in the next five or six weeks."

"Will he go to Fond du Lac first? Or come here?"

"I dinna ken." Reid took Charlotte's hand again. "I wish I could tell you more." He opened his arms, and she entered his embrace. "I wish I could protect you better—but I dinna think you want to hide in the storage room until Stephen arrives."

Despite the dire situation, Charlotte smiled.

"You'll need to sleep in the storage room tonight, though," Reid said against her hair.

"I'll be fine."

"I'll see that you are."

The candle popped and sputtered but held its light.

Pulling away, Charlotte looked up into Reid's face. He was so dear to her—dearer than anyone had ever been.

He touched a curl that had come loose from her queue. "Your hair is growing."

"It always grew quickly."

"Do you ken what makes me the saddest some days?" He lightly wrapped the curl around his index finger.

"What?"

"That I might never get to see your hair long again." He looked away from her hair and into her eyes. "I well remember the morning in Montreal when you stood in Mrs. Mallarme's old nightgown, your bonnie hair tumbling over your shoulders like a waterfall of auburn curls."

Warmth filled Charlotte's cheeks at the reminder. It was the first time a man had seen her in a nightgown—though she'd been seen in far worse since then.

"Even though I'll never forget that moment, I still wish I could see you like that again."

Pleasure quickened in her midsection, and she had to force herself to breathe.

"Good night, Lady Charlotte." Reid leaned forward and placed a kiss on her forehead. He lingered there for a heartbeat and then left the trading room, the feel of his kiss still sweet long after he'd gone.

# Chapter Eighteen

The days passed by at a rapid pace as Charlotte spent her time in the trading room with Reid. She was amazed at how quickly she'd learned basic Chippewa words, though she was never left alone to trade with the Indians. When the trading room was open, he was with her. If he could not communicate with someone who wished to trade, he would call in their translator. Either way, Charlotte spent hours listening to the men speak.

She kept a close tally on the numbers and kinds of fur brought in and recorded the goods given to the Indians. Some Indians came into the post looking for goods without fur, and Reid offered them credit. It was Charlotte's job to record those transactions as well.

The rituals surrounding the trade were new and unusual to Charlotte. Some of the lesser chiefs and leaders who entered came with great fanfare. They would send a few of their men into the fort ahead of them to procure tobacco and other small gifts from Reid. After they were satisfied, they would discharge their guns outside the stockade. Reid's men would answer the call with a few shots of their own, and then the Indians were allowed to enter the fort after giving their guns over to Jacques. When the leader would come into the trading room, he and Reid, and sometimes the interpreter, would share a pipe and speak about matters other than trading. This ceremony could take upwards of an hour or two before the official trading would begin.

Along with the gift of tobacco, the Indians also expected alcohol as part of their ritual. Reid gave each man a dram—but no more. When they asked for more, Reid was adamant in his refusal. He couldn't abide drinking and only did so when absolutely necessary.

Daanis continued to visit Fort McCoy almost every day. She spent hours in Noemie's cabin, though she often stopped in the trading room to speak to Reid before she left. She ignored Charlotte, for the most part, but her intentions were clear. She was there to entice Reid into a marriage.

Noemie did her best to encourage the relationship as well, talking about Daanis every chance she could. She often told Reid how much he would enjoy a female's companionship, and when she did, Reid only smiled.

Though Noemie spoke about Daanis often, Reid rarely brought up her name. He did mention other things that bothered him, though.

In the evenings, when the weather was fair, they sat on the bench facing the river and the sunset, and he spoke to her about the trade. His numbers were already far behind where he'd hoped at this time of the year. Granted, the majority of trapping took place in the middle of the winter, when the animals' fur was at its thickest, but there were those who brought fur at all times of the year—and those were the transactions that were lacking.

"I dinna understand," Reid said to Charlotte early one morning as she put away their breakfast dishes. "We should have more fur in our storage room by now."

He sat at the table, the ledger Charlotte used to record their transactions open in front of him. Every morning before they went into the trading room, he looked over the books—and every morning he complained about the problem.

He ran his index finger down the column. "We have half the numbers I hoped for by now."

"Do you think my arithmetic is wrong?" She glanced at the book over his shoulder.

"No. The numbers look correct."

She hated to voice her concern—but surely he had thought the same thing. "Perhaps the Indians are taking their furs to the XY post."

Reid slammed the book closed, and Charlotte jumped.

"Why?" Frustration and worry creased his brow. "Curly Head told me he has encouraged his men to trade with me."

Charlotte put away the last dish and leaned against the cupboard, knowing he was not angry at her—but at the problem. "Perhaps Lachlan is paying more."

Shoving his chair back, Reid stood and grabbed his coat off the hook. The weather had turned chilly, forcing him to wear his coat in the morning to go into the trading room where it would be cold. "We shall see about that."

Scrambling to join him, Charlotte put on her coat as well. They would need to light the fire in the trading room to chase away the chill before they could start to trade. She took a candle and lit it from the fireplace and then banked the fire. She held her hand in front of the candle to keep it lit and followed Reid down the hall, through the storage room, and into the trading room to begin her daily tasks.

The voyageurs usually kept the wood box full, but this morning, there was not enough kindling to get the fire started.

Reid stood at the counter with the ledger open before him again, his eyebrows furrowed.

Not wanting to bother him, Charlotte slipped out of the trading room and walked around the row house to the woodpile on the south side of the building.

As she gathered the sticks, Noemie's soothing voice traveled on the still, morning air. Peeking around the corner of the row house, Charlotte saw Daanis bent over near Noemie's cabin, retching onto the ground as Noemie rubbed her back.

A pang of envy touched Charlotte's heart as she watched Noemie care for her friend like a mother. Charlotte had often admired their closeness, making her long for her own mother. It had been months since Charlotte had spoken to another woman as herself, and she ached for that female companionship.

Noemie was kind and patient as she waited for Daanis to finish, and when she did, Noemie embraced her. Her voice was low and troubled as she patted Daanis's back. "Does your father know?"

"No. He will be very angry if he learns the truth."

Charlotte didn't want to eavesdrop, so she reached for another stick of wood, trying to finish her job before she heard more.

"How far along is the pregnancy?"

Pregnancy? Charlotte's eyes grew wide and her hand stilled. Was Daanis expecting a child?

"Maybe two months."

Charlotte's curiosity was now piqued, and she couldn't help looking around the corner again to hear the women better.

Noemie put her hand on Daanis's shoulder. "Does Lachlan know?"

"I'm afraid to tell him. He is already angry at my father for keeping us apart."

"Are you still meeting with him, even though your father forbids you?"

Daanis wiped her mouth and nodded.

"You are putting yourself and your child in danger by meeting him." Noemie spoke with a stern voice. "I would caution you to stop."

"I cannot." Daanis's answer was spoken softly. "I love him."

"All is not lost." Noemie's voice was clear and certain. She stood up straight. "If you convince Reid to take you in, there's still time to make him think the baby is his."

Charlotte's heart thudded at Noemie's words. Would Daanis do that to Reid? Why would the older woman suggest such a thing?

"I fear it is too late," Daanis said. "Mr. McCoy does not want me."

"It will work out." Noemie placed her arm around Daanis, directing her back into the cabin. "It always does."

Charlotte stood near the woodpile. What should she do with the news? She shouldn't have listened—should have walked away—because now she would have to decide whether to tell Reid what she'd heard.

Did he need to know Daanis was pregnant with his brother's child? What would it benefit him if he did? He had no plans to marry Daanis—even if she continued to make herself available. Besides, it wasn't Charlotte's news to share. She'd overheard two friends discussing something very personal. It wasn't her place to spread gossip. If Reid needed to know, she'd tell him—but if he didn't, she'd keep the information to herself.

Relief should have flooded her at making the decision, but instead sorrow filled her heart. Whether Reid had plans to marry Daanis or not, the chief's daughter was in love with his rival. A man who had brought Reid a lifetime of pain.

She hoped and prayed he would not continue.

Reid stood in the quiet trading room, his arms crossed as he leaned against the front side of the counter. It had been a week since Charlotte had suggested that the Indians were going to the XY post because Lachlan was paying more for fur. The silence pounded in his head like a war drum, blurring his vision. It was the fourth day in a row that no one had come to trade. If something didn't change soon, Reid would have no chance at becoming a shareholder in the North West Company. His books were more dismal than Fraser's.

With nothing to occupy their time, Reid had told Charlotte she was free to spend her afternoon as she wanted, so she had taken her cassette into her room to work on her drawings. She'd created several more since they'd opened the post. She'd shown him one she'd drawn of their trading rituals. He encouraged her to publish them when she returned to England, but he wondered if she would.

Part of him also wondered if she still had the picture she'd drawn of him without his shirt. Would she keep it, even after she left?

He thought a lot about what would happen to Charlotte when she married Stephen. But today was not a day to worry about Charlotte. Today, he needed to learn why he was losing his trade, and the only way to do that was to confront Lachlan.

Reid pulled his coat over his shoulders and buttoned up the front to ward off the October chill. Gray clouds covered the sky, and a northwesterly wind tore the red, orange, and yellow leaves from the trees beyond the fort. Small whitecaps appeared on the Mississippi, blowing the surface of the water upstream.

Without telling Charlotte where he was going, he put on his hat and left the trading room. Jacques stood in the stockade yard around a campfire with three other voyageurs, visiting with one of the Indian wives as she washed their clothing in a large caldron. The scent of wood smoke carried on the cold wind.

"Jacques." Reid called to his trusted friend, turning his back to the wind.

Jacques left the warmth of the fire and jogged across the yard to Reid. "Oui, Bourgeois?"

"I am going to visit the XY post. I need you to assist Mr. Crawford in the trading room while I'm gone."

Jacques rubbed his hands together. "Should I join you?"

In any other post, the assistant clerk would be more than capable of overseeing the trading room alone—but Reid did not want to put Charlotte in that position, especially if Rutherford should happen to come earlier than expected.

"No. I want you to stay here. I will go alone." It was time he faced his brother by himself.

Jacques knew better than to question his bourgeois, so he simply nodded.

"Mr. Crawford is working in his room. I dinna tell him I am leaving, so please tell him when you see him. Close the trading room and the post gates in an hour if no one comes to trade."

"Oui." Jacques left Reid and entered the trading room.

Charlotte would probably be angry that Reid didn't tell her he was leaving, but if he had, she would have tried to talk him out of going—and he needed to go.

It was a long, cold walk to the XY post. The wind pushed at his face and ran down his collar to chill his neck. He pulled his collar up and put his hands in his pockets, trying to stay warm.

Light rain started to fall, but it didn't bother him. His anger propelled him forward.

He walked around Curly Head's village so he would not have to speak to anyone he knew—especially Daanis. She continued to visit him at his fort, spending more and more time in the trading room. Her desperation had increased, and he wondered if she was being pressured by her father to make a match. He would prefer it if she stayed away, but he didn't want to anger Curly Head, so he allowed her to continue her visits.

Lachlan's post came within sight, and Reid pushed himself forward.

The post gate was open, so Reid walked in without hesitation. Voyageurs stood around campfires inside the stockade, much like they did in Reid's post. Instead of one row house, there were three separate buildings in the XY post. One was the trading room, one was a sleeping house for the voyageurs, and the other was for the bourgeois.

Men looked up at his arrival, but no one approached him.

He walked directly to the trading house and opened the door. Seven Indian men stood within the room, a pipe smoking in one man's hand. All the men held cups while the clerk poured a liberal amount of alcohol into them.

They spoke loudly in their own language, and one of them laughed. It was evident that they had been drinking for some time.

They hardly glanced at him.

Was this why the Indians were coming to Lachlan's post and not Reid's? The free alcohol? There were no laws to stop Lachlan from serving the Indians alcohol—at least not yet, though several mission societies were working on abolishing the practice. Reid used alcohol as a trade good, but he only gave each man a small amount as a gift. He couldn't abide a trader who inebriated the Indians to manipulate them—or used alcohol to draw them to his post.

"Mr. McCoy." The clerk quickly set the jug on the counter and left the Indian men. "What can I do for you?"

"I'm here to speak with Lachlan."

"He is busy, but I can assist you."

"No." Reid shook his head. "I've come to see Lachlan." He turned to leave the trading room, knowing he'd find Lachlan in his quarters. "I'll go to his home."

The clerk rushed forward and stepped between Reid and the door. "He is not in the post."

Reid almost tripped over the eager man, a frown pulling his eyebrows down. "Where is he?"

"At Curly Head's village, I believe." The clerk stammered. "But I could be wrong."

Irritation prickled Reid's skin. "When will he return?"

"I'm not sure." The clerk shrugged. "I'll tell him you came."

Reid pushed past the clerk and opened the door. "There's no need. I'll wait until he comes back." The rain fell harder now. Reid leaned against the side of the trading house and crossed his arms.

The voyageurs left their fires and went to their house, but Reid remained.

Soon, a figure entered the fort, and Reid instantly recognized Lachlan. He was walking quickly—and when he spotted Reid, he stopped, though he didn't look surprised. Had he noticed Reid when he had gone by Curly Head's village?

Reid pushed away from the building and faced his brother in the yard, the cold rain falling between them.

"What do you want?" Lachlan asked.

"I've come to see why the Indians are choosing to trade with you."

Lachlan took his time as he moved toward Reid, a gleam of victory in his eyes. "They prefer me over you." He gave a pompous bow. "They are not the only ones."

Reid knew he meant Daanis, but he would not give Lachlan the satisfaction of becoming angry. It mattered little to him if the chief's daughter was in love with his brother.

"They do not prefer you," Reid said instead. "They come for the free alcohol."

Lachlan shrugged. "I do what I must."

Reid's skin crawled with irritation. Though he hated the idea of using alcohol to bribe and lure the trade, he was getting desperate and would do whatever was necessary. He would stop at Curly Head's village on the way back to his post, and he would spread the word. Anyone who chose to trade at the North West Company post would be given as much alcohol as they desired.

Reid walked past Lachlan and out the gates of the post without a farewell.

Lachlan's laughter followed Reid until he was out of earshot, but the sound of it echoed in his mind long after the XY post was out of sight.

His brother thought he had bested Reid, but he was sorely mistaken.

# Chapter Nineteen

Rain spattered against the roof of the row house. Charlotte sat in the living quarters alone, eating the rubbaboo she had prepared over the fire. Heat from the hearth warmed her, but the chill of not knowing when Reid would return sent a shiver up her spine. Jacques had told her that Reid had gone to the XY post, but that was his only information.

There was still a hint of daylight in the sky, though the clouds made the day darker than usual. Charlotte couldn't stomach the stew, so she pushed it away. She needed to do something to keep occupied as she waited.

She walked across the room, her shoulders tense, wondering what had taken Reid away. What if he'd been hurt—or worse? If she could look through the oiled paper windows, she'd glance outside to see if Reid approached, but that was useless. She'd have to open the door to check, and that would let the heat out and the cold, wet air in—a prospect she didn't welcome.

Her paper and charcoaled pencils beckoned her, but it was hard to be creative when she was worried. Maybe there was work to be done in the storage room. She took a candle and went down the hall to the room at the end.

It was cold and dark, and the candle gave only a scant light. A pile of fur needed to be counted, and she had planned to rearrange some of the trade items, but the thought of starting a project so late in the day didn't appeal to her either.

She was too restless to concentrate.

Sighing, she started to leave the room when her eye caught on an exquisite gown hung on a peg in the corner. It was a trade item like the dress Reid had given to Daanis the first time he'd visited Curly Head's village. She walked across the room and lifted the candle to look at it closer. She'd admired it many times over the past couple of weeks but had forced herself not to dwell on the rich blue fabric or the delicate stitches.

Tonight, she didn't have the same self-control. Running her hands along the soft muslin fabric. How she longed to wear a gown like this one again—to feel like a woman, even if just for a few minutes. The binding she had worn almost constantly these many months suddenly pinched and dug into her skin.

Nibbling her bottom lip, she touched the silk ribbon just under the bust of the empire-style waist. What would it feel like to try on the gown?

Reid would probably not return for some time. If Charlotte brought the gown to her room and tried it on there, she might enjoy a few stolen moments to bask in the female delights once again.

Without giving it a second thought, she slipped the dress off the hook, left the storage room and went down the hall into her bedchamber. She didn't have the proper undergarments to wear with the gown, but she could do without a corset and petticoats this once.

Closing her door, she listened for Reid a moment, then set the candle on the small side table next to her bed.

Excitement made her tremble as she began to undress. She couldn't deny the freedom of trousers—but she missed being feminine.

After her pants, suit coat, and shirt were removed, she stood in her long underpants and tight linen binding. She'd only removed it momentarily a few times in the past few months. Now, she untucked the edge and unwound the material, letting out a long sigh as the last of it slipped loose and the cool air sent gooseflesh racing across her bare skin.

Not wasting a moment, she lifted the gown and slipped it on over her head. She wiggled the dress down the length of her body and smiled when it fell into place. The dress fit like it was made for her, the material soft and luxurious against her skin.

Tears gathered in her eyes as she did a little twirl. The skirt of the gown was not wide, but straight, coming down from the high waist tucked up under her breasts. She worked on the buttons and was able to get them fastened, and then she tied the bow in the back.

Oh, how she longed for a mirror!

She let out her queue, and her hair touched her shoulders. She ran her hands through the curls to soften them. If only she had a ribbon to tie around the crown of her head—but that was an impractical thought, much like wearing this gown.

Impractical or not, she had not felt this beautiful or feminine in many months. Pinching her cheeks for extra effect, she laughed at being so frivolous.

If only she had a ball to attend or a friend to visit. She walked across her room and took a seat. She ran her hands over the exquisite blue material and shook her head in awe. How had she ever taken such a simple thing as a gown for granted?

"Charlotte?" Reid's voice filled the living quarters unexpectedly.

She jumped from the chair, her heart pounding wildly. What would he think if he saw her playing dress-up?

She tugged at the buttons at the back of her neck and tried to get them undone, sweat gathering under the material as she turned in circles.

"Charlotte?" Reid's voice was closer—in the hallway—concern tightening the sound. "Are you in your room?"

"Reid!" Charlotte's voice was higher than usual. "I-I'm here."

"Are you well?"

"I'm fine." She tugged at a button and sidestepped, bumping into the chair. It fell with a crash.

Reid stood outside Charlotte's door, his pulse picking up speed when he heard the crash within her room. Was she being attacked? Memories flashed of Calum's body pressed against her, and his anger flared. He turned the doorknob and slammed the door open.

But his feet faltered, and he stumbled to a stop.

Charlotte remained perfectly still, standing in a beautiful blue gown, her arm reaching behind her neck.

She swallowed as she dropped her arm to her side and then remained still.

His pulse quickened for an entirely different reason now. The dress transformed her in every possible way, accentuating her small waist and her feminine curves. Not since the morning she'd stood in his home in Montreal had he seen her in such fine form—and not even then, since everything had been hidden beneath Mrs. Mallarme's modest nightgown.

But now? Every inch of her well-formed body was presented to him in the most becoming way he could imagine.

His eyes traveled from her face down to her hem and back up again. For the first time, he noticed her hair was no longer pulled back, but hanging loose. It softened her face and made her brown eyes luminous.

"Charlotte." His mouth was dry, and the word got stuck in his throat.

"I'm sorry." Her eyes were filled with remorse as she finally moved forward. "I only meant to try it on—I was going to return it before you came back—but I couldn't get the buttons undone."

"You dinna need to be sorry." His voice was gravelly as he forced his feet to move forward. The candlelight flickered, sending shadows dancing along the walls and over the planes of her beautiful face. "You are stunning."

He couldn't stop himself from drawing closer to her—and she didn't move away. It was dangerous, this attraction he had to her. It over-whelmed his every thought, coursed through every muscle and sinew in his body, and made him forget everything and everyone else. It was easier to ignore when she was dressed like a man—but now, seeing her this way, it reminded him that she was very much a woman, and he was very much a man.

She breathed deeply and her chest rose and fell, pressing against the fabric of her bodice. It was evident that she did not have on a corset. Her binding did a good job hiding her figure, but her binding was no longer in place.

"Charlotte." He said her name again. "I—"

He didn't finish his words, capturing her mouth against his.

She came to him willingly and allowed him to wrap his arms around her. The pressure of her body against his made him lose all reason, and he deepened the kiss, allowing his hands to slip up her back and into her hair. The curls were soft under his touch.

Charlotte responded to his kiss as she put her hands on his face and let her fingers splay over his ears, the tips dipping into his hairline.

Pleasure coiled tight in his belly and spread out through his limbs. He lowered his hands and encircled her waist, drawing her upwards, pressing her tighter to him. He found himself moving toward the bed—and it was at that moment that his reason returned, and he pulled back, stepping several feet away from her.

Her eyelids were heavy, and she blinked several times before her gaze focused. Lifting her hands, she placed them on her bright red cheeks, her eyes growing wide.

"I'm sorry." Shame covered her face. "I should have never put on this dress." Tears gathered in her eyes, and she wiped at them in frustration.

"Och, lass." Reid ran his hands through his hair. He knew how he felt about her—knew that he could not have her—but had almost done the unthinkable because he was weak and foolish. "'Tis not your fault. You're a woman and you belong in a dress." He turned the chair upright and took a seat, putting his face in his hands. "I had no right to kiss you simply because you look so bonnie."

"But if I hadn't put on this dress—"

"'Tis not just because you're bonnie, Charlotte. You ken that well." He looked up at her, wanting to tell her he loved her because she was brave and kind and good—but he could never say what was on his heart. "I canna deny that I'm attracted to you—but 'tis not only because of the way you look."

She wiped the tears away and took a shaky breath. "I'm sorry, Reid." She lifted the hem and let it fall to the ground in a silent cascade of fabric. "I just wanted to feel feminine again."

"You felt very feminine to me." Heat washed over his skin at the thought of her female curves pressed against him.

"I think it would be best for me to change back into my other clothes," she whispered.

He couldn't agree more—though he longed to see her remain in that dress for good.

"Aye." He pushed his hands against the armrests and forced himself to stand and move to the door. He turned around one last time and took a full look at her again.

Without another word, he stepped out of the room and closed the door soundly.

# Chapter Twenty

The wind was now howling around the eaves of the row house, blowing the rain against the side of the building. Reid stood by the fireplace, waiting for Charlotte to emerge after changing out of the dress and into her suit again.

Every one of his muscles still thrummed from their encounter, and he had to force himself to cool his thoughts. It had been one thing to imagine what Charlotte looked like dressed as a woman—but now that he had a clear picture in his mind, he wasn't sure he'd ever be able to get it out of his head again.

The encounter had almost made him forget about his experience at Lachlan's post and then his visit with Curly Head. He'd told the chief he would serve alcohol to those who traded with him, but he hated that he'd been forced to make the offer.

The door to the hallway creaked open, and Charlotte stepped into the room, fully clothed like a clerk.

It didn't matter. In his mind's eye, she was still in that gown, with no corset, her hair kissing her shoulders.

"Why didn't you tell me you were leaving today?" she asked.

It wasn't what he thought she would say after what had just happened—but it was safe.

"I dinna want you to try to stop me."

Charlotte walked over to the fireplace and stretched out her hands.

He did the same, standing close at her side. His head told him to keep distance between them, but his heart would not obey.

As they stood side by side, he couldn't help but think about Stephen and Rutherford, wondering when they might reach the post—and who would arrive first. If it was Stephen, he and Charlotte would have to leave immediately and go to Fond du Lac. If it was Rutherford, Reid would have to do everything possible to keep her hidden from him. He'd already spoken to several of his trusted men who were keeping an eye on the fort gate for the arrival of an Englishman. He wouldn't be hard to spot, since there were so few in the district.

Even with those safeguards in place, he still didn't want to let her out of his sight. Hopefully today would be the last time he'd have to leave her side until he could hand her off to Stephen.

But the thought of placing her in Stephen's care didn't sit well with him either. She wouldn't be safe from Rutherford until she was married, and there was a great distance to travel from his post to Fond du Lac. Could Stephen keep her safe?

"Why did you go to the XY post?" she asked.

"I needed to see for myself why the Indians are choosing Lachlan's post over mine."

"And?"

"He's using alcohol to lure them."

"How can you compete with that?"

"I canna." He let out a long, low sigh.

"What will you do?"

He shifted a log with his foot. It sent a cascade of sparks up the chimney. "I will do what needs to be done to win the trade. That's why I've been sent here."

"You'll sacrifice your morals?" There was accusation in her voice.

Reid tilted his head and frowned. "Isna that what you've been doing all this time?"

Putting her hands on her hips, she faced him. "How?"

"Dressing as a man, lying about who you are, sleeping in a tent—alone—with me for weeks?"

"That's different."

He crossed his arms. "How?"

"If I didn't, Roger would force me to marry him."

"Marrying someone you dinna love is not the worst thing that could happen."

Her mouth slipped open in shock. "For me it is."

"And losing to Lachlan would be the worst thing for me. So it looks like both of us will sacrifice our morals to get what we want."

She stared at him for a moment, her mouth trembling, and then turned and left the living quarters. Her bedroom door shut before he allowed himself to realize how crass he had been.

Was sacrificing his morals ever worth the trade-off? Was it worth disappointing Charlotte and God?

He briefly closed his eyes, knowing he'd hurt her again. He wanted to blame his foolishness on everything that had happened that day, but he couldn't justify his thoughtless words. He was angry with Lachlan and the trade—and his own weaknesses—but not with Charlotte.

Beating Lachlan and proving to his father he was worthy were not the same as escaping a ruthless guardian and fighting for her life.

He banked the fire and lifted the candle off the table. He would apologize to her before he went to bed, or he wouldn't be able to sleep.

A knock sounded at the front door.

Frowning, Reid went to the door and opened it. A blast of cold air blew into the room. Daanis stood there, her hair and clothing soaked, her face filled with unmistakable grief.

Concern shifted Reid's emotions as he opened the door wider. "Come in, lass."

She entered the room, and Reid closed the door behind her, fighting the wind.

"Here." He quickly set the candle on the table then removed the ashes from the coals. He placed new logs on the embers, and blowing against them, he was able to coax a warm fire for her.

"Come by the fire," he said.

She did as he instructed, her body shivering uncontrollably. She allowed him to help her remove her wet coat, but her dress was just as wet.

"What's wrong, lass?"

"I'm so cold," she said through chattering teeth.

He left her side and went into his room and grabbed a blanket for her. He also went to the storage room and found the dress Charlotte had worn, now hung back on its peg. The feelings he'd experienced seeing her in the dress resurfaced and he hesitated for a moment before removing it.

When he returned to the main room, he placed the blanket over Daanis's shoulders and laid the dress on the back of a chair. "You should get out of those wet things."

The fireplace blazed with heat and light, sending firelight dancing over her face. She glanced at the dress and nodded.

"I'll be back after you've changed."

He left the living space again and went into his bedroom. He questioned if he should tell Charlotte that Daanis was there but thought better of it. It wasn't worth disturbing her after everything that had passed between them. If she was feeling anything close to what he was experiencing, she'd need just as much space as him.

After waiting for several minutes, Reid reentered the main living quarters again and found Daanis sitting in a chair, facing the fireplace, with the blanket wrapped around her shoulders. Her wet dress was on the back of the chair.

"Would you like something warm to drink?" he asked.

"Yes, please."

He busied himself with preparing the tea, glancing over his shoulder from time to time to look at Daanis. She sat perfectly still, watching the flames. It was growing late, but he still didn't know why she had come.

When the tea was finally ready, he brought her a cup and held one for himself. He drew a chair up to the fireplace beside her.

"Can you tell me why you've come?"

Her dark brown eyes revealed nothing. How different they were from Charlotte's expressive eyes. He almost always knew what Charlotte was thinking when he looked at her.

Without a word, Daanis set her cup on the table nearby. Her blanket slipped off her shoulder, revealing her dark, silky skin.

Reid's pulse picked up speed, and he swallowed hard. She had taken off her wet dress, but had not put on the clean, dry one. It was on the seat of the chair, bunched up under the wet one.

He looked away, but she made no motion to cover herself again.

"I've come to offer myself to you," she whispered.

Panic rammed against Reid, and he leapt to his feet, putting the chair between them. His senses were already heightened from his encounter with Charlotte.

Daanis allowed her blanket to drop even lower as she watched him.

"You need to leave, Daanis." His voice was filled with panic, and he didn't try to hide it. "I canna give you what you want."

Daanis allowed the blanket to completely fall away from her shoulders and pool around her bare waist. "Why not?"

Reid moved so quickly his teacup fell out of his hand and crashed to the floor. He tripped on his own feet in his haste to get away. He went to the other side of the room, and it took every bit of self-control not to look back at her. She was a beautiful woman—stunning. But she was not his, nor did he want her to be.

Between Daanis and Charlotte, never in his life had he been tempted like he'd been this evening. Was this a test? He'd been flippant in his comments about sacrificing his morals to get what he wanted. Was God trying to see how far he'd go?

Charlotte's words filled him with apprehension. He might forfeit some of his morals—but he could not sacrifice the one he held most dear. Marriage was sacred to him, and he would not compromise that belief for a moment of pleasure.

"Why don't you want me?"

Movement behind him suggested she had covered herself again, so he chanced a glance over his shoulder. The blanket was now wrapped tightly around her body, and she was standing with her back to the fireplace. Pain and sadness pinched her face.

He prayed Charlotte was asleep and that she would not suddenly appear to find them in such an awkward situation. How would he ever explain?

"You are a bonnie lass," he said quickly, his throat dry. "But I dinna love you." He swallowed, the words coming of their own accord. "I'm in love with someone else."

She pulled the blanket even tighter around her shoulders and sank back into her chair, sobs wracking her body.

Reid froze. What should he do? He didn't want to encourage her—but he couldn't let her suffer alone.

He went back to the fireplace and took the seat beside her again. "Why are you trying so hard, lass? You dinna need to come to me this way."

She turned her head away from him and wiped her cheeks. "My father is angry with me. He thinks I have done something to displease you."

"No." He shook his head. "This is not about you. I made my decision about marriage before I even met you. I should have had the courage to tell you and your father." He paused. "What do *you* want, Daanis?"

Taking a deep breath, Daanis finally looked at Reid. "I want a home and children of my own."

Things she had probably hoped Fraser would give to her but had failed to do. Things she might want with Lachlan, if her father would allow it.

"I'm sorry, lass. I canna give you what you want."

She wiped her face again, her eyes pleading. "Is it too much to ask?"

"No." Compassion softened his voice. "But I'm not the man who can give it to you."

After a quiet moment, she stood and lifted her wet dress off the chair.

"You may take the dry gown and spend the night with Noemie," he said. "But in the morning, you'll need to return to your faither."

"He will be angry with me when he learns the truth." Her eyes grew hard, and her lips thinned to a straight line. "I don't know what I'll do."

"I willna tell him you came here tonight." He wanted to reassure her. "But you canna come again."

She didn't seem to hear him as she started walking toward the door, and he sensed she was upset about something deeper than her visit.

Reid wished he could help the lass, but it wasn't in his power to give her what she wanted.

Charlotte entered the living quarters the next morning and found Reid sitting at the table, a bowl of porridge set before him. The ledger, which was usually his morning companion, was still on his desk near the door.

The rain had not let up. It continued to pour outside the row house, sending rivulets of water down the oiled paper windows.

"Good morning," Charlotte said as she walked to the fireplace. She usually rose before him and made breakfast, but today, a pot of porridge warmed near the hearth.

"I couldna sleep, so I made breakfast," he said.

"Thank you." She took a bowl from the cupboard and filled it with a scoop of porridge. When she was done, she sat across from him.

His shoulders were bent, and his hands hugged the bowl, though he didn't eat. Fatigue rimmed his eyes, and the lines around his mouth were troubled as he met her gaze.

Concern tightened her chest. "What's wrong?"

"I'm sorry for what I said last night. I wanted to apologize before I went to bed, but—" He looked down at his porridge, his eyebrows wedged together. "I waited too long, and you were asleep."

Their heated words had made him this upset?

She reached across the table and laid her hand over his. "You don't need to be sorry, Reid. We were both upset."

"It doesna excuse my poor behavior."

"Nor mine."

He nodded absently, and she pulled her hand back to reach for the maple syrup.

But his mood did not lighten as he looked back at his porridge.

The longer the silence stretched, the more certain she became that he was upset about something other than their little fight, though he didn't tell her what.

As she stirred the syrup into her porridge, he rose from the table and went to his desk to retrieve the ledger. "If you dinna mind, I'll open the trading room."

"It's still early."

"I'm expecting more trade today."

She opened her mouth to ask why, but then she remembered their conversation from the night before. Lachlan was offering free alcohol. Would Reid serve it as well?

Instead of asking him about the trade, she nodded at his bowl. "You didn't eat your breakfast."

"I'm not hungry."

"Then I'll join you." She started to stand. "You shouldn't have to do my job."

Reid put his hand on her shoulder. "Finish your meal first, lass. I'll start the fire."

He left the living quarters, and Charlotte sank back into her chair. She longed to ease Reid's burdens but didn't know how. She dipped her spoon into the porridge he had made, unsure if she could eat.

There were so many things conspiring against her and Reid, not only to be together, but to get what they wanted most in the world.

Would either of them ever be truly happy again?

# Chapter Twenty-One

T he evening had worn on and the sun had fallen, but the campfires in the stockade yard still burned bright. Rain no longer fell, but the air was cold, and the yard was full of mud. Laughter filtered through the open door into the trading room, where Reid worked on his ledger by the light of a candle. His voyageurs were enjoying the company of about a dozen Chippewa men and women who had come to trade at the post that day, making it the most successful day Reid had had since arriving at Crow Wing.

But it had come at a cost, and Reid was angry with himself for giving in to the alcohol.

Instead of leaving when the trading had been complete, the Indians had stayed to share the rum they had been given in exchange for their fur. Reid's men were more than happy to relieve them of their alcohol, and they had been celebrating ever since. Jacques was among them, not because he was drinking, but because Reid had asked him to keep the peace and if anything escalated out of control, to let Reid know.

Two voices rose above the others, and Reid paused in his work to listen. One was the voice of a voyageur and one of an Indian. If he was correct, they were having words about one of the women in the gathering.

Concern tightened Reid's muscles as he waited. Would the argument continue? Or would they find a resolution to whatever had caused their anger?

Standing, he went to the open door and looked out at the yard. Two campfires were lit inside the stockade gate. Both were encircled with men and women standing in their capotes and furs. A dog lay in the mud near one of the Indian men, and two children sat huddled together along the stockade wall, all but forgotten in the cold night air.

Reid stepped out of the trading room, and several of the voices quieted as people watched him approach. He hated that they were still drinking, but he'd made his choice. His job was to get the trade. The only way to get the trade was to give the trading Indians what they wanted, and many of them wanted alcohol. If Reid couldn't do what was necessary to get their business, then he had no reason to be in the interior.

But the children shouldn't suffer.

Jacques left one of the fires and approached Reid. "Bonjour, Bourgeois."

"Who is arguing?" Reid asked.

"Robert. He has taken liberties with a woman who did not offer them."

"Call him to me." Reid would send Robert to bed so he would cause no more trouble.

"Oui." Jacques bowed.

"And who do those children belong to?"

Jacques glanced in the direction Reid pointed. The surprise on his face suggested he hadn't even noticed the small boy and girl.

"I am not sure. I will ask."

"I would like to bring them into the trading room to stay warm until their parents are ready to leave." He might not be able to keep their parents from being drunk, but he could offer them some heat and a bit to eat. "Have Robert and the children come into the trading room."

"Oui." Jacques left, and Reid returned to the trading room to wait. Though he had a fire blazing in the hearth, he continued to keep the door open to monitor the campfires.

The door from the storage room creaked open, and Charlotte entered the trading room.

"I told you to stay inside." Reid walked over to Charlotte and took hold of the door, shielding her from the people around the campfires.

"You didn't join me for supper." She held a plate of pork and beans. "They're getting cold."

"Thank you." He took the plate and set it on the counter but doubted he would eat. Maybe he'd give the food to the children.

Charlotte looked toward the open door, her lips thinning with displeasure.

"You should go to bed," he told her. "We'll have an early morning again."

"Will it be like this every night?"

He hated seeing the disappointment in her eyes. He was disappointed enough with himself.

"Not every night. But most."

"I have Robert and the children." Jacques entered the trading room, a disgruntled Robert at his side. The short voyageur was as grizzly as they came, with long whiskers and small, sharp eyes.

"You're not needed," Reid said to Charlotte. He tried to close the door, but she saw the children and wouldn't budge.

"They're cold," she said with compassion.

"Aye."

The children still clung to one another, their large brown eyes filled with uncertainty as they took in Reid, Charlotte, and the trading room. They couldn't be more than four and five years old.

"Come here," Charlotte said in Chippewa. "Warm yourself by the fire." She moved away from Reid and walked toward the fireplace in the corner of the room. She knelt on the ground near the hearth and motioned for the children to join her.

Jacques nudged the little girl forward, and she came warily into the room, the little boy at her side.

"What do you want with me?" Robert asked impatiently. "I'd like to return to the fire."

"You won't be returning tonight." Reid crossed his arms. "I want you to turn in early. Tomorrow you'll be sent to hunt at daybreak."

Robert smelled of rum, and his eyes were glazed from the effects of the alcohol. He grunted. "I'll be fine in the morning."

"I disagree." Reid stepped between Robert and the three at the fireplace.

Charlotte took Reid's plate of food and handed it to the little girl, whispering words of encouragement to her and the boy. Either she was oblivious to the drunken voyageur, or she was trying to distract the children. Either way, he was thankful she was taking care of the boy and girl.

"I want you in your bunk now," Reid said to Robert, his voice filled with warning. "I'll not have you disobeying orders."

"And I said I'd be fine in the morning." Robert turned and stumbled out of the trading room.

"Robert!" Reid called to the man.

But Robert didn't respond. Instead, he strode back to the campfire and stopped next to a woman who didn't look pleased to see him again.

Sighing, Reid nodded at Jacques to return to Robert. "I'll be there in a minute."

Jacques left the trading room, and Reid turned to Charlotte.

She glanced at him, but didn't speak. Instead, she turned her attention to the children and smiled.

The little girl helped feed her brother while watching Charlotte and Reid closely.

"They're beautiful," Charlotte said quietly. "But they look so scared."

"They are freezing." Reid took a blanket from a pile on a shelf and wrapped it around the children.

Charlotte set another piece of wood on the fire and sat on the ground across from the boy and girl. Her face had softened in a way he'd never seen before.

"Do you hope to have a family one day?" he asked.

A tender smile curved her lips as she looked at the children. "One day."

She would make a good mother. She had all the qualities a mother needed. Courage, selflessness, kindness, and patience.

"Do *you* hope to have a family?" she asked, finally looking up at him.

He had not thought about a family of his own over the past fifteen years. He'd been too preoccupied with his career. But more importantly, he'd not found someone he wanted to create a life with.

Until now.

He inhaled at the thought, trying to push aside his feelings, though they were growing stronger with each passing day. He had to remind himself that it was an impossible match, not only because he was a bourgeois in the North West Company and she was an English lady, but also because her fiancé was on his way to claim her.

Yet he couldn't help but wonder. If Stephen hadn't been on his way, would Charlotte even consider marrying him? Did her feelings for him run as deep as his did for her?

It was a pointless thing to consider. What would he do if they married? He was so close to becoming a shareholder that it would be ridiculous to leave the trade now. And besides, he couldn't let Lachlan win—not now, not when he was so close to finally proving to himself and his father that he was the better man. He had a responsibility to the North West Company to secure the trade. And it would be impossible to marry Charlotte and then leave her. It would drive him mad. Yet he couldn't keep her in the interior either. Not only was it against the rules for European women, but it was no life for her—and if there were children, he could not keep her identity a secret.

"Reid?" She watched him carefully, questions in her beautiful brown eyes.

It wasn't the first time he'd contemplated these thoughts, but it should be the last. It was too hard to feel a moment of hope and then dash it with all the reasons why it would never work. Not to mention that she might never agree to such a match. She'd chosen Stephen, and it wasn't Reid's place to ask her to make a different choice.

"What did you ask me?"

"Do you want a family?"

He nodded, his smile sad. "Aye. But only with the right lass."

She studied him for a moment, and his insides warmed at the look in her eyes.

Voices rose in the stockade yard again, and this time, they were louder and more forceful than before. Someone screamed, and the hair on the back of Reid's neck rose.

"Go," she said. "I'll stay with the children."

He wanted to remain with her, but he had no choice. He must deal with Robert—and the consequences of allowing alcohol in his trading post.

Charlotte's body was weary from another restless night. She lay in the living quarters, near the fireplace, early the next morning. Her eyes burned, but she was unable to sleep. The little boy and girl were asleep on a pile of fur beside her, their parents having either forgotten them or passed out in the fort yard, despite the cold and the mud.

She had never seen anything like the night they had just endured and had no desire to witness it again. Surely Reid would not allow the men to drink after this.

The sun was nearly kissing the horizon, but the revelry had just died down. Perhaps Charlotte could catch a few minutes of sleep before everyone awoke. Hopefully Reid had found some sleep in the trading room, because she had not seen him for hours.

Would he rouse the men and put them all to work at first light? If she had her way, there would be no rest for anyone at Fort McCoy this day.

The front door creaked open. Charlotte raised her head, expecting to see the children's parents, but it was Daanis who entered the room. She tiptoed inside and gently closed the door behind her.

Charlotte didn't move.

Why had Daanis come so early in the morning? And why had she come into Reid's quarters?

The table and chairs were between Charlotte and Daanis, shielding Charlotte and the children as Daanis silently walked across the room and went into the hallway leading to the bedrooms.

Frowning, Charlotte raised herself on her elbow. Should she go after Daanis and ask her what she needed? Uncertainty weighed Charlotte to the spot.

After a few moments, the hallway door opened again, and Charlotte lay down on instinct. She closed her eyes and listened as Daanis walked back across the room and left the row house.

Charlotte finally stood and went to the door. She opened it slowly. Several people were asleep in the yard, but Reid was not there.

Daanis walked around the side of the row house and sent a glance over her shoulder toward one of the smoldering campfires. Charlotte frowned. Where was she going—and more importantly, why had she come?

Charlotte grabbed her coat off the hook and slipped it over her shoulders as she left the row house to follow.

Daanis moved behind Noemie and Jean-Paul's cabin, further perplexing Charlotte. There was a small gate at the back of the post for easy access to that side of the fort, but it was rarely used.

Charlotte stepped lightly through the slippery mud and hugged the side of Noemie's cabin as she peeked her head around the corner. The early dawn offered enough light for Charlotte to watch Daanis slip out of the fort through the small gate.

Now more curious than ever, Charlotte walked to the gate and pushed it open. She looked right and then left—and that's when she saw Lachlan. He stood near a tree, not far from the post.

Daanis handed something to him, but they were too far away for Charlotte to see what it was.

Her heart beat hard as she peered around the gate.

After Daanis handed him the object, Lachlan put his hand on her stomach and said something that Charlotte struggled to hear.

Daanis nodded and looked as if she wiped away a tear.

What were they discussing?

Charlotte's pulse picked up speed, drumming loudly in her ears. What had Daanis taken from Reid? And why did Lachlan want it?

Her limbs trembled, and she wished she had not followed Daanis. She began to retreat, but the mud oozed under her shoes and made her foot slide. She braced herself against the gate, trying not to fall.

"Who's there?" Lachlan asked.

Panic overwhelmed Charlotte, and the need to flee overcame her, but she couldn't get her feet to move.

Daanis screamed.

Charlotte turned toward the sound.

Lachlan had a pistol pointed at her. Before Charlotte could cry out for him to stop, the pistol fired and a searing pain tore through her right shoulder, forcing her backward into the ground.

Her head struck something hard, and the world started to fade.

# Chapter Twenty-Two

The crack of a pistol sounded in the stillness. Reid's head snapped up as he waited to hear another shot.

Who would fire a pistol in the early morning hours?

He set aside the iron poker as the fire popped and sizzled. He hadn't bothered to let it die the night before and wouldn't let it die now. He'd been up all night guarding the storage room, where he'd put Robert on arrest, while keeping an eye on the men and women in the stockade. It had been a long, arduous night, and he had no desire to live through another like it. His head pounded, his eyes were gritty, and his stomach growled from having missed supper the night before.

But there would probably be more Indians at the post in the coming hours, and he'd need to be ready for them.

Most of the men were asleep in the yard, though he couldn't account for all of them. Had one of them left the stockade and gotten into a brawl with one of the Indians?

Reid left the trading room, his pulse ticking a steady rhythm as he surveyed the stockade.

Nothing moved in the front yard, but the sound of the pistol had come from behind the post.

Jogging to the back of the row house, he scanned the area but could find nothing amiss.

Jean-Paul's door opened just a crack, and Noemie looked out at Reid. She was still in her nightgown, but her eyes were wide. "Did you hear that?" she asked.

"Aye." Reid continued toward the back gate, his hand on the pistol he wore in a holster at his side. He had kept it ready all night but thought the need for it had passed.

He silently stepped around Jean-Paul's cabin, his senses on high alert. He had no wish to come between two people who might be fighting with pistols—but he couldn't let this argument pass without trying to intervene.

A body lay on the ground near the gate. Alarmed, Reid rushed to his side—and noticed the auburn curls.

The earth shifted beneath his feet as he dropped to his knees, shaking his head. "It canna be."

But then he saw her face, and there was no denying it was Charlotte.

Terror squeezed the breath from his lungs as he lifted her head in his shaking hands. He'd never known such fear or dread in all his life. Blood soaked the right side of her brown coat, and her eyes were closed.

"No," Reid said on a breathless prayer. "Please, God." He put his trembling fingers to her neck, feeling for a pulse, and almost collapsed with relief. She was still alive.

Without thinking, he lifted her into his arms and ran through the fort, his feet sliding in the thick mud. Rushing past Jean-Paul's cabin, he called out to Noemie.

She opened the door again, her eyes growing wide at the sight of Charlotte's limp body in his arms.

"Hurry! Charlie's been shot!" Reid didn't wait for Noemie to respond but continued around the row house, his heart crying out to God.

Noemie followed him and opened the door to allow Reid into his living quarters. The children were still asleep on the fur, so Reid nodded toward the door. "Charlie's room."

Noemie opened the other door, and Reid pushed past her to lay Charlotte on her bed.

"Stoke the fire and set some water to boil," Reid commanded Noemie. "Get as many clean rags as you can find and bring my medicine chest."

Noemie left the room to do as he bid.

Reid took off Charlotte's coat, though it wasn't easy. She was unconscious and felt like a rag doll in his hands.

"Dinna die, lass," he frantically whispered into her ear as he pulled her close to his chest to remove her arm from a sleeve, wishing he could give her his strength. "I willna let you die."

He prayed in fervent, broken, desperate words as he gently laid her down, cradling her head in his hand. When he pulled his hand away, there was blood from the back of her head.

Had she hit her head when she fell?

There was a hole in Charlotte's shirt on the right shoulder at the center of all the blood. He put his finger into the hole and pulled, ripping the fabric away from the wound—but then he remembered her binding and forced himself to stop tearing. He could still clean her wound and keep her shirt on. He only needed to tear the fabric away from her shoulder.

Noemie rushed into the room with a handful of rags. "We must stop the bleeding."

Reid grabbed several and pressed them against the wounds.

Blood stained the blanket beneath Charlotte's shoulder. He felt behind her back, where her skin was sticky with blood.

"I think the bullet passed through. Hand me another rag." He took the rag Noemie handed him and pressed it to the back of Charlotte's shoulder as well.

"What happened?" Noemie's shirt was untucked, and her silver-streaked hair was in disarray as she knelt across from Reid.

"I dinna ken." Reid knelt awkwardly beside Charlotte, both hands pressed against her shoulder.

"Who would hurt Mr. Crawford?"

None of it mattered right now. Reid just needed to get Charlotte better. Once she was well, he could ask her what had happened, but until then, he would focus his energy on taking care of her.

"He hit his head," Reid told Noemie. "We need to stop the bleeding there too."

Noemie rolled up her sleeves. "We'll get Mr. Crawford well again. You do not need to worry."

Reid hoped she was right—but dread filled his gut, and he felt nauseous from the fear.

He continued to pray. It was the only thing that would save Charlotte.

Charlotte forced herself to open her eyes. The light hurt, so she closed them again. She tried to move, but pain shot through her shoulder and head. What happened? Was she having a bad dream?

The pain suggested otherwise.

As she took a deep breath, fragments of images floated through her mind. Lying on the fur with the Indian children. Daanis entering the room. Following her to the back gate.

She tried to open her eyes again, and this time she was able to focus on the person in her room.

Daanis.

She sat on the chair beside Charlotte, her hands clasped in her lap. "You're awake."

Charlotte closed her eyes again. The gate. Lachlan.

*Lachlan.*

Charlotte's eyes flew open as everything returned to her with blazing clarity.

Lachlan had shot Charlotte because she'd caught him and Daanis—but what had Daanis been doing?

Panic clawed at Charlotte. Where was Reid? Why would he leave her alone with Daanis?

Daanis stood and took a cup of water off the table by Charlotte's bed. "You're probably thirsty."

She put her arm behind Charlotte's back and helped her take a sip of water.

The liquid felt wonderful sliding down her throat, but the pain from moving almost made her pass out again. Her forehead broke out in a sweat, and she had a hard time not whimpering.

Charlotte tried to look past Daanis to the closed door. Had Reid gone after Lachlan? Did he know Daanis had been there too?

"Mr. McCoy is in the trading room." Daanis took a seat again.

Relief flooded Charlotte and she felt weak. Reid was still here.

"How long have I been like this?" Charlotte asked, her voice hoarse.

"Three days."

Three days? She briefly closed her eyes again.

"Before you go back to sleep, we need to speak." Daanis leaned forward. "I haven't gone back to my village since you were shot, waiting for you to wake up."

Charlotte wished Reid was in the room. She didn't want to talk to Daanis alone.

"I know you saw us," Daanis said, swallowing hard. "We didn't know you would be there. It was a mistake. He wouldn't hurt you on purpose."

As Daanis spoke, Charlotte wondered if she was trying to convince herself just as much as she was trying to convince Charlotte.

Charlotte tried not to show her fear. "Does Reid know?"

"No. And he mustn't know."

Charlotte wanted to shout for Reid to come. She needed to tell him the truth. That Daanis had snuck into the row house, then met Lachlan and handed him something in the woods.

"I know what you're thinking." Daanis walked to the end of Charlotte's bed. She put her hands on the footboard, as if for support. "But you mustn't tell him."

"I will—as soon as I can get him—"

"I know who you are—or at least, what you are."

Charlotte's breath stilled. She wanted to sit up and face this woman, but she could never sit up on her own.

"Mr. McCoy tried to see to your every need." She crossed her arms. "But I started to get suspicious when he wouldn't let Noemie or me alone with you, so I came in here when he passed out, exhausted. It didn't take me long to discover the truth. At least I know why he wouldn't have me."

Panic raced through Charlotte. She had to tell Reid that Daanis knew about her. Had she already told the others? Had she alerted Reid's superiors? Were they already on their way to apprehend him?

"Don't worry." She dropped her arms to her sides as empathy filled her voice. "I won't tell anyone."

Charlotte frowned. "Why not?"

"Because you won't tell anyone what you saw in the woods—or who shot you."

Charlotte stared at Daanis, her pulse ticking.

"Do you understand?" Daanis asked.

She did understand. Completely. "Yes."

"Good." Daanis looked Charlotte over from head to toe, a frown marring her face. "Does it please you to dress like a man?"

Tears gathered in Charlotte's eyes and slipped down her cheeks. "No."

"Then you must love him very much."

Charlotte didn't bother to wipe the tears away as she whispered, "I do." But saying it out loud made it feel more real. More pressing.

And more impossible.

To protect Reid from losing his job, she could not tell him the truth.

There had to be another way.

# Chapter Twenty-Three

The trading room felt overly warm. Smoke from the fireplace mingled with the stale scent of alcohol and sweat as Reid stood with six Indian men haggling over the price of the fur they had brought to him. Jacques and the interpreter were also there, prolonging the exchange.

All Reid wanted to do was to return to Charlotte.

For three days, he had spent almost every moment by her side. Noemie and Daanis had insisted on staying with him around the clock, for which he was grateful, but he couldn't risk leaving Charlotte alone with either one of them.

This morning, when Jacques told Reid it was vital that he meet with this group of Indians, Reid had sent Noemie and Daanis to Curly Head's village to retrieve herbs from his healer for a poultice.

Thankfully, Charlotte had been resting peacefully when he'd left her not more than twenty minutes ago—but it was twenty minutes too long.

"Mr. Crawford is awake."

Reid turned away from the men and found Daanis standing in the door to the storage room.

"You were with him? I thought you went with Noemie." Momentary panic filled his chest. Had she guessed Charlotte's secret?

Daanis nodded but didn't seem alarmed or concerned, so perhaps she hadn't.

"Thank you." Reid left the trading room without excusing himself, pushing his way past Daanis.

Charlotte was finally awake.

He'd never been more relieved in his life.

Smoothing his hair away from his face, he suddenly felt nervous to see her again. Would she remember what happened the day she was shot? There had been no witnesses or clues, nothing to help him learn the truth. The marks in the mud near the stockade were unhelpful because of all the foot traffic coming and going from the fort that day.

Pushing open the door, he stepped into the small room, then closed the door behind him for privacy. Charlotte was on her bed, the blankets pulled up to her chin. The air was cool, and the heat from the fireplace in the main room did not reach her here.

Thankfully, she did not burn with fever, though that could still happen. He'd bled her twice since she was shot. His medical instruction book told him it was the best thing he could do for a bullet wound. He would do whatever it would take to make her well.

At the sound of his footsteps, she opened her eyes.

The love he felt for her became so strong and so sweet in that moment that he couldn't help but kneel beside her bed and pull her hand out from under the blanket and press it against his lips. "Charlotte." He breathed out her name. "Thank God you're alive."

She squeezed his hand, and though it was a weak grasp, he briefly closed his eyes with relief.

"How are you feeling, love?" he asked, searching her beautiful face.

"Love?" she whispered.

He swallowed and touched the curls lying on her pillow. "You must ken the truth."

Tears gathered in her brown eyes, and she blinked several times, but they slipped down her cheeks.

He wiped one away with his finger and tried to smile, but he was too overcome with the reality of what he was confessing. He'd never loved anyone the way he loved Charlotte. It was both freedom and vulnerability, ecstasy and torture. It consumed him so fully, there was nothing he could do but tell her.

"Reid—" Charlotte tried to move but winced.

"Shh." He put his hand on her healthy shoulder to keep her still. "You dinna need to speak." He ran the backs of his fingers down her cheek, loving the feel of her soft skin. "You had me scared these past three days, and I told myself if you survived—" He paused, hating how terrified he'd felt while she'd been unconscious. He was in love with her, and nothing could change that fact.

"If I survived?"

"If you survived, I wouldna keep my feelings hidden from you any longer."

She nibbled her bottom lip in a way that had become as dear to him as everything else about her.

"I—" She blinked again and swallowed. "I don't know what to say."

His chest constricted, and he realized that he had wanted her to tell him that she loved him too. It was a foolish desire, and he'd been unwise to share his heart. The last thing he wanted was for her to feel obligated to respond. "Dinna say anything, lass. I shouldna spoken—especially not now when you're still recovering." He pushed away from her bed and pulled the chair close beside her. It would be better to talk about something that didn't concern his feelings for her. "Now that you're awake, can you tell me what happened the day you were shot?"

She opened her mouth, then closed it again, her eyes hooded with uncertainty.

"What is it?" he asked.

Licking her lips, she slipped her hand back under the covers. "I don't remember."

He'd been afraid of that. She had hit her head hard and been unconscious for days. Maybe he could help her remember.

"Have you left the stockade alone before?"

"No."

"Then why did you decide to go that day?"

She was quiet for a moment. "I don't know."

"You dinna remember?"

She was so still as she lay on the bed, her face pale. "No."

Reid nodded. He wanted to know what had happened, but it wasn't as important as having her return to him. "If you remember anything about that day, please tell me."

"I will."

He hated to know that whoever had shot her was on the loose somewhere, but hopefully they were far away. He'd do everything he could to protect her from this day forward.

"I'm just happy you're awake." He moved one of her curls off her forehead. "I've been praying for you night and day."

"Thank you." Her eyelids started to lower with exhaustion.

"Sleep," he said. "I'll be back in a wee bit with some broth."

He stood and walked to her door.

"Reid?"

He turned. "Aye?"

"Promise me you'll be careful."

"Careful?" He frowned and walked back to her bed. "About what?"

"Everything."

"Lass?" He knelt by her side again, confused. "What aren't you telling me, Charlotte?"

"I just want you to be careful." She took a deep breath. "Don't trust anyone. Promise me." Her voice was so full of pleading, how could he say no?

"Of course. I promise."

"Thank you." She closed her eyes and took a few deep breaths.

He left her room, his heart heavy with the words she'd spoken—and those she'd left unsaid.

It was two weeks before Charlotte was able to get out of bed. Another week before she didn't feel as weak as a newborn lamb, and a week after that before she felt almost like herself again.

And in those four weeks, she kept the truth about Daanis and Lachlan to herself. She never spoke of the day she was shot, and Daanis didn't return to the post to tell the truth about Charlotte.

After Reid's confession in her sickroom, he never spoke about his feelings for her again, either, though she often saw them in his eyes and in the way he cared for her. She loved him too, more now than ever, but she refused to let herself dwell on her feelings. It would only hurt worse if she confessed her heart to him. Both Stephen and Roger were well overdue. One day soon, they would appear, and she must be prepared for either.

October had turned to November and the land took on a death pall. Where there was once lush green foliage, now bare brown branches reached to the pale sky. The Mississippi was low—so low a few of the men had waded across to Crow Wing Island in water barely above their knees.

One afternoon, Charlotte stood outside the row house on her way back from the necessary and paused as large white tufts of snow fell from the sky. She lifted her hand, and one dropped into her palm and began to melt. As they fell to the cold, frozen ground, they collected, soon covering her whole world in a soft blanket.

The ugly brown earth was fresh and new again.

With a smile, Charlotte pushed open the door into the trading room and stepped inside.

Reid and Jean-Paul looked up from a piece of paper on the counter and stopped talking.

Charlotte stilled with her hand on the doorknob.

Reid's face was red with fury, and Jean-Paul's eyes were clouded with concern.

"Come in and close the door," Reid said, his voice hoarse. "This concerns you."

Her heart hammered as she closed the door.

The rage in Reid's face mixed with something more—panic? He looked as if he wanted to gather her in his arms, but he couldn't do that with Jean-Paul present.

"What's wrong?" she asked.

"An anonymous note slipped under the door moments after you left." Reid clutched the piece of paper in his hand. "Someone saw Lachlan and Daanis together the morning you were shot—and they saw Lachlan pull the trigger."

Charlotte's mouth slipped open. Who saw? And why had they waited so long to share the truth? Worse, what would keep Daanis from revealing Charlotte's secret now that Reid knew about Lachlan?

"Do you remember anything?" Reid asked. "Do you remember Lachlan shooting you? All I have is this note—and 'tis not even signed. 'Tis my word against his, unless you remember something. If we can prove he shot you, we can have him removed from his post and brought to trial for attempted murder."

And Reid would win the unseen war he battled with his half brother and father.

The desire to tell him the truth nearly choked her, but how could she? If she did, Daanis would reveal the truth about Charlotte, Reid would lose his job, and if Roger came, he'd force her back to England.

Reid moved around the counter and came to stand directly in front of Charlotte. "Do you remember who shot you, Charlie? 'Tis a simple question."

Her hands trembled and her stomach turned, but she had to look him in the eyes and lie. "No."

He studied her, his jaw tight. "I dinna believe you."

"Mr. Crawford is not on trial," Jean-Paul said to Reid, his voice patient and calm. "We will have to investigate this claim to see if it is true. I will ask Daanis to meet with us, and we can question her."

Reid clenched his jaw. "I willna get the truth out of her either."

It was the first time she saw disappointment in his gaze directed at her, and it hurt deeply.

Without another word, Reid grabbed his coat and hat off a hook.

"Where are you going?" Charlotte asked.

"I am going to speak to my brother and get the truth out of him."

Alarm seized her, and she put her hand on his arm to stop him. "Don't go, Reid."

"It isn't wise." Jean-Paul strode across the room. "You are angry, and you'll only make things worse."

He yanked his arm away from Charlotte and pulled his coat over his shoulders. "I willna let him get away with this." Reid met Charlotte's gaze, pain and anger mingling with fear. "He could have killed you, and for whatever reason, you're letting him get away with it. I won't."

"If you insist on going, let me come with you," Jean-Paul said.

"No." Reid grabbed his hat. "This is between me and my brother."

Charlotte gripped Reid's arm again, heedless of Jean-Paul. "Don't go. I beg you."

Reid did not listen—or if he did, he chose to ignore her, because he pulled away and left the row house without looking back.

The XY post stood before Reid in the falling snow like a formidable fortress, its tall pickets pointing toward the heavens like sentinels. Rage burned deep within his gut and propelled his feet to carry him over the distance on the frozen ground.

Reid didn't know what made him angrier, that Lachlan had shot Charlotte, or that she would lie about it. Why would she want to protect his brother?

The gates were open, and Reid walked into the stockade yard. One campfire burned to his right, and a woman stood near it, stirring dirty laundry in a cauldron. The snow fell into the water, melting before it touched the surface. She didn't pay him any attention as he crossed the yard and walked into the trading house.

Lachlan stood alone in the room, behind the counter, a ledger before him. When he glanced up, his eyes focused on Reid, and he braced his hands on either side of the book. "What do you want?"

Reid planted his feet and crossed his arms. He wasn't sure if he was older than Lachlan, or Lachlan was older than him—but it was clear that his father had created two families at the same time. Did either wife know about the other at the time? "I came to tell you I ken you shot Mr. Crawford."

Lachlan did not react, his chest rising and falling with deep breaths.

"And I willna let you get away with it," Reid said.

Lachlan straightened. "You have no proof."

"I have an eyewitness as well as Mr. Crawford's testimony." Reid took a step toward Lachlan, his hands balled into fists. "You will hang for attempted manslaughter."

"It will be your word against mine." Lachlan snorted in disgust. "Besides, this isna about your clerk. This is about our faither and your need for revenge."

Reid didn't respond.

It was about both.

"There are others," Lachlan said evenly. "I have three sisters and two brothers."

His father had six other children—besides Reid?

"He sent my brothers and me to Montreal to school." Lachlan walked around the counter to stand before Reid. "I saw you, many times at church and other places—and I laughed every time, because I knew that our faither chose to stay with me when he could have returned to you."

Anger blurred Reid's vision and made his hands shake with the need to punch the smug look off Lachlan's face.

"I wasna the only one to laugh." Lachlan looked Reid up and down, a smirk on his lips. "All my friends laughed too. You were a great joke to all of us."

Reid caught Lachlan's chin with his right fist, snapping his brother's head back. Lachlan fell against a shelf, sending several trade goods scattering to the floor. He touched his jaw and then barreled into Reid's gut, pinning him to the opposite wall.

Energy raced through Reid's limbs as he lost his footing and fell to the ground. Lachlan sat on top of him and threw punches into Reid's face, but Reid rolled and tossed him aside.

His brother scrambled to his feet and Reid followed, but Lachlan threw a punch before Reid could steady himself. It connected with Reid's nose. Blood began to flow from his nostrils. His jaw ached, but he would not back down.

This was about more than Lachlan. It was about all the years of pain and heartache his father had inflicted upon Reid and his mother. Reid had felt so helpless—until now. For the first time in his life, he could do something with his anger. He fought in a blind rage until the door flew open and three of Lachlan's voyageurs entered the trading room. They lifted Reid off the floor and held him as Lachlan rose, wiping blood from his lip.

Lachlan approached and punched Reid's gut several more times. Reid knew the moment his rib cracked. It sent searing pain through his chest, and he doubled over, his breath rushing from his lungs.

"Toss him out of the fort," Lachlan demanded. "And if you see him anywhere near here again, show him what happens to the unwanted trash."

"I will prove you shot Mr. Crawford," Reid gasped. "And you will hang."

Lachlan laughed and then winced, holding his side. "You canna prove anything."

The voyageurs pulled Reid from the trading house before he could respond to Lachlan and threw him onto the frozen ground just beyond the fort gates. Reid tried to stand, but stumbled and fell, gritting his teeth from the pain.

Lachlan came to the open gate, hatred seething from his face. "This is not the end. You will hear from me soon—and you will regret coming here."

Reid pulled himself from the ground, breathing hard. His brother could threaten all he wanted, but the truth would prevail, and Lachlan would be removed from his post. It might take time, but eventually Reid would win the trade war.

And he'd finally be able to face his father as the victor.

# Chapter Twenty-Four

Charlotte paced in front of the fireplace as she waited for Reid to return. Since there had been no visitors, she had closed the trading room and stoked the fire several times in the living quarters, but there was little else to do. She wasn't hungry, but she began to prepare a simple meal of rubbaboo. She boiled water, added the pemmican, allowed it to break down, and then added some root vegetables and flour to thicken it into a stew. The smell wafting from the pot should have made her stomach growl but turned it, instead.

With a sigh, she moved the stew out of the flames and set a cover over the pot before she began to pace again.

Finally, the door opened, and Reid stepped into the row house.

Charlotte stopped pacing and stared at him as he closed the door. She moved forward, but her breath stilled at the sight of him. Dried blood covered his lips, his chin, and the front of his coat. A bruise darkened the side of his face, and a cut on his eyebrow swelled. Snowflakes covered his back, shoulders, and bare head.

She went to the medicine chest, but he stopped her with his low, dark voice. "Dinna." He limped to the chest, holding his ribs with his right hand. "I'll see to my own wounds."

"Let me help." She opened the chest.

He slammed the lid closed and she jumped back.

"I said no." He lifted the chest in his left hand and cringed as he walked to the door leading to the hallway.

He opened the door and walked through, slamming it shut with his foot.

Silence filled the living quarters, and Charlotte was left alone once again.

Despite his anger, he would need help, even if he didn't want it. But would he turn her out if she offered? She hated that she had lied to him—and hated even more that he was angry and hurt because of her.

She walked into the hall, not giving him a choice. Opening his door, she found him with his shirt off trying to wrap binding around his ribs. It slipped off and he growled.

"Leave me," he said.

"You need help."

"I'd rather not have your help right now."

Charlotte walked across the short space to where he stood by his bed. "I know you're angry with me, but don't let your stubbornness cause you more pain." She took the binding from his hands and started to wind it around his chest. "Besides, I know a thing or two about doing this."

He let out his breath and gritted his teeth, but he allowed her to help him.

She walked around him, pulling the fabric tight, glancing up at his face at each pass. He held his arms high to allow her to move freely.

Even with bruises, his chest was just as magnificent as it had been those weeks they'd slept in the same tent.

"I'm sorry I lied to you."

He kept his face free from emotion or reaction and did not respond.

When she finished with the binding, she went to his trunk and found a clean shirt. She helped him pull it over his head. "Did you hurt him?"

"Not as much as I had hoped."

Slowly, she buttoned the top half of the shirt, her knuckles brushing against his chest. He tensed each time she grazed his body—but not from pain, she was certain.

"Sit and I'll tend to your wounds." She finished the last button and nodded at the chair.

He sat and she went to the living quarters to get some fresh water and rags.

When she returned to Reid, he watched her cross the room, his brow furrowed. "Though I've been guilty of it myself, I canna abide lying, Charlotte."

She closed her eyes at the sting in his words, then dipped the rag into the water to clean the blood from his face. "Daanis knows I'm a woman. If I had told you who shot me, she would have told everyone my secret."

He sighed and closed his eyes briefly. "If I accuse Lachlan, Daanis will reveal the truth about you?"

She nodded.

"You did it to protect me?"

Again, she nodded.

He didn't speak or move for several moments. "I canna beat him." He took the rag and wiped his lips and chin.

When he was done, he handed her the rag and she rinsed it, then cleaned a spot on his chin that he missed. She took out the witch hazel and drenched a piece of lint to dab at his cuts.

She stood between his knees and placed her left hand on his shoulder as she used her right one to work on his face.

He exhaled another deep breath and set one hand on her hip.

She briefly closed her eyes at his touch, feeling the weight of his hand all the way to her heart.

"I ken you're sorry—and I apologize for reacting the way I did." His thumb rubbed the front of her belly. "My anger was mostly for Lachlan, but I never suspected that you would lie for him."

"I didn't want to lie for him, but I didn't have much choice."

He nodded and put his other hand on her right hip, pulling her slightly toward him.

She dropped her hand away from his face and set it on his shoulder. She should have known that being this close to Reid would lead to more intimacy. How could it not? They were drawn to one another like a wave to the shore.

Reid set his forehead against her stomach and wrapped his arms around her. "Charlotte, I find myself leaning on you in every way. What did I do before you were a part of my life? Who did I turn to in times of trouble?"

"I've caused you even more trouble since the day we met."

He shook his head. "You have been a balm for my weary soul. What will I do without you?"

"We can't think about the future," she whispered, her voice breaking. "Or the past."

"That's all I can think about. My future looks as bleak and barren as the winter without you by my side."

He tugged her until she sat on his knee and then he put his hands on either side of her face and looked deeply into her eyes. "Marry me, lass. We'll find a way to make it work."

Pain and yearning warred within her chest, stealing her breath. "It would never work." She knew, because she'd lain awake for hours over the past few months trying to find a way.

"I love you." He leaned forward and captured her mouth with his. This kiss was not breathless and passionate, like the others, but slow and sweet. It wasn't longing that fueled his lips—but love, pure and honest.

Charlotte was the one to pull back, though she did not pull away from his hands.

"Say you love me, Charlotte, even if you canna marry me." His hand was still on her cheek. "I see it in your eyes, but my heart aches to hear the words."

Tears gathered in her eyes as the truth warmed her entire being. She did not need to be prodded to tell him. "I love you, Reid. I've loved you since the night we danced under the stars."

His face softened, and he kissed her again. "Then marry me."

"You know it would never work. You're married to the fur trade."

"I would give it all up for you."

She could see in his eyes that he meant it.

"I could never ask you to do that." He loved the fur trade—had devoted fifteen years of his life to it.

"You wouldna need to ask me. I'd do it because I love you and I never want to leave your side. There is nothing on this earth more important than you."

"You would give up your dream and return to England with me?"

"I would go to the ends of the earth with you."

"What about Lachlan?"

Sudden, unchecked rage passed over his face, and he stiffened.

"You can't leave—not when you're so close to your goal." Charlotte knew it well. "And I need a husband now. I need to return to England as soon as possible and reclaim my inheritance." She dropped her gaze and tried not to cry. "More importantly, I've made a promise to Stephen. I couldn't break that promise in good conscience—and neither could you."

"I hate Stephen," Reid said quietly.

"You do not," she chided him.

"I hate that he found you before I did."

"You would have never found me if I hadn't come looking for him."

He didn't respond.

"Stephen is a good man." She tried to convince herself. "He will make a good husband."

"Will he kiss you the way I do?" He captured her mouth again, this time with a fervency that both thrilled and frightened her—not because Reid scared her, but because she might never experience such passion again.

"No one will ever kiss me the way you do," she said as she pulled away, breathless.

"And no one will ever love you like I do." He removed the strap of fabric holding her hair back and ran his fingers through the curls.

Charlotte briefly closed her eyes and leaned into his touch, knowing that their time together could not last, but wanting to hold him close for as long as possible.

"When Stephen comes for you, I will try to convince him not to marry you," he promised. "I will not hide my feelings from him. He will know I want you."

She offered him a sad smile.

"But he willna listen," Reid said. "Not when you are the prize, lass."

Charlotte rose and placed her palm against his cheek. "Try to rest."

He turned his head and kissed her palm.

"McCoy!" Loud pounding came from the front door. "Open up!"

Reid frowned as they both stood.

"Who is that?" she asked.

The front door slammed open, the shouts of several men filling the air.

Moving with surprising speed, given his tender state, Reid left his room. Charlotte followed, tying her hair back again.

Lachlan stood in the living quarters, a dozen of his men standing outside. The sun hung low in the sky, offering enough daylight to allow Charlotte to see the cuts and bruises on his face.

"Why have you come?" Reid demanded.

The men moved to the side, revealing a limp body in the center of the stockade yard.

"I am here for justice," Lachlan said.

"Justice?" Reid's lips curled in anger.

"I'm here to see that you hang for the death of Nicolas LeBlanc." Lachlan's eyes were narrowed, and his breath came fast.

"The death of who?" Reid's confusion was swift.

"Nicolas LeBlanc, the man you killed at my post this afternoon." Lachlan lifted his chin. "I have a dozen witnesses who saw you plunge your knife into his chest."

"I did no such thing."

"What's the meaning of this?" Jean-Paul pushed his way through the crowd, which now included some of Reid's men. His alarmed gaze passed over the dead body.

"I'm here to charge Reid McCoy with the death of Nicolas LeBlanc." Lachlan's steely gaze never wavered from Reid's.

Jean-Paul frowned and looked at Reid, a question in his eyes.

"I dinna ken what he's talking about." Concern deepened Reid's brow.

Daanis pushed her way through the crowd and joined Lachlan, fear and uncertainty in her eyes as she looked at him.

"Reid would never do such a thing," Jean-Paul said.

"Look at him." Lachlan pointed at Reid. "He's clearly been in a brawl."

"With you," Reid snarled.

Jacques was the next to push his way into the living quarters. He stood beside Reid and glared at Lachlan.

"Leave this post immediately," Jean-Paul said to Lachlan with authority. "Reid is innocent."

"You believe him innocent?" Lachlan asked.

"As innocent as myself." Jean-Paul lifted his chin. "I've never known Reid to lie. He's the most honest man I know."

"If he's so honest"—Lachlan's gaze turned to Charlotte—"then why has he kept his mistress a secret from everyone for these many months?"

Charlotte's mouth slipped open, and her heart rate escalated while Reid took a protective step toward her.

"His what?" Jean-Paul turned to see who Lachlan was looking at—and his gaze collided with Charlotte's.

"Mr. Crawford is not who you think he—she is." Lachlan walked across the room and rounded Charlotte. "She is his lover."

"I am not." Charlotte's indignation rose, but even as she denied Lachlan's claim, guilt and shame burned her cheeks as she remembered the stolen moments she and Reid had shared.

Jean-Paul moved closer to Charlotte, looking at her with new eyes. "You're a woman?"

Charlotte met Reid's troubled gaze. There was no way to keep the truth hidden any longer. Despite her best efforts, everyone would know that they had been lying.

She couldn't look at Reid any longer. "Yes."

Jean-Paul's face grew pale. A hush fell over the crowd as every eye turned to Charlotte.

"You knew this?" Jean-Paul asked Reid.

Reid's jaw clenched, causing his cheek muscles to jump. "Aye—but 'tis not what you think. She is not my mistress. She came to find her fiancé."

"Apprehend them both!" Lachlan cried. "And turn them over to your superiors."

Lachlan's men yelled out their agreement, while Charlotte's legs grew weak and Daanis grabbed Lachlan's arm, shaking her head frantically.

Within seconds, Charlotte was in the custody of several dozen angry voyageurs who now knew she was a woman.

The days and nights were arduous and freezing as they traveled by canoe from Crow Wing to Fond du Lac, at the far western tip of Lake Superior. The journey that had taken them seven weeks in the middle of summer only took a week when traveling without cargo or dozens of men. There were no packages to haul over portages, no need to stop for illnesses or injuries, and no mosquitoes to contend with.

Charlotte was kept away from Reid and forced to sleep in a tent with Daanis, who had been ordered, along with Lachlan, to be a witness at Reid's hearing. They were also separated into two canoes. In Reid's canoe, Lachlan and Jean-Paul kept him under guard with four voyageurs to paddle. In Charlotte's canoe, she was guarded by Jacques and Daanis, along with three other voyageurs who paddled the twelve-hour days.

Though it was cold and had already snowed, the lakes and rivers were still open and navigable, though there were fringes of ice along the edges of most of them.

They had left at first light the morning after Reid had been accused of murder. Charlotte and Reid had been allowed to bring along their own possessions, but all she had were her drawings and three pairs of clothes. When Jean-Paul had asked her if she'd like to change into a dress, she chose to travel in her suit, which was warmer and more conducive to canoeing.

At night when they stopped to camp, Daanis prepared their meals, and the thirteen of them sat in utter silence. Reid's and Lachlan's bruises had turned from a deep purple to a greenish, yellow color. Though he was healing, Reid's ribs still bothered him, and he often winced when he got in and out of his canoe, or when he had to sit or rise from the ground. Charlotte wanted to ease his pain, but she was completely helpless. The best she could offer was a smile now and again, but even that was not enough to lighten his dark mood.

On the afternoon of their seventh day, the fort at Fond du Lac appeared on the edge of the St. Louis River Bay, which emptied out of Lake Superior. Charlotte had seen it before, when they had left Grand Portage and entered the deep interior. But shrouded in snow, with stormy gray clouds hanging low overhead, it looked inhospitable—especially because she and Reid would have to face harsh charges once they stepped inside those stockade walls.

Charlotte shivered in her wool coat as the canoe glided to a stop at the pier positioned at the base of the fort. It was four times as large as their

post at Crow Wing and housed the region's manager, Mr. Joseph Mc-
Donnell. It was one of the largest inland depots, besides Grand Portage,
and was at the head of the Folle Avoine District.

Jacques jumped out and offered his hand to Charlotte and then to
Daanis. Just behind them, Jean-Paul held the other canoe to allow Reid
and Lachlan to disembark. Since Reid had not resisted his arrest, they
did not wield any weapons to keep him or Charlotte in line, so they both
walked up to the fort's gates of their own free will.

Reid drew up beside her. "Dinna fash, lass." His face was without
emotion as they continued up the banks of the river. "I willna go down
without a fight."

That was what worried her. She knew Reid was innocent—but he had
no witnesses to speak on his behalf, and the only people who could speak
for his character would also have to admit that he had hidden a woman
among his men all these months. He would have to fight for his life if he
hoped to go free.

If he was found guilty, he could face imprisonment in Montreal—or
the gallows at Fort Fond du Lac. It would be at the discretion of Mr.
McDonnell.

Over a hundred people called Fond du Lac home, and an island just
off the shores of Lake Superior, within sight of the fort, was home to a
large village of Chippewa Indians. The two groups intermingled, which
meant several dozen women and children were also at the fort that day.

Their arrival did not stir up much interest, though Mr. McDonnell
was summoned by a voyageur. When he exited his two-story home, a
smile of greeting lit his face, which told Charlotte that he had no idea
why they had come. But how could he?

"Mr. McDonnell?" Lachlan broke apart from the group and approached the fort commander.

"Aye?" Mr. McDonnell extended his hand. "And you are?"

"Lachlan McCoy of the XY Company post at Crow Wing." He did not take Mr. McDonnell's hand. "I am here with Reid McCoy as my prisoner."

Mr. McDonnell's smile disappeared, and he looked sharply at Reid. "What is this about?"

Reid took a step forward, but Jean-Paul put his hand on Reid's arm.

"Can we speak somewhere privately?" Lachlan asked Mr. McDonnell.

"Of course." Mr. McDonnell motioned for the group to enter his home.

The voyageurs in their company stayed outside, except for Jean-Paul, so it was just Reid, Lachlan, Daanis, Charlotte, and the guide who entered McDonnell's home.

The front room was wide and long and contained several pieces of furniture. Plank floors ran from one end to the other, and large rag rugs were situated around the room, giving it a surprisingly comfortable feel—though Charlotte felt anything but comfort at the moment. An enormous fireplace dominated the end of the room with a fire crackling within.

"What is going on, Reid?" Mr. McDonnell's gaze slipped over the group assembled and landed on Charlotte. A question flashed within his eyes before he looked back at Reid.

"This man forced his way into my post seven days past," Lachlan said to Mr. McDonnell, "with the sole intention to attack me."

"Is that true, Reid?" Mr. McDonnell asked.

Reid stood with his feet spread apart, his eyes hard. "Aye."

"Why?"

"We have had better success with the trade," Lachlan said, "and he was angry."

"That is not why I attacked you." Reid almost spat out the words. "I was there to confront you about shooting my clerk."

"'Tis a lie," Lachlan said. "He is jealous and wanted a reason to attack me."

Mr. McDonnell took a seat and told the others to sit as well. "Why have you arrested him?" he asked Lachlan.

"While he was at my post, his anger was directed at several of my men." Lachlan stopped and swallowed, as if it was hard to speak. "He stabbed one of my voyageurs, Nicolas LeBlanc, who later died from his wounds."

"It isna true," Reid said, his jaw tight. "I did not touch anyone but Lachlan—and I dinna have my knife that day. I dinna ken where he got my knife."

Daanis dropped her gaze, and Charlotte suddenly knew where the knife had come from. Daanis had come into Reid's post that long ago morning before Charlotte had been shot. She'd probably taken it then as part of Lachlan's plans to frame Reid.

"I am here with three of my men who all witnessed the event," Lachlan said.

Mr. McDonnell's eyes were sharp and squinted. "You expect me to believe that one of my most trusted men killed an XY voyageur—based solely on your word? I've known Reid for over a decade and have never seen him hurt anyone. There isna anyone I trust more than him."

Lachlan shook his head, as if all of them were daft. "Then how do you explain the woman he's kept as his mistress this year?"

Every eye in the room turned to Charlotte—except Reid's and Daanis's. Even Mr. McDonnell seemed to know exactly who to look at—as if he already suspected as much.

"Is it true?" Mr. McDonnell asked Charlotte.

"I am not his mistress," Charlotte said evenly, prepared to defend herself and Reid. "I am Lady Charlotte Fairfax, and I sought Mr. McCoy in Montreal to help me find my fiancé, Stephen Corning." She took a deep, steadying breath. "Reid owed Stephen a debt for saving his life. He agreed to take me as far as Grand Portage, where I was supposed to meet with Stephen, but Stephen had been ill and remained at the Upper Red River fort."

"And where is Mr. Corning now?"

Charlotte shrugged. "He was supposed to come for me at Crow Wing, but he has not arrived." She leaned forward, trying to beseech the man. "Reid was not keen on taking me, but I gave him little choice. If anyone is to blame, it is me."

Mr. McDonnell let out a long, weary sigh. "Reid, you ken the rules."

"Aye," Reid agreed. "But I also ken she was in grave danger if I dinna take her along."

"Danger?" Mr. McDonnell asked.

"From my guardian," Charlotte offered. "I was forced to flee my home in England where he kept me a prisoner."

Mr. McDonnell frowned, the lines between his eyebrows deep and unforgiving. "I've been entertaining an English gentleman for several weeks. When he first arrived, he was so ill, I advised him not to go looking for you."

Alarm hammered in Charlotte's heart as she held her breath.

"But he's well now and would very much like to learn you're here." Mr. McDonnell crossed his arms. "He's come a long way to find you. He's concerned for your safety, lass. The fur trade is no place for a lady. You belong back in England under his watchful care."

So, Roger had charmed Mr. McDonnell into believing his lies. Anger and panic brought her to her feet. "He doesn't care about me—only about my inheritance." Charlotte swallowed the fear racing up her throat.

Mr. McDonnell stood and strode to a doorway leading into the next room. "Mr. Rutherford?"

Roger had been in the next room the whole time?

Charlotte's legs shook as she started to move toward the front door. Her desire to flee was fierce—but Lachlan stepped into her path and stopped her.

Roger appeared, a look of hatred and triumph mingling on his arrogant face. He started toward Charlotte, but Reid sprang from his chair and grabbed Roger by the lapels of his expensive coat. He pushed Roger against the wall, and Charlotte screamed.

Jean-Paul and Mr. McDonnell leapt to action and pulled Reid away from Roger.

"Stay away from her," Reid warned Roger.

Roger straightened his lapels and stretched his neck. "I've come too far and withstood more than my fair share of hardship to leave her here." He continued toward Charlotte. "You are a spoiled, vain child, and you will return with me to Blissfield Manor immediately. I have employed several guides who will take us to Montreal, posthaste. We will return home and be married by the Church of England."

"No." Charlotte shook her head. "I will not go with you."

"You don't have a choice, Charlotte. I am your legal guardian, and until you are twenty-one, I oversee your affairs." He smiled, his mustache twitching with delight. "The law is on my side—and these men cannot do anything to stop me."

Reid tried to pull away from Jean-Paul and Mr. McDonnell, but they held him tight. His face pinched with pain, and she wanted to beg him to stop trying—to stop hurting himself—but she also wanted his help.

"Thank you for your hospitality," Roger said to Mr. McDonnell. "But I plan to leave in the morning with Lady Charlotte."

"Is that what you desire, Lady Charlotte?" Mr. McDonnell asked, concern on his face.

Before she could speak, Roger stepped between her and the fort commander. "She has no say in the matter."

"I will marry her," Reid said, trying to pull free.

"You have other things to worry about right now," Mr. McDonnell said, resolve replacing his concern. "Mr. Rutherford must take Lady Charlotte home where she belongs."

"What will you do with Reid?" Lachlan asked Mr. McDonnell.

The older man sighed and looked toward Reid. "Perhaps you did help Lady Charlotte out of obligation to your debt—but a rule is a rule, and you have broken it. I have no choice but to apprehend you and charge you with two crimes—both of which require a trial." He looked disappointed and saddened. "You are charged with bringing a European woman into the interior without consent, and you are accused of the murder of an XY Company voyageur. Both charges will strip you of your job with the North West Company, and one will hold the penalty of death or imprisonment, if proven true."

Charlotte wanted to scream or cry, to throw herself on the mercy of Mr. McDonnell—but there was nothing she could do to change Reid's fate. Jean-Paul, Mr. McDonnell—and even Daanis—looked like they were just as upset as Charlotte. It was only Lachlan and Roger who were triumphant.

# Chapter Twenty-Five

Reid had not slept all night. From his room in Joseph's home, he had a view of the St. Louis River Bay and massive Lake Superior beyond. The windows were made of real glass, and he was able to watch the day approach, though the low-lying clouds hid the rising sun.

Below him, several voyageurs were already awake, building fires, hauling wood, and carrying water. Beyond the stockade, near the bay a small party had gathered to begin a long voyage back to Montreal. This was the group that kept him near the window.

As winter set in, it was inadvisable to travel—but a good guide would have no trouble navigating the landscape. Reid just prayed that the guides Rutherford had hired were the best.

He pressed his forehead against the cold glass as he watched Charlotte enter a canoe with Rutherford. She glanced behind her at the stockade—but she was so far away, there was no possibility she could see him, especially with the lake's reflection on the window. He could see her, though. She was still dressed in her clerk's clothing for the journey, and she carried her bag. Had she taken her pictures? Did she have the one of him? Or had Rutherford made her leave that behind?

Reid felt helpless, locked in this room, unable to save her from a life of unimaginable pain and unhappiness. He had thought about his options last night and had found no other course but the one set before them. If he had escaped with her, they would be tracked down and returned to this same spot—but with more speculation as to their innocence. She was so close—yet out of reach in every way possible. His own uncertain future meant little to him compared to hers.

"Mr. McCoy?" Someone called to him as the door was unlocked. "Mr. McDonnell would like to see you."

Reid hated to pull himself away from the window—to not watch Charlotte for as long as possible. But he did not want to anger Joseph, so he looked at Charlotte one more time and then stepped through the open door to follow the clerk down the hall. They came to a set of stairs, which they took to the lower level, and walked through another hall to Joseph's office. This room also faced the St. Louis River and the pier where Charlotte was about to leave with Rutherford.

Joseph sat at his desk, his face lined with fatigue. When Reid appeared, he motioned for him to have a seat and excused his clerk to allow them some privacy.

"You have brought me a great deal of strife." Joseph steepled his hands together and touched his fingers to his lips. "I believe you when you say you dinna kill the XY man—but your honesty is now in question because of the lass."

"Aye." Reid glanced out the window. Charlotte's canoe was just leaving the pier. His chest felt as if it would split open from the wrenching pain that jarred him at seeing her leave. It was one thing for him to never see her again—that alone was the greatest sorrow of his life—but it was another entirely to know she was with Rutherford and Reid could no longer protect her. He'd failed Charlotte, and that was something he couldn't bear.

"I have sent two couriers to nearby posts where shareholders are wintering," Joseph said. "I have also sent couriers to two XY posts to ask for representatives, since the man who was murdered was in their employ. When everyone arrives, they will help me oversee your trial." Joseph dropped his hands into his lap. "I canna be impartial. Hopefully they will arrive within the next week or so."

A week or more before his trial? He'd been hoping that if he could have his trial sooner and prove his innocence, maybe there would still be time to go after Charlotte and save her from Rutherford. "Until then?"

"Until then, you will be on house arrest. You canna leave this building under any circumstances, but you will be free to move about." Joseph leaned forward. "I am allowing you this privilege because I believe you are innocent. Do not make me think otherwise."

Reid appreciated his friend's offer. It would help speed his week if he was not confined to a room—or worse. But it didn't matter where he resided. With Charlotte gone, it would be the longest, hardest week of his life.

"I also sent my fastest courier to your post." Joseph stood and walked to the window. "I sent him to look for other witnesses who would speak on your behalf about this incident."

"You will not take Lachlan at his word?"

Turning, Joseph gave Reid a scathing look—hopefully it wasn't meant for him but rather for the XY man who had accused Reid.

"I am hoping that my courier will arrive at your post within a few days and will come back with one or two men who can shed more light on this matter."

"I received an anonymous letter from someone who claimed they saw Lachlan shoot Charlotte. I have the letter with me."

"That will not prove your innocence."

"No, but it will prove he is heartless and a liar." Reid clenched his jaw. "What if your courier can find no other witnesses to speak on my behalf?"

Joseph put his hand on the window frame and leaned against it while he watched his small kingdom beyond the house. "Then I will only have the statements from Lachlan and his voyageurs to take into consideration."

Reid prayed it would not come to that. Lachlan would say and do anything to see Reid hang.

A northwesterly wind whipped at the canoe, which hugged the shoreline of Lake Superior. Charlotte bent her head low, dipping her chin into the top of her coat, trying to stay warm. The four voyageurs who paddled the canoe had fought against the strong wind and waves all day. Though it had been almost nine hours since they had left Fond du Lac, they had not gone far. The guide, Bernard, was an old, wrinkled voyageur. He had tried on several occasions to get Roger to pull to shore, but Roger had adamantly refused, wanting to make as much progress as possible.

Whitecaps formed on the lake, and the gray clouds overhead started to let loose the snow.

"We will camp," the guide called out in Chippewa.

Charlotte understood his order, but Roger did not, so when the boat started to move toward shore, he yelled at the men to keep going.

None of them listened.

"Our lives are in danger," Charlotte said to Roger. "The guide has told them it's time to camp."

"But there is still daylight." Roger turned to address the guide, who sat behind them in the small canoe. His movement caused the vessel to tip from side to side, and Charlotte held on to the edge, trying to help balance it, so they wouldn't turn over in the deep, frigid waters.

"He will not be swayed," Charlotte said. "It's too hazardous to stay on the water. The waves are only getting worse."

Roger didn't listen to her but started making demands of the guide—who completely ignored him.

Charlotte was thankful that they would make camp and get out of the wind. Her fingers and toes were numb from the cold, and her teeth had not stopped chattering since they'd left early that morning. She had tried to dress for the elements but found very little to keep her warm sitting for hours on end in the canoe.

She didn't mind being numb. She was afraid that if she allowed herself to think about Reid and everything he faced, she would start crying and never stop. Her own dismal future paled in comparison to the thought of him being found guilty of murder. So she had sat, almost lethargic, as the canoe had plied through the tumultuous waters of Lake Superior.

They found a pebbly beach with a steep cliff hanging overhead, creating a sheltered alcove away from the wind. As before, the voyageurs would not land the canoe on shore, for fear of puncturing the thin birch bark, but this time—since they knew Charlotte was a lady—they did not allow her to step out of the boat into the water. The voyageurs stepped out first, and without their weight to hold it down, the boat floated higher on the water, allowing them to pull it closer to shore, so she could jump out on a nearby rock. She thanked them for their thoughtfulness, conscious that her treatment toward them could go a long way in how painful or pleasant her journey might be—if pleasant was an option.

Roger's wrath had been simmering all day, and every time he met her eye, she saw the promise of retribution within their depths. He would not let her behavior go unpunished—but what did he plan to do to her? She didn't want to care about him or anything else.

"You two start a fire, while you two pitch my tent," Roger demanded of the men. He'd hired them, so they were at his command.

One of the men produced a steel and flint, while another gathered bits and pieces of tinder from the driftwood scattered around the pebbly beach. Charlotte started to help, but the voyageur shook his head. "No, my lady. I will gather the wood."

For the first time that day, she noticed how the men glanced shyly at her.

"Are you a real lady?" the one with flint and steel asked.

"Do not speak to Lady Charlotte unless absolutely necessary," Roger snapped at him.

Obviously embarrassed, the man returned to the growing pile of wood and struck the flint against the steel, creating sparks, which soon caught the tinder on fire. Slowly, and patiently, he fed that small flame until it was a roaring campfire. Charlotte and Roger stood beside it, drawing heat, while the men started a second fire for themselves.

The tent was also pitched in record time, and their few belongings were brought inside. Charlotte had taken all her pictures and carefully rolled them and tied them with a piece of string. They were in her one bag, which the second voyageur moved from the canoe to the tent as if it held the most precious jewels in the world.

"I want you inside the tent," Roger said to Charlotte when the men had finally moved to their own campfire to begin the evening meal.

"Now? Before bed?" She didn't want to be in the tent with him—didn't know what he planned to do with her once they were out of sight. Memories of the night she had fled Blissfield Manor returned, and she shook from more than just the cold.

"Do not test my patience, Charlotte. We are in this godforsaken place because of you."

She nervously moved away from the warmth of the fire and glanced over her shoulder at the other fire. All five men watched her.

Frowns and uncertainty met her gaze—but none of them tried to interfere.

Roger followed her into the tent and tied the flaps closed. It was much like the tent she had shared with Reid, though there were no cots within—just several layers of furs and blankets on the ground.

When he finally turned to her, his entire body was rigid, and he breathed heavily. "I cannot begin to tell you how much money this little foray has cost us."

Us? It was her money he was using. He was as poor as a tenant farmer—and might be reduced to one if he did not marry her.

"You have stolen nine months of our lives—months we could have been enjoying at Blissfield Manor as husband and wife."

"I would never enjoy being your wife."

He struck her with the back of his hand.

The sting was so sharp—and so sudden—it took the air out of her lungs.

"You will never address me with such disrespect again—do you hear me?"

She stared at him, her hand holding her burning cheek.

"We will not wait for England—in case you try to run again. I will be your husband the moment we arrive in Montreal." He came close to her, his foul breath burning her nose. "You will obey me, or I will be forced to punish you."

"I will not obey you," she said in defiance. "I will do everything in my power to escape again and again."

He struck her again, harder, and this time she stumbled over the blankets. She fell with a thud, jabbing her elbow and hip into the frozen ground, and cried out in pain.

Tears stung the back of her eyes. "I will despise you until the day I die."

"I don't care if you despise me—I hope you do. It will make it more enjoyable for me if you hate me."

"Let her alone," a voice called out from the other side of the tent.

Someone grabbed the flaps and tried to tug them loose, shaking the whole structure.

"Leave us alone!" Roger yelled. "This is between me and the lady."

"Exactly," someone said, tearing the flap open. "She's a lady."

All the men, including the guide, stood outside the tent. Bernard reached inside and pulled Roger out by the nape of his neck. "You will not hurt the lady," he said in French.

"Unhand me!" Roger's face was red, and his eyes bulged with anger. "It's none of your business what I do. I'm paying you to transport us and nothing more."

"It's our business if you hurt the lady." Bernard was old, but he was thick in the chest, and Roger would be no match for him. He turned and looked at Charlotte. "Do you wish to go with this man?"

Tears streaked down Charlotte's face as she shook her head. "I want to go back to Fond du Lac."

The guide nodded. "I will take you back in the morning."

"No." Roger struggled to get away. "She is my ward and will do as I say."

"We are not in England anymore," another voyageur said with a smile. "We are in the northwest wilderness, where there are no laws, and women are free to come and go as they please."

Everything Charlotte had learned about the Indian women told her he was right—and these men would honor that culture, even though she was an English lady.

"Merci," she said to them, her tears falling unchecked, though she wished she could say and do more.

"I will guard him during the first watch." Bernard still held Roger by the back of his coat. "And you will rest, Lady Charlotte."

"I will take the second watch," said another.

"In the morning," the guide told Roger, "we will leave you here with your tent and some food and take the lady back to the fort."

Roger stopped sputtering in anger. The color drained from his face. "You cannot leave me here alone! You are my employees."

"Not anymore." The guide went to his belongings and found a rope, which he brought back to their small gathering. "We have no respect for a man who mistreats a lady. You will spend the night tied to a tree, so you cannot harm her anymore."

Charlotte's mouth fell open at the plan.

"The lady will have the tent," the voyageur said. "Alone."

The men carried Roger off to the nearest tree, where they tied him. He yelled obscenities and threatened to have them all hanged—though the men just laughed. They were courier du bois—independent fur traders and voyageurs who answered to no man but themselves.

Charlotte sat around their fire as they prepared her a meal. They were sheltered from the worst of the wind and snow in their little alcove. Though she was dressed like any number of clerks they must have met over the years, the men continued to treat her like royalty.

But now that her identity was known, Charlotte didn't try to hide her femininity any longer. On the way from Fort McCoy, she had quickly reverted to her old mannerisms, and she found herself enjoying the men's attention, given the circumstances.

Best of all, the thought of returning to Reid in the morning made her almost happy. Though, the only way she would be truly glad was if he was free from Lachlan's accusation.

Just as they were about to eat and Roger had finally quieted, a lone canoe paddled toward them, hugging the shoreline. Snow and wind continued to beat against the lake, but the canoe made good time.

Two men sat in the canoe, both paddling.

Bernard stood and called to the men to join them on shore.

When they were finally within sight, Charlotte's breath stilled, as her heart skipped a beat.

There, sitting in the bow of the canoe, was a man she would recognize anywhere—though she hadn't seen him in five years.

"Stephen."

He saw her at the same moment.

Their gazes connected, and she suddenly felt faint. He had finally come to marry her—and it wasn't too late.

She stood on shaky legs, the voyageurs hovering around her, and walked toward the shores of Lake Superior.

When the boat was close enough to land, Stephen jumped into the water at the same time as the other man, and they hoisted the canoe over their heads to bring it on shore. Water dripped from the sides of the canoe, raining down around them as they walked.

Stephen was no longer the boy she remembered. He carried himself with confidence and authority. He was broader and more muscular than she remembered, and his face had matured into that of a grown man.

Though she wouldn't call him handsome, neither was he unpleasant to look upon. His blue eyes were like that of the lake on a clear, bright day, and his hair had darkened, though most of it was covered under his hat.

He wore the clothes of a bourgeois. Tight trousers, tall black boots, a dark wool coat. Once he set the canoe on the ground, he moved toward her, his powerful legs steady and sure.

"Charlotte." He said her name like a prayer—one she was sure he had breathed countless times in the past two years.

Though he felt like a stranger in some ways, in others, he was as real and familiar and dear to her as he had been when they were children. She ran to him and threw every precaution aside. When she entered his embrace, it was not romance or protection she sought but familiarity and understanding. Besides Reid, Stephen was her greatest ally, coming all this way to marry her and keep her from Roger's grasp.

He smelled of campfire and cedar, and though it was good to finally be with him, it also felt awkward to be in his arms. He felt nothing like Reid—and he did not elicit any of the same feelings she had when she was standing in Reid's arms—but he was the man who had promised to marry her and save her from Roger.

"Am I too late?" he asked.

She pulled away and looked up into his worried face. "No. You've come just in time."

He tried to smile—but the concern in his eyes was far too great. "Just in time to marry you?"

"Yes—but just in time to help me prove Reid is innocent as well." Because she knew of one way she might gain Reid's freedom—though it would take another miracle—one she prayed she would receive.

# Chapter Twenty-Six

The next morning, the storm had not let up, but Charlotte could not wait another day to return to Reid.

"Are you sure you want to go now?" Stephen asked as they stood huddled around a campfire in the early morning light.

"The wind will be at our back?" she asked.

"Yes—but the waves look formidable." He was gentle with her—far too gentle—almost like a skittish lamb. Part of her wanted to test the limit to which he would allow her to push him, because she longed for him to take command. But he didn't.

"How long will it take us to return to Fond du Lac?" she asked Bernard.

"Maybe six hours, since the wind will be at your back." Bernard ate from a cup, the warm rubbaboo steaming into the frosty air. "But I will not go back with you." He nodded at Stephen and the guide Stephen had hired to get him from the Upper Red River to Crow Wing, where they had learned that they had missed Reid and Charlotte by two days.

"Where will you go?"

"The men and I have decided to take Monsieur Rutherford to Montreal, as he requested." He smiled at Charlotte, and his eyes danced. "He hired us to take him there, and that is what we will do."

Roger was still tied to a tree, though he had been fed and given a blanket to ward off the worst of the chill. He stared at Charlotte now, his eyes filled with hatred.

"You will be free to return to the fort and be married by the priest." Bernard nodded encouragingly.

Roger was close enough to hear, and he spat on the ground.

Charlotte stepped away from the fire and went to stand before her guardian. "Do you hear that? I will marry Stephen and will return to England as the rightful heir of Blissfield Manor." Now that she was free of his threats and power over her, she almost felt sorry for him. "You are not allowed to step foot on my property. I am sending a letter with Monsieur Bernard, which will be delivered to my solicitor in London. He will see that my wishes are carried out." In her letter, she would tell her solicitor to fire all the staff Roger had hired—and those who had conspired against her. Only Stephen's parents would be retained. A whole new staff would have to be hired. The thought was a bit daunting but also felt like a fresh start.

Roger turned his head away from her, as if he did not see her or hear her.

"If you will excuse me," she said to Bernard and Stephen, "I will write my letter and then we can be off."

She went into her tent where she had paper and the charcoals Reid had given her when they moved into the row house at Crow Wing. She wrote her letter as quickly as she could and folded it. She did not have an envelope or a seal, but she hoped Bernard would honor her privacy and not read the contents.

Even if he did, it mattered little. Once she and Stephen were married, she would have complete control of her fortune. By the time the letter arrived in England, she would probably be on her way there as well.

She came out of the tent and handed the missive to Bernard. "Merci, monsieur. You do not know what a godsend you have been to me."

"It is my pleasure, my lady." He bowed, then directed his men to start breaking camp.

"We are ready to leave," Stephen said to Charlotte.

She took her bag to the canoe waiting for her, and without looking behind, she stepped into the vessel.

The wind pushed at them for hours, numbing her fingers, toes, and face. Stephen and his guide paddled without ceasing. Guilt ate at her for asking them to go to such trouble, but she did not suggest they stop, because she cared too deeply for Reid. She did not know how much time they had—or if it was too late. They might have already held his trial and found him guilty. At this very minute, he might be hanging from a noose.

Charlotte swallowed the fear and kept her chin down to ward off the chill.

Finally, the stockade of Fond du Lac fort was visible in the St. Louis Bay. It was still far off, but she could see the NW flag flying in the snow and knew they would be there soon.

Upon arrival and before they drew any attention, Stephen directed the canoe to the shore and got out to help Charlotte disembark, then he allowed the guide to continue without them.

"Are you certain this is the only way?" Stephen asked her.

She nodded and held her bag close to her side. They would approach the fort from behind and make a quiet entry into the stockade. What she hoped to do would only work if they were not spotted.

They climbed over rocks and crevices, down into ravines and up the side of a steep hill before coming to the back of the stockade. A guard stood near the back gate, but he didn't seem too alarmed at their arrival. When Stephen told him who he was, the guard allowed them to enter without any fuss.

The fort was busy with activity, even in the midst of the storm. Snow swirled around them, gathering in wind-swept piles along the eastern edge of the stockade. Mr. McDonnell's house was the tallest building in the fort and easy to locate among the other dependencies.

"We will enter at the back of the house, and I will ask for Daanis," Charlotte told Stephen as they crossed the yard. She had already told him who Daanis was and why she wanted to speak to her. "Hopefully, we can get her alone." It was the only hope.

They made it to the servants' entrance, and Charlotte stopped for a moment to take a deep breath. Stephen stood beside her, quietly, waiting for her to proceed. Again, he did not take the lead or try to stop her but simply allowed her to go forward—much as he would if he were her servant, which was exactly what he had been their whole lives. Gone was the authoritative bourgeois who had walked toward her yesterday. Over the past day, Stephen had become the cook's son again, his face turning red each time she caught him watching her.

"I will pray for you," he said.

If that was all he had to offer, then she would gladly take it. If she had learned anything this past year, she had learned that she was far braver and stronger than she'd ever believed, and that God was worthy of her trust. He's proven to her over and over that He had gone before her, answering prayers she hadn't even uttered. Bringing Reid into her life to protect her and fight for her. Knowing it was her turn to fight for

Reid gave her the courage to move forward without Stephen's leading. "Thank you."

Entering the house, she found the kitchen busy with activity. The midday meal would be upon them soon, and with several guests now in residence, there were three ladies at work.

"May I help you?" one of the ladies asked when she saw Stephen and Charlotte.

Charlotte was still dressed as a clerk and had no wish to be known, so she resumed the mannerisms she'd adopted as Mr. Crawford. "I'm here to see a guest you are entertaining."

The lady lifted an overgrown eyebrow, impatiently going back to the bread she was kneading. "I'm no maid. Go find him yourself. And use the front door the next time you come."

If Charlotte remembered correctly, Daanis had been given a room on the bottom floor, not too far from the front room. But she had not been in the kitchen and didn't know how to get there from here.

"What way to the front room from here?" she asked.

"Through that door and down the hallway to the right." The woman pointed at one of the three doors in the room.

"Thank you." Charlotte led Stephen to the door and opened it cautiously. If someone saw her, they would alert the whole house. But her plan depended on the element of surprise, so she didn't want Daanis to know they were there.

Peeking around the corner of the door, Charlotte found the hallway empty. Voices drifted to her from a room at the opposite end of the house, but she could not make out who spoke or what was being said.

She didn't bother to close the door but walked quietly to the right. Several doors ran down the length of the hall, and a staircase sat in the middle. If she was correct, Daanis's room would be at the end of this hall.

Charlotte motioned for Stephen to follow her, and when they stopped at the last door, she took a steadying breath and knocked lightly.

"Yes?" a woman asked.

It was Daanis. Charlotte breathed a sigh of relief. Before she turned the knob, she pointed at the opposite end of the hall and nodded at Stephen to do what they had planned.

He returned the nod and started toward the sound of the voices. When he was almost at the office of Mr. McDonnell, Charlotte turned the knob and entered Daanis's room.

Daanis sat on a chair near a window, staring out at the endless woods beyond the stockade. At the sound of Charlotte's entrance, she turned.

Her eyes grew wide, and she stood. "Charlotte." She swallowed hard and moved to stand behind the chair. She looked as if she'd been crying. Her face was swollen, and she had big dark circles under her eyes.

"Is it Reid?" Charlotte choked on the question. "Has he been sentenced already?"

Fresh tears gathered in Daanis's eyes, and she shook her head. "No. Mr. McDonnell is waiting for other shareholders to arrive before they have a trial."

Charlotte prayed Stephen had had time to get Mr. McDonnell to leave his office and stand outside Daanis's door—because she was ready to draw the truth out of Daanis and she needed Reid's superior officer to hear.

"Why are you so upset?" Charlotte asked, staying where she stood, not wanting to alarm Daanis any more than necessary. "You have everything you want, don't you?"

Daanis wiped her face and took an unsteady breath. "I didn't think it would come to all this."

"What do you mean?"

"This," she said impatiently. "I never wanted to hurt Reid—I just wanted to choose my own path, to be with the man I love."

"Lachlan?"

"Yes." She nodded.

"Because you are carrying his child?"

She stared at Charlotte. "How do you know?"

Charlotte didn't bother to answer. "Do you think your father will let you be with Lachlan if Reid is found guilty of murder?"

Daanis paced over to the window and looked out. "Reid will simply be replaced by another bourgeois, and my father will make me stay with his replacement. He is loyal to the North West Company."

"Then why did you frame Reid for murder?" Charlotte's heart pounded hard, and she had to focus on breathing, afraid she would push too fast—too soon. Her hands shook so violently, she clenched them together. "He is a good man. He does not deserve to be punished."

"I did not frame Reid." Daanis gripped her skirt in her balled fists. "That was Lachlan's idea. I didn't even know he was going to do it until it was done."

"Until you were on your way here with him?"

"Yes. He told me while we were traveling here."

"Where did he get Reid's knife?"

Daanis looked down at her hands.

"Did you give it to him?"

"He asked me to take it from Reid's quarters. But it happened so long ago, I'd forgotten he had it."

"Is that what you were doing the morning I was shot by Lachlan?"

Nodding, Daanis pressed her lips together.

Charlotte needed Mr. McDonnell to hear her confess the truth. "So you gave Lachlan Reid's knife? And then didn't tell anyone when he shot me?"

"Yes." She looked at Charlotte with wild eyes. "But I didn't know what he planned to do with it and he didn't kill you, so I didn't see the need to tell anyone who pulled the trigger."

"I believe you." And she did. Daanis was acting out of love and desperation.

Charlotte hoped and prayed Stephen and Mr. McDonnell were on the other side of the door, because she would never get Daanis to admit this to them in person. "Lachlan used the knife to frame Reid for murder so he would be out of the way and you two could be together?"

Daanis clasped her hands together and paced back to the chair. "It wasn't simply for us to be together. To gain my father's respect, Lachlan needs the trade. He needs to prove the North West Company men are not trustworthy."

"Yet Lachlan is the one who is not trustworthy." Charlotte felt sad for Daanis and the child she carried. "Why did you support him in this?"

"Because I love him." Daanis finally met Charlotte's gaze. "You understand—it's why you've done what you've done, because you love Reid."

Charlotte didn't respond, not wanting to confirm Daanis's statement for fear of what Stephen might think.

"There is no excuse to frame another man for murder," Charlotte said.

"Lachlan would do anything to have me."

"Even murder Monsieur LeBlanc and then frame Reid?"

She looked down at her hands again, and Charlotte's heart broke for her. "Yes. He told me he sent the anonymous letter to Reid that morning, claiming to be a witness who saw him shoot you, because he knew Reid would go to his fort to fight him. It was the perfect way to accuse him of murdering Monsieur LeBlanc."

The door opened, and Mr. McDonnell stood on the other side. Stephen stood beside him, with Lachlan in his grasp. Two other men Charlotte did not know were also there.

But Reid was not with them.

"I've heard enough," Mr. McDonnell said. "Lachlan McCoy, you are charged with the murder of Nicolas LeBlanc and the attempted murder of Lady Charlotte Fairfax. You will be transported to the nearest XY Company post where you will be handed over to their authority."

Daanis inhaled a sharp breath and ran toward Lachlan, but she was intercepted by Mr. McDonnell. "The young lady will be transported back to her father's village immediately."

"This is all a lie," Lachlan said. "Daanis is upset and dinna ken what she was saying."

"Take him away," Mr. McDonnell said to Stephen and the other two men.

Lachlan tried to get away, but they held him fast.

Mr. McDonnell addressed Daanis. "You must stay in your room until I can organize your transfer."

Daanis crumpled onto the chair with a wave of fresh tears.

Charlotte wanted to comfort her, but the other woman would never accept her compassion now. To free Reid, Charlotte had been forced to reveal Daanis's secrets. Any hope Daanis had of marrying Lachlan was now dashed.

"And Lady Charlotte?" Mr. McDonnell raised an eyebrow. "I think you have some explaining to do as well. Will you join me in my office?"

Charlotte bit her bottom lip as she cast one more glance at Daanis.

"I'm sorry," she said and then quietly left her room.

She had freed Reid from his charges—but she must now convince Mr. McDonnell not to fire him from his post.

It was the very least she could do for all that he had done for her.

A knock sounded at Reid's door. "Supper is served."

Reid had not been downstairs since the morning meal. Sitting at the same table as Lachlan and Daanis had turned his stomach sour, so he had avoided the midday meal. Though he was hungry, he would rather starve than see them again. He didn't bother to rise from the chair where he'd been sitting, trying to read to pass the infernal hours.

But all he could think about was Charlotte and how she was faring in this storm—at Rutherford's side.

Reid closed his book, saving his place with a finger. "Please tell Mr. McDonnell I am unwell."

The door opened, and it was Joseph who stood over the threshold. "I think you'll want to be at this meal."

Reid frowned. Why had Joseph summoned him personally? He had sent a clerk the other time. He stood and set his book on the chair.

"I'll wait for you to put on your best coat," Joseph said.

"My best coat?" Reid could care less about his appearance.

"We're having a party tonight."

A party? While he was waiting for a murder trial? "What kind of party?"

"A wedding feast—though the wedding won't take place until the morning."

Lachlan and Daanis? "I'd rather not attend."

"I think you'll be pleased that you did." Joseph smiled, and it was the first time since Reid's arrival that the smile reached his eyes. "I have some good news to share at the party."

Now Reid was intrigued—at least to hear the good news. He reached for his coattails and ran his hands through his hair but did nothing else.

He followed Joseph through the hall, down the stairs, and into the spacious front room. There were about two dozen people in attendance, many of them clerks and their wives, people he knew from Grand Portage and other places where they'd mingled in the past.

A long table had been set up in the middle of the room and chairs were gathered around it. The table was laden with wild rice, bread, roasted vegetables, venison, and other good things to eat, though Reid doubted he'd enjoy the food.

Standing at the head of the table, a man drew Reid's attention, and he had to blink twice before he recognized him.

"Stephen?" Reid left Joseph's side.

Stephen offered his hand and took Reid's in a hearty shake. "It's good to see you again, McCoy."

The reality of Stephen's timing hit Reid like a boulder. He staggered from the force of it and put his hand on Stephen's arm. "You must go after her. She isna more than two or three days away."

Stephen smiled and clasped Reid on his shoulder. "I found her. She's here."

It took a moment for Stephen's words to make sense. "Charlotte is here?"

"Yes." He grinned. "And she proved your innocence and convinced McDonnell to give you a second chance back at Crow Wing."

"What?" Reid frowned, uncertain that he'd heard Stephen correctly. "She proved my innocence?"

Stephen explained how Charlotte was able to get Daanis to confess the truth while McDonnell and he had stood in the hallway to listen.

"Lachlan is already on his way to the nearest XY post, and Daanis will be on her way back to her father's village in the morning."

Reid stared at Stephen. "Charlotte has done all of that?"

"She has." Stephen's cheeks were ruddy. "She's a courageous woman."

"And she's here?" Reid looked around the room but could not see her.

"She'll be here any minute."

Just then, a woman entered the room from the hall. Her beautiful auburn curls hung loose around her face, with a green ribbon encircling her head. The dress she wore matched the ribbon and was the bonniest gown he'd ever seen. It was even more attractive on her than the one back at his fur post. This one fit her like it had been sewn just for her, and this time it was evident that she wore all the right undergarments to keep it modest and shapely.

Her dark brown eyes searched the room, and when her gaze landed on him, her face softened into the most beautiful smile he'd ever seen.

His heart thrummed with joy as he realized she was free from Rutherford. His own freedom didn't compare to hers.

She moved toward him with such grace and poise, he wondered how anyone had ever believed she was a man.

He met her in the center of the room as all else faded around them.

"Charlotte." He shook his head, unable to believe what he was seeing and what he had just heard. "Stephen told me—"

"Are you happy?" she asked with a smile as she put her hands on his arms.

"Happy?" He wanted to throw her high into the air and swing her around the room. "I never imagined." Reid swallowed the emotions and took her hands in his. "Now I owe you a debt for my life."

"Just be happy," she said quietly, squeezing his hands, her eyes filling with tears. "That's all I ask."

There was a different air about her now—one he liked very much. She was more than feminine, she was a highborn lady, and it reminded him how far apart their worlds really were. Everything she had endured in the wilderness was even more impressive as he saw her in this light. There was not another woman like her in all the world.

The sounds of the room pushed their way back into his consciousness as the guests glanced their way. After all this time, he was finally standing with Charlotte in a room of people who knew she was a woman.

Stephen joined them then, and Reid let go of Charlotte's hands.

"Thank you," Stephen said to Reid. "For bringing Charlotte safely to me."

Reality crashed back on Reid. This breathtaking lady before him was betrothed to another man. Reid forced himself to smile. "'Tis the least I could do to repay you for saving my life."

"I was hoping you'd agree to one more favor." Stephen stood proudly next to Charlotte and faced Reid. "Would you be my best man in the morning?"

Charlotte's smile fell, and she turned troubled eyes to Reid. "I'm sure Reid wants to be on his way back to Fort McCoy as soon as possible."

"I don't know anyone else but you," Stephen said with a little embarrassment to Reid. "I'd be in your debt."

How could Reid turn down the request? Yet how could he stand beside the man who would become Charlotte's husband?

"Please?" Stephen asked.

Reid nodded. "Aye. You saved my life, after all."

Stephen smiled, but behind his smile Reid could see apprehension. Was he nervous about marrying Charlotte? Reid couldn't imagine being nervous to take her as his bride. If it were him standing beside her tomorrow, he would have no uncertainty.

# Chapter Twenty-Seven

After supper, the tables and chairs were moved to the edges of the room for a dance to celebrate the impending wedding in the morning. Reid stood near the door, watching Charlotte with Stephen. Though there was an awkward newness to their relationship, there was also an undercurrent of familiarity that could not be denied. During the meal, which Reid couldn't stomach for different reasons, there had been a lot of uncertain smiles, flushed cheeks, and hesitant glances—but mingled in between those moments were deep laughter, nods of understanding, and animated conversations that suggested they were recalling old memories and shared experiences.

Occasionally, Charlotte had glanced in Reid's direction, and he had tried to smile for her—but there was so little to smile about he struggled to do her that small favor. He knew she was doubtful, that she felt obligated to follow through with her promise to marry Stephen. He'd once told her that he would try to convince Stephen not to marry her, but it would be a futile attempt. Stephen and Charlotte were good and honorable people. They would do the right thing. It would only make them uncomfortable and unhappy if he tried to interfere.

"Reid?" Joseph moved to stand beside Reid. "May I have a word with you?"

"Aye." Anything to give Reid the excuse to leave the party.

He followed Joseph to his office, where a candle flickered on his desk. Outside, the storm still blew forcefully and without ceasing. Even if he had wanted to leave before the wedding, he would be hard pressed to travel right now.

"Have a seat." Joseph motioned to one of the chairs across the desk from where he sat. "I'd like to speak to you about your post."

Stephen had mentioned that Charlotte had already spoken to Joseph on his behalf, but he hadn't told him the details or what Charlotte had said.

"Lady Charlotte was very persuasive." Joseph's smile was large. "I can tell she cares a great deal for you. She said you saved her life several times and defended her honor as well."

Reid didn't speak. What could he say? Charlotte's word was just as good—if not better—than his.

"She has convinced me that you were only acting as a gentleman on her behalf—and since she is a lady, I am honor bound to believe her." He leaned forward. "'Tis still against the rules for her to be here, but in this instance, with your impeccable reputation and service to the North West Company—and Lachlan McCoy's arrest—I've decided to overlook your behavior."

Reid sat perfectly still, unsure how he felt about Joseph's decision. He had been expecting a dismissal from the North West Company, and now that it was not forthcoming, he felt—disappointed, even frustrated. Had he wanted to be dismissed? But why? Hadn't it been his desire to become a shareholder? It was the only thing that had driven him these past fifteen years.

Or had it been something else entirely?

Did he want to be a shareholder—or did he simply want revenge? All these years, he'd thought the only way to show his father he was the better man was through his ascension in the North West Company. Now that Lachlan was in custody facing murder charges, there was nothing else to prove. His desire to continue in the fur trade no longer held the same appeal.

And without Charlotte at his post, the years ahead suddenly felt bleak and meaningless.

But what else could he do? Returning to Montreal without the income from being a shareholder meant he'd have to start over in a different trade. That didn't sound appealing either.

He leaned forward and put his elbows on his knees. "I dinna expect you to say that."

"You thought I'd send you home to Montreal?"

"Aye."

"You look disappointed that you're staying."

Reid tried not to look disappointed. He had no right to be. He was a fur trader, and Charlotte was an English lady. It was foolish to wish for things that were not meant to be.

"Reid." Joseph studied him carefully. "Staying in the fur trade is not worth the sacrifice."

Reid frowned. "What do you mean?"

"I mean Lady Charlotte. I have eyes, and I can see how she feels about you." He smiled. "I dinna ken until now how you felt about her."

Was it that obvious? He straightened and set his face. "I'm a fur trader."

"And she's not a fur trader's lady?"

Reid was unwilling to discuss it further. There was little choice. Reid must return to his post and continue with his plans—though he no longer had the same burning desire to capture the trade from the XY Company.

Joseph didn't press any further but reached for a letter on the corner of his desk. "I have started to pen a letter to McTavish, Mackenzie, and Pond to recommend you as a shareholder when we gather at the Rendezvous in July." He turned it for Reid to see. "I have always been impressed with your hard work and dedication to the North West Company, and barring this one instance with Lady Charlotte, you have been above reproach."

He should have been relieved—or even proud. But he felt nothing.

"Now that we've settled our business," Joseph said, "shall we return to the party?"

"'Tis been a long day. I think I'll go to bed." Reid stood, not tired, but needing to stay as far from Charlotte as possible tonight.

Joseph nodded with understanding and clapped him on the back. "You deserve some rest."

Reid parted ways with Joseph and started down the hall to the stairway—but then he saw the door leading into Daanis's room, and he took a deep breath. He couldn't simply dismiss her without speaking to her first. Yes, she had aided Lachlan's scheme, but he also knew she had been a victim of her circumstances. If anyone needed a bit of reassurance or hope tonight, it was Daanis.

He knocked on her door and when she answered, he opened it wide.

She sat in a chair, a blanket wrapped around her shoulders, staring out the window at the dark. Snow swirled around the window frame, but the candle on the small table near her elbow reflected off the glass and didn't allow much to be seen outside.

When she saw it was Reid, she sat up straighter, fear tightening her face and shoulders.

"Dinna fash," he said quickly. "I willna harm you."

She pulled the blanket tighter. "What do you want?"

He kept her door open but entered the room to stand before her. "I want to help you, lass. However I can."

Her dark eyes filled with uncertainty. "Help me?"

"I ken you're just as innocent as I am." Though innocent wasn't quite the right word. Both had made choices that had not been wise, though they had done it for the people they loved.

She stared at him. "Does this mean you will take me as your wife?"

He sighed. "No, lass, but I will speak to your faither on your behalf. And I will give you aid whenever 'tis in my power."

Tears gathered in her eyes. "My father will be angry with me."

"I suppose he will. But he will forgive you." He tried to smile. "And I hear you have a wee bairn coming."

She nodded and looked down at her stomach. She rested her hand there, and her face softened. The baby would be hers, and she would love it and care for it under the protection of her father. Hopefully, in time she might find a man to love and help her raise the baby. But until then, she'd have Noemie's friendship to see her through the difficult days ahead.

"We will wait until this storm passes and then head back to Crow Wing with Jean-Paul and the other men," Reid told her.

Daanis finally looked up at him, tears in her eyes. "I'm sorry for everything. I was only trying to please my father."

"I ken, lass, and I'm sorry too."

There was nothing left to say, so he exited her room and closed the door.

The hallway was dark and empty, making the sound of revelry all the louder. With a sigh, he turned toward the stairs and went to his cold room.

He wouldn't sleep for many hours, so there was no reason to go to bed. Instead, he did as Daanis had been doing and took a seat near the window without lighting a candle. Below him, long rectangles of light spilled onto the snowy yard from the front room. Music and laughter filtered up through the floorboards, making him think about the woman who was celebrating down below.

Would he ever find a way to forget Charlotte?

He sat there for several minutes, thinking about the day she had shown up at his house, then the day she had cut her hair to join him in the fur trade. Of the nights they had lain in the tent, talking for hours on end, or the day he'd discovered she could draw—and had found the picture she'd drawn of him. So many memories returned, each one a gift he'd treasure as long as he lived.

A knock sounded at his door, bringing him out of his reverie.

"Aye?"

"It's Charlotte." There was a brief pause. "May I come in?"

Reid's pulse thrummed at the sound of her voice. Was she alone or was Stephen with her?

Part of him wanted to run to the door and yank it open to see her—the other part wanted to send her away. Seeing her and not being able to hold her would be torture.

But he could never turn her away. Rising, he crossed his room and opened the door.

She stood there in the green gown, her chest rising and falling, her eyes large and luminous as she searched the darkness for his face. Her curls looked as soft and inviting as ever, brushing her shoulders.

Neither one spoke for a moment. "May I come in?" she asked again.

"Is it proper for an English lady to be in the room of a single man on the eve of her wedding?"

"I think this is the least of our transgressions." Her voice was low and teasing, though there was truth to her words that sobered him.

"Aye." He stood back and opened the door wider.

She entered his room, the heels of her shoes clicking on the wood floor. She moved with an elegance and grace that looked foreign in this far-off fur post.

"Would you like me to keep the door open?" he asked.

Charlotte turned and tilted her head. "Do we need to worry about propriety? We slept in the same tent together for over three months."

He left the door open. "Things are different now, lass." The room was dark, but his eyes had adjusted, and he could see her plainly. She had a sad smile on her face.

"I wish they weren't."

"Why have you come?"

"You don't need to be Stephen's best man tomorrow morning. Anyone can fill that role."

"Aye." Someone else could do a better job as best man—and as Charlotte's husband. Once again, he was second best when it mattered the most. First with his father, and now with Charlotte.

Looking down at her clasped hands, she nibbled her bottom lip. "You don't need to come to the ceremony tomorrow."

"You dinna want me there?"

"I think, given the circumstances, it would be best if you stayed away."

Neither one spoke for a moment. He didn't want to be there when she promised her life to another man, but he didn't want this to be goodbye either.

She stood only three feet from him, but she felt a world away. Every-thing within him wanted to hold her one last time, to feel her in his arms.

"Is this goodbye then?" he asked.

Her eyes were rimmed with tears when she finally looked up at him. One slipped down her cheek, trailing across the smooth skin. "I think so."

His chest tightened, and he struggled to take a deep breath.

She moved around him toward the door, the sleeve of her gown brushing his hand as she passed. He longed to reach for her, to pull her into his arms, but he simply flexed his fingers.

She stopped at the door and then turned around. With a small cry, she rushed back into his arms.

He wrapped her in a tight embrace, pressing his lips against her curls. "Charlotte." He whispered her name. Though it was but one word, it held every emotion he felt.

Her arms were around his waist, her pounding heart pressed against his torso.

"I love you," she said on a breath.

And then as quickly as she came to him, she was gone.

Tears streamed down Charlotte's cheeks as she walked through the dark hallway toward her room at the opposite end. She had no heart to stay at the party and had excused herself from Stephen's side to say goodbye to Reid. She had thought it would make her feel better somehow, but she felt worse than before and wanted nothing more than space to be alone and cry the pain from her heart.

"Charlotte?" Stephen appeared at the top of the stairs, a candle in his hand, uncertainty on his face. "Is something wrong?"

She quickly wiped her cheeks and tried to smile, but her lips wobbled with the effort. "I'm fine."

He frowned but didn't press her for more information—not like Reid would. He would have tried to find the answer for her, to heal her, to make her feel better, but Stephen simply stood there, awkwardly shifting his weight from foot to foot.

"Is there anything else I can get for you before I retire for the evening?" he asked.

She closed her eyes at the request, hating that he sounded like her servant and not her fiancé.

"Can we speak for a moment?" She needed him to understand his role as her husband. She needed a lord for her manor—not another servant. He must find the confidence he lacked before they returned to England, or she feared he would never take his rightful place as the head of their family.

"As you wish." He gave a slight bow. "Where shall we go?"

"My room?"

His eyes grew wide. "Before we're married?"

She had to fight impatience as she walked to her door and opened it. "There are few other places that will offer as much privacy."

"Should I get a chaperone?"

"Stephen." She said his name with more irritation than she intended and then paused to take a steady breath. "I have been living as a man in the northwest wilderness for the past seven months. Having you in my room the night before our wedding is the least of our worries right now."

He nodded nervously and followed her into her room, looking up and down the hall before closing the door.

His candle sent shadows dancing on the walls and over the bed. When he saw where she slept, he turned so suddenly the flame flickered and almost died—and he ended up facing the wall.

"Why don't you have a seat?" She took his arm. "Over here by the window."

He sidestepped across the room until he reached the chair and waited until she sat on the one opposite.

After he sat, he set the candle on the table nearby. His hands shook so violently the clay candle holder tapped against the wood until he let it go, then he clamped his hands tight between his knees.

Her impatience was mounting, and she didn't know how to tamp it down.

"There are things we should discuss before tomorrow." Charlotte was not nervous. Her feelings had been raw and tender with Reid, but now that she faced Stephen, she felt almost nothing.

Stephen struggled to meet Charlotte's gaze.

"First, I want to thank you for coming all this way for me." She was truly grateful. "But I need to know if you plan to return to the fur trade or if you will go home to England with me."

"Whatever you wish."

She frowned. "I want to know what *you* want."

He opened his mouth, but then he closed it again. "I want to make you happy, Lady Charlotte."

As he sat before her, she couldn't stop thinking about what it would feel like to sit across from Reid and discuss her future. She couldn't imagine him being this uncomfortable or rigid—or indecisive.

Stephen's discomfort made Charlotte uncomfortable. How long would it take before she was used to his company? Would she ever long to be with him, like she did with Reid? Would she crave his love and affection, his tender embrace? What would it feel like to be kissed by Stephen?

The thought of consummating their marriage the following day made her feel physically ill. How could they go from hardly knowing one another to sharing something so intimate? Shouldn't they at least kiss?

Nerves bubbled in her stomach, but she stood. "Will you kiss me, Stephen?"

He looked up so quickly, she was afraid he had hurt his neck. "Kiss you?"

Charlotte nodded.

"Do you think it proper? Here, alone in your room, before we're married?"

"Of course it's not proper." She reached out her hand to him. "But I would very much like for you to kiss me right now."

He stared at her for a heartbeat, then took her hand and stood. His palm was cold and moist.

Stephen was a tall man, but not nearly as broad shouldered as Reid. When he stood before her, she had to look up at him.

They faced each other, and she waited for him to make the first move—but he didn't. His hand shook and he cleared his throat.

She lifted her eyebrows.

"Now?" he asked.

Nodding, she tipped her head back a little farther so he could easily reach her lips.

Stephen did not step closer but bent at the waist and puckered his lips. He closed his eyes and bobbed like a chicken pecking at cornmeal. The brief touch of their lips carried no passion whatsoever. His lips were dry and scratched her skin.

Dropping his hands to his side, he took a step back, putting even more space between them.

Charlotte's eyes stung with unshed tears. What was she doing with this man, when there was another down the hall who loved her passionately and with abandon? If she had not committed to marrying Stephen and asked him to come all this way, she would run back to Reid's arms, no matter the obstacles that faced them.

Stephen swallowed and looked like he might become ill. But why? Surely, kissing her couldn't be as bad as that.

"Do you want to marry me?" she asked quietly.

"Of course I do." He backed up until he was behind the chair and put his hands on the top. He clutched the wood until his knuckles turned white.

"Why?" she asked.

He frowned. "What do you mean?"

"Why did you come all this way to marry me? Do you love me?"

"I would be a fool not to marry you. You're the lady of Blissfield Manor."

"But do you love me?"

"I am fond of you," he said tentatively.

"Fondness is not love."

"Won't love grow in time?" he asked, as if he really needed to know.

"I'm not sure." She thought about the love she felt for Reid and was more concerned about the love she needed to forget than the one she needed to find. "Have you ever been in love before, Stephen?"

He dropped his gaze, and a smile lifted the corners of his mouth. "Yes." When he finally looked at Charlotte, sadness and joy mingled within his gaze. "I have loved someone very deeply."

"What happened?"

He didn't speak for a moment, then said, "I left her to come to you."

Charlotte's mouth cracked open. "You're in love with someone right now?"

"I didn't mean to fall in love." His voice was apologetic. "She nursed me back to health when I was sick last summer. I met her after I wrote the letter to you."

Charlotte walked across the small space and put her hand on his arm. "Why did you leave her?"

"Because I made a promise to you, and I'm a man of my word."

Charlotte's breath caught at the declaration. "Do you still want to be with her?"

Pain pinched his eyebrows together. "I could never do that to you."

Shaking her head, Charlotte laughed with joy. "You do not need to marry me, Stephen."

"But your guardian—"

"There is someone else who has asked me to be his wife." Yet even as she said the words, she wondered how she and Reid could ever make such a marriage work. He would stay with the trade, and she would need to return to England. The thought of being apart was almost unbearable. Yet—if she had to give up Blissfield Manor for him, she would. She could always sell the property and stay in Montreal. At least then, she would be closer to him, and it would not take as long for him to come to her when he had his leave.

Stephen took a tentative step away from the chair. "You do not need me?"

"I would never want you to marry me out of obligation when you are already in love with someone else." Tears formed for a different reason this time. "I know what it feels like to be separated from the person you love, and I could not bear to be the reason you are apart from the woman you wish to marry."

He took her hands, and this time they were warm. "Do you mean that, Lady Charlotte?"

"I mean that with all of my heart." She smiled. "And I will compensate you for your efforts in coming to my aid."

"No." He shook his head. "Having your blessings to pursue Marguerite is all the compensation I need."

When he took her into his arms, it was the hug of two old friends.

"It was good to see you again," Charlotte said. "When I see your parents, I will send them your love and tell them they have a courageous and honorable son."

Stephen stepped back and gave her a slight bow. "It's been my honor to serve you, my lady."

"Thank you."

He walked across her room and opened the door. Then, he turned and smiled at her before slipping out into the dark hallway.

Charlotte took a deep breath and faced the flickering candle. If Reid refused to marry her, she'd be at a loss with what to do with her life. She still needed a husband to keep Roger from forcing her to marry him. If Reid said no, she would have no choice but to marry a stranger.

But it was a risk she was willing to take.

# Chapter Twenty-Eight

Another sleepless night kept Reid on his feet praying while pacing across the length of his room. The snow continued to fall, even when the sun warmed the horizon and brought light to the gray day. He had hoped it would let up enough to depart for Crow Wing, but it would force him to stay at least one more day. What would people think if he didn't attend Charlotte's wedding? He could feign illness, but that felt like the coward's way out. She had said it would be best if he stayed away, so would she be angry if he came?

The scent of fried bacon found its way to Reid's room, and he realized he hadn't eaten since yesterday morning. His stomach growled and he realized he could never fake sickness when he was this hungry.

He dressed in his best clothing, taking time to shave, comb his hair, and brush his coat. If he attended breakfast, surely he'd be expected to witness the wedding, and if so, he wanted to look presentable. If not for Charlotte's sake, then for his own pride.

There was little activity in the house, which was a surprise. With the wedding soon upon them, he expected to hear furniture moving, animated voices, and footsteps up and down the length of the room below him. But all was silent.

Reid left his room and walked down the hall, his gaze resting on Charlotte's closed door. Was she in there now, preparing herself to be married? Would she wear the same green gown, or had someone found a different one for her? There were several mixed-blood women at the post, including Joseph's own wife. Was someone helping her dress?

No sounds came from Charlotte's room, either, but he wasn't sure what he expected to hear. Girlish laughter? Shared confidences?

Assuming the meal would be served in the large room, he walked down the stairs and opened the door into the space.

The first thing he saw was the furniture. It was back in its original places, a seating arrangement near the fireplace, the large rugs spread out over the floor, a table in one corner.

The second thing he saw was the woman standing near the fireplace. She faced the crackling flames with her back to him. She wore the green gown again, the same ribbon secured around her head, the sash of her gown tied snug at her small waist.

Reid paused, his pulse racing at the sight of her. He hadn't expected to find her alone—hadn't expected to see her at all.

Charlotte turned, and when their eyes met in the light of day, he could do nothing but smile. By candlelight, she was stunning—but surreal. In the daylight, she was the same Charlotte he'd fallen in love with—only she was dressed as the bonnie lass she was meant to be.

Her lips lifted into a beautiful smile, and he was certain his chest would explode from the bittersweet pleasure it brought to his heart.

He didn't move from his place near the door, uncertain if he should stay or leave. Was she waiting for Stephen?

"I've been waiting for you," she said. "For hours."

"Me?"

"Aye," she said with a Scottish brogue and a gleam in her brown eyes.

He closed the door and walked across the room to stand before her, anticipation filling his chest.

She inhaled, as if she was taking the first breath in a long while. And when she looked up at him and met his gaze, her eyes swam with a tenderness that made his knees weak.

"What are you about this fair morning, lass?" he asked, his own brogue thickening. "Is there not a wedding to plan and attend?"

Charlotte touched the cravat at his throat and repositioned one of the folds.

He wanted to take her hand in his and press it against his beating heart, hoping to somehow still the rhythm. But he didn't touch her.

She lowered her hand and rested it by her side. "There is no wedding planned at the moment."

He frowned. "What do you mean?"

"I mean, I called off the wedding."

Instead of growing more still, his heart beat even harder. "Why?"

"Because Stephen is in love with another woman." She looked up at him, tears gathering in her eyes. "And because I'm in love with another man."

He touched the curl at her temple and ran his finger down the side of her cheek, pleasure and relief and love filling his heart until he thought it might burst.

"And does he love you?" he asked.

She searched his gaze. "I believe he does. I hope he does."

"Aye." His voice caught, and he slipped his free hand around her waist, drawing her closer to him, feeling this moment was too good to be true but not caring. Her body pressed against his, and he lowered his lips to capture hers in a kiss unlike any other. Every desire and longing in his heart poured into the kiss, but it was the freedom in holding her, in not being ashamed or guilty for the pleasure he felt, that made the moment sweet. After he thoroughly kissed her, he ran his thumb over her swollen lips. "I love you more than life itself, lass."

She rested her cheek against his chest. "What will we do?"

"Whatever we need to be together."

"Are we being unrealistic?"

He pulled back, so she had to look into his eyes. "Charlotte, there is nothing on this side of heaven that I love or value more than you. It was unrealistic of me to think I could return to my former life and find any joy there without you."

"I will give up Blissfield Manor and live in Montreal, so you don't have to travel as far to see me when you have leave."

He placed his hands on either side of her precious face. "I would never let you give up your home. If you'll have me, I would love to see it for myself—to make it my own."

She blinked several times. "You'd give up the fur trade for me?"

He kissed her forehead and then wrapped his arms around her. "I thought I had lost you, and I couldna imagine how I would live the rest of my life with you in England in the arms of another man."

She pressed her cheek against his chest again as her arms encircle him.

"I'd give up everything for you." He kissed the top of her head. "From this day until the one I die, I dinna want to leave your side ever again."

"What about becoming a shareholder?" She looked up at him and frowned. "It's what you've wanted for years."

"I wanted retaliation and vengeance." He sighed. "And now that I have it, I feel numb toward the fur trade and numb toward my faither."

"Do you know where your father lives?"

"Aye." Reid hated to admit the truth. "He lives near Grand Portage."

Her eyebrows lifted. "And you didn't go to see him when you were there?"

"He's lived in the same spot for the past fifteen years, and not once did I go to see him."

She stepped out of his embrace. "You need to go."

He reached for her again, grasping a bit of fabric on her dress. "I dinna want to see him."

"I think you should." She took his hands in hers and brought them to her lips to kiss his knuckles. "Will you introduce me to him?"

He frowned, never contemplating such a thing. "Would you truly like to meet him?"

"I would." She rubbed the tops of his hands with her thumbs. "And I think you might enjoy seeing him too."

"It means I would have to meet his country wife."

"I know."

She was right, even if he wasn't ready to admit the truth. He needed to see his father, at least one more time. There were things they needed to say to one another before he left for England.

Letting go of Reid, Charlotte stepped back and clasped her hands together. She stood before him, a smile on her lips. "Well?"

He wanted to hold her again but stayed where he stood. "Well, what?" he asked with a smile.

"Is there something you need to ask me?"

There were a great many things he wanted to ask her, but only one thing that mattered in this moment.

"Aye, there is." He put his hands behind his back and offered a slight bow. "I've heard there is a priest who is coming to the post today to perform a wedding."

She nodded.

"I've also heard there is a bonnie young woman who is dressed in a pretty gown, waiting to be married." He took her hands in his and brought them to his lips. "But more importantly, there is a man who canna wait another moment to take a bride."

Her brown eyes sparkled.

"I love you, lass." He lowered her hands. "Will you marry me?"

Her smile was brighter and more beautiful than any he'd ever seen.

"Aye. I thought you'd never ask."

Standing outside the great room on Joseph McDonnell's arm, waiting to join Reid, Charlotte felt so many things, yet peace was foremost. She had many questions, but there was no doubt in her mind that she was meant to be Reid's wife. Her entire journey, from escaping her bedroom at Blissfield Manor until this moment, each step had been orchestrated by a God who loved her and wanted her best, even if her best came through hardship and trials.

"Are you ready, lass?" Joseph asked.

Charlotte met his happy gaze and nodded.

"You're a bonnie bride—the first European lady to marry in the northwest wilderness."

An honor, indeed.

Joseph's wife, Nicolette, opened the door, and Joseph led Charlotte into the great room. Two dozen guests had gathered, but Charlotte hardly knew them. The only person in the room who mattered stood near the fireplace beside the French priest, wearing his best mauve-colored tailcoat and the brightest smile she'd ever seen.

She returned the smile, hoping her face was as bright and just as full of hope.

The green dress she'd borrowed from Nicolette felt as if it had been tailored for her. It fit snug across her bosom and was cinched just below her chest with a sash. The skirt was straight and had a matching ribbon along the hem. She had taken a bath and used Nicolette's lavender-scented soap and hoped Reid liked the smell. She hadn't felt this beautiful since before her parents had died—and it was all because of the man who waited for her near the crackling fire. Even at her worst, he had made her feel lovely—but now, standing before him, she felt as if no one in the world was as desirable or attractive as her.

When they arrived at the fireplace, Reid extended his hand, and Joseph gave her to the fur trader.

He took her to his side, wrapping his arm around hers, and pulled their clasped hands near his heart. He'd also bathed and smelled of wood smoke and sandalwood as he stood tall and proud beside her.

"Dearly beloved," the priest began in French. His words faded away as Charlotte gazed up at Reid. She tried to listen to the priest, wanted to hear the words he was speaking, but Reid's eyes were communicating in such a way she could hear nothing above the sound of his love.

"Do you, Lady Charlotte Fairfax, take Mr. Reid McCoy to be your lawfully wedded husband? To love him and honor him, in sickness and in health, until death do you part?"

"I do."

"And do you, Mr. Reid McCoy, take Lady Charlotte Fairfax to be your lawfully wedded wife? To love her and honor her, in sickness and in health, until death do you part?"

The longing in Reid's eyes made Charlotte's cheeks burn with anticipation.

"Aye," he said. "I do."

"Do you have rings?" the priest asked.

Reid slipped his fingers into his vest pocket and removed a simple gold band. "It was my grandmither's ring," he said to Charlotte. "I hope it doesna disappoint ye."

How could it disappoint, when it represented his love and commitment? "I'm very glad to wear her ring."

The priest smiled. "Please say after me—with this ring, I thee wed."

Reid put the ring on her fourth finger. "With this ring, I thee wed."

It was still warm from his pocket, and it slipped on easily.

"I also have an old Celtic vow of my own I'd like to speak," he told the priest.

When the priest nodded, Reid turned to Charlotte and took both her hands in his. "I, Reid McCoy, in the name of the Spirit of God that resides within us all, by the life that courses within my blood and the love that resides within my heart, take thee Charlotte Fairfax to my hand, my heart, and my spirit, to be my chosen one." His eyes brimmed with love, and she could not contain the tears any longer. They trailed down her cheeks, but she did not wipe them away.

"To desire thee and be desired by thee," he continued, speaking only to her, as if no one else was present, "to possess thee, and be possessed by thee, without sin or shame—" His voice broke at this declaration, and he took a moment to collect himself before he continued. "For naught can exist in the purity of my love for thee. I promise to love thee wholly and completely without restraint, in sickness and in health, in plenty and in poverty, in life and beyond, where we shall meet, remember, and love again. I shall not seek to change thee in any way. I shall respect thee, thy beliefs, thy people, and thy ways as I respect myself."

She finally released his hand to wipe her tears, and she whispered, "I love you."

The priest closed his Bible with a contented smile. "I now pronounce you man and wife. You may kiss your bride."

Reid slipped one hand around her waist and the other he placed on her cheek, then he kissed her as if it were the first time. Pleasure coursed through her, and she forgot about the others until they clapped and cheered.

He pulled back and rested his forehead against hers. "Our union is not only blessed but also celebrated." He smiled. "And now I may kiss you whenever I like, and I may hold your hand and proclaim to the world that you are mine."

She took his hand in her own and returned his smile. "And I do not have to hide my love or withhold it from you any longer." The knowledge that they could openly love each other was a wonderful gift. "I will never take that privilege for granted."

Joseph and Nicolette insisted on giving them a wedding feast. They ate, laughed, and held hands through the whole meal—but when the sun began to set and the food had been cleared away, Reid pulled Charlotte to her feet.

"'Tis time we take our leave, my love. I canna wait any longer." He kissed the back of her hand, his eyes proclaiming a promise that her heart could hardly contain.

"You'll not stay for the dancing?" Joseph asked the couple as he met them at the door.

"No." Reid shook his head, and that was all he said to their host.

"Good night, then," Joseph called to them as they left the room behind, a knowing laugh in his voice.

Her heart began to pound as they walked down the hallway and up the stairs, side by side, hand in hand. Reid held a candle aloft, allowing her to see the next step.

They did not speak, but from time to time, they caught each other's eye, and a tender smile passed between them.

Her belongings, the few she owned, had been moved into Reid's room, so he led her to the room at the end of the hall and opened the door.

She stepped into the large space, and he followed and closed the door behind him.

A fire had been laid in the hearth, and it popped and sizzled. Smoke drifted up the chimney, and just outside the window, the snow continued to fall.

Reid set his candle on the windowsill, his hand steady, his purpose clear.

When he turned, their gazes met, and she suddenly felt like the young lady who had started off on this journey with him seven months before. Shy, uncertain, a little scared, yet completely confident that she was doing the right thing.

"How many times did I lay beside you in that tent and hope that one day you would be my wife?" He walked toward her, his eyes taking in her body from head to foot without shame or hesitation.

A thrill of excitement raced up her spine as she reveled in the feel of his desire. They'd denied their feelings for so long, there was freedom in knowing they could take pleasure in one another. She smiled at him, hoping he saw the love and longing in her eyes.

His hand went to her curls, as they so often did, but this time, his touch lingered. "I canna wait until your hair is down to your waist again."

The words were barely out of his mouth before he kissed her, taking her breath away.

This time, he did not hold anything back as he pulled her to himself, his muscles flexing and jumping where they touched her body.

Her own senses became alert as her skin tingled from his touch.

The kiss was long and deep and left her shaking and wanting more.

"Do you still have your drawings?" he asked when he pulled back for a moment.

"I do."

"And do you still have the one of me?"

Her cheeks warmed at the question, but she nodded. "I do."

He slipped off his coattails and set them over the back of the chair. Then, turning to her, watching her, he began to unbutton his shirt. The firelight danced in his dark brown eyes. "Why did you draw that portrait of me, love?"

It was her turn to walk toward him. With a boldness she had acquired in the wilderness, and a confidence she had gained through his love, she slipped her hands inside the front of his shirt and finally allowed herself to enjoy tracing his muscles with the tips of her fingers. "Because I had never seen anything as beautiful as the sight of your body."

It was all she needed to say. With a groan deep inside his throat, Reid lifted her into his arms and walked her to the bed.

# Chapter Twenty-Nine

Large snowflakes drifted down from the light gray sky in a lazy cadence. They covered the tall pine trees, weighing down the branches, until some of them touched the ground. Three weeks after his wedding, Reid enjoyed the stillness of the woods as he and Charlotte trekked across the snowdrifts, wearing intricately woven snowshoes strapped to their feet. A guide he'd hired at Grand Portage led the way through the dense forests, claiming the walk to Sean McCoy's cabin was only a day's journey from the fur post.

It was just the three of them making this frozen pilgrimage. Just ahead of him, Charlotte kept up the pace like a seasoned voyageur, though she'd never worn a pair of snowshoes before in her life.

She glanced over her shoulder and offered a steady smile, though it did little to boost his confidence in this trip. He'd almost decided against coming when they'd reached Grand Portage, but Charlotte had insisted, and he hated disappointing her so soon after they were married.

Instead of thinking about the reception they might receive when they reached his father's cabin, he thought, instead, about all that he'd enjoyed as Charlotte's husband. They had spent two days in their room after their wedding, reveling in the newness of their union, before Reid had declared the weather safe enough for travel. It had taken them two and a half weeks to navigate Lake Superior to reach Grand Portage. They'd been fortunate not to contend with November storms upon the water, though it had still been a frigid journey.

But in the evenings, when they had pitched their tent and were curled up beside one another under all the blankets and furs, talking long into the early morning hours, Reid knew there was no better place to spend the honeymoon period with his bride. He marveled that he and she were in a tent once again, and he didn't need to deny his feelings.

In those two and a half weeks of travel, with nothing hindering them, he'd come to know Charlotte even better than before, and his love for her grew stronger with each passing day. There was no doubt that he'd made the right decision to leave the fur trade—yet, he had some unfinished business he needed to attend to before he left for good.

"There," the guide said in Chippewa.

A cabin was barely discernible among the thick trees. It blended with its surroundings in such a way he would have missed it had the guide not spoken.

They continued to walk, but this time, Reid kept his head up, watching the cabin as it came into view. It wasn't a fancy home, but it was snug and permanent. There was only one floor, but it had real glass windows and two chimneys, which belched out smoke.

When they came into the clearing, the door in the center of the building opened. A tall, broad-shouldered man stepped into the opening. His dark hair was worn long, with a thick beard covering half of his face.

Though Reid had not seen him for almost twenty years, he knew for certain it was his father, Sean McCoy.

Cold sweat gathered under Reid's shirt, and his pulse began to thrum. All the pain and anger he'd harbored over the years threatened to push their way to the front of his emotions, but he forced himself to stay calm.

The words Charlotte had asked him one night while he held her close beneath the covers in their tent returned.

"What do you wish to say to your father?"

"For a long time," Reid had said, "I wished to tell him I hated him and did not need him in my life."

"And now?" she'd asked.

He was married to a woman who made him want to be the best version of himself—and if that meant forgiving Sean McCoy and moving on with his life, then that was what he would do. "I want to tell him I did need him but found a way on my own."

"And will you tell him you hate him?"

"No." He had pulled her closer. "I will tell him I love him—and forgive him—despite the heartache."

Charlotte had kissed him, and he had become lost in her embrace.

But now, looking at Sean McCoy in the flesh, would he have the courage to forgive him like he had promised his wife?

"Welcome," Father called to them with a wave. "Come, warm your-selves by my fire."

As they drew closer to the cabin, his father continued to watch them. Reid did not take his eyes off him—and because of that, he knew the moment Sean McCoy recognized him.

Shock rippled across his features, soon replaced with disbelief. A heartbeat afterward, remorse weighed down the lines of his face.

"Reid?" His father trudged through the snow to meet him.

"Aye."

Charlotte stopped, and Reid walked up beside her.

Father's disbelieving gaze moved from Reid to Charlotte.

"I'd like you to meet my wife, Lady Charlotte."

"A lady? In the wilderness?" Father stared in bewilderment.

"Aye." Reid's knees felt weak, but he was thankful his voice was strong.

"Come in." Father seemed to return to his senses. He motioned toward the cabin door—where a woman now stood.

She was a mixed-blood woman with long black hair, as straight as the horizon on Lake Superior. Soft, almost sad eyes watched them with curiosity, and age lines marred her once beautiful face.

Reid reached down and unfastened his snowshoes while Charlotte did the same. When they were off, the guide took them and hung them on nails secured to the side of the cabin.

Father led them into the warm home. The main room was spacious with a fireplace, a table, several chairs, a thick bearskin rug, and an ornate cupboard. Two young women stood from the table when they entered, the sewing projects in their hands all but forgotten.

"Let me take your coats," Father said. "So you can warm yourselves by the fire."

Reid helped Charlotte remove her coat, while everyone in the room stared at her. She wore a wool dress, given to her by Nicolette. It was more serviceable and warmer than the green one she'd worn at their wedding. This one was a beautiful burgundy color, and she wore warm leggings hidden underneath.

When she took off her hat, her curls were unbound and lay against her shoulders. She smiled at each person but offered Reid the best smile of all.

"Come," Father told Charlotte and took her by the arm and led her to the fire.

Reid's body went rigid at the sight of his father touching his wife—but he forced himself to remain calm. His father meant her no harm, nor did he act out of unkindness.

Taking off his coat, Reid handed it to his father's country wife, who gave him a nod.

"Come by the fire, son," his father said. "We have much to say."

Father's face glowed with happiness, though Reid could not imagine why. How could he be happy after so many years of absence?

The two young ladies at the table watched Reid closely, as did their mother.

Reid took a seat beside Charlotte, and she captured his hand. Her fingers were cold, so he rubbed them gently.

Father sat across from them, looking Reid over, shaking his head in disbelief. "I never thought I'd see you again."

Charlotte smiled up at Reid, nodding her encouragement.

"I dinna think I'd ever come," Reid said honestly. "Charlotte suggested we stop here on our way to England."

"England?" Father leaned forward and clasped his hands. "There is much catching up to do. How did you meet? Where are you coming from?"

Reid did not answer but turned questioning eyes to his father's wife.

Father's mood sobered as he held out his hand to the woman who had shared most of his life in the interior. "Reid, I'd like you to meet Esme, my wife." He motioned the young ladies to come over from the table. "And my daughters—your sisters."

With a steadying breath, Reid rose to meet his father's family.

Father smiled at the women, the pride in his face warming the whole room. "This is Catriona and Isobel." His chest puffed out, just a bit. "My other children, Lachlan, Gavin, Jamie, and Moira, are either married or serving in the fur trade."

At the mention of Lachlan, Reid stiffened.

Catriona and Isobel curtsied, but neither one said a thing. After Esme nodded her greeting, she excused herself and went to the cupboard to prepare some tea.

"It does me good to see you, Reid." Father settled back into his chair, his face growing sober. "How is your mither?"

Reid also sat and clasped his hands as Charlotte wrapped her arm through his. "She is—" He didn't want to lie, neither did he want his father to know how pitiful she had become because of his betrayal. He wanted his father to know exactly what he'd done to them. "She is doing as good as can be expected." He met his father's gaze. "You hurt both of us deeply when you dinna return."

Father dropped his chin and stared at his hands for a moment. "Aye. And I'm sorry for that." He finally looked up again. "If I could go back, I'd do everything differently."

"Why?" Reid asked quietly. "Why did you leave us?" He felt like the fifteen-year-old boy all over again, waiting for months for his father to return, only to receive a short letter telling him he would never come back.

Father glanced over his shoulder at Esme, and then he sighed. "I was pressured to take a country wife, and I folded under that pressure."

Before now, Reid would not have understood that pressure as keenly as he did.

"And then," Father continued, "I found myself with a country wife and a son—Lachlan—and I felt such shame that I struggled to face your mither." He stood and walked to the fireplace, where he put another log on the flames. "When I returned to Montreal, I couldna find the courage to tell your mither the truth. And when I came back to the interior, I couldna abandon Esme and Lachlan, so I returned to my life with them, and then Esme had another child and another." He turned and faced Reid and Charlotte. "I'm not excusing my behavior, simply explaining it."

Charlotte squeezed Reid's arm, reminding him she was there for him.

"The second time I visited your mither, I told her about Esme, and she told me I had to make a choice, I could no longer be married to both." He put his hands behind his back and paced across the front of the fireplace. "By that time, I had four children with Esme, and I loved her and the children just as much as I loved you and your mither."

Reid hated to hear his father share these details, but he couldn't deny that he'd also made a fair share of mistakes. Who was he to blame his father for falling short?

"I couldna leave Esme any more than I could leave your mither—but I ken your mither and you were being taken care of. I could send money to you and you had your home in Montreal, but if I abandoned Esme and the children, they would be destitute." He stopped pacing and met Reid's gaze. "So I made the hardest decision of my life—not because I dinna love you, but because I thought it was best at the time."

Reid had nothing to say, so he simply stared down at his clasped hands.

"When I heard you were in the fur trade, I sent word to you. Did you receive my letters?"

"Aye."

"Yet you dinna come?"

"I couldna."

Father nodded. "I understand."

Did he? Reid wanted to tell his father how hard those years had been, but he suspected his father already knew. He hadn't made the decision because Reid wasn't good enough, he'd made it out of obligation to a family fully dependent on him. How was that any different than Reid making the decisions he had made when he knew the success of the Crow Wing post was his obligation? How much more so for a family?

Reid would need to tell his father about Lachlan, though it would come as a shock. "I met Lachlan."

"Oh?" Father took his seat again. "Did he ken who you were?"

"Aye." He knew exactly who Reid was and had hated him because of it. "Our posts were only a couple miles from one another in the Folle Avoine District."

"He's in Crow Wing." Father scooted forward on the chair. "You were there too?"

Reid nodded and glanced at Charlotte. The love in her brown eyes reassured him. After Joseph learned that Reid would not return to Crow Wing, he'd sent one of his senior clerks back with Jean-Paul and Daanis to oversee the post. With Lachlan's arrest, Reid was certain the North West Company would win the trade war in the Folle Avione District.

"Lachlan framed me for murder," Reid said without preamble. "But it was discovered that he was the one who committed the crime, and he's now in custody, facing charges."

Father stared at Reid for several heartbeats, and the women became still.

"Murder?" Father asked.

"Aye. One of his own men."

Father stood and clasped his hand behind his neck. He faced away from Reid and Charlotte.

No one said anything for a long moment.

Reid finally stood, his heart heavy. "I'm sorry I was the one who had to tell you."

"I would have heard eventually." Father turned back to face Reid. "I'm sorry he tried to blame you. He was always an angry child, and I tried to show him how to control that rage—but I couldna reach him. I sent him to school in Montreal, hoping he'd find a different path, but he only came back angrier. He was lonely there, without a single friend." Sean sighed. "And when he saw you with your mither, he was so overcome with jealousy and bitterness, he was asked to leave his school. He came back here in shame."

Then the story Lachlan had told him about his friends laughing at Reid was not true.

"I'm happy you came, Reid." Father walked the short distance across the room. "I hope you'll find it in your heart to forgive me and stay with us for as long as you can."

Reid had expected his father's anger after telling him about Lachlan—but instead, his father had asked for forgiveness.

When Reid looked to Charlotte to see what she wanted, he found her nodding.

"Aye," Reid said. "We'd like to stay."

Sean smiled and reached out to pull his son into his arms.

At first, Reid stiffened in his hold—but then he wrapped his arms around his father and accepted his embrace, as if he were fifteen again.

Brilliant stars sparkled in the cold night air as Charlotte stood watching her breath fog out in front of her face.

They had been staying with Sean and Esme for over two weeks, and though the visit had been pleasant, the cabin had become overly warm after supper, so she'd stepped outside to take a deep breath.

She'd enjoyed getting to know Reid's father and enjoyed watching her husband let go of the bitterness that had held him captive for so many years. Though Reid was kind to Esme, he had not warmed to the woman, and Charlotte didn't blame him. It was one thing to forgive his father and another to embrace the woman who had come between his parents.

"Charlotte?" Reid slipped on his coat as he stepped outside, closing the door behind him.

She was snuggled warmly in her fur-lined coat and smiled at him when he came close to her.

"Are you ill, lass?" Concern lined his eyes. "You hardly touched your supper."

"I'm fine." She put her arms around him and loved when he put his around her.

Behind them, the cabin was warm and bright, but before them, the deep northwestern wilderness spread out for what felt like an eternity.

"Why do the stars look more brilliant in the winter?" she asked.

He was watching her closely, but after her question, he looked up into the heavens. "I suppose the air is clearer and the—"

Across the wide expanse of sky, brilliant green lights reached up and over their heads. The lights danced, waving back and forth, shimmering in the clear night air.

"Aurora borealis," Reid breathed in amazement.

Awe filled Charlotte's chest. "I've heard of them," she said quietly, as if speaking loudly might scare them away. "But I had no idea how dazzling they were."

The lights shifted, sending purple spiking up into the green.

"What a wonder this world is," Reid said. "And what a gift from our heavenly Father."

"Will you miss the wilderness?"

"I suppose I will." He pulled her closer and kissed her forehead. "But I willna mind. I'm thankful for the years I had here, but I'm more excited about the ones to come."

Her own heart skipped a beat as the future beckoned, with more than one surprise on the horizon.

"Reid," she whispered.

"Aye?"

"I think." She paused, wondering if she should wait until she had spoken to a doctor.

"You think what, love?"

In her heart of hearts, she knew her secret was true and she didn't need to have a doctor confirm it. She looked up at her husband's face, warmth and love and excitement filling her chest. "I think we might be expecting a baby."

The wonder on his face was even more intense than when he'd looked at the aurora borealis. "A wee bairn?"

Tears filled her eyes, and she nodded. "I'm not completely certain—but I-I've had several symptoms."

A smile spread across Reid's face that would rival any sunrise or sunset she'd ever seen. "I couldna think of anything that would make me happier, lass."

The tears in her eyes slipped down her cheeks as wonder filled her heart.

A wolf howled in the distance and the cold air nipped at her nose, but she had never been so happy or felt so safe in her life. Despite the pain and uncertainty of her journey, God had brought her to a place of peace and contentment.

"Are you ready to go back inside?" Reid asked.

She looked up at him and smiled. "Let's stay out here a little longer. I like being alone with you."

He grinned and pulled her closer.

Charlotte nuzzled into her husband's chest, marveling that she had become a fur trader's wife. She wondered what might happen once they returned to England, but she chose not to worry about the things yet to come. God had proven that no matter what they faced, He would be by their side, guiding them, protecting them, and teaching them how to love and trust Him.

And through it all, He would bless them, just as He always had.

# Epilogue

ENGLAND,
MAY 1804

The moment Blissfield Manor came into view, Charlotte's heart began to pound. Reid sat beside her in the coach, holding her hand.

Sunlight glinted off the gray exterior, making the large home appear to glow. It had never looked more beautiful or more welcoming than it did at that moment.

"We're almost there," Charlotte said to her husband and her mother-in-law, who sat across from them.

Reid's mother had been overjoyed when they'd arrived at her home almost a year to the day after they had left. She had not expected to see Reid for two more years, and when he told her that he and Charlotte had been married and they were planning to take her to England, she had become like a young woman again. Her health had improved so drastically she almost bounced when she walked. Just like Reid and Charlotte, Mother McCoy was ready to start afresh, and England would be the perfect place.

Before traveling to Blissfield Manor, they had stopped at the North West Company's London office, where Reid had presented a letter of recommendation from Simon McTavish. Not only had Reid become a shareholder in the company, but he would now work for the company from England. After they settled things at Blissfield Manor, they would return to London to secure a townhome. It would be a far cry from his years in the northwestern wilderness, but he was excited for a new challenge, and Charlotte was eager to live in the city. They would keep Blissfield Manor for summers and holidays.

The child within Charlotte's womb leapt and she put her hand on the swollen rise. A foot or elbow pushed against her, and she smiled. Did the baby know they were almost home?

"It's bonnier than you let on, lass," Reid said to Charlotte. "I dinna ken it was so grand."

Her ancestral home spread out before them, nestled among gradually rolling hills and green trees. A long gravel drive welcomed them to turn off the main road, causing Charlotte's pulse to race faster.

"I hope they received our letter," Charlotte said.

"I'm certain they did." Reid's reassurance made her breathe easier. "But even if they dinna, we will soon set everything to rights."

Charlotte's gaze roamed the land of her childhood, and she was suddenly reminded of the night she had fled from Roger, down this very road. She'd been so afraid and uncertain. How wonderful it felt to return with courage and certainty—alongside her husband. And to know Roger would never bother them again.

Soon after their arrival in London, Reid had inquired about Roger and learned that he had set sail for Bombay as a new employee of the British East India Company. With no hope of acquiring Charlotte's inheritance, and the threat of embarrassment when people learned what he had done, Roger had left England for good.

The front door of Blissfield Manor opened, and an older man and woman appeared. Behind them, a handful of women in black gowns and white aprons and mob caps followed. Along with the women, four men exited in black suits. They formed a line in front of the house, with Mr. and Mrs. Corning at the head of the group of servants.

The coach came to a stop and Mr. Corning, though he wasn't the butler, stepped forward to open the door.

Reid exited first and then turned to offer his hand to Charlotte. He was no longer in the wilderness, but he looked as natural and confident in the English countryside. When she took his hand, he winked at her and communicated his complete confidence in her with a smile.

It was awkward to maneuver inside the coach with her growing waistline, but she managed and stepped down from the vehicle to greet the shining faces of her old friends, the Cornings.

Mrs. Corning curtsied, and Mr. Corning bowed, but Charlotte refused to stand on formality this one time, and she went forward to embrace them. First, Mr. Corning, and then Mrs. Corning. "I do not know how to thank you," she said. It was because of them that she had escaped that long-ago night.

"No need," Mr. Corning said with a stoic face.

"Just a word or two about our boy would suffice," Mrs. Corning added with a laugh.

"Indeed, you shall hear a great deal about him." Charlotte's chest warmed at the love she felt for these people. "He was just as kind and selfless as you. I owe him—and you—a deep debt of gratitude."

The Cornings blushed but nodded their understanding.

Reid helped his mother step down from the coach, and she took in the manor and the staff with one quick, approving glance.

"Reid," Charlotte said, "may I present Mr. and Mrs. Corning?"

"'Tis a pleasure to meet you," he said to them and then introduced his mother.

"And we'd like you to meet your new staff." Mr. Corning took Charlotte and Reid down the line of servants, and they met each one with a nod and a smile.

"Shall we go inside?" Mrs. Corning asked.

Charlotte took a deep breath as Mr. Corning opened the door.

With one hand wrapped around Reid's arm and the other resting on her rounded stomach, Charlotte stepped over the threshold, the mistress of her family home.

After the servants scattered to their work, Charlotte took Reid and Mother McCoy on a tour of Blissfield Manor. Though she was tired, she was eager to make them feel comfortable.

She could not show them the entirety of the home in one day, but she could show them her favorite rooms. The north parlor, the music room, the dining room, the ballroom, and the hall of portraits showcasing her ancestors. Finally, when they came to Mother McCoy's room, Charlotte made sure she had everything she needed, and then she and Reid entered the hall.

"Where is our room?" Reid asked with a twinkle in his eye.

"Room?" Charlotte asked innocently. "Don't you mean *rooms*, Mr. McCoy?"

He shook his head and took her hand in his. "I mean room—singular. I willna sleep apart from my wife."

Her cheeks warmed, but she didn't chastise him. She had no plans to sleep apart either.

"What will the servants think?" she whispered.

"They'll think their master and mistress are madly in love, and they'll be right."

With a smile, she led him to the room her father had used when she was a child. It had a connecting room, which her mother had slept in, and a dressing room between them.

On the way down the hall, the door to her childhood bedroom caught her eye, and she paused.

"What's wrong?" Reid asked when he saw her face.

Charlotte still held his hand. He squeezed it now, concern etching between his eyebrows.

"My room," she said.

"Would you like to see it again?"

Memories from the night she had fled Blissfield Manor washed over her, and she shook her head. "No." She smiled at him. "I have no wish to look back. Only forward."

One day, she would return to the room to retrieve her old drawings, but that day could wait. She had more important things to occupy her mind and heart. The drawings she had made in the northwestern wilderness were being published in a book Reid had written about the fur trade on their journey across the ocean. After stopping at the North West Company office, they had gone to a publisher who had known Charlotte's father. The book would be released later that summer, and the publisher had already asked the McCoys for a second volume.

Charlotte and Reid continued walking, and eventually she took him into their new bedroom, which had been prepared by the servants for their arrival. A large bed dominated the room, and floor-to-ceiling windows lined one wall, allowing the bright sunshine to fill the room with light.

Reid reached behind Charlotte and pushed the door closed, giving them the privacy they craved.

"Welcome home, Lady Charlotte." Reid took her hand and lifted it to his lips.

"No." She placed her other hand on his and stood as close to him as she could with the baby between them. "My name is Mrs. Reid McCoy."

He encircled one of her curls around his finger, love and joy in his eyes. "Thank you for inviting me to live this life with you, lass. I couldna be happier."

"Neither could I," she said as she entered his arms.

Once again, Blissfield Manor had become a sanctuary—for her and her growing family.

# Author Note

Every story I write is sparked by a bit of history that fascinates me. As I delve into my research, and learn more about the setting and events, I begin to imagine the characters that will populate my story and how they will interact with the history I've learned.

*The Fur Trader's Lady* was birthed from my fascination with the North American Fur Trade. I live on the banks of the Mississippi River in central Minnesota and, growing up, I often heard of the fur trade reenactment groups that would rendezvous at nearby Crow Wing State Park or further away at Grand Portage on the North Shore of Lake Superior. As an employee of the Minnesota Historical Society for ten years, I was very familiar with the Snake River Fur Post (formerly North West Company Fur Post) in Pine City, MN and visited it several times.

Like most history, I think I have a good grasp of it until I start to dive deep, and I quickly realize that my knowledge is woefully lacking. The fur trade is such a complex subject on so many levels. It impacted thousands upon thousands of lives and crossed cultures between Europe and North America, creating a subculture of people known as the *Métis*. I could study this subject for decades and never have all the information

I would need to create a story that captures the true essence of the fur trade and its people. I tried, to the best of my ability, to represent all sides with respect and accuracy. If there are any mistakes within the story, they are unintentional.

One of the most fascinating things I learned about the fur trade is that it existed for over 200 years, and it employed thousands of men across Canada, the United States of America, and Europe. It was a well-oiled machine with a social hierarchy and culture that was unique to its time and place. French, British, Scottish, and native North Americans played equally important roles as they brought European goods to North America and traded them for fur. I don't touch the economic impact the fur trade had on America, Canada, and Europe, but it was phenomenal and made many people very rich.

Because Eruopean women had been banned from the fur trade by the Hudson's Bay Company by 1683, the French, British, and Scottish voyageurs and fur traders often took native wives in *à la façon du pays,* or in the custom of the country. These relationships were desirable from both sides since a native wife could help a fur trader with trade relations and local customs, and a fur trader could provide comfort, convenience, and protection to his wife. The husband had no rights to the children born from these relationships and either party could come and go as they pleased without formal separation. Many of the male children were sent back east or to Europe for education and then returned to become officers in the fur trade. Many men chose to leave behind their fur trading families when they retired, but others stayed in the interior and remained with them for life. I cannot begin to do this subject justice, so I highly recommend a book to explore in more depth called *Many Tender Ties,* by Sylvia Van Kirk.

When I set out to write this story, I came across several research gems. Because I had no idea how a voyageur would get from Montreal to Grand Portage and on to Crow Wing in central Minnesota, I relied heavily on a book called *A General History of the Fur Trade from Canada to the Northwest* by Alexander Mackenzi which is a compilation of writings printed in 1801. Mackenzi was a Scottish explorer and fur trader for the North West Company. It was through his detailed descriptions of his voyage from Montreal to Grand Portage that I was able to recreate Charlotte's journey. Almost all the details I offer from what they ate and wore, to how they carried cargo, how they cleaned themselves, and what they did at each stop, comes from this book. Even the unusual practice of the Algonquins the evening Charlotte and Reid visit Rideau Falls is described. I tried to use Mackenzi's spellings for place names as accurately as I could. Another book I read was *The American Fur Trade, Its Trappers, Traders, and Companies, 1605-1855* by Hubert Howe Bancroft. It's not as detailed but gave me a better picture of how the fur trade grew.

As often as possible, I try to visit the places I'm researching. While writing *The Fur Trader's Lady*, I had the opportunity to go to the Rendezvous in Grand Portage, MN. If you're ever in Minnesota the second weekend in August, I highly recommend attending! The massive fort has been reconstructed and costumed interpreters teach you everything you've ever wanted to know about the fur trade. All the descriptions of Grand Portage in *The Fur Trader's Lady* came from my visit to this beautiful place. Check out this link to learn more: https://www.nps.gov/grpo/planyourvisit/grand-portage-national-monument-rendezvous-days.htm

There are two other great historic sites I recommend visiting if you get the chance. The Snake River Fur Post in Pine City, MN has a recreated rowhouse, trading room, and stockade (my inspiration for the one in *The*

*Fur Trader's Lady*). They also have an Ojibwe Indian encampment, as well as a great museum about the French voyageurs, Ojibwe people, and British fur traders at the site of an 1804 North West Company fur post. The other place to visit is the Milles Lacs Indian Museum in Onamia, MN. It has fascinating history about the Mille Lacs Band of Ojibwe. My favorite part of the museum is the Four Seasons Room where you can see how the life and activities of an Ojibwe tribe changed with each season.

And, finally, I want to talk about Crow Wing State Park. This is where I set Reid's fur post and fort in 1803. It is not too far from where I live on the banks of the Mississippi River and was the site of a trading post starting in 1823, twenty years after my story. To my knowledge, there was no North West Company or XY Company posts there in the early 19th century, but it isn't out of the realm of possibility. And because I know this place so well, I wanted to use it. You will see a more accurate depiction of the Crow Wing area in the 1860s in an upcoming book in the Ladies of the Wilderness Series.

Thank you for going on this wilderness adventure with me. There are so many other things I'd love to tell you about the real history behind this story, but this note would get too long. I hope that you are intrigued to do your own research and learn more about this fascinating bit of time.

Happy Reading,

Gabrielle

# About the Author

Gabrielle Meyer lives in central Minnesota on the banks of the upper Mississippi River with her husband and four children. As an employee of the Minnesota Historical Society, she fell in love with the rich history of her state and enjoys writing fictional stories inspired by real people, places, and events. You can learn more about Gabrielle and her books at gabriellemeyer.com.

# Other Books by Gabrielle Meyer

**Timeless Series**

**American Brides Series**

GabrielleMeyer.com/books

www.ingramcontent.com/pod-product-compliance
Lightning Source LLC
Chambersburg PA
CBHW030102310726
48970CB00004B/1112